Dear Mystery Reader: **S0-ADR-111**

Walter Satterthwait is probably one of the most well-reviewed authors going today. Satterthwait's latest, MASQUERADE, has had its fair share of glowing raves. Everyone from *The New York Times Book Review* to *The Boston Globe* has sung the praises of this exhilarating look at the decadence and deceit of Paris in the 1920s. Dashing sleuth Phil Beaumont and his seductive British sidekick, Jane Turner, are sent to the City of Love to hunt down the killer of a wealthy American and his mistress.

American publisher Richard Forsythe had always been a bit of a cad. Handsome, poetic—every woman's dream during the golden days of the early 1920s. However, his caddish ways abruptly come to an end when he and his paramour of the moment, a sensuous German named Sabien von Stuben, are found dead in their Paris hotel room. The police say the lovers made a suicide pact. Forsythe's mother back in the States doesn't buy it. She hires the Pinkerton Agency's finest sleuths, Beaumont and Turner, to get to the bottom of this deadly mess. As they wade through a long list of suspects, they also stumble across some of the finest figures of the roaring 20s. Hemingway, Gertrude Stein, Picasso...they're all in town. Of course Phil and Jane don't have much time to mingle—they've got fabulous French food to eat—and a killer to find.

With MASQUERADE Walter Satterthwait has captured the essence of an era that has long since passed, and created a fun, fast-paced mystery along the way. Whether you're a mystery fan, a Francophile, or just in search of a good read, you've come to the right book. Enjoy!

Yours in Crime,

Joe Veltre

Joe Veltre
Associate Editor
Dead Letter Paperback Mysteries

Other titles from St. Martin's **Dead Letter** Mysteries

SAND DOLLARS by Charles Knief
THRONES, DOMINATIONS
by Dorothy L. Sayers and Jill Paton Walsh
AGATHA RAISIN AND THE WELLSPRING
OF DEATH by M.C. Beaton
THUNDER HORSE by Peter Bowen
A SCORE TO SETTLE by Donna Huston Murray
A SHOOT IN CLEVELAND by Les Roberts
DYING ON THE VINE by Peter King
AN UNFORTUNATE PRAIRIE OCCURRENCE
by Jamie Harrison
THE DOCTOR DIGS A GRAVE by Robin Hathaway
A HOUSE BY THE SIDE OF THE ROAD
by Jan Gleiter
WINGS OF FIRE by Charles Todd
CANAPES FOR THE KITTIES by Marian Babson
MASQUERADE by Walter Satterthwait
MURDER IN THE MAP ROOM by Elliott Roosevelt
TIME AND TROUBLE by Gillian Roberts
A VEILED ANTIQUITY by Rett MacPherson
A BITTER FEAST by S.J. Rozan
INVITATION TO A FUNERAL by Molly Brown
A COLD DAY IN PARADISE by Steve Hamilton

Dead Letter is also proud to present these
mystery classics by Ngaio Marsh

DEAD WATER
HAND IN GLOVE
THE NURSING HOME MURDER
KILLER DOLPHIN

RAVE REVIEWS FOR WALTER SATTERTHWAIT

MASQUERADE

"We simply cannot think of a more delightful way to spend a hot summer afternoon than curling up and reading MASQUERADE."
　　　　　　　　—Tom and Enid Schantz, *The Denver Post*

"Intelligent, amusing, marvelously written . . . Great good fun."　　　　　　　　—*St. Petersburg* (FL) *Times*

"A notch above most historical mysteries . . . Satterthwait does a fine job of recreating Paris in the post-World War I."
　　　　　　　　—*The Herald* (Rockhill, SC)

"Wonderfully rich in detail and atmosphere . . . a delightful mix of high society and the demimonde . . . a terrific imaginary junket." —*Publishers Weekly* (starred review)

"Decorative, dizzying . . . chock-full of the stuff that made the Twenties roar."　　　　　　　　—*Kirkus Reviews*

"Offers something for everyone. . . . Satterthwait . . . succeeds admirably."　　　　　　　　—*Booklist*

"A welcome escape to an exciting time and place."
　　　　　　　　—*Library Journal*

"Mystery and light social history, both underscored with sophisticated humor and nimble prose . . . Enticing."
　　　　　　　　—*The Poisoned Pen*

ESCAPADE

"A classy and classic whodunit . . . A seemingly effortless, beguiling style, and a mesmerizing story, smartly told . . . What more could a mystery lover ask?"
— *The Los Angeles Times Book Review*

"A convincing period piece with a droll modern sensibility . . . A book that pleases from the first page to the last."
— *The Wall Street Journal*

"A stunning success . . . It is hard to praise Satterthwait highly enough."
— *The Houston Chronicle*

"One of Satterthwait's best . . . Anyone who catches even half the playful references is bound to have a good time."
— *The Boston Globe*

"Thoroughly civilized, thoroughly pleasurable entertainment."
— *Kirkus Reviews*

MASQUERADE

Walter Satterthwait

St. Martin's Paperbacks

MASQUERADE

Copyright © 1998 by Walter Satterthwait.

All rights reserved. No part of this book may be used or reproduced in any manner whatsoever without written permission except in the case of brief quotations embodied in critical articles or reviews. For information address St. Martin's Press, 175 Fifth Avenue, New York, N.Y. 10010.

ISBN: 0-312-96989-9

Printed in the United States of America

St. Martin's Press hardcover edition/July 1998
St. Martin's Paperbacks edition/May 1999

10 9 8 7 6 5 4 3 2 1

This book is for my brother, Paul Satterthwait,
without whose help, and whose computer expertise,
it might have vanished into the ether.
Thanks, Paul.

Acknowledgments

IN THE STATES, thanks to Bill Crider, Valerie DeMille, Sam Gottlieb, Sparkle Hayter, Feroze Mohammed, Jonathan and Claudia Richards, Jeanne Satterthwait, Joan Satterthwait, Roger Smithpeter, Ann and Michael Theis, Polly Whitney, my ever-smiling editor, Reagan Arthur, and to my agent, Dominick Abel.

In Scotland, thanks once again to Dr. Olga Taxidou.

In France, thanks to Kristi Jaas, Timothy Linwood Brown, Alyssa Landrey, Helene Colon, John Baxter and Marie-Dominique Montel, and to Helene Almaric and the folks at Le Masque. I'm very grateful to all of you for giving me, in one way or another, a glimpse of Paris.

In Germany, thanks to Thomas Worche and to Nele Morkel.

In Switzerland, thanks to Gerd Haffmans, Herwig Bitsche, and to Tilo and Anja Edkardt.

Here on Aegina, thanks to old Paros friends David and Vanessa Grant, and to Jim Wilkinson and Ellen Boneparth.

This book has been read in manuscript by Olivier DeParis, by the remarkable Sarah Caudwell, and by my remarkable wife, Caroline Gordon, and I thank them all profusely for their suggestions and comments.

Special thanks to Brad Spurgeon, at the International Herald Tribune, who has been, throughout, an unfailing source of useful information and a very nice guy.

Sometimes one heard the curious dry sound of wild geese flying in formation to Norway or wherever it is they go.

—DIANA MOSLEY
A Life of Contrasts

BOOK ONE

Dear Evangeline,

Yes, *Saint-Malo!* Yes, *France!*

C'est un miracle, non?

I'm terribly, terribly sorry, Evy. I am prostrate with apology. I know that I should have written to you long before this. But I did tell you—I know I did—that I was about to be assigned my first real 'case' as a Pinkerton operative (unless you count The Adventure of the Incontinent Dowager, which, for obvious reasons, I do not), and that I might be unable to do so.

Now, at last, snuggling down beneath the French covers of my snug little French bed in my snug little French room, a French oil lamp snugly glowing on the quaint (if somewhat wobbly) French night table, I can finally pour out my trembling heart, as all English spinster ladies are required by law to do whenever we find ourselves, *zut alors,* in France.

But a few drams of trembling heart is honestly all I can offer. The trip across the Channel has left me quite ragged. When we were some ten miles out, the wind turned suddenly vicious and began to hurl huge grey tattered waves at our little boat. We corkscrewed up and down them, plunged and rose, turned and twisted, lurched in every direction possible, lurched in some that were most unlikely, and then lurched in a few that were altogether absurd. I have never been so spectacularly ill in my entire life. I feared for a while that I might die; and then, for an endless time, I feared that I might not.

It is sheer bliss to lie here on this unmoving, stable, and remarkably snug (if somewhat lumpy) mattress. (Which is French, by the way: have I mentioned that?)

But bliss, however sheer (and despite what the poets say) is apparently soporific. I feel myself drifting off. Enough. I will finish this, slip it into an envelope, and then lie for a time in bed and stare dreamily at the charming (if not terribly accomplished) print of the Eiffel Tower that decorates the far wall. I will pinch myself a few times, to be sure that I am not in fact dreaming; and then I will blow out the lamp; and then, soon, in my French bed, in my French hotel room, in my French town, in my French France, I shall (in fact) be dreaming.

In the morning, I'll ask Madame Verlaine, the owner of the hotel, to post this letter. Tomorrow, when the children have calmed down, I will discreetly pilfer some time from my murder investigation to write another.

Murder investigation? I hear you say. Children? I hear you say. Whatever is she doing, our Jane? Well, I'm afraid that you must wait to learn the answer. Tomorrow I will tell you all.

All my love,
Jane

P.S. Before I left London, I heard a rather interesting rumour. Do you remember Phil Beaumont? The tall American who helped shape me into the legendary sleuth I have become? It seems that he may be returning from the United States to Europe. Perhaps we shall meet again, he and I. There are one or two matters which, for some reason, we never got round to discussing. Ah, Evy, I see you smile, you vixen. If only you weren't quite so right, quite so often.

How is that charming brother of yours? And the dashing Mr Hammond?

Love,
J.

One

PEOPLE MOVED THROUGH the huge train station the way they always move through train stations, more hurried than careful, and more harried, most of them, than carefree.

The train from London had been early. I had been standing by the Information Booth for ten minutes.

"Monsieur Beaumont, I presume."

I turned. He was a brightly wrapped little package, for seven o'clock in the morning.

"That's right," I said. In the air was a faint smell of bay rum. It hadn't been there before.

"I am Ledoq," he said, and he bent his head forward in a small quick bow. He might have clicked his heels. I couldn't swear to that.

He smiled primly and he added, "Welcome to Paris."

"Thanks," I said.

He was in his late thirties or early forties. He was maybe five feet, two inches tall, but he was slim and erect. He wore a black three-piece suit that was beautifully cut and made from a lightweight wool that was probably cashmere. He wore a black bow tie that was probably silk, a crisp white false collar, and, draped across his flat stomach, a heavy watch chain that was probably gold. His black hair was slicked back over a slightly oval skull and two small, slightly pointed ears. Like the hair, his carefully trimmed goatee was black, and so were his small round eyes. In his left hand he held a pair of black leather gloves. In his right, clutched flat against his chest as though he were standing on parade, he held a black bowler hat. There wasn't a spot or a speck on him, anywhere.

"You have additional baggage?" he asked, and nodded toward the valise I carried.

"Just this," I told him.

He raised his left eyebrow a fraction of an inch, and then he nodded. *"Bon,"* he said. "How wonderful, to travel with so few encumbrances." It was one of those compliments that are designed to hide a smirk, but not hide it very well.

That was all right. He didn't have to like me, and I didn't have to like him.

A young woman passed by, fluffing her shiny brown hair with one rapid, delicate hand as her heels clicked quickly at the floor. The tails of her expensive coat swung with the rhythm of her stride, revealing a pair of slender ankles, a pair of contoured calves. Ledoq admired these thoughtfully for a moment, and then he turned back to me. "And have you eaten?"

"Not since last night."

Another nod. "You were wise to avoid the railway food. It is often treacherous." No smirk there. He took his food seriously. "But just across the street, not a hundred meters away, is a passable brasserie. We could enjoy some coffee, and perhaps a croissant or two, while we discuss the case."

"Fine with me," I said.

"I commend to you," said Ledoq, "the bilberry jam. It is from Alsace, and excellent."

From where we sat, at the front of the restaurant, we could see through the wide window across the busy boulevard to the Gare du Nord, tall and broad and dark, its brick walls streaked and stained. Among the vehicles out there were a few large carts, pulled by big stolid drays that weren't paying much attention to all the honking horns around them, or to the shouting red French faces leaning from the automobile windows behind. The people on the sidewalks weren't paying much attention either. Some of them had obviously just gotten up. Some of them, furiously bustling along, looked like they hadn't gone to sleep, ever, and never would.

"What I'd like," I told Ledoq, "is some bacon and eggs."

"Ah," he said. A bit sadly, as though I'd somehow let

him down. But he recovered quickly, shrugged, and signaled the waiter. Carefully, slowly, like a professor lecturing an idiot, and with a lot of precise gestures, he gave the man what looked to be very detailed instructions in French. I heard him use the word *"Américain."* Ledoq shrugged after he said it. Then the waiter shrugged. I felt like shrugging too, but I didn't let it get the better of me.

Ledoq interrupted his lecture to turn to me. "How would you prefer your eggs to be prepared?"

"Fried," I told him. "In butter, if they have it."

Irritation flickered briefly across his face. "Of course butter. But the yolks? Liquid or firm?"

"Liquid is fine."

He turned back to the waiter, and he spent another half hour explaining how to fry an egg. The waiter took this pretty well. He sighed only a couple of times. Finally, with a brisk nod, Ledoq finished. The waiter left, wiping his hands on his white apron. He didn't roll his eyes as much as I'd expected. Maybe he was waiting until he got back into the kitchen and he could really let go.

Ledoq turned to me and said, "You have been to France before?"

"A few years ago," I told him.

"Ah," said Ledoq. "The War."

"Yeah."

Ledoq shook his head sadly. "A terrible thing, the War. You spent time in Paris?"

"A few days."

"A pity. That was not time enough to see much."

"There were other things on my mind. Tell me about the gun."

"Ah," he said. He sat back, adjusted his cuff. "The gun. It was, I understand, the small Browning, of twenty-five caliber."

"The Baby Browning."

He shrugged yet again, dismissively. If it were called such a thing, that was no concern of his.

I said, "There's no question it was Forsythe's gun?"

"None whatever. It was of a unique design. Silver plated,

with an ebony grip. Monsieur Forsythe's name was engraved
along the back of the butt.''

"Very classy," I said.

Once again he raised his left eyebrow. And then, abruptly,
he smiled. "Irony, Monsieur Beaumont? Before breakfast?"

I smiled back. "Did he always carry it? The gun?"

"No." He seemed a bit more friendly now. Maybe it was
the irony. "Normally," he said, "it was kept in a drawer, in
his flat on the Rue de Lille. The wife, she insists that she had
no idea it was missing."

He glanced up as the waiter brought the coffee. We
watched him pour it into our cups, then watched him set down
the pot and walk away.

"Where are you getting your information?" I asked Ledoq.

"From the accounts in the newspapers. And from people
who knew the Forsythes."

"Okay," I said. "What about the German woman?"

He nodded. "Sabine von Stuben. A beautiful girl, despite
the name. And, for a German, quite stylish in her way. But
she was apparently from a good family. Her father was a
baron." He sipped his coffee.

I sipped some of mine. It was very good coffee. "What's
her story?"

Ledoq frowned. "Her story?"

"What did she do?"

He smiled. "She was an aristocrat. She wore clothes well.
She spent money."

"Uh huh. And how did Forsythe meet her?"

"I do not know. She arrived in Paris some six months ago
and began appearing everywhere. The Opéra, the balls, the
chic cafés. She was rumored, for a time, to be involved with
the Count De Saintes. And then, approximately two months
before her death, she became involved with Monsieur Forsythe."

"She was involved with the Count De Saintes?"

He shrugged. "So rumor has it. You know of him?"

"I know the name."

"I know little more myself. Few do. He is something of
a cipher, the count. Young, rich, charming, a hero during the

war.'' He smiled. ''And, consequently, an extremely annoying man. But otherwise a cipher. The family is a very old
one. They fought with Charlemagne.''

''They were angry with him?''

He looked at me for a moment, bemused. ''Please, Monsieur Beaumont. We shall get along much better if you refrain
from making bad jokes until after the noon hour.''

I smiled.

''There is also a sister,'' he said. ''Eugénie. Younger still,
and very attractive.

''Her, I know somewhat better.'' He shook his head sadly.
''A terrible waste.''

''How so?''

''She is a lesbian. But a very pleasant person, I hasten to
add. They are having a masquerade party on Saturday, at their
house in Chartres. I have an invitation. You may join me if
you like.''

''Masquerade parties aren't really up my alley.'' Someone
else, another Pinkerton, would be handling the Count De
Saintes and his sister. ''Did Forsythe's wife know about her
husband and von Stuben?''

''Yes, of course.'' With a faint thoughtful frown, he leaned
forward. He put his elbows on the table and he tented his
fingers, a doctor about to present his diagnosis. ''They were
an unusual couple, these Forsythes. They conducted many
affairs, each of them. And always, I believe, with the full
knowledge of the other. And not affairs only. There are stories
of orgies. The two of them and other women. Other men.''

He sighed slightly, disapproving. ''At their château near
Chartres, at their flat here in Paris, even in the Bois de Bou-
logne.'' He gave me significant glares. ''In the beam from
the headlights of their automobiles.''

He paused. ''They were, I should say, obsessed with sex.''

Two young women walked by the table, heading for the
door. With his lips pursed, Ledoq studied them carefully. He
looked over to me. ''English. One can tell by the clothing.
Very attractive, *non?*''

''The clothing or the women?''

He smiled. ''What is clothing? Merely the setting for the
diamond. Some settings are more stylish than others—yes, of

course—but the diamond is the thing, eh?'' He sat back, raised his coffee cup, sipped. He looked off for a moment, as though he were giving some serious thought to everything he had just said. Then he nodded, as though he had decided to agree with it.

''I very much appreciate the English women,'' he told me. ''They possess a reserve which I find infinitely intriguing.'' He shrugged again, lightly. ''It is another form of clothing, really.''

''Right,'' I said. ''You knew him. Forsythe.''

''But of course. Paris is a large city, *mon ami,* but the community in which they lived, the Forsythes, it was quite small.''

''Which community was that?''

Before he could answer, the waiter arrived with our food. I got my bacon and eggs. Ledoq got some croissants and some white porcelain crocks of butter and jam.

After the waiter left, Ledoq carefully pulled away the end of a croissant. He picked up his knife and said, ''The community of artists. Writers. Painters. Many of these—the writers in particular—are Americans. They come to Paris for the inspiration it offers.''

''And you're a member of that community,'' I said. I cut some bacon.

Buttering his croissant, he glanced up at me. ''My father possessed a head for business that enabled him, over the course of a long and rather dreary life, to accumulate considerable wealth. He also possessed a wonderful sense of timing and died while I was still young enough to enjoy it.''

He smiled. ''The money has permitted me to indulge my interest in books, in painting, in the theater.'' He spread a dollop of blue jam on the croissant. ''And it has permitted me, from time to time, when I find it amusing, to take on a little adventure for your friend, Monsieur Cooper, in London.'' Deftly, he bit into his croissant.

''Do you figure Forsythe for a suicide?''

He chewed on that, and the roll, for a moment. He swallowed. ''Yes,'' he said. ''Like sex, death was one of his obsessions. He spoke of suicide often.''

"He ever mention murder?" The bacon was good. So were the eggs.

"He spoke of a suicide pact. Of the beauty of two souls uniting themselves in death, for all eternity."

"And that's what the police think happened here," I said.

His croissant stopped halfway to his mouth so that Ledoq could shrug again, and then it waited for him to finish. "The door was locked from the inside. The windows were locked from the inside. The two of them were alone in the suite. The pistol belonged to Monsieur Forsythe. Their wounds, his and the girl's, they were entirely in keeping with the notion of a double suicide. What else could the police think?" He popped the croissant into his mouth.

"No one heard the shots."

He frowned, and then he swallowed. Judging by his wince, he had probably swallowed sooner than he'd planned. "They were fired in the middle of the afternoon. The other guests of the hotel were out and about."

"According to the desk clerk, Forsythe and the woman were in there for nearly four hours. What were they doing?"

He looked at me sadly. I'd let him down again. "Surely, my friend," he said, "that is obvious."

"When they were found, they were both wearing clothes."

"They dressed themselves, afterward. For the benefit of their families, I imagine."

"Forsythe's family doesn't buy that."

Another frown. "Buy it?"

"Accept it."

"Ah. Well. A family is, of course, as a group no more likely than its individual members to accept reality. Perhaps, as a group, it is less likely to do so."

"According to the autopsy report, there were two hours between the time the woman died and the time that Forsythe did."

"Perhaps, after assisting Sabine with her suicide, he entertained second thoughts about his own. And let us suppose that he did. That he wished to change his mind. How, in the circumstances, could he do that?"

Theatrically, he gestured toward the floor, holding his croissant as though it were a searchlight. He lowered his eyebrows. "There is the beautiful Sabine. Quite dead, and by his hand. If he retreats now, he will be forced to confront not only the police, distasteful enough, but also his own conception of himself."

"Which conception is that?"

"The man who never retreated. From extremes. From life. From death."

"It would only be a retreat," I said, "if he's the one who killed the woman."

Once again, Ledoq swallowed sooner than he'd planned. "But the door was locked."

"It was locked when the bodies were found. But the two of them were in there for at least an hour before the girl died. And afterward, Forsythe was in there for another two hours, before he died. And then another half an hour passed. A regiment of people could have gone in and out of that suite."

"No such regiment was seen."

"Like you said, it was the middle of the afternoon."

He nodded once, a quick, sideways, agreeable nod. He sat back, rubbed his hands together, and then put them flat along the arm of the chair. "*Bon*. So. If I may summarize? Monsieur Forsythe and the girl enter the suite at noon. They dally for a time, perhaps. Yes, almost certainly they dally. Then they dress. And then, at approximately one o'clock, a third party enters. He removes the pistol from Monsieur Forsythe, who by happenstance has it on his person, and who offers no resistance. This third party shoots the girl, who also offers no resistance. He then hands the pistol back to Monsieur Forsythe, tips his hat, and leaves. Monsieur Forsythe sits there and contemplates the situation. After two hours of puzzlement, he at last decides to shoot himself. Do I have it?"

"No one has any idea what went on in that room," I said. "No one heard the shots. There was no note. Forsythe made a phone call at about one o'clock. No one knows who he was calling."

"The desk clerk misplaced the record."

"I'd like to talk to that desk clerk."

Ledoq shrugged. "Unfortunately—"

"Unfortunately," I said, "the desk clerk is dead."

"And you find that suggestive."

"Yeah."

Still another shrug. "He lived near the Seine. He was drunk that night, as he often was. Walking home, he slipped and fell."

"A week after the bodies were found."

"His death was ruled an accident."

"And Forsythe's was ruled a suicide."

Suddenly he smiled. "It occurs to me, my friend, that you possess a fine grasp of the details of the story. There was really no need, was there, for us to have this little chat?"

I smiled back. "I thought we should get to know each other."

His smile grew wider. *"Bon."* He nodded. "And so we have. *Un peu.* A little. But a beginning, isn't it? And now, would you care to freshen yourself before your first appointment of the day? I have taken the liberty of obtaining for you a room in a rather pleasant hotel, not far from my own apartment. We can discuss this further in the taxi. Is that acceptable?"

"Fine with me."

He nodded and turned to signal the waiter. When the man arrived, Ledoq spoke for a while in French. Maybe he was explaining exactly how much he liked the bilberry jam. Finally, the waiter took a small notepad and a pencil from his pocket, scribbled something in the notebook, tore off that sheet and placed it on the table.

As he walked away, Ledoq leaned forward, picked up the slip of paper, and handed it to me without looking at it. He smiled. "You are being reimbursed for your expenses, of course."

"Right," I said. I glanced at the bill, calculated the exchange rate. It came, in dollars, to less than twenty cents.

It wasn't only inspiration that Paris was offering Americans.

In the taxi, we did talk about the case, but not for long. Ledoq wanted to point out the sights.

"There we have the Opéra," he said, leaning toward my window and nodding at an ornate gray building on the right. "It was designed during the Second Empire, by Charles Garnier. The interior is very lavish. Gobelin tapestries, gilded mosaics, a chandelier that weighs five tons. Enormous. In 1896, it fell upon the audience.''

"They get their money back?"

He sat back and smiled. He glanced at his watch. "Still before the noon hour. They did not. But no doubt they were consoled by the knowledge that they had suffered in the cause of art. Incidentally, there is a passable café, just back there, to the right. The Café de la Paix. They serve an admirable *chevre chaud*. A salad with warm goat cheese. Perhaps one day you will join me there.''

"We'll see."

He kept on with the tour. "And here we have the Place de la Madeleine. The construction of the Madeleine began in 1764, at the command of Louis the Fifteenth . . . and here we have the Place de la Concorde . . . and here, the Champs-Elysées . . .''

Everything was covered with soot and streaked with grime, but that was true of everything in New York and everything in London. You don't use steam power, and the coal that fuels it, unless you're willing to live with a little soot and grime.

And this was very grand, all of it. Grander than New York, grander than London. The streets were wide and the buildings were imposing, the kind of streets and buildings that got put up by people who wanted to make sure that no one would ever forget them (and who hoped that no one would ever ask who put up the money).

We crossed the Seine, broad and brown and flat between its embankments of stone, and then we turned left and drove alongside the river for a few blocks. Out on the water, long low barges slowly slid by. Smaller boats, some with sails, dashed and darted between them.

We turned right. Ledoq pointed out some more sights. Most of these were restaurants.

"Down there," he said, "is the Tartuffe. You see the yellow awning? They do an excellent *caneton à l'orange*. Duckling with a sauce of oranges. They use only Rouen duck, of course . . . There, up that street, is the Bonne Chance. A *crê-perie*. You are familiar with the *crêpes* of Normandy?"

"No."

He nodded as though he weren't very surprised by my ignorance. "You must permit me to introduce you to them."

"We'll see."

"Here on our left," he said, "we have the Deux Magots, a tolerable café. They do a nice *citron pressé*. A lemon press. And there, that large building, the church, that is Saint-Germain-des-Prés. Saint Germain in the Fields. On this very spot there was once a temple dedicated to the goddess Isis."

"Not recently," I said.

"No, no. Thousands of years ago." He glanced at me, and then he smiled. "Again the irony, eh?"

A few blocks beyond the church, the taxi turned left, and then threaded its way through a few narrow streets.

"Further down," said Ledoq, "is the Café Procope, one of the first cafés in Paris. Voltaire drank forty cups of coffee there, every day, as he finished *Candide*. They still do an acceptable *café au lait*. And their *crème brulée* is more than adequate."

The taxi stopped in front of a narrow, four-story brick building. A small sign over the door, carefully hand-painted, said that it was L'HÔTEL VICTORIEN.

Ledoq leaned forward, spoke to the driver, then turned to me. "Five francs. You will want a receipt, naturally. To account for your expenses."

I pulled some notes from my pocket, handed one over. He passed it to the driver, said something else in French. The driver grumbled, searched around the cab of the taxi, found a scrap of paper, then grumbled again as he scratched at it with the point of a pencil. Grumbling once more, he handed it back to Ledoq, and Ledoq handed it to me. "*Voilà*," he said.

I stuck it into my jacket pocket, opened the door, stepped out. Ledoq passed me my valise and then stepped out himself. Holding hat and gloves in his left hand, he brushed himself lightly with his right. "And now," he said, "your room."

Ledoq waited in the small lobby while a bellboy who had probably fought with Charlemagne now fought with a rickety open elevator that had been old when Charlemagne was born. He had wanted to take my valise but I held on to it. I didn't know how to call for an ambulance in French.

The elevator lumbered slowly upward, clanking and rattling, and faintly squealing, as though a very large mouse were being tortured somewhere along the shaft. The old man turned to me with an expression that was infinitely sad and he said, *"Américain?"*

"American, yes."

He nodded sadly and looked away. He had expected that, too. Probably not a lot of things happened that he didn't expect to happen.

The elevator clanked, shuddered, clanked again and continued to rise. Far off, the mouse squealed again. He turned to me. *"Parlez-vous francais?"*

"No. Sorry."

He nodded sadly.

With a final clank, a final faint gasp from the mouse, the elevator stopped at the top floor. The old man opened the gate and gestured for me to get out. I did. He shuffled from the cage, then gestured for me to follow him. We went down a narrow corridor. Pale green paint on the walls and red carpet on the floors, slightly worn along its center. At room 404, the old man stopped, reached into his left pocket, frowned, reached into his right pocket, pulled out a key, fumbled it into the lock and kept fumbling with it for a bit. A good second-story man could have opened and closed that door eight or nine times while the old man struggled with the key. Finally the door opened and he gestured for me to step in.

He followed me and then he stood there, waiting, as I looked around the room.

Except for a print above the bed, a painting of the Eiffel Tower, it could have been a room in any decent hotel in Pittsburgh or Portland or Peoria. A nightstand on either side of the bed. A white bedspread. A small dark-wood writing table and an uncomfortable-looking dark-wood chair. A throw rug covering part of the wooden floor. A door leading to a bathroom.

"C'est bon?" said the old man.

"Fine," I told him. I reached into my pocket, pulled out a note. Five francs. I handed it to him.

He glanced at it, looked at me, and said, *"Merci."* He

handed me the key and turned to go. Then he stopped and turned back to me. "Ah," he said, his eyebrows raising. *"Le bidet."*

He shuffled into the bathroom and signaled for me to follow. Once again, I did.

"Voilà," he said, pointing a trembling finger. *"Le bidet."* It stood beside the toilet, across a floor of small black-and-white tiles from the bathtub.

"Yeah," I said. "I know."

He said something in French, noticed my frown, then began to use hand signals as he chattered. Slowly, rheumatically, his body stiff, he mimed what I was not supposed to use the bidet for. *"Non, non, non!"* he said. He wagged a finger at me.

"I know," I told him.

He mimed something else I wasn't supposed to use the bidet for. This was more complicated.

"I know," I said. "I've been in France before."

He got as much out of my English as I'd gotten out of his French. Still chattering, he went on to mime what I was supposed to use the bidet for.

"I know," I said.

For the first time, there was something other than sadness in his face. If it had been more animated, I would've called it worry. Sometime in the past, probably, he'd dealt with Americans who'd never seen a bidet, and who'd made a mistake.

"Comprenez-vous?" he asked me.

"Yes," I assured him. I nodded. "Yes," I said, and I nodded some more.

He glanced at the bidet, glanced at me, and then, finally, he nodded back. He didn't seem very convinced.

I set my valise on the bed, unpacked it. At the bottom was my notebook. I took it out, opened it, glanced at the names on the first page. Rose Forsythe. Gertrude Stein. Jean Aubier, the Count De Saintes. Eugénie Aubier, his sister. Ernest Hemingway. Aster Loving.

The Agency had gotten most of the names from Richard Forsythe's mother, the rest from a Pinkerton operative who was working under cover, traveling with the family of Mrs. Forsythe's brother-in-law. All the names, according to the information I'd been given, belonged to people who were suspects in the death of Richard Forsythe.

All of them but the first name on the list. Auguste La-Grande. The Prefect of Police. The Head Cop in Paris.

He would be the first person I saw. My first appointment of the day, as Ledoq had put it.

I undressed, washed up under the faucet in the bathtub, put on some clean clothes, and left the room.

In the false bottom of my valise there was some American currency and a small .32 Colt automatic pistol. I left them there. I had enough money for the time being, and carrying a gun right now was probably a bad idea. American cops don't like it when you carry one into their offices, and I was pretty sure that French cops felt the same way.

Two

"There," said Henri Ledoq, "that is La Bonne Femme. They do a lovely *truite*—trout—in a crust of bread crumbs, parmesan cheese, and herbs."

"Uh huh," I said. "Tell me about your prefect."

"Ah."

We were in another taxi cab, driving back toward the river along the Boulevard Saint-Michel.

"You must understand," he began, "that the Prefect of Police is responsible for more than simple crime and punishment. He is accountable for public health, maintaining sanitary conditions within stores and hotels, control of the capital's doctors—"

"I'm more interested," I said, "in LaGrande himself."

"Ah. Yes, of course." He stroked his goatee. "Well, then. Our Monsieur LaGrande is a man who publicly prides himself on his incorruptibility."

I nodded.

"And correctly so," he added. "For one cannot corrupt that which is already corrupted, and LaGrande has been corrupt for his entire life. He will not, of course, accept bribes. That would be gauche. But if one desires a favor from Monsieur LaGrande, one need only donate money to the charity operated by his wife, the Society for the Safety of Orphans. There is no Society, of course. There are no Orphans. There is only Monsieur LaGrande."

"And his wife."

"A nonentity. Ah, there, you see it?" Leaning toward me,

he pointed out the window, out across the broad brown river. "The Cathedral of Notre-Dame. You see, behind it, that other island? The Ile Saint-Louis. On it is a restaurant, Au Paradis, that serves a first-class *berdonneau à l'impériale*. This is turbot, cut into slices, poached in milk, arranged with crayfish tails, and then delicately coated with a sauce of truffles. It is a lovely dish. You must, while you are here, enjoy it at least once.''

"We'll see," I told him.

The prefect was in his middle fifties. He was a big man who moved at the slow steady pace of someone who refused to waste his energy but who didn't worry very much about his time, or yours. He wore an expensive black suit that fit his heavy body as though it had been tailored just after breakfast. His thick black hair was pomaded, parted in the middle and combed back. His black mustache was waxed and its pointed ends were curled toward the ceiling. His face was round and ruddy, with small pouches under his sleepy brown eyes and a slightly bulbous nose over a thin, hard mouth that looked like it might smile once or twice a year, probably at funerals.

Sitting behind an antique mahogany desk the size of grand piano, he spoke for a while to Henri Ledoq in French. His voice was low and flat, and his speech was slow. He kept his hands, fingers interlocked, on his broad stomach.

Ledoq turned to me. So did the prefect. But not by much—he only shifted his sleepy brown eyes to the right, very slightly. "Monsieur le Préfet welcomes you to France," said Ledoq, "and wishes you a pleasant stay. He is always, he says, pleased to cooperate with a crime-fighting agency like the Pinkertons, an agency which he personally holds in the highest regard. But he assures you that your inquiry will be fruitless. The investigation conducted by the Judiciary Police was thorough and correct, he says. There is no doubt whatever that Richard Forsythe shot the von Stuben woman and then turned the pistol on himself."

"Tell him thanks for the welcome," I said. "And tell him I'm sure that the Paris police did a fine job. Tell him the Pinkertons think that the Paris police are a fine bunch of people, and we know that they always do a fine job."

Behind those sleepy eyes, LaGrande was watching me.

"But we've been hired," I said, "by Richard Forsythe's mother, Mrs. Claire Forsythe, and Mrs. Forsythe doesn't know as much about the Paris police as we do. Richard was her son, after all, and sometimes a mother can't see what's obvious to everyone else. Tell him I'm sure that any investigation of mine will confirm what he's just said. But as a Pinkerton operative, I've still got to conduct it."

"*Bon,*" said Ledoq, in agreement or approval, and then he turned to LaGrande.

I looked around the office. It took up a corner, a large corner, of one floor of the Prefecture. Running along the high ceiling, up to the gilded chain that supported a sparkling crystal chandelier, were ornate golden moldings. On the cream-colored walls were framed plaques and certificates and old portraits of people who were probably dead now. On the gleaming white marble floor, embroidered antique rugs, pale green and cream. Throughout the room, more pale green antique furniture, all of it light and spindly—an upholstered divan, a few upholstered chairs like the pair that Ledoq and I were sitting in. A mahogany coffee table, a mahogany secretary spangled with brass fittings. A couple of glass-covered mahogany bookcases, the books inside looking like they hadn't been opened for a hundred years. Along one side of the room was a row of tall windows that gazed out at the Seine. Along another side, a second row gazed out at the truncated towers of Notre-Dame.

It was a nice piece of real estate.

"Monsieur le Préfet," said Ledoq, "fully understands your position. What do you wish to know?"

I said, "Could I get transcripts of the police reports on Forsythe's death? Including the autopsy report?"

LaGrande nodded faintly and said, "*Mais oui.*"

"Yes, of course," said Ledoq. He added, "These will be in French, naturally."

"We'll get them translated. I'd also like transcripts of the reports on the death of the desk clerk from that hotel."

LaGrande spoke without changing his expression. His glance shifted to me when Ledoq turned. "As you wish," said Ledoq. "But Monsieur LaGrande is curious as to why you might be interested in these."

I shrugged. "Just to confirm that he died by accident. Part of the job."

LaGrande nodded, then spoke.

Ledoq said to me, "Very well. Is there anything else?"

"I'd like to talk to the inspector who did the actual investigations. Of Forsythe's death and the desk clerk's. It's the same man, isn't it, who did both?"

"Yes," said Ledoq. Still without changing his expression, LaGrande spoke for a while.

Ledoq said, "Monsieur LaGrande regrets to tell you that the Paris Police Department is these days greatly preoccupied. They fight not only against crime, which seems always to increase, but also against enemies of the state. To remove this officer from his duties now, to ask questions about two investigations which have already been concluded, would be to waste valuable time and incur considerable expense."

"Tell Mr. LaGrande that I'd only talk to the officer while he was off duty."

LaGrande spoke, and they both turned to me. "Monsieur LaGrande says that the police of Paris, if they are doing their job properly, are never off duty. This particular inspector is particularly concientious, and would therefore be reluctant to cause his department any loss of time or money."

"Right," I said. "Tell him that the Pinkerton Agency understands. I know that it wouldn't be right for me to offer any money to the police department, or to the inspector, for his time. But maybe the inspector and I can work something out. Maybe there's some charity group we could agree on. The Pinkerton Agency could thank him for his cooperation by making a donation to the group."

"An excellent notion," said Ledoq, and he stroked his goatee. "I commend you." When he finished translating, LaGrande answered him.

Ledoq turned back to me. "It happens that there is, in fact, such a charitable group. It is called the Society for the Safety of Orphans."

"Orphans?"

"Yes. Orphans are close to the hearts of all the policemen of Paris."

"No kidding," I said. "That's great."

He nodded. "It is most admirable, yes."

"Fine. Tell Mr. LaGrande that if it's all right with him, I'll make a donation to this society, in the name of the Pinkertons. Let's say two thousand francs."

About a hundred dollars. Claire Forsythe would be paying. Money was no object, she had said, and she had meant it.

Ledoq spoke to LaGrande, who spoke back. Ledoq turned to me. "Monsieur LaGrande says that is most generous of you and the Pinkertons."

"It's the least we can do," I said to LaGrande. LaGrande nodded his appreciation. I think that's what it was.

"Would I be able to meet the inspector tomorrow? And, if it's possible, I'd like to meet him at the hotel where Forsythe died."

LaGrande nodded and then answered. Ledoq said to me, "Would noon be convenient for you?"

"Fine."

"Monsieur le Préfet," said Ledoq, "will see to it."

"Thank him for me," I said. "And tell him I appreciate his help."

LaGrande spoke again. Ledoq turned to me. "It is Monsieur le Préfet's pleasure."

"But I'll need to see those reports first."

Ledoq listened to LaGrande's answer, then said, "Monsieur le Préfet has anticipated you. They are with his secretary, awaiting us. All of them. We may obtain them as we leave."

"Thanks."

LaGrande spoke for a while. Ledoq turned to me. "Once again, it is Monsieur le Préfet's pleasure. And, once again, he hopes you enjoy your visit to Paris. At the moment, however, he regrets to tell you that he must return to the demands of his office."

I stood up. "Could I ask the prefect one more question?"

"Of course."

"He knows about the case. What's his personal opinion of Richard Forsythe?"

Before Ledoq could translate, LaGrande said in English, "He was useless." It was pretty good English, I thought. His expression, what there was of it, hadn't changed. "A dilettante. And a pervert."

"Thanks," I told him. "I'll be sending a bank check to that Orphan Society tomorrow."

For the first time, LaGrande smiled. "I never doubted it, Monsieur Beaumont," he said.

"*No kidding*," said Ledoq.

"It means—"

Smiling, he put up his hand. "Yes, yes. I know what it means. I was merely savoring it."

We were coming down the steps of the Prefecture. It was a fine day, the sun shining, the air warm. Blossoms bloomed on the chestnut trees.

"You suprise me, Monsieur Beaumont," he said. "I had believed Americans to be invariably straightforward and open. I had no idea that they might be so practiced at duplicity."

"For a Pinkerton," I said, "it sometimes comes in handy."

He laughed. "Come. We shall enjoy a coffee."

We sat outdoors at a small café on the Rue de Rivoli, under a red and white striped awning, not far from an English-language bookstore. The street bustled with people, and none of them looked likely to starve to death anytime soon. The men wore well-cut dark suits, and they wore them well. The women wore well-cut light-colored dresses, and they wore those well. The dresses showed more of their legs than you might see in New York or London, but that didn't bother me much.

It didn't bother Ledoq either. He kept looking up from the folder that held the reports LaGrande's secretary had given us. He would purse his lips and narrow his eyes and contemplate a pair of calves as they smoothly clenched and unclenched their way down the sidewalk.

"Those are summaries," I said, nodding to the folder.

He had been contemplating. He looked over at me. "But

of course. One cannot expect a bureaucrat to surrender a genuine document. To do so would be like surrendering his liver.''

''We'll need to get them translated before I meet that inspector tomorrow.''

''I will arrange it. If necessary, I shall translate them myself.'' He tossed the folder to the table. ''With great reluctance, however. The prose is stupefying.''

I sipped my coffee. ''Tell me some more about La-Grande.''

''What sort of information do you wish?''

''Anything that might be important.''

''But who can say what that might be?''

''Whatever you know.''

''Ah. Well.'' He stroked his goatee. ''First of all, Monsieur le Préfet is a man of the right.''

''The right?''

''In America you have two parties, isn't it? Republican and Democrat. Here in France, things arrange themselves rather differently. We possess not only parties, and many of these, but societies, leagues, clubs, unions, syndicates, all of them sprinkled along a spectrum that proceeds from the right wing to the left.''

''What separates the right from the left?''

''The center,'' he said, and he smiled. ''But only theoretically. In fact, many of these groups, right and left and center, share similar outlooks and similar goals. Attempting to tell them apart can be quite frustrating. I am not a man of politics myself, you understand. I believe that in the end, all governments, right and left, are aristocracies. So far as I can determine, the only real difference between the right and the left is that the right wishes power to be placed in the hand of one individual.''

''And the left?''

''Does not.''

''You think LaGrande wants power for himself?''

''But, *mon ami,* what more power could he possess? Already, if he wished it, without consulting any higher authority, he could order the arrest of virtually anyone in Paris.''

''And outside Paris?''

"For Monsieur LaGrande, I suspect that no such place exists."

I nodded. "It's funny, then."

"Funny?"

"Strange. How'd you set up the meeting today?"

"I telephoned the Prefecture, two days ago. I explained, to an august personage, what I required. I was told to telephone another august personage. This happened several times. Finally I was told to do so once again, by one of the prefect's assistants, a personage whose augustness was almost palpable. I did so, and within minutes I was speaking to Monsieur LaGrande."

"That doesn't seem strange to you?"

He frowned. "I was most persuasive, I assure you."

"I'll bet. But why would the Prefect of Police spend any time with us? Why bother with a couple of deadbeats who're interested in Richard Forsythe? A pervert and a dilettante. A dead dilettante."

Ledoq shrugged. "He was curious, perhaps."

"But why? And why show up himself? He could've sent an assistant to see us."

Pensive, Ledoq pursed his lips. *"Deadbeats?"* he said.

"It means—"

"Yes, yes. I question its aptness, merely."

"Another thing."

He raised an eyebrow. "Yes?"

"Two thousand francs," I said, "is chicken feed to a guy like LaGrande. He never asked for more."

He pursed his lips again.

"Something else," I said.

He raised both eyebrows. "There is more?"

"Did you know that LaGrande could speak English?"

"Non. Not at all."

"So he sucker-punched us. Why?"

"Mon ami, what exactly are you are saying?"

"I'm saying that LaGrande is up to something. He's got reasons of his own for talking to us, and for letting us talk to that inspector. And I think he wants us to know it."

"And what might those reasons be?"

My turn to shrug. "We'll have to wait and see."

He looked at me for a moment. At last he smiled. He said, "Beaumont. Of course. You are of French descent."

I smiled back. "A long time ago." I reached into my pocket, pulled out my watch. Nearly twelve. "I should get over to the Forsythe place," I said.

"She lives directly across the river. We can be there in only a few minutes, with the taxi."

I nodded. "Look, Mr. Ledoq—"

Smiling, he waved his small hand. "No no no. It is *Henri*. Please. And I will call you . . . Phillip?"

"Phil. Fine. Look, Henri, she's an American. I won't need a translator. I'll give her a call, and I'll go over there on my own."

His smile faded as he sat back, away from me. "Very well," he said stiffly.

"I think," I said, "that she'd be more likely to talk to just one of us. Two of us, it looks like we're ganging up on her."

He pursed his lips again, considering this.

"And she knows you," I said. "She knows that you already know her story. She won't be able to lie."

"And her lying to you, that is a good thing?"

"Lies are always interesting. Just as long as you know they're lies."

He studied me again for a while, and then, abruptly, he smiled. "I believe," he said, "that it was not so long ago, this descent of yours from French ancestors. *Bon*. But we shall share the taxi. There is a small café not far from her house. I will await you there. And then we will have lunch together, you and I."

"Fine," I said.

I telephoned Rose Forsythe from a tobacco shop. She was in, and she said she'd be happy to see me.

Sharing the taxi with Ledoq didn't mean splitting the cost, I found out. I paid, and Ledoq got the driver to give me a receipt.

At the Rue de Lille, number 27, I walked across a flagstone courtyard past a large white marble fountain that was dry now, the bottom of the basin stained brown beneath a few dead leaves curling in the sun. The building was an old stone townhouse, broad and impressive, six or seven stories tall, with high mullioned windows and a massive wooden door flanked by thick sandstone columns. In the center of the door was a flat stylized brass skull, about two inches thick, life-size, and beneath that was a stylized brass bone about a foot long, hanging vertically. The upper joint of the bone was hinged to the base of the skull, and the lower joint rested on another piece of brass. That was the knocker. I knocked on it.

After a moment or two, the door opened.

Dear Evangeline,

Today the sky has opened, like a huge door, and the sun is out, brilliant yellow in a pale blue seamless sky. The Channel is as flat as a lake. It seems impossible that only yesterday that same body of water, so tranquil and still this morning, was heaving and snarling, lashing us with spray, hurling our boat to and fro as though it were a shuttlecock.

The boat, by the way, was a private yacht, The *Meltemi,* a two-masted sailboat of teak, perhaps sixty feet long, very handsome if you like that sort of thing, which I never shall again. It belongs to the people by whom I am pretending to be employed. Well, by whom I am in fact employed; but in a kind of pretence. I am Not What I Seem, you see. Even more so than usual, I mean to say. This is all very easily explained, Evy, I assure you; and I shall explain it in a moment.

I must tell you, though, that it is absolutely wonderful to have a few hours to myself. Here I sit on a tiny cane-backed chair at a tiny zinc table draped with a red-and-white chequered cloth under a tiny green awning before the tiny Café le Figaro, on a square situated along the cobblestoned Rue Brussous, a hundred feet from the sedate and stately cathedral of Saint-Vincent.

Saint-Malo is gorgeous, Evy—*absolument ravissant!* The grey towering stone wall which encircles the town is wide enough for a brigade of spinster ladies to promenade along its top, twenty abreast, twirling their parasols as they gaze romantically out at the Channel, at the narrow strip of tawny beach, at the port with its tiny bobbing fishing boats; or, across a broad blue harbour where bright white sloops glide towards the brown ragged distant cliffs of Saint-Servan, perhaps a mile away.

The thick ramparts, even here inside the town, where you cannot see them, make the narrow winding streets seem sheltered and snug, as cosy as my room in the hotel. This particular square is delightful. Across the street from where I sit, neatly arranged in a single stone building, are a baker's shop, a greengrocer's, and a florist's, all their doors and window frames painted a lovely cerulean blue. Everything is so perfectly charming and quaint that one might suspect that this was in fact a stage set, designed to persuade the dubious English traveller that she has at last arrived in France.

There are but a few people about, most of them women; and most of these—like Madame Verlaine, the owner of our hotel—wearing widow's black. (The War, while it never actually reached Saint-Malo, still tore its pound of flesh from the town.) They march from shop to shop, wicker baskets hanging from their arms, their backs proud and straight. Outside the greengrocer's, they pore over and they probe the onions, the garlic, the potatoes with the care and concentration of a Harley Street physician examining the wealthiest of hypochondriacs.

There *is* a handful of men in town. But the owner of the café, Monsieur Guillaume, Madame Verlaine's brother, is under the strictest of orders from Madame to intercept any amorous or even genial or even congenial advances from male passersby.

At this he succeeds splendidly. Whenever a man approaches (as several have, Evy!), he lumbers from inside, leans his broad back against the jamb of the tiny door, folds his meaty red arms above the immaculate white apron that hugs his round proud belly and, stroking the end of his elaborate handlebar moustache (Frenchmen take their moustaches very seriously), he fixes them with a fierce glower. This basilisk stare reduces them all, not to stone, but to jelly; and they wobble off, down the street, towards the port; or up it, towards the cathedral.

I confess that most of these men were already somewhat jellied at the start: slick and slippery and slack. One of them, however, was dashing in a way that Mrs Applewhite might have described, with that little gleam in her eye, as 'rather *aggressively* masculine.' He was

young, virtually a boy; and a fisherman, or so I assume
from his nautically broad shoulders and nautically bare
brown arms. But he carried himself with a grace that
was very nearly feline, and just barely turning the corners of his broad red lips was a small elegant Gallic
smile; and beneath a tousle of dark black Gallic hair his
eyes were feline, too, Evy, as green and as knowing as
a cat's—

Ah well. Confronted with Monsieur Basilisk, the
smile withered and a pair of long black nautical lashes
fluttered over the feline eyes, and their owner slunk
away with them, down towards the harbour.

I haven't mentioned that he was wearing black san-
dals and brown trousers, these rolled up at the cuffs to
expose strong brown nautical ankles, and a black one-
piece shirt of jersey that had affectionately moulded itself to the contours of his nautical chest. Have I
mentioned that his eyes were green?

Yes, I see that I have.

It's the coffee, perhaps. Three cups of it this morning, strong, heady, delicious French coffee. Possibly the
coffee would explain the giddiness that seems to trem-
ble just beneath the surface of my skin. My heart, which
has not yet *actually* begun to flutter, seems poised (and
determined) to do so.

Perhaps it's the scents of Saint-Malo, of France,
scents that curl and wisp along the sun-splashed square:
garlic and sage, thyme and rosemary, roasting meats
and baking bread. And, behind them all, the scents of
the sea, of brine and fish, of travel and promise.

Or perhaps it's those green eyes.

Enough.

What am I doing here? you ask. I am 'on assign-
ment', I answer. I am working 'under cover', which
makes it sound rather more cosy than it is. On the face
of things, I am the nanny for two American children,
Edward ('Eddy') and Melissa ('Sissa', I'm afraid) Forsythe. Edward is eight years old; Melissa, ten.

You might believe that these children ought be in
school just now, rather than romping about the Conti-

nent with a spinster Pinkerton. It seems, however, that their (American) parents distrust British schools, all of them, and have engaged private (American) tutors to guide them through the Halls of Learning. This educational *chauvinisme* has of course its disadvantages: Melissa will never acquire those valuable skills which you and I acquired at Mrs Applewhite's Academy: sewing, and comportment, maintaining a piquant but unassailable virginity until overtaken by marriage or death. Nor will poor Edward ever acquire those skills which Eton might have provided him: how to wear a silly hat; how to endure one's inferiors and cherish one's canings; how to accommodate, within a busy academic day, an occasional jolly bout of boyish sodomy.

But it has, too, this *chauvinisme*, its advantages. For one, it permits them (and their Pinkerton nanny) to romp about the Continent.

There is another sibling, Neal. He is eighteen years old and will, next autumn, be attending university (in America, of course); and he is—in theory, at least— long past the need for a nanny. I say in theory because he is a very strange young man and I am unsure precisely what his needs might be—although I must say, from furtive glances cast in my direction, that I have my suspicions. (What a *femme fatale* I have become, *n'est ce pas*, Evy?) He is tall and thin and pale, and he dresses invariably in black. He carries with him, at all times, a small leatherbound edition of Baudelaire's *Les Fleurs du Mal*, in an English translation.

And what is wrong with Baudelaire, you ask? Nothing whatever. Very clearly (and fondly) I recall those nights at Mrs Applewhite's when (under a very different sort of cover) you and I sighed and giggled at the poems. But Neal has taken them a bit more to heart than we did. He has convinced himself that he is an aesthete, and so inclines towards a brooding, self-conscious world-weariness that fits his young self like a hand-me-down coat: threadbare and ungainly; and, yes, too long in the sleeves.

But to return to our Dramatis Personae. Also a mem-

ber of this merry band of travellers is Mrs Alice Forsythe, mother to the three. Her husband, George, in
Paris now, is a banker, with businesses and homes not
only there but in New York and London. He owns, too,
a 'perfectly dreamy little chateau' (to quote Mrs Forsythe) in St Piat, near Chartres, for which we are all
bound. We leave tomorrow, 'as soon as silly old Reagan
shows up with that silly old car.' (Ibid. Silliness is a
trait shared by nearly every item or person which wan-
ders, unwitting, into Mrs Forsythe's narrow world.)

Oh dear. I'm being catty again. And I promised myself I wouldn't be, that I'd try—

Speak of the devil. Or devils. First Neal arrived, and
then *Maman* herself, with the rest of the tribe. They all
await me outside the post office. I have time enough
only to scribble these few words and then post this,
along with my report to Mr. Cooper in London. More
later.

>   All my love,
>   Jane

Three

I'D SEEN A photograph of her, but in it she had looked taller than she actually was, probably because she was so well proportioned. Her hair was cut short, a glossy black helmet on her small, perfect head. Shiny black bangs fell to the small, perfect arches of her narrow black eyebrows. Her lashes were black with mascara and her eyes were blue, a dazzling blue that reminded me of a woman I knew in England. Her lips were red. She was wearing a caftan of black silk, and a black silk scarf loosely knotted at her slender throat. Her left hand held the door and her right was resting, fingers splayed, between her small, perfect breasts. Her delicate wrist was so slender I could have circled it with my first finger and thumb. I knew that she was thirty years old, but she could have been ten years younger.

"Mr. Beaumont?" she said.

"Yes. Mrs. Forsythe?"

"*Rose*," she said, and showed me a set of small, perfect teeth. "You really *must* call me Rose. *No one* calls me Mrs. Forsythe. Ever, ever, ever." She had a bright open smile. "Please, come in."

I went in and she closed the door and turned to me. She took her hand from her chest and crooked a finger. On its small, perfect nail, the red lacquer exactly matched her lipstick. "Come along. We'll sit in the sitting room, shall we?" Cocking her head, she smiled once more. "Don't you think that's a good idea?"

I did, and said so. I walked behind her, in the trail of a perfume that smelled of gardenias.

The sitting room was three stories tall, maybe twenty feet wide and forty feet long. Light drifted down from the mullioned windows, high up there along one wall. It was a big space, but everywhere you looked there was something waiting for you to look at it. There were animal skins on the polished wooden floor, zebra and lion and tiger. There were sea chests and model ships. There were statues and urns. There were leather drums and leather shields. There were smoky paintings of harem girls and belly dancers on the white walls. There was a yellowish skeleton standing upright in one corner, a top hat clamped to its skull, a limp condom dangling from its opened mouth like a long lolling tongue. In the opposite corner was a hollow elephant leg that held nine or ten African spears. The furniture was oversized, with heavy wood frames and plump embroidered cushions of black and yellow.

She led me over to the sofa. In front of it, on a coffee table the size of a door, were bottles and glasses, a bucket of shaved ice, a bottle of mineral water, a teapot and a coffee pot and saucers and cups.

"Now you sit there," she told me, and pointed at the sofa. "And I'll sit here," she said, and lowered herself to another plump cushion, this one red, on the floor opposite me. She crossed her legs and put her elbows on the table and she clasped her hands together beneath her small, perfect chin. She smiled up at me. "Isn't this cozy? And I got out all these *things*." She waved at them.

I noticed that her eyes were shiny and her pupils were dilated, and I wondered what drug she was on.

"I wasn't sure what you'd want," she said. "There's bourbon and scotch and gin." She pointed to each bottle, her arm upraised, her wrist bent. "And cognac and armagnac and calvados. And absinthe. Do you like absinthe?"

"Not much." If it were cocaine, she'd begin to wind down pretty soon.

"Good," she said. "Me neither. It's awfully icky, I think. They say it's an aphrodisiac, but I've honestly never needed one." She said this as though she were talking about a pair of galoshes. "And there's tea and coffee. So"—she held up her hands, palms open, and she cocked her head and smiled again—"what's your poison?"

"Water will be fine."

Pouting, she dropped the hands and clapped them against her lap. "Oh how *boring*! Only water? You're sure?"

"I'm sure. Thanks."

"Spoilsport," she said. She sighed heavily, lifting and dropping her shoulders in mock resignation. "Oh well," she said, "if you *insist*." She lifted the bottle, poured some water into one glass. "I suppose I should have some, too." She poured water into another glass. "I'll probably need my wits about me, if I'm going to *survive* this interrogation of yours." Smiling cheerfully, she handed me a glass.

"It's not an interrogation, Mrs. Forsythe."

"Please. It's *Rose.* It's *always* been Rose." That was a lie, or at least not the whole truth. Until she'd gotten married, her first name had been Polly. "I *hate* being called Mrs. Forsythe." She raised her glass, held it out. *"Slainte,"* she said. We clicked glasses.

I took a sip of water.

She said, "So tell me, are all the Pinkertons as good-looking as you are?"

"All of them," I said. "It's a requirement."

"Oooh. How *wonderful*! And will *more* of them be coming here?"

She was more playful than seductive, and there was no real invitation in the playfulness. Probably it was just a habit of hers. Like using drugs. I had the feeling that if I responded to her as though she were being seductive, she would've gone along with me. But that would have been out of habit, too.

I smiled at her. "I doubt it."

"Oh *drat*." She gave me another bright cheerful smile before she sipped at her water.

"Rose," I said, "you know that your mother-in-law hired us to look into your husband's death."

"Poor Claire," she said, suddenly sorrowful. "How is she?"

"She's fine. But she's still convinced that your husband didn't commit suicide."

"Well, of *course* she is. Claire always thought that Dickie was *kidding*. When he mentioned suicide, I mean. She thought it was just one more *terrible* thing he was trying to shock her with. She'd always laugh and say, 'Richard, darling, do *stop* that!' '' She looked down and her sleek black hair swung forward. "Poor Claire," she said. She looked up. "She's very sweet, I've always liked her, and she loved Dickie very much, but she really didn't know him at all."

"He wasn't kidding," I said. "About suicide."

"Absolutely *not*. It was something he really, truly believed in."

"When did you first meet your husband, Rose?"

"*Ages* ago. We were children together. Our parents were *very* close." She leaned forward like a conspirator and she said, "That's because they were also very, *very* rich." Smiling brightly, she sat back. "The rich stick together, you know. Dickie always said that. And he always said that it was wrong *and* inevitable."

"When did he start talking about suicide?"

"After the War. Dickie was a hero in the War. Did you know that?"

I nodded. "An ambulance driver."

She nodded, pleased. "That's right, first for the French and then for us, the Americans. The French gave him a *very* important award. A medal. And that was even before the United States came *into* the War. He was at Verdun—do you know about Verdun? The big battle? It's famous."

"I know about it."

"He was there, with his ambulance, and he and his best friend were standing right next to it when it got hit by a shell. It blew up, the whole thing! And his friend, Harry, the poor man, he was cut right in half! Right across the middle! It was *horrible* for Dickie. Well, of course it was horrible for Harry too, *obviously* it was, but the thing is, Dickie didn't have a single scratch on him! Not a one. The explosion knocked his hat off, that's all. Can you *imagine*?"

She took a long deep breath, and then looked around, blinking, as though she had just realized where she was. She exhaled the breath in a slow sigh and looked up at me and she smiled and said, "Would you excuse me for a minute?" The brightness had seeped from her eyes. There was still some of it left in her smile, but now it seemed forced.

"Sure."

She rose gracefully, without using the table to support herself. I started to stand, but she waved her hand at me. "Don't bother. Please. I'll be right back."

She moved off, the small, perfect head held high. For a few minutes I looked around the room and admired all the admirable things, like I was supposed to.

When she returned, the brightness was back in her eyes and a small framed photograph was in her hand.

"Here," she said, and she handed me the photograph, slowly, reluctantly, as though she were handing me her heart. "That's Dickie," she said. She sat down. "The second from the left."

The photograph showed four men, three of them leaning against a boxy Field Service ambulance. The standing man was Richard Forsythe, and even if he hadn't been standing, you would have noticed him first. The other three were slumping, their bodies heavy with exhaustion, their faces gaunt. But Forsythe stood tall and slender and vibrant, and he wore his stained field coat as though it were a smoking jacket. His hands were in his pockets and a cigarette dangled from the corner of his amused smile. It was a pose—the cigarette had been lit just before the photograph was taken—but it was a pose that worked.

"The man on Richard's left," she said, "with the mustache, that's poor Harry. The photo was taken at the Somme, before Verdun . . . Where was I?"

I laid the photograph on the table. "You were saying how horrible it was for Richard, when Harry died."

She put her hand onto the edge of the table, as though it were a lectern, and she leaned slightly forward. "It was *awful*! Dickie said it was the *randomness* of it that really struck him. He was alive, not even *touched*, and poor Harry was dead, and so horribly, too. And not just horribly, but *suddenly*. In an instant, the blink of an eye! It was frightening, Dickie said, the randomness, but it was also liberating, in a way. It opened things up, he said. And he said he decided, then and there, to live out his life as a poem."

"A poem."

She sat back and let her hands fall to her lap. "Exactly. A poem has themes, recurrent themes, Dickie said, and recurrent images, and he said he wanted to live his life that way. As a beautifully constructed poem. And he said that when he'd achieved that kind of perfection, he'd end it. If anything happened to him before he finished, another random accident—if he got hit by a comet or something—then the poem would go unfinished. But even unfinished poems can have power and beauty—look at 'Kubla Khan.' But if nothing happened, if he could finish it, then he'd be able to make it a work of art."

"His life."

She smiled. "Exactly, yes."

"When did he first tell you all this?"

"When he asked me to marry him. When he came back from the War. I was still married at the time, to my first husband, but Dickie knew he was a terrible brute. Everyone knew. It wasn't his fault, Stefan's, not really, there was madness in the family, hereditary, but it was awful for me, and Dickie *rescued* me from it all. He *saved* me. He asked me to marry him, and I said yes. Even if I hadn't been married, I would've said yes. I love to say yes." She smiled brightly, but again there was no invitation in the words. "Especially to Dickie. It always made him so *happy*."

She took another deep breath. "And so I got a divorce," she said, "and Dickie and I got married and we came here to Paris. And it was wonderful. We lived a beautiful life together. We had the most *marvelous* time, the two of us. We did things, fabulous things, and we went to fabulous places— to Marrakesh and Rome and Berlin. The Greek islands. *Everywhere*." She giggled suddenly, remembering something. "Once we drove across France, Dickie and I and another couple, they were *lovely* people, the Fitzgeralds, Scott and Zelda, and we stopped for a drink at every town that had a one-syllable name. Every single one of them. Isn't that *perfect*?" She giggled again. "We had such fun. We *always* had fun."

"Then why," I said, "did he commit suicide?"

She winced. Not with pain. With frustration at my denseness. "Because the poem was *finished*. Dickie'd done everything he wanted to do, and he'd done it all so beautifully, and he was happy with it—happy with his life. With the *shape* of it, the form of it, and he decided to end it then and there, while everything was still beautiful and pure.''

"What about Sabine von Stuben? Was she happy with the shape of it?''

"Poor Sabine," she said. "She was absolutely smitten. Totally infatuated with Dickie. She would've done anything he asked.''

"Including die?''

Another wince. I was being dense again. "Of *course*. Dickie thought that a suicide pact was the perfect ending. Two people, two separate souls, united forever by the act of a single moment. And Sabine thought so, too. *Obviously*.''

"Uh huh. How did they meet, Rose? Your husband and Sabine.''

She frowned. "Meet? You mean for the first time?''

"Yes.''

"At a party. At the Count De Saintes's house, in Chartres. Jean has—do you know the count?''

"No." I smiled. "I just got into town today.''

"Oh, of course. Well, Jean—he's a *dream* of a man, by the way, incredibly handsome and incredibly charming—he has a really lovely house in Chartres, a beautiful place, not far from the cathedral. And Dickie and I were in Chartres for Christmas—we have a little place near there, in the country, nothing like Jean's, of course, but very nice. Anyway, Jean threw a big dinner party, and he invited us. This was in January. Jean was there, of course, and so was his sister, Eugénie, who's *incredibly* chic, and so were Dickie's aunt and uncle, Alice and George. And the Prefect of Police, Auguste La-Grande, and his wife.''

"He's a friend of the count's? The prefect?''

"I don't know if he's a *friend*, exactly. I don't really think that Jean would have a *policeman* for a friend. But they know each other. I only mentioned him because I saw him talking with Sabine a few times. But *everyone* was. People were all *over* her.''

She frowned. "I didn't really like her, you know. She was very pretty, I admit that, and she was very smart—she was wearing a Jean Patou—but she seemed so *political*. I mean, men don't want to hear a woman talk about *politics* all the time, do they?''

I smiled. ''Probably depends on the men. And the politics.''

''Well,'' she said, ''*I* don't think they do. And I know Dickie didn't. Politics bored him to *tears*. That's why I was just flabbergasted when he started to see her. Started having an affair, I mean. I said, 'But Dickie, she's so *political*, doesn't that drive you *crazy*?' And he just smiled and he said, 'I think I can cure her.' ''

She paused. ''And he was right, too, you know. In a little while, she forgot politics, and all she cared about was Dickie.''

''So you knew about them. Sabine and Richard.''

''Well, of course. We never kept secrets from each other. Dickie had lots of other women, and sometimes I had other men, too. It was something we did, the two of us. It was open and honest, and it was *pure*, really.''

''Uh huh. Did she come here, to the house?''

''No. Never. I just never liked her, and I asked Dickie not to bring her here.''

''Let me ask you this, Rose. Why Sabine and not you?''

Her face went slack. ''You mean why didn't I do it with him?''

''Yes.''

She looked down at her water glass. She reached out her right hand and touched its rim with her fingertips. She moved the glass an inch, toward her. Staring at it, she said, ''He asked me. To do it with him. About a month before . . . he did it.''

She looked up. Her eyes were shiny now, but not from the drug. A tear rolled from the corner of her eye and left a slick dark trail of mascara over her cheek. ''I couldn't,'' she said. ''I didn't have Dickie's courage.''

She sniffed once. Then, abruptly, she stood up. ''Excuse me. No, stay there, please. I'll be right back.''

She left, and for a few more minutes I admired all the admirable things.

When she came back, she looked as though she'd never

been unhappy in her entire life. She'd fixed the mascara. Smiling brightly once more, she lowered herself to the cushion. "I'm sorry. Sometimes I get silly and selfish and I forget that Dickie was happy when he did it. That he did exactly what he wanted to do."

"Tell me about that day, Rose. Did you have any idea what he was planning?"

Her eyebrows rose. "Not a *one*. Dickie was *incredibly* clever about everything! Afterward, when I looked back at it all, I was just *furious* at him." She smiled, delighted. "But that was Dickie. He'd *always* been clever."

"What happened that day?"

"Well, we had breakfast in bed, like we always did—Dickie *loved* to eat in bed. Sometimes we'd lie around all *day*, reading and writing and making plans, the two of us. Anyway, that morning we had cornbread and eggs and flapjacks with maple syrup—Dickie taught Marie, our cook, how to cook American, and she's *wonderful* at it—and then he took a bath and dressed. And then he came and kissed me good-bye and said that he'd see me before the opera."

She took a sip of water. "We were supposed to go to the opera that night. *Carmen*. And then, around four-thirty, I got a telephone call from Sybil Norton, and she told me what'd happened. That Dickie and Sabine were dead. I got dressed and I took a taxi over to the hotel. The Grande Bretagne. That's where it happened. Where he did it."

She blinked and then looked down.

"Who's Sybil Norton?" I asked her.

She looked up. "You haven't read her books? I thought *everybody* had. She writes mystery novels, and they're really *wonderful*. Well, the first one is. *The Mysterious Affair at Pyles*. That's my favorite. She has this clever little French detective who runs around and solves crimes. I didn't really like the second one as much. *Death Gets Knocked Up at Nine*." She leaned toward me, conspiratorial again. "The narrator is the murderer, but you don't find that out until the end." She frowned. "I don't think that's fair. Do you?"

"I don't really read many mystery stories," I said. "How did Sybil Norton know Richard?"

"She was one of Dickie's women," she said. She found

another bright smile. "Dickie always had women. Women were crazy about him."

"Uh huh. And you were here all day?"

"Yes, that's right. All day. Until I got the phone call from Sybil."

"And there are witnesses who can verify that?"

She frowned in mild exasperation. "You know, the inspector asked me the very same thing. The one from the police."

"It's something they usually ask, in this kind of an investigation."

"I suppose so. But it just seems so strange. I mean, it wasn't *my* idea for Dickie to commit suicide."

"No," I said. "But there were witnesses?"

"Well, naturally there were. Marie the cook. And Sylvie. She's the maid. And Paul, the gardener. And the inspector talked to them all, too." She was still resentful about that.

I nodded. "Does Sybil Norton have a telephone?"

"Yes, of course. Do you want the number?"

"Please."

She gave it to me. I took out my notebook and pen and I wrote it down.

I looked up at her. "Does the name Aster Loving mean anything to you?"

She blinked. "No. Should it?"

"I don't know. It's a name that's come up."

"Aster Loving? I would've remembered that, I think."

"Okay. Did your husband have any enemies that you know of?"

"Enemies?" She frowned, as though the word were part of some foreign language.

"Anyone who wouldn't mind seeing him dead. Anyone—"

"But everyone *loved* Dickie. Everyone. Men, women. *Everyone.*"

"I heard he had some disagreements with a couple of writers. Ernest Hemingway. Gertrude Stein."

"Oh, that." She waved a dismissive hand. "Writers. They're such *babies*. They say that what they want is recognition—for the *work*, they say—but what they *really* want is adoration for *themselves*, and they want it from *everyone*. And they want *money*, too—don't let them fool you with all that *Art* business they're always talking about. Dickie published some things of theirs, little collections of short stories, and he put them out in *beautiful* editions, leather bindings, *lovely* paper. And were they grateful? Not Ernest and Gertrude. They both *demanded* free copies, hundreds of them, so they could give them away to all their friends. And then they turned around and yelled at Dickie because he wasn't *selling* enough copies. Can you *imagine*?''

I nodded.

"Ernest even tried to *punch* Dickie once. In the library, upstairs. He can be incredibly charming, Ernest, and he's fabulously handsome, in a kind of brutish way. But he's really a *terrible* bully, and he's ever so much bigger than Dickie was. But Dickie was a boxer at Princeton, before the War, a champion, and he just backed away a little bit, and Ernest missed him, missed hitting him, and then Dickie took a step forward and punched Ernest right on the nose.''

She smacked a small, perfect fist into a small, perfect palm. "*Pow*!" she said, and then she giggled happily. "Just like he deserved. And Ernest fell down—I thought he'd been hurt, but he was more surprised than anything else. *Startled*, I guess. And when he got up, his face was as red as a beet, and he said, 'We'll talk about this some other time. When there are no ladies present.' He said that because I was there—he sort of nodded toward me. But that hadn't stopped him from trying to hit Dickie, obviously.''

She giggled once more. "I think he just wanted to leave without getting punched in the nose again. And Dickie told him, 'Whenever you like.' And Ernest left, and Dickie never talked to him again. I mean, can you *blame* him?''

"What about Stein?''

"Well, Gertrude never tried to *punch* Dickie.'' She smiled. "Although I think she would've done a better job than Ernest did.'' Her face became serious. "But no. She and Dickie were cool to each other for a while, but then they made up and they were friends again.'' She looked at me and then she said, excited, as though she'd just remembered where she'd hidden the family gold, "Would you like to meet her?''

"I think I'll have to," I said.

"You can come with *me*, then. Tomorrow night. I'm going there. To her house, I mean. She *always* has people there. Writers and editors and all the important people in town. And painters, too. Gertrude is crazy about art, the place is *filled* with paintings. I don't really like them all that much, it's that modern stuff, everything all jumbled up, but a lot of people do."

"Fine," I said. "We'll go there together."

She clapped her hands and she made a delighted little bounce against the cushion. "*Wonderful!* You can pick me up at seven." She frowned, concerned. "Is seven all right with you?"

"Seven is fine."

"Oh good!" She touched the fingertips of her right hand to her temple, lightly. "But would you be terribly upset if we stopped this now? I think I'm getting a teensy-weensy headache."

"Not at all." I had some other questions, but they could wait until tomorrow night.

"I'm terribly sorry," she said, and she looked terribly sorrowful, "but once I start getting one of these, the only thing I can do, honestly, is go lie down for a while." She sighed and then she lifted her small, perfect head and she smiled bravely.

"It's okay," I said.

"Thank you," she said, "for being so understanding." She stood up, and so did I.

I found Henri Ledoq sitting outside the small café, a folded newspaper on his lap, watching the women come and go. On the table were his bowler hat, his gloves, and the folder that held the police reports.

Aside from Ledoq, only a few people were out there. A young couple ignoring their coffee and staring into each other's eyes. An old couple ignoring each other and staring into their coffee. And, off by himself at a far table, a fat man wearing a tight gray suit and reading a magazine.

Ledoq noticed me just as I reached him. He smiled and

stood up, flipping the newspaper to the table. "And how is Madame Forsythe adapting to widowhood?"

"Pretty well." I said. "But the cocaine probably helps."

He frowned. "She used cocaine while you were there?"

"Not in front of me. But she used it."

He nodded. "You must tell me all about it, on our way to lunch. I will obtain a taxi." He glanced around.

"Where are we eating?" I asked him.

He was still looking for a taxi. "I suggest that we try the Lipp. It is a brasserie on Saint-Germain, not far from here. Alsatian food. Not especially subtle, but very satisfying."

"If it's not far, let's walk."

He turned. Once again he looked at me as though I'd let him down. "Walk?"

"Walk. You put one foot in front of the other, and then you do it again."

"Ah." He smiled. Sadly. "Perhaps your French ancestors are farther back in time than I imagined."

"Could be."

He sighed. "Very well. We shall walk." He turned, picked up the bill, examined it carefully, set it down, then reached into his pocket and pulled out some coins. Carefully, he counted out a few, set them on top of the bill, and then slipped the rest back into his pocket. It was the first time I'd seen him spend money. I had begun to wonder whether he ever carried the stuff.

He picked up his hat, put it on, picked up his gloves, put them on, and then picked up the folder. He tucked it under his arm and turned back to me. "*Bon*. Let us undertake this famous walk."

As we strolled down the Rue de Lille to the Rue des Saints-Pères and turned right opposite the School of Fine Arts, I told him most of what I'd learned from Rose Forsythe.

The buildings along the Rue de Lille were posh. But as we came to the Boulevard Saint-Germain, the neighborhood changed. The buildings were the same height, six or seven stories tall, the usual brick and stone darkened with the usual soot. But they were less stately than the buildings to the west of us, and less elaborate than the proud, plump buildings along the Rue de Rivoli.

And the people we passed were less prosperous. There
were fewer men than women, and most of these were workers
and storekeepers and students. On the Right Bank, watching
the men in their sleek suits, you could believe that no War
had ever taken place. And maybe, for many of them, it hadn't.
Maybe they'd been too well dressed for the government to
risk losing them.

But things were different on Saint-Germain. Along with
their shabby jackets and baggy pants, some of the men wore
their own personal souvenirs of battle. A ragged scar, maybe,
or a limp. A cane, or a pair of crutches. An empty sleeve
folded back over a missing arm. At the broad intersection of
Boulevard Raspail, a haggard man in the uniform of a French
soldier, the jacket tattered, the pants soiled, shuffled slowly
across the street, his lips moving soundlessly, his eyes still
dazed by what they'd seen.

The Brasserie Lipp was a big place, brightly lit and filled with
the buzz and clatter of hungry people. Henri Ledoq held his
bowler in one hand, his gloves and the folder in the other,
while he consulted with a waiter. The waiter was tall and slim
and regal and his black hair was slicked back by the same
pomade that everyone in Paris seemed to use. His nose was
large and bony and, in its shade, he was growing an enormous
mustache. The tips of the mustache curled into perfect circles
and made it look like a strange, inverted pair of spectacles.
Frenchmen took their mustaches seriously.

Finally, marching as stiffly and as formally as a British
Guardsman, the waiter led us to a table in a distant corner.
Ledoq put the hat, the gloves, and the folder on one of the
three empty chairs, and we sat down in the other two. The
waiter handed him a menu, reverently, like the high priest of
some stern religious cult passing down a sacred text. Then,
reverently, he handed one to me. He said something to Ledoq.

Ledoq turned to me. "You wish an *apéritif*?"

"No thanks. Maybe some water."

"I believe I shall have a small Ricard. Do you know this
drink?"

I nodded. "I'll stick with the water."

He spoke to the waiter. The waiter nodded formally and then he turned and marched away.

Ledoq opened the menu, and he sighed a large contented sigh. I put mine on the table. Ledoq glanced at me. "Shall I order for you, *mon ami*?"

"Sure," I said. "Whatever you think's good. But nothing exotic. No liver. No organ meats."

He smiled. "Very well." For a moment he studied the menu with the same attention he usually paid to women. "Ah." He turned to me. "They are serving a special dish today. *Andouillettes à la tourangelle*. These are a kind of pork sausage, marinated in armagnac and then cooked in a hot oven with sliced mushrooms and just a bit of Vouvray wine. Quite delicious, if properly prepared."

"Fine," I said.

He closed the menu. "*Bon*. And I will have the skate with black butter and capers. As for the wine, I suggest that we share a bottle of Montrachet. It will go well with both our meals. The 1919 vintage is particularly good. Still a tad young, perhaps, but very drinkable."

"Fine."

"A small salad?"

"Sure."

He smiled. "Such nonchalance toward food. Perhaps you were adopted, my friend, and have no French ancestors at all."

"Could be. Do you know of a woman named Sybil Norton?"

"Yes, of course. An Englishwoman. A writer. One of the few, here in Paris, who actually supports herself with her work. She writes novels of crime. Why do you ask?"

"According to Rose Forsythe, she was having an affair with Richard Forsythe."

He raised his eyebrows. "Indeed." Suddenly he smiled. "Remarkable. The man has been dead for two months, and yet he continues to surprise me."

"And," I said, "according to Rose, she was the one who called, from the hotel, and told her that Richard was dead."

"Oh yes?" He considered for a moment. "I do not recall this being mentioned."

"It's not in the police report?"

"Not that I remember." He picked up the folder, opened it, riffled through the sheets inside. "No. Here, it says only that the manager of the hotel informed the police. Madame Norton's name is never broached."

"Interesting," I said.

"But why——" He stopped. The waiter had reappeared, and he was carrying a tray. He set a pitcher of water in front of Ledoq, and then a long spoon and a tall glass that held a couple of inches of yellowish Ricard. He set a bottle of mineral water in front of me. And then Ledoq gave him detailed instructions in French for half an hour or so, gesturing and frowning, before he let the man leave.

When he was out of earshot, Ledoq said to me, "But why would no one mention Madame Norton?"

"I don't know. But like I say, it's interesting."

He poured some water into the Ricard, clouding it. "And there is another question, *mon ami*, one equally as 'interesting.' "

"What was she doing there."

"Exactement."

"What do you know about her?"

He shrugged. "As I said, she is a writer of crime novels. She apparently makes an excellent living from them." He smiled again. "Oh, and she was involved in a scandal while she was still in England."

"What kind of scandal?"

"It has become a famous story. She discovered, you see, that her husband was having an affair. A common enough situation, of course. But she dealt with it in a unique manner. She knew that the husband intended to stay for the weekend at the home of some friends, and she knew that the other woman, the mistress, would be there also. On Friday, she wrote a letter to the local police in which she professed to be in jeopardy. She did not specify what sort of jeopardy. Late that night, she drove her car into the moors and abandoned it near a pond. The pond was—purely by happenstance, of course—locally famous because several poor souls had drowned in it, and their bodies had never been recovered. Inside the car, Madame Norton left a suitcase. This was opened, as though it had been rifled. And then she simply vanished.''

''She set him up. The husband.''

Ledoq smiled. ''*Exactement*. The next day, when her servants reported her missing, the police made inquiries about the husband. They found him with the mistress at his friends' house. As the house was only a few miles away from his own, the police reasoned that he could easily have skulked away during the night, gone home to his wife, killed her, and then disposed of the body.''

''Where was she?'' I asked him.

''Somewhere in the north of England. At a resort hotel. Registered under the name of the mistress.'' He laughed.

''Nice,'' I said.

''Is it not?'' he said. ''Well, for a week the police searched the moors. They dredged the pond. And, of course, they followed the husband's every move. They investigated his bank account—a joint account, with his wife—and they discovered several serious irregularities. Both those and the fact of his mistress were reported in the press. It was a huge embarassment for him.''

''How did it end?''

''One of the musicians at the hotel recognized her. By then her photograph had been published in every newspaper in England. The police were called in. She claimed, when questioned, to be suffering from amnesia.''

Another smile. ''Within a month, she had instituted a divorce claim. It was granted. Shortly afterward, she came to Paris. That was perhaps a year ago.''

''What happened to the husband?''

''He married the mistress.'' Ledoq shrugged. ''I suspect that, in order to salvage some small fragment of his self-respect, he had no choice.''

I nodded.

''I have read one of her books, the first one. *The Mysterious Affair at Pyles*. It was clever, but I felt no compulsion to read the next of them.''

He glanced around the restaurant and then turned to me. ''You said that you wished to speak with the journalist? Ernest Hemingway?''

"Yeah."

"He has just come through the front door. Shall I fetch him for you?" He smiled. "I warn you. He is a catastrophe."

"In what way?"

"You shall see. And if we invite him to the table, he will pay for nothing he orders. He is legendary for this."

"That's all right. Let's talk to Mr. Hemingway."

Dear Evangeline,

Here I am, finally, back in my legendary little room, after a long afternoon and a short evening with the children.

Maman Forsythe is a witch. This is a scientific observation, unfiltered through any feline bias on my part.

Where was I?

Yes. Neal was just about to put in an appearance at my little table before the Café le Figaro.

I must tell you that I was so engrossed in inscribing all those penetrating psychological insights in my earlier letter that I failed to hear him approach. Suddenly he was there, at my shoulder.

'Um,' he said. (This is, by the way, the youthful American's equivalent of 'Pardon me, madam, but may I trouble you for a moment?')

I looked up. As usual, he was carrying his Baudelaire and wearing his black: shoes, socks, trousers, and a shapeless cotton jacket that sported, in lieu of buttons, one of those ingenious American fastening devices, a 'zipper', two rows of small, interlocking metal teeth, one row on each side. This was half opened, or half closed—I am unacquainted with the linguistic rules that apply to zipperhood.

In any event, only his shirt and his skin were white, and they were of nearly identical hue. But he is not really an unattractive boy. If only he would stop playing at Decadence.

I smiled and, at the same time, with the nonchalance of a bank teller who has been embezzling for the whole of his life, I casually turned over the pages of my letter and their penetrating, etc. 'Hello, Neal.'

Monsieur Guillaume had obviously recognised Neal; and, for the moment, at least, he remained inside the café. But through the window I could see him watching

us warily from behind the counter, ready to leap over
it (or around it, considering his bulk) and to sprint to
my defence should the boy suddenly lunge at me with
lust in his eyes and foam on his lips. It's a terrible
burden, Evy, being a *femme fatale*.

'Can I sit down?' he asked.

A *femme fatale*, even one masquerading as a nanny,
a *nanny fatale*, must never criticise a young man's
grammar. 'Of course,' I told him.

He sat, glancing around him, and set the copy of
Baudelaire on the table. He looked at me, then looked
away, toward the cathedral. He was brooding, evidently.
It was clearly my responsibility to keep the conversation, such as it was, alive.

'How are you this morning?' I asked him.

He glanced at me. 'Okay, I guess,' he said. He has
some difficulty in meeting my gaze—unlike my young
fisherman, before that champion was reduced to nautical
jam—and again his glance twitched away. Then, in an
instant, as though remembering his manners, he glanced
back and asked me, 'And how are you, Miss Turner?'

'Very well, thank you.'

He glanced away, and commenced to brood again.

I asked him, 'And where's your family this morning?' I was actually beginning to feel more like a nanny
than I ever do with Edward and Melissa.

Frowning slightly, he shrugged. 'My mother's with
the kids. Shopping.' He looked back toward the cathedral, and frowned again. 'Like always.'

I nodded, concealing my envy of his mother uncom-
monly well, I believe. 'Are you enjoying Saint-Malo?'
I asked him.

He looked at me. 'This place?' A faint note of scorn
curdled his voice. 'It's really boring, don't you think?
I mean, the only interesting thing is the grave of what's-
his-name. Out on the island.'

'Chateaubriand,' I said. 'On the Ile du Grand Bé.'
You can always rely upon a nanny for accurate geographical details.

'Yeah,' he said, 'and you can't get there except at

low tide.' He glanced at me, glanced away. 'And Chateaubriand was kind of a bore anyway.'

'Do you prefer Chartres?' I asked him.

Another frown. 'I used to. But Richard's gone now—
my cousin. He had a house there. Not far from ours.
It's really an incredible place.' Then he realised, I believe, that he was speaking in the present tense about a
life, and a way of life, that now existed only in the past.
He looked away again, and he shrugged—a bit hopelessly, or so it seemed to me; but attempting to disguise
hopelessness as indifference. I felt badly for him, and
not a little guilty for what I was about to do.

(I must interrupt this, Evy, to tell you that it is precisely to investigate the death of Richard Forsythe that
I am masquerading as a nanny. Here, at this moment in
our conversation, the Pinkerton in me began to rise,
shark-like, slowly to the surface.)

'It won't be the same now,' he said. 'Chartres, I
mean.'

Monsieur Guillaume emerged from within the café
then, wiping his big hands on his apron. He glanced at
Neal, looked at me. *'Et pour le garcon? Qu'est-ce que
ce sera?'*

Neal blinked at up him, clearly uncomprehending.

'He wants to know,' I said, 'whether you'd like
something. A coffee, perhaps?'

'Oh. Yeah, sure.' He looked up at Monsieur Guillaume. 'One of the big ones.' Then, to me, he said, 'But
without any milk in it.'

'Un grand café,' I told Monsieur Guillaume. *'Noir,
s'il vous plaît.'*

'Bien, mademoiselle,' he said, and lumbered back
inside.

I said to Neal, 'Your cousin Richard. Your mother
mentioned to me that he died in March.'

'Yeah.'

'You liked him,' I said.

Neal nodded. 'He was an incredible guy. Really incredible. He was the smartest guy I ever met. He knew
just about everything. And he could do *anything*.'

This was the first time I had ever heard Neal express an enthusiasm. It wasn't—well, it wasn't *nautical*—but I thought it was quite nice.

I said, 'He was a poet, your mother told me.'

'Yeah, and a really good one. But he was a whole lot more than just a poet. He was a publisher, too. He had his own publishing house in Paris.'

'He must've been someone quite special.'

He nodded. 'He was, yeah.'

'I understand that there was some mystery involved in his death.'

He had recovered, it seems, from his attack of zeal. Possibly talk of Richard's death had saddened him. Or possibly he had realised that zeal conflicted with the pose he likes to affect. Now, sitting back with an elaborate casualness, he shrugged. 'No mystery,' he said. 'He killed himself. He wanted to die, and he did it his own way.'

'You say that,' I told him, 'as though you admire him.'

'I *do* admire him,' he said. A tiny rivulet of enthusiasm had trickled back into his voice. 'He lived his life on his own terms, and his death, too.'

'But he was married, wasn't he? Did he stop to consider how his wife might feel?'

'Rose? Rose loved him, I guess. But she knew him, you know? She knew everything about him. She even knew about all the women he was seeing.' He said this with a man-of-the-world casualness which immediately belied itself. And then he frowned. 'Well, except for one of them.'

'Who was that?'

His answer was forestalled by the arrival of Monsieur Jean, who set a white saucer and steaming white cup of coffee on the table.

'Thanks,' Neal told him.

M. Jean nodded and lumbered off.

'And who was that, Neal?' I repeated. (With the idle and amiable interest of a nanny, naturally, and not the prying persistence of a Pinkerton.)

Casually he reached for his coffee—and then snapped his hand away from the hot cup. Wincing, he shook his fingers in the air.

Poor Neal. This is the problem with poses, of course: they are so easily undone by the malice of the props we use to maintain them.

I glanced into the café. I am certain that Monsieur Guillaume was grinning as he turned his expanse of back to me and busied himself with his bottles.

Undone, too, by the jolly malice of provincial café owners.

'Aster Loving,' Neal said. 'She's a singer. She sings on a barge on the Seine, in Paris. Richard took me there once, to meet her. She's a Negro.' He glanced at me as though he expected me to swoon away in astonishment. We nannies, of course, are made of sterner stuff.

'That was why,' he said. 'Why he never told Rose about her, I mean. Rose doesn't like Negroes. Aster's really nice, though. And she's really beautiful.'

'But Rose knew about the other women? And she accepted them?'

'Sure.'

'And she accepted the idea of Richard committing suicide?'

'Richard told her he was going to do it. He told her more than once, she said. He wanted to die beautifully. And he wanted to die together with someone. A suicide pact.'

'And Rose approved of that?'

'Sure. Like I said, she knew Richard. Sure she approved.'

Although not to the extent, evidently, of dying with him herself.

'The woman who died with Richard,' I said. 'Sabine something. Had you ever met her?'

'Sabine von Stuben. Yeah, I met her in London. She came over with Richard in February. My parents didn't know. They don't—they didn't really approve of Richard, so sometimes I'd see him without letting them know. In Paris, or in London when he came over. Anyway, he was there, in London, and he telephoned, and I went to meet him at the Savoy. Do you know the Savoy?'

I smiled. 'Only by reputation, I'm afraid. How did you like Sabine?'

'I don't know. She was really beautiful. And she was nice . . .' He frowned. 'But . . .'

'What?'

'Well, I thought she was kind of . . . strange.'

'Oh? In what way?'

He reached out for his coffee, thought better of it, and sat back, crossing his arms over his chest. 'The way she looked at Richard. It was like she idolised him or something. She followed him around, like a dog. I mean, I guess I can understand—Richard was an incredibly good-looking guy. You ever see a picture of him?'

'No,' I lied.

'He was tall, you know, taller than me, and he always looked great. He was . . . elegant. He always wore double-breasted suits, really well tailored. And black, all of them. He always wore black.'

Ah.

'And he was clever and witty, always saying funny things, and he was a really generous guy, so I guess I can understand why she'd be nuts about him. But there was something about the way she acted. She couldn't stop looking at him. It was like she had a fever, almost. Her face would even get a little red, and it was like she couldn't breathe, like—'

He stopped, suddenly a little red himself, and reached out for his coffee. He tested the cup, tentatively, with the tips of his fingers, then lifted it. 'She was really political, too,' he said.

'Political?' I said. 'In what way? She was a communist?'

'No, no,' he said. 'Exactly the opposite. She hated the communists.' He sipped at his coffee. He set down the cup, reached for the sugar bowl, scooped out a spoonful of sugar, dropped it into the coffee. 'Really hated them. She said the communists were trying to destroy Germany, just like they'd destroyed Russia.' He added two more spoons of sugar to the coffee, then stirred it. 'She's a member of some new party in Germany. The National Socialists. They want to get rid of the communists and the Jews. And everybody else, too, it sounded like.' He set down the spoon, raised the cup to his mouth, sipped at it. 'I thought it was all pretty boring.'

'I'd always thought that socialism was an international phenomenon.'

'Not the kind in Germany, I guess.'

'And Richard,' I said. 'He felt the same as Sabine? His politics were the same?'

Neal laughed. 'Richard? He didn't give a da—' He blinked, glanced away, then sipped again at the coffee. 'No. Richard didn't care about politics at all. He was smiling at everything she said. He told me, another time, that politics was the last refuge of the lethally tedious. He wouldn't trade one good poem, he said, for all the politicians in the world. He was the guy who told me about Baudelaire. He gave me that,' he said, and nodded toward the copy of *Flowers of Evil*.

Ah.

He placed the coffee cup in its saucer. 'You know what Baudelaire says about poets?' He leaned slightly forward and put his hand on the book, as though it were a bible and he were about to take an oath. He recited, ' "The poet is like the prince of the clouds, who rides out of the tempest and laughs at the archer." '

' "*Exilé sur le sol*," ' I quoted, ' "*au milieu des huées, Ses ailes de géant l'empêchent de marcher.*" '

Neal had sat back, frowning. I translated: ' "But exiled from the sun, amidst the clamour, his giant's wings prevent him from walking." '

'You know it?' he said, blinking in surprise. 'In French?'

I smiled—with that disarming modesty one expects of a nanny, albeit one who is also a Pinkerton, and a *femme fatale*. Secretly, however, I was rather pleased with myself. It has been over a decade, as you know, since we read the poems, you and I.

'I learned it years ago,' I told him. 'I'm surprised I can still remember it.'

I must be very careful with young Neal, Evy. In his stare now was a mixture of awe and something (I suspect) considerably more physical. Any additional poetry, so much as a single line of it, in any language, and I fear he would have clambered over the table and pitched himself into my lap.

Back to the investigation. 'For how long,' I asked him, 'had Richard known Sabine?'

He blinked again, but like someone waking from a daydream. 'Sabine? Oh. For a couple of months, I guess.'

'Before he died, you mean?'

'Yeah,' he said. Once again, he glanced away, towards the Cathedral of Saint-Vincent. Suddenly he frowned and quickly looked back at me. His voice was hurried and low, with something like panic pushing at it from beneath: 'It's my mother. Don't tell her we were talking about Richard. Okay?'

'Of course,' I assured him. I smiled sweetly—while two (less than altogether sweet) thoughts hurtled through my Pinkerton mind: first, that Mrs Forsythe might well have some secret (i.e., suspicious) reason for wanting Neal to remain silent about this; and, second, that by agreeing not to reveal the discussion, by creating a secret of our own, I had also created a debt which Neal could repay, if I so wished, by further discussion.

One discovers quite a lot when one is a Pinkerton, and some of this pertains to other people, and some of it pertains to oneself; and not all of it, in either case, is necessarily wholesome. Or welcome.

Ah well. Better a professional dissembler, I have come to believe (or persuaded myself), than an amateur.

In any event, I put on my spectacles to look, and it was indeed Mrs Forsythe, and the children, who were ambling down Rue Broussous from the direction of the Saint-Vincent.

Above brown brogues and brown socks, young Edward wore pale brown short trousers of corduroy, a matching blazer, unbuttoned, and a white shirt so brittle with starch that it buckled over his belt. Melissa wore a white cardigan, also unbuttoned, and a lemon yellow dress, white socks, and white patent leather shoes.

Mrs Forsythe's outfit was considerably more *soigné*. In one hand she carried her parasol of tasselled white silk; in the other, dangling from thin but robust leather straps, a linen shopping bag, packed with recent purchases. She was wearing, perched jauntily on her (rather *aggressively*) blond hair, a white toque, silk as well, but brocaded. Her dress was a trim white linen affair that reached midway down her slender calfs, and her jacket was of the same material, the shoulders draped, the hem just brushing the lowered waistline of the dress. Around her slender neck, inside the opened collars of dress and jacket, she wore still more silk, a flowing white scarf, loosely knotted. On her feet, white silk stockings and white pumps. Not patent leather, however, the pumps; they were lambskin. She had bought them, so she told me, in Paris. I was not even remotely jealous, of course.

She wore all of this, I regret to say, very well.

Edward noticed us before the others did. He waved his hand and shouted, *'Hey!'*, and then immediately began to scramble towards us.

'Eddy!' his mother called after him. *'Edward!'*

Ignoring her, he scurried down the cobblestones, his brown hair flopping, his small angled arms ferociously pumping. He arrived at the table in a rush, and stopped himself, very theatrically, by smacking the palms of his hands against the table. *'Whoa!'* he said. Crockery clattered. A dollop of coffee leapt from Neal's cup and splashed against the tablecloth.

'Hey!' said Neal, backing away.

'Miss Turner,' said Edward, panting as though he had just run from Marathon, his eyebrows raised so high they disappeared behind the fringe of his hair, 'you know what we saw? We saw a guy beating on an *octopus*! He kept *hitting* it and *hitting* it against a rock!

Just hitting it, for *hours*!' He turned to Neal and abruptly stopped panting. He grinned widely. 'Boy, are *you* in trouble. Mom looked all over for you. She's *really* mad.'

Neal's face crinkled with distaste. 'Why don't you go away?' he asked his brother.

'*Make* me,' said Edward, and stuck out a pink tongue.

'Edward,' said Mrs Forsythe, coming up behind him (as Edward retracted his tongue and transformed his face into a mask of rigid innocence), 'you mustn't run like that. Running is common. Isn't that right, Miss Turner?'

'Extremely common,' I told Edward. Especially among young children.

'You see?' said his mother. She turned to her oldest son. 'Neal, where *were* you this morning? We looked all over for you.'

Holding on to the table with one hand to support himself, lest his paroxysm of glee topple him to the ground, Edward held his other hand to his mouth and dramatically failed to smother an evil chortle.

Neal was blushing. 'I had some things to do.'

'I'm sure you did,' said *Maman*, 'and I'm sure they were *extremely* important, but it was very rude of you to disappear like that.' She turned to Edward. 'And do stop making that noise, Eddy. You sound like some silly barnyard animal.'

'Maybe,' said Melissa, and ran her tiny hand through her long straight blond hair, 'maybe Neal was looking for Miss Turner.' This she said with a perfect reasonableness in her voice and a perfect blandness on her ten-year-old face.

'What silly barnyard animal?' asked Edward.

Mrs Forsythe had glanced from Melissa to Neal, whose blush had spectacularly deepened, and then to me. Her blue eyes narrowed slightly, but only for the briefest of instants before she turned back to Neal and smiled at him sweetly. (As sweetly as I had, if this suggests anything to you.)

'*What* silly barnyard animal?'

'Hush, Eddy,' said *Maman*. 'Neal, come along now, would you, dear? I need some help with these things.'

Behind her, Melissa's blandness dropped like a veil and she grinned wickedly at Neal. Glee rippled once again through Edward.

(At one time in my life, you know, I actually prayed for a brother and a sister.)

Neal was blinking. 'But—'

'Come along, dear.' She turned to me and offered me the same sweet smile. 'I know I promised you some time off, Miss Turner, and I know you're exhausted after your experience yesterday on that silly old boat. But I wonder if you'd be willing to take care of the children for a while. I've got so many things to attend to right now.'

'Of course,' I said. Even a genuine nanny would have said the same. As a counterfeit, I had virtually no choice.

'But I haven't paid yet,' said Neal. 'For my coffee.'

'I'll handle it, dear,' she told him, and held out the bag. 'Be a darling, would you? I'm the teensiest bit exhausted myself.'

Neal stood, blinking, and accepted the bag. Awkwardly. (Have you noticed that whenever a woman gives a bag of any sort to a man, even a young man, he will instantly begin to display a truly massive maladroitness? It's as though, by their utter ineptitude with things feminine, men feel that they somehow demonstrate their own masculinity.)

Mrs Forsythe breathed a large sigh of relief and briefly fanned her face with her slender hand. 'Thank you, dear.' She leaned towards the bag (Neal moved his eyes heavenward) and she dislocated packages until she found a white lambskin handbag.

She looked at the other children. 'Don't wander off, now. I'll be right back.' She looked at me and again smiled sweetly. 'I'll handle your bill, too, Miss Turner,' she said. 'You just relax.'

'But—' I said. This is, however, a woman accus-

tomed to 'But—'s. She strode off, into the café. Neal
glanced at me, glanced away.

Edward placed his elbow on the table casually, a
polo player resting between chukkas, and then looked
up at me and asked, hugely serious, 'Miss Turner, how
come an octopus has eight testicles?'

Melissa hooted with laughter. Convulsing, clutching
at her side with her left hand, she pointed the finger of
her right directly at him. 'You *dope!*' She hooted some
more and then sucked in a great blissful breath of air.
'It's *tentacles*, you idiot. Testicles are *balls.*'

Edward wheeled on her. 'They are *not!*' He wheeled
on me. 'Are they, Miss Turner?'

I considered (carefully) a number of choices; but at
last I plumped (as all nannies must) for Truth. 'Well,
yes, Edward, I'm rather afraid they are, actually.'

He looked up at Neal. Neal nodded, smiling, then
glanced at me, stopped smiling, and blushed once more.
Edward turned to Melissa, then to me again. He pursed
his lips, then wrenched them thoughtfully to the side,
lowering his eyes. And then, abruptly, he looked up and
grinned. '*Whoops,*' he said.

And, all at once, everyone was laughing—including,
I must confess, the nanny.

And then, all at once, as Mrs Forsythe came striding
back from the café, everyone stopped laughing and began to look about the square with a quite extraordinary
insouciance.

Mrs Forsythe looked down at me. 'Are you coming,
Miss Turner?'

And so—after my hurried run into the post office, to
post my letter to you—we all returned to the hotel. I
spent the rest of the day with the children, reading
books and telling stories. (None of which involved tentacles or, you may be sure, testicles.) Mrs Forsythe
packed, a formidable task, and Neal was sent scurrying
off on various errands, all of them no doubt momentous.
After dinner, I trundled up the stairs to bed.

I confess, Evy, that I do not like the woman. A few

moments before she arrived at the café, young Neal and I had been simply a pair of people, pleasantly chatting to each other. (We might possibly, each of us, have possessed some clandestine personal reason for chatting; but is this not, perhaps, the human condition?) In an instant, however, *Maman* had deliberately reduced us to the roles that she was determined we ought play. The Son and the Nanny.

A Pinkerton's lot is not a happy one. And neither, it would seem, is a Son's.

I grow, Evy, a trifle weary—just the teensiest bit exhausted. This letter has turned into an opus. Surely I have repaid any lingering debt?

I do wish that *Maman et la famille* had not arrived when they did. I should have liked to learn more about this Sabine person. And more about the woman who sings on barges, Aster Loving.

I will mention her name in my next report to the Pinkerton Agency; perhaps it shall prove useful.

But in fact it was not to interrogate the Forsythes, any of them, that I was assigned to my current lofty position. It was, rather, to obtain information about a certain Count De Saintes, in Chartres, and his sister. Yes, a count. Mrs. Forsythe, the mother of the dead young man, believes that they may be somehow responsible.

In any event, soon I shall be able to say that I count a count among my acquaintances. But I shall endeavour, for your sake, to avoid doing so. I am, of course, entirely in earnest about this.

        All my love,
        Jane

Four

ERNEST," I SAID.

"Call me Ernie," he said. He grinned as though he'd never been more pleased to meet anyone in his life, and he began to squeeze my hand to a pulp.

I smiled and tightened my grip.

"A real pleasure," he said.

Beneath the thick mustache, he was still grinning. It was a grin that showed a lot of healthy white teeth, a grin that crinkled up the corners of his sparkling brown eyes and dug deep dimples into his broad tanned cheeks. He was young, in his early twenties, and he was big, as tall as I was, but wider, with heavy square shoulders pushing at the corners of a battered brown wool sport coat. He wore a brown work shirt and brown cotton pants and brown brogues. The clothes were drab, maybe, but you were so busy being impressed by the person inside them that you didn't really notice. His voice boomed a bit more than it needed to, maybe, but it boomed with sincerity.

Rose Forsythe had said he was incredibly charming and fabulously handsome. He was all that, and then some.

He released my hand but he kept grinning. "Henri tells me you're a Pinkerton, hey?" He shook his big head in admiration. "Jesus," he said. "That must be fascinating work."

Henri Ledoq stood off to the side, watching us with a small smile on his lips.

"Sometimes," I said.

He said, "You look very fit, hey? Ever do any boxing?"

He lowered his left shoulder and raised his hands and he turned them into big brown fists, then moved them in small quick circles in front of his grinning face. The bottom of his coat slapped against a salt shaker and sent it twirling to the floor. It bounced, without breaking, against the tiles.

"Damn," he said, and he swooped to pick it up and he smacked his forehead against the table. Silverware rattled. He grabbed at the table to stop it from falling, but he grabbed too hard, jerked it, and Henri's water pitcher toppled over. It shattered against a butter dish and water exploded across the tablecloth.

"Damn," said Hemingway, and reached forward.

Ledoq cut him off. "Please, Ernest," he said. "Do not trouble yourself. We will move to another table."

"Okay, swell," said Hemingway, who didn't seem very troubled. Lightly, he rubbed his forehead, then looked down at his fingers. No blood. As Ledoq signaled for a waiter, Hemingway turned to me and grinned and put up his fists again. "Hey? Ever go a few rounds?"

"A few," I told him. "A long time ago."

"Yeah? Swell! Let's spar sometime, hey?" He did a quick shuffle with his feet and slammed the back of his right leg into one of the chairs. It was the chair that held Ledoq's hat and gloves and the police folder. The folder sailed off the seat and it flapped itself open and sheets of paper flew out and spun and fluttered in different directions to the floor.

Hemingway bent forward, but Ledoq put his small hand on the man's large arm and said, "Ernest. Please. Over there." He pointed to an empty table. "I will deal with this."

"Sure." He grinned at me. "C'mon."

We moved toward the other table. "I work out," Hemingway said, "in a gym not far from here. Bags, jumpropes. Come by sometime, we'll fool around. Hey?"

"Sure," I said.

There were four seats at the table. I sat down in one, and Hemingway sat down to my right. He put his big hands on the tablecloth and he knocked over the salt shaker. "Damn," he said, and he righted it. He grinned at me again. "Henri said you wanted to talk to me. What about?" All of his attention was focused directly on me, and he had a large amount of attention. Journalists usually do, or pretend they do.

I said, "The Agency's been hired to investigate the death of Richard Forsythe. I need to find out as much as I can about him."

"Hey, happy to help. Anything I can do. I mean it. But what's to investigate? Guy committed suicide."

Ledoq joined us. He glanced around the circular table, taking in the seating arrangement, then sat to Hemingway's immediate right. He placed the folder, the gloves, and the hat on the last remaining chair, out of the journalist's reach. *"Bon,"* he said.

"His mother," I told Hemingway, "thinks differently."

"Nice lady," he said. "Got a lot of class. I always liked her." He grinned. "But she's wrong, hey? He took the easy way out."

"Out of what?" I said.

"Want to know what I think?" he said, suddenly serious, and he leaned forward and clasped his big hands together. Ledoq glanced down and eyed the hands warily.

"Sure," I said.

But the waiter with the mustache arrived then, carrying another menu. He handed the Sacred Text to the journalist. Hemingway opened it and knocked over the salt shaker. As he reached for the shaker, Ledoq's hand darted forward, snapped it up and swiftly shifted it to the far side of the table. He set it down firmly, released it, and sat back, folding his arms over his chest. The waiter and his mustache looked on, impassive.

Hemingway studied the menu. "Hey! They've got *andouillettes*. Swell!" He turned to the waiter and spoke for a while in rapid French. The waiter listened, nodded, took back the menu, and marched away.

"They do a true *andouillette* here," Hemingway said. "Very good. Very fine. They use—"

"What was it you were saying, Ernest," interrupted Ledoq, "about Richard Forsythe?"

"Yeah, right." Again he leaned forward and clasped his hands together. He took a quick look around the room. When he spoke, his voice was lowered. It wasn't low, but it was lowered. "He was a fairy."

Ledoq laughed. "Ernest, he made no secret of the fact that he sometimes slept with men."

"Exactly," said Hemingway, and he sat back, opening his hands to show us his broad palms.

"But he slept," said Ledoq, "more often with women."

Hemingway put his arms along the arms of the chair. "More women around. The War. Simple mathematics, hey?"

Ledoq said, "Ernest, I admit that I find bisexualism to be in questionable taste, but—"

"I don't get it." Hemingway sat back and shook his big head. "Bisexualism. How's it work, hey? Tuesday you wake up and you decide that today you're gonna grab Rosie O'Grady? Wednesday you wake up and you decide you're gonna grab Barnacle Bill? How's that work?"

Ledoq smiled. "I do not know. But I can tell you what Richard Forsythe said about it."

"What's that?"

" 'Skin is skin, flesh is flesh.' "

"Yeah, yeah. Very pretty. But it's window dressing. And that's what the women were, too. Window dressing, hey? Deep down, he was a fairy, plain and simple." He leaned forward again, put his arms on the table again. "Here's what I think happened. He was with What's-her-name, the German girl—"

"Sabine von Stuben," said Ledoq.

"Right," he said. He turned to me. "Good-looking girl. Crazy about him, too, followed him around like a bitch in heat." He shook his head. "Terrible waste. Anyway. They're together that afternoon, the two of them, up there in that hotel room, hey? *And Forsythe couldn't get a hard-on.* Old Mr. Love-Twig had gone belly up. And what probably happened, she made fun of him, von Stuben—you've gotta watch those German girls, tough as nails, all of them. Anyway. He went well and truly nuts. And he pulled out that sissy little Browning and he blew her brains out. And then he saw what he'd done, and he turned the gun around and used it on himself." He sat back. "It's obvious, hey?"

Ledoq smiled. "There are, of course, several difficulties with that theory."

"What?" said Hemingway. "What difficulties?"

The waiter and his mustache reappeared then. Food for Ledoq and me, a bottle of wine in a silver bucket.

Ledoq and Hemingway waited, hushed, while the waiter uncorked the bottle. He offered the cork to Ledoq, who sniffed it thoroughly and thoughtfully and then nodded his approval. The waiter poured a half an inch of wine into Ledoq's glass. Ledoq tasted the wine, nodded at the waiter again.

The waiter poured wine into my glass, then into Hemingway's, then again into Ledoq's. He put the bottle back into its bucket, tucked a napkin carefully around its shoulders, and marched stiffly off.

Ledoq lifted his wine glass. Hemingway and I held up our glasses. *"Salut,"* said Henri. He moved his wine glass toward Hemingway's, thought better of it, and said, *"Salut,"* again and put it to his mouth and drank. Hemingway and I said *"Salut,"* and did the same.

Hemingway smacked his lips together lightly, cocked his head and narrowed his eyes, and he said, "A Montrachet. The 1920?"

"The 1919," said Ledoq.

"A very good wine. A very fine wine. What difficulties?"

Ledoq picked up his knife and fork. "They were both wearing their clothes. If they had in fact made love, the *contretemps* you mention would have occurred some time previously." He cut a bit of his fish, and put it in into his mouth.

Hemingway shrugged his heavy shoulders. "So she said something afterward. Those German girls are tough."

I tried the sausage. It was very good. Very fine, too.

"And," said Ledoq, "according to his wife, this was the first time that Richard Forsythe had ever carried the pistol with him." He smiled. "Are you suggesting that he suspected, beforehand, that the von Stuben girl would question his virility? And that he intended to prove it, unequivocally, by shooting her? And then himself, of course."

Hemingway shrugged again. "So he was carrying the gun. Maybe he carried it more often than Rose thought he did. Or said he did."

"And there were two hours," said Ledoq, "between the time of her death and the time of his."

"Probably took him that long to work up the guts to do it."

Ledoq raised an eyebrow. "But you said that the act itself was an act of cowardice."

Hemingway narrowed his eyes and announced, "Sometimes, to be a coward, you've gotta have guts."

"And what does that mean, precisely?"

"No idea," said Hemingway, and he laughed, a big booming laugh. He threw himself back in the chair, still laughing, and his elbow hit the wine stand and the thing clanged like a bell and began to topple. Darting sideways, Ledoq grabbed for it and snatched the bucket. Frowning impatiently, he set the bucket back in the stand, then moved the stand away from Hemingway.

"How did you know," I asked the journalist, "that the gun was a Browning?" I took another bite of sausage.

"Everybody knew. He used to keep it in a drawer in his library. Used to pull it out all the time, show it off to people. Sometimes he'd take potshots at a big stuffed bear he kept across the room." He frowned. "He was a pretty good shot, got to admit. Never missed that damn bear." He grinned. "But it was a *big* bear, hey?"

"Rose Forsythe said that you and Richard had an argument there. In the library."

He scowled. "Bastard was cheating me. He published a book, a collection, some of my short stories. He paid me an advance—not much, couple of hundred bucks, but at the time, all I was thinking about was getting the work in print. Later, I started to stew about it, hey? He hadn't paid me another dime. So I went over there, to talk to him. He said there wasn't any more money. Told me there weren't any copies left. Had the nerve to say it was *my* fault—that I'd given them all away. That's a crock, and he knew it. We got into an argument." He looked at me. "But that was all it was, an argument, hey? No big deal."

"Rose Forsythe said you tried to hit him."

He laughed again. "She said that? Nah! He swung at *me*. He missed, and *then* I swung at him. Damn carpet tripped me and I fell down. And that was it, hey?"

I'd seen his relationship with inanimate objects and I could believe his story. But I could also believe Rose Forsythe's.

Suddenly his handsome brow furrowed and he said, "Hey. Wait a minute. All these questions. You don't think *I* had anything to do with that? Forsythe and the German girl?"

"No," I said. "It's just what I do. Ask questions. But now that you mention it, where were you that day?"

"The day he killed himself? At the races. With about ten other people I know."

I nodded.

He squinted at me for a moment, as though trying to decide whether I were okay. Finally he decided I was. Once again he shook his head in admiration. "Must be fascinating work."

Just then, the waiter and his mustache returned, this time carrying Hemingway's lunch. He set the food down, picked up the bottle of wine, topped off all our glasses, eased the wine back into the bucket, and marched away.

Hemingway picked up his napkin, unfolded it. He tucked a corner of it into his collar and spread the rest of it out over his shirtfront. "But here's the best part of the story." He picked up his knife and fork and cut himself a chunk of sausage. He put his hands on the table, both of them fisted, his right holding the knife, his left holding the fork with the piece of sausage skewered on its tines. "He sent me back the contract we'd signed. Afterward, hey? After the argument? He'd written 'null and void' on it and signed it. Few weeks later, I sold one of the same damn stories, and a couple of new ones, and some poems, to another publisher here in Paris, Bob McAlmon." He grinned. "And because Forsythe canceled out the contract, he never got a penny from the deal. So, hey, sometimes the good guys *do* win." He grinned again, and then stuck the piece of sausage into his mouth.

"Admirable," said Ledoq.

Chewing, Hemingway nodded. He swallowed and said, "Yeah." He looked over at my plate, which was empty now. "How'd you like your *andouillettes*?"

"Very much."

He nodded. "It's something, hey, what the French can do with pig guts."

Ledoq leaned quickly forward. "When are you going to Spain, Ernest?"

"End of the month."

"What was that," I asked Hemingway, "about pig guts?"

Ledoq pursed his lips.

Hemingway was chewing. He swallowed. "The *andouillettes*." He tapped the blade of his knife against the sausage. "Some of them are made from veal, hey? But the best ones, the true *andouillettes*, they're made from the intestines and belly of a pig. They're very fine, hey?" He took another bite.

"Yeah," I said. I looked over at Henri Ledoq. No organ meats, I had told him. A kind of pork sausage, he had said. "Very fine," I agreed.

Ledoq's lips were still pursed. Mostly, I think, to stop himself from smiling.

"Been to Spain?" Hemingway asked me.

I turned to him. "What?"

"Spain. Been there?"

"No."

"Me neither. We're going down to take a look at the bullfights. I've got a theory about bullfights."

"What is that?" said Ledoq.

He put down his knife and fork. His face grew very serious. "Now that the War's over, the bullring is the only place where a man can confront Death truly and well. And the matador, he confronts it every day. With skill and grace, hey? With bravery. He courts the possibility of his own death, as a gesture of human pride and dignity and style. *Panache*, hey? He confronts Death every day, and he defeats it."

Ledoq smiled. "Only for a time, *mon ami*."

"Defeats it, I said—not escapes it. Nobody escapes it. Not in this world." He turned to me and grinned. "Little Dickie Forsythe sure didn't." He picked up the fork, and he finished off the last bite of sausage.

I said, "You knew that Forsythe used drugs?"

He swallowed. "Everybody knew."

"You know where he got them?"

"They're all over the place. Marijuana. Cocaine. Heroin." He grinned again. "Me, I prefer this." He reached over, plucked the bottle of wine from the bucket. It was nearly empty. He poured what was left into Henri's glass, then asked him, "Another one?"

"Not for me, no," said Ledoq. "Thank you."

Hemingway turned to me. "You?"

"No thanks. Where did Forsythe get his?"

He leaned over and plunked the bottle back into the bucket. The stand wobbled and Ledoq reached out to steady it. He sighed wearily.

Hemingway said, "From someone at the Hole in the Wall, probably. It's a dive, over in the Ninth Arrondissement. Filled with scum, hey? Dope dealers, deserters. Dickie went there all the time." He grinned. "Probably felt right at home."

I asked Ledoq. "You know the place?"

He nodded. "It is as Ernest says."

"Do you know anybody there?" I asked him. "Anybody who might've known Forsythe?"

"I know of one," he said. "An American, but originally Irish. John Reilly. He is involved, I am told, in the drug business."

"In a lot of things," Hemingway said. "Supply sergeant during the War, hey? Got into smuggling, the black market, just about everything. Tough as nails. Story is, he made more money than the chiefs of staff."

"Yes," said Ledoq. "He returned here, to Paris, immediately after the War. He is something of a luminary now, among the criminal element."

I turned back to Hemingway. "Do you know a woman named Aster Loving?"

"Sure. Nigger jazz singer, hey? Sings on a barge on the Seine. I heard her once. She's good."

"Did you know that she was involved with Forsythe?"

"Yeah?" For a second he looked interested. Then he shook his head, and waved his hand at me. "Ah, that's window dressing. Like I say, the guy was a fairy."

He reached into his pants pocket, pulled out a watch, glanced down at it. "Damn. I've gotta go. An appointment with a friend." He slipped the watch back, put his hand inside his coat, frowned, reached around for his back pocket. "*Damn*," he said. He looked at me, thunderstruck. "I left my wallet at home."

"Forget it," I said. "The Agency will take care of the bill."

"I was *sure* I had it with me. I remember, just before I left—"

"It's okay," I said.

He grinned. "Damn white of you. Next time I pay."

"Fine."

He stood up and his chair tumbled backward and clattered against the tiles.

"Leave it, Ernest," said Ledoq.

Hemingway nodded. He turned to me and grinned once again and held out his hand. "Great to meet you. Hope I see you again." Once again, he tried to squeeze my hand to a pulp.

"Me too," I said.

"Henri, good to see you."

They shook hands. Ledoq narrowed his eyes and did something with his mouth that was either a brief smile or a brief wince.

And then, with a wave of his big brown hand, and another bright white grin, Hemingway turned and walked into the back of a Frenchman who was spooning up some soup.

As Hemingway apologized in French, Ledoq stood, bent forward, picked up the fallen chair, and righted it.

Hemingway turned, grinned again, waved again, and strutted off.

Ledoq sat back down and leaned toward me. "Forsythe was having an affair with Aster Loving?"

"Yeah. You know her?"

"Of her. I have heard her sing. She is very talented. Rose Forsythe told you of this affair?"

"No. He kept it a secret from his wife."

"From everyone, it seems." Smiling, he looked off and he shook his head. "What a devil he was, that Forsythe. Sybil Norton. Aster Loving." He frowned. "But how, then, do *you* know of his connection to Aster Loving, *mon ami*?"

"From Forsythe's cousin."

"The son of the financier?"

"Yeah. The family's in France right now, in Chartres, and the Agency's got someone with them. Forsythe told his cousin about the woman. The cousin told our operative. The report came in just before I left London.''

"My admiration for your Mr. Cooper increases. And whom has he placed with the family?''

"I don't know. But I'd like to talk to this Aster Loving.''

"And who could blame you? She is most attractive.''

"When does she start singing?''

"At midnight, I believe.''

"Okay. We'll go see her.''

He nodded. "I look forward to it.'' He sat back. "And what did you think of Monsieur Hemingway?''

"You want the long version,'' I said, "or the short one?''

"The short, I think.''

"I thought he was a jerk.''

He laughed.

"I noticed,'' I said, "that he never gave me the name of that gym of his.''

"No, no, of course not. You are much too large a personage for him actually to spar with you. He prefers shorter partners. Did you notice, also, that he neglected to recall his rendezvous until after it became clear that there would be no more wine?''

"I noticed.''

Ledoq said, "You do not believe that he was involved in the death of Richard Forsythe?''

"No. I don't think he ever killed anybody.''

Ledoq nodded. "I believe that this is one of the great regrets of his life.''

"He was in the war?''

"The ambulance corps. In Italy. He was wounded early on.''

"I can see why.''

Ledoq laughed again. "I think that the buffoonery, the clumsiness, is the result of his spending all his energy attempting to be something he is not. The brave and manly hero. I suspect that at one time he was a very sweet and sensitive boy. I suspect that, beneath the muscles and the bravado, he still is. I suspect, too, that he would despise me for thinking so.''

He took a sip of wine and then leaned forward. "And you know,'' he said, "he is in fact a remarkable writer. I read one of the stories in that little book, the one published by Monsieur Forsythe. It concerned itself with a young man fishing, alone in the Great American Forest. No dialogue, no other characters. Just the young man, and the forest, and the river, and the fishes. Nothing of much import happens. The young man walks through the forest; he arranges a camp for himself. He loses some fish and he catches some others. He eats the fish—very simply prepared, of course. He sleeps, he awakens. But all this is detailed in a language that is so powerful—so apparently simple and precise, and yet so evocative—that the story becomes quite profound. Somehow the reader knows, without the writer ever having said so, that the young man has recently returned from the War and its many horrors. I was most impressed.''

''Why didn't you read the others?''

''Pardon?''

''You said you read one of the stories in the book. Why didn't you read any of the others?''

''Ah.'' He sat back and he shrugged. ''The man is a jerk.''

I laughed.

''And now, *mon ami,''* he said. ''Shall we have some coffee?''

''Sure,'' I said. ''Nothing I like better than coffee, after a meal of pig guts.''

''But was the *andouillette* not good?''

''It was good,'' I admitted.

''Well then . . . ?''

''Let's have the coffee.''

I sat back then, myself, and for the first time I looked around the room. At the high ceilings, the slowly moving fans, at the other tables, the other customers.

Ledoq signaled for a waiter, then looked back at me. ''What plans have you for this afternoon?''

''Well,'' I said, ''first off, I'd like to find out why we're being followed.''

He frowned. ''Followed?''

''Don't look now. But behind you, over by the column. The fat man in the gray suit. He was at the café. Near Rose Forsythe's house.''

He thought for a moment. Then he said, ''I recall that gray suit. It was a disaster.'' He stroked his goatee. ''What shall we do?''

Dear Evangeline,

Today we were very nearly overcome by a disaster.

Now that it is safely tucked into the past (where *Maman* cannot find it), now that the day is over and everyone is safely tucked into bed, I can gather my wits, such as they are, and tell you what happened.

First, however, I must tell you about Mont-Saint-Michel. It is splendid, Evy. It is as remote and dramatic and as wonderfully romantic as I remember it from my childhood. Perched on a jumble of rock in the middle of nowhere, the flat empty sea on one side, the flat empty sand on the other, it soars spectacularly up into the clear blue Normandy sky, like a hope, or a prayer. Despite what happened today, I love it. If I were on my own, I should stay here for weeks and weeks. I should amble endlessly up and down the narrow Grande Rue, peering into all the quaintly cramped little shops, buying lace from this one, wooden gewgaws from that. I should settle into some cosy roost near the Cloisters, up top, and watch the tide come roaring in across that huge blank sweep of sand. (They say it travels, as it rushes eastward, 'at the speed of a galloping horse'; and they say truly.) I should wander with a flickering candle through the tunnels in the living rock beneath L'Église and I should imagine myself a contessa seeking her bold young lover, or an aging but still unruly nun seeking her no-doubt weary confessor. The nun would of course require less imagination.

As it happens, we have tarried here longer than *Maman* Forsythe had planned. Madame Verlaine served us oysters last night, at the hotel in Saint-Malo, and it seems that one of *Maman*'s had spoiled. This morning when Reagan, the driver, arrived at the hotel, she was already complaining of a stomach upset.

Maman's upset stomach was not the disaster. I shall

be getting to the disaster. I am not trying to be mysterious, Evy; but I am, after all, a Pinkerton. I do know how to report my disasters.

As for Reagan, he is something of a near disaster himself. God knows where he had been hiding before he materialized at breakfast. Possibly within a Dickens novel. Tall and gaunt and stooped, he wore a long white linen driving coat, powdered with dust; and, clamped to his forehead, like a second pair of eyes, a pair of dusty goggles. His grizzled brown hair sprang off in every direction, like tufts of ticking from a mattress; but somehow amidst that tangle he was always able to locate a tuggable forelock.

I am being harsh, you say. But as we prepared to leave this morning, and I was clambering up into the automobile, the lickerish old swine *pinched* me on the buttock. 'Whoops,' he said. 'Mind those door handles, miss.'

He's English, I'm ashamed to admit.

In any event, when we drew near Mont-Saint-Michel, *Maman* began to breathe deeply and clutch at her middle; and, as soon as we arrived, I was dispatched to find shelter for us all. So here we all are, at the Mère Poulard, whose sole recommendation is its uniqueness: it is the only hotel on the Mont. At the moment—just gone eleven at night—Edward, Neal, and the Swine are sharing one room, and Melissa and I (she fast asleep on the other bed) are sharing another. *Maman*, of course, is gallantly recovering in a room of her own.

Her ailment did, however, provide me an opportunity to learn more about Richard Forsythe and his circle. From her sickbed, *Maman* asked me to lead the children on a tour of the Mont—ostensibly to broaden their knowledge of French culture but in truth to remove them from her presence, so she might suffer in peace.

Neal was with me when she made the request, and he volunteered to accompany us. The idea clearly troubled her. She is concerned, I believe, about a threat to someone's virtue, but I am unclear as to whose, Neal's or mine. Neal's, I suspect. From the moment she discovered our tête-à-tête outside the café in Saint-Malo,

she has been keeping us apart, deliberately, and sometimes none too subtly.

And so now, lying there along the bedspread in her
sportif outfit, both hands pressed against her stomach,
Maman tried to invent some objection to his coming,
when suddenly another nasty cramp attacked her. Wincing, she waved us away, then lurched up from the bed
and hurried off to the lavatory.

And so we wandered, the four of us, through the
Abbaye; through the Merveille (and marvelled at it);
through the Réfectoire; through the Salle des Hôtes with
its two massive fireplaces, each large enough to roast a
brace of oxen; down through the deliciously gloomy,
echoing tunnels; and then out into the giddy air again
and back down the steep giddy steps. Then down the
winding Grand Rue, and finally out La Porte de
l'Avancée to the sand and the sea. The tide was low,
and Melissa and Edward began to build castles, perhaps
fifty feet to the south of us, while Neal and the nanny
made themselves quite uncomfortable on some lumpy
rocks at the base of the Mont. (The nanny keeping,
while she did so, a practised eye on the young archi-
tects, lest they wander off and disappear beneath the
quicksand rumored to lurk in the area.)

'Really a nice day,' said Neal, glancing at me, then
glancing away.

'Yes, it is,' I said. 'It's glorious.' It was indeed; and
there was no one else about. Between our rocks and the
sea lay an expanse of lovely brown sand that was infinitely wide and, before it met the water, perhaps a
hundred feet long.

'Um,' said Neal, and looked off towards the horizon.

Neal is not, as I've said, the most forthcoming of
conversationalists.

'Neal,' I said, 'when we were talking yesterday, you
mentioned something about a woman, a singer, who
was . . . involved with your cousin Richard.'

He glanced at me again, blinked, glanced away, then
nodded. 'Aster Loving. Yeah.'

'Was she still involved with him at the time of his death?'

'No. He hadn't been seeing her for a long time.' He frowned slightly. 'How come you're so interested in Aster?'

I gave him one of my most charming, most duplic-itous smiles. 'It's not really Aster who fascinates me,' I said. 'It's Richard. From everything you've told me, he sounds a remarkable person.'

He smiled brightly, delighted at this revelation of a shared respect, and I felt a small, quick, nanny's stab of guilt. Which was immediately, and almost entirely, stifled by a Pinkerton's firm sense of duty.

He said, 'He was, yeah. Like I say, he was just about the most amazing guy I've ever met.'

'Was it Aster who ended the relationship?'

'No.' He looked down, then up, then over to me. 'See, the thing is, Aster takes drugs. A lot of drugs. That doesn't mean she isn't a really, really nice person. She is. I really liked her. And Richard liked her, too. But he didn't like the drugs. He didn't like her taking them, I mean.'

'That's strange,' I said. 'Because from something your mother mentioned, I'd assumed that Richard had used drugs himself.'

He looked surprised. 'My mother said that?'

'Well, I confess, it was more something she *didn't* mention.' She hadn't mentioned anything, of course.

He nodded. 'She didn't like Richard. She thought he was a bad influence.'

(You will please note that the nanny, while attempt-ing to glean whatever facts she can from Neal, has rather foolishly neglected her surveillance of the other children, whom we last observed gambolling near the water. Perhaps you can begin to anticipate the disaster.)

'Did he in fact use drugs?' I asked Neal.

'Yeah, he did. But only cocaine. That's not such a big deal. A lot of people take it—a lot of the people that Richard knew, anyway. And he only took it, he said, so he could stay awake long enough to enjoy his champagne.' He smiled at this *bon mot,* hopefully, wanting me to smile as well, and to share with him again.

I smiled. 'Had he ever given you cocaine?' I asked him.

'No.' He sounded disappointed—not surprising, I suppose, in a youth with an exemplar like Richard for a cousin. 'He said that he'd give me some when I finished my first year at college.'

In lieu of a firm handclasp and a hearty 'Well done!' presumably.

'Which drug was Aster using?' I asked him.

'Heroin. Richard didn't approve of heroin. And Aster, well, she used a needle, I guess you have to, with heroin, but she didn't like to, um, inject herself. So Richard had to do it for her.'

'How on earth did she become an addict,' I said, 'if she couldn't inject herself?'

'It wasn't that she *couldn't.* Richard said she just liked it better if someone, a man, I mean, if a man, um, injected her.' The word *injected* was giving him a terrible time. I wasn't enjoying it overmuch, either. I was nodding, fairly calmly, I think; but I suddenly felt myself a great distance from Sidmouth and from Mrs Applewhite's.

'How is it that Richard told you all this?'

He shrugged. 'We were friends. I've known him since I was a little kid. And he knows I'm interested in the same stuff that he's interested in. Poetry, I mean. And books and things.'

'The other woman. The woman who died with him. Sabine?'

'Yeah. Sabine von Stuben.'

'Did she use drugs as well?'

'No. I don't think so. Maybe cocaine, but like I say, everyone uses cocaine.'

Everyone? I wondered. Mrs Applewhite? The Archbishop of Canterbury?

'For how long had he known her?' I asked him.

'I dunno. Not for long, I think. He called her his "new friend" when he introduced her.'

'And that was in February, you said?'

'Yeah.'

'Do you know how they met?' I asked.

Before he could answer, I heard a distant childish scream of pleasure and I looked toward Edward and Melissa.

They hadn't moved from their position, but the tide had come in and the sea was now up to Melissa's waist, and it had climbed beyond Edward's.

It had come in so quickly that its edge, rabidly foaming, turbid with sand, was a mere thirty feet from the rock where we sat, Neal and I. It was still coming, an encroaching monster, inexorable, moving visibly as I sat there, immobile and disbelieving.

Edward and Melissa were having a grand time, thrashing and splashing about as the water rushed around them. They slapped at it; sprayed it at each other. Their clothes were soaked; their hair was dripping.

I saw all this in less time, I expect, that it has taken you to read it, and then I was up, screaming at them: *'Edward! Melissa! Come over here right now!'*

The looked at me, laughing, and splashed each other again.

'Edward!' I cried.

He turned to me, laughed, made a small reluctant movement toward the rapidly diminishing shore, and then he tripped on something, and suddenly he was gone. Melissa shrieked.

I do not know how long it took me to reach him. I have no recollection, now, of crossing the sand, entering the water, splashing through it. All at once, it seems, I was there, snatching at that small sodden bundle in the grey churning sea. Somewhere close by, someone was screaming: Melissa. The water came as high as my own waist now, and my legs were frozen to the bone. I dug my feet into the sand, bracing myself against the current, and I ripped his head free. He gave a great shake, arms flailing, and then he coughed, spasmodically, wretchedly; but I was thrilled. It meant he was alive.

I was somewhat less thrilled half a second later, when he began to writhe madly about, screeching, wailing, twisting with panic in my arms. His hand smashed against my face. (You have no idea how powerful a small terrified boy can be.) He smacked at me again and I darted back my head, which put me off balance, and all at once I lost my purchase and I went under, dragging Edward with me.

I was caught in a whirl of muddy grey, as cold as the grave, the stuff of nightmares, and my ears were filled with a dreadful howl. For a tumbling, demented moment I felt the same terror Edward must have felt. And then at last I came up, sputtering, gasping for breath. And Edward was coughing again, and wailing again, louder and more piercingly than before, and he was trying with all his tiny, superhuman strength to kill us both.

'*Sshh,*' I hissed at him.

Had I been out there on my own, I should have been in no real peril. The tide was, after all, hurling me exactly where I wished to be hurled, towards the shore. Alone, I should have merely swum along with it until I reached the causeway, and then scrambled up into La Porte.

But Edward's panic-stricken behavior made that impossible. He was kicking, punching, whipping his hands at me, desperately trying to escape his own terror. And I was trying to calm that terror and also to bring myself back upright by digging the heels of my shoes into the sand. But the sand was moving, too, and in the opposite direction, and very swiftly.

'*Shhh,*' I said. 'It's all right, it's *all right*.' I glanced quickly around and saw that Neal was out there, too, bless him, and that he had Melissa. He had been pulling her towards shore, but he hesitated now, watching me.

'*Get her in,*' I cried, as Edward shrieked again and jerked against me. My right arm was wrapped around his body, pinning his left arm to his side, but suddenly, with his right hand, he bashed me again.

It was at this point, I believe, that I went somewhat insane.

It occurred to me, in a sort of sudden cold flash, that the situation was utterly ridiculous. This was a bright sunny cloudless day in France, perhaps the most civilized country in Europe; and civilization, in the form of, say, a *salade Niçoise*, was no farther away than a hundred yards (I don't know why I thought of a *salade Niçoise*); and I was about to die in less than five feet of seawater. Mrs Applewhite, who had herself pinned the swimming ribbon to my proud bodice, should have been quite miffed at me.

Somehow I managed to stab both of my feet into the shifting sand. I whirled against the current and grabbed Edward with both my hands and swung him up from the water, and I shouted in his dripping, twisted, pallid face, as loudly as I could, *'No more sticky buns!'* (He quite likes sticky buns, you see.)

Instantly he snapped shut his opened mouth. His hands stopped flailing, his legs stopped kicking; his body, all at once, drooped. He looked at me and—Evy, I swear—he began to pout.

'Calm yourself,' I said, 'and we'll be out in a moment.'

After that, it was simply a matter of towing him towards the causeway, where Neal and Melissa awaited us. Edward lay there in the crook of my arm as calmly as in his own bed. When we reached the causeway, Neal offered his hand, helping Edward up, then assisting me. As I arose from the sea, not unlike Aphrodite, he glanced at my front, where the material of my dress clung to my skin, and he blushed and nearly dropped me. When I was back on land again, he blushed and blinked and turned away. I wrapped my old cardigan, now dripping and drooping, around me.

We were all of us soaked through, naturally, and I felt as exhausted as I might feel if I'd run a hundred miles. I sat down—plopped down, really—on the steps of the Porte de l'Avancée. The children sat on either side of me, Edward to my left, Melissa and Neal to my right. The water spilling from us made an oddly syncopated patter against the stone beneath.

For a moment no one spoke. Then Melissa took a deep breath. *'Wow,'* she said. 'That was *great.'*

I looked at her. Her canary yellow pinafore was waterlogged, her blond hair was dark now and matted to her skull, but her eyes were shining, her mouth was smiling widely, and her face was alight with a wild, invincible excitement.

This time it was I who began the laughter. I couldn't help myself. Then they took it up, the children, even Edward, who was shivering uncontrollably at my side. There was relief in the laughter, of course, and perhaps even some hysteria; but I suspect that, for all of us, it felt better than drowning would have done.

Then Melissa leaned around me and said, to Edward, 'You're such a big ba—'

I turned and gave her a glare that would have stunned a Gorgon. She never finished the sentence.

It was Edward who spoke next. He looked up at me and through chattering teeth he said, 'Mom's going to kill us.'

Yes. *Maman* might be less than pleased that her children had been nearly washed from the landscape.

'I believe we can prevent that,' I said. It was clearly as much in my own interest as in theirs that *Maman* never learn of the dunking; not that the children needed to know this. 'Come along. Let's get you out of those damp clothes.'

Monsieur and Madame Boyle, the owners of the hotel, made an enormous fuss over the soggy crew, but I prevailed upon them to keep the incident from Madame Forsythe. Madame's heart, I explained, was delicate, and no matter how comical and harmless the incident had been *actually*, ha ha, her learning of it might damage that organ irreparably. We all bathed and changed into dry clothes, and Madame Boyle washed the wet things and set them on the line to dry, which took very little time in today's clear sunlight. She ironed them for us, as well. (I paid for all this with my Pinkerton emergency francs, to prevent the charges appearing on the bill at our departure.)

And so by dinnertime, when *Maman* joined us, we were all dressed very much as we had been.

Only my cardigan and all of our shoes were unsalvagable; these had been ruined. The children had an abundance of shoes in their luggage, and I had a pair of boots in mine. *Maman* didn't notice that everyone was wearing different footgear; and, if she noticed that I was wearing a different cardigan, she failed to comment on it.

She had begun to recuperate by this time, but she was still weak. She barely touched her food before she drifted back to her room, sighing bravely.

But I had no chance to learn anything further from Neal. Melissa and Edward kept hovering about the hotel lounge, where Neal and I sat. They were very sweet. Both of them talked about the afternoon's dunking in terms that an adult might use—mere spot of bother, really, quite amusing in retrospect—when Edward was (I suspect) secretly rather fearful that the tide might surge up the Grande Rue, rip the front door from its hinges, and lunge for us across the carpet in a great engulfing wave; and Melissa was (I suspect) secretly rather hoping that Edward was right. Just after nine o'clock, *Maman* made another wan appearance and suggested that everyone retire. Tomorrow, she said, we should be making an early start.

After Melissa fell asleep, I left the hotel, and wandered up to the entrance to L'Église. The streetlamps had been lit and the narrow passageway was empty as it climbed in a slow steep spiral around the hill towards the distant peak. Some of the little houses that edged against the Rue were illuminated from within, promising a familial cosiness which I myself can only barely remember. At the rampart below the church I stood and looked out at the flat black sea, which surrounded the Mont now, transforming it into an island in the center of a magical, moonlit lake. Overhead, a million stars were burning. I stood there and I thought about Richard Forsythe.

What sort of man is it, I wondered, who discusses his mistresses with his young cousin? Who talks about giving one of them injections of heroin? Who promises the boy a gift of cocaine?

Children are charming when they pretend to be adults. (Melissa and Edward are occasionally charming, at any rate. I often wish that Neal would forgo the pretence.) Adults who pretend to be adults are less charming.

I am coming round to the conclusion that I do not like the man.

Never fear, Evy, I shall perform my duties properly. If he has been murdered—the police are satisfied that he committed suicide—then I will do my utmost to discover who was responsible. But I am beginning to believe that I shall have more sympathy for the perpetrator than for the victim.

Enough. I must sleep.

All my love,
Jane

Five

I WAS ASLEEP when someone knocked at the door.

I opened my eyes, remembered where I was, and rolled off the mattress, my feet slamming to the floor. I hadn't bothered to take off my shoes before I lay down.

Someone knocked again. I stumbled to the door and opened it.

It was Ledoq, carrying his gloves and hat. When we split up, outside the hotel, I had taken the police folder. Ledoq might get busy, and I didn't want him to lose the thing. It rested now on the room's nightstand, beside the bed. "You were sleeping, *mon ami*?"

"That's okay. Come on in."

He stepped in and I closed the door. "Grab a seat," I said, and nodded toward the writing table. He set the gloves and hat on the table, pulled out the uncomfortable-looking chair, turned it around, and sat, putting his hands on his thighs. I sat on the bed.

"What happened?" I asked him.

"As you suggested," he said, "I attempted to discover whether our friend in the poorly cut gray suit was following me. I was able to determine, rather quickly, that he no longer was. I doubled back—very discreetly, of course—and found him watching the entrance to the hotel. He stood just outside the lobby of the apartment building across the street, reading a newspaper. I took great pains to make certain he did not see me."

Ledoq crossed his legs, right thigh over left. "He remained

in place for quite some time. And so, *naturellement,* did I. Finally he entered a nearby *tabac.* From the window of this he could still maintain his surveillance of the hotel entrance. He used the telephone inside, briefly, then returned to his post. Within twenty minutes another man appeared. This one wore a suit of black, but it was cut just as poorly as the suit of the other. The coat was tight across the shoulders, the trousers were too short, with no break at the hem, and—''

''Right,'' I said. ''And what happened?''

He looked at me as though I'd let him down once again. ''Yes. The first man handed him the newspaper and departed. He obtained a taxi and entered it. The second man remained there. He remains there still, and continues to read the newspaper. It must be an extraordinary newspaper.''

''So you lost the first guy,'' I said.

He smiled, pleased with himself. ''*Au contraire.* I obtained a taxi of my own and I followed him.'' Raising an eyebrow, he leaned slightly forward. ''Would you care to know where he went?''

''He went to the Prefecture. He's a cop.''

Ledoq sat back. ''If you already knew what the outcome would be—''

''I didn't. Not for sure. But it made sense. Besides the cops, who knew I was in town? Only Rose Forsythe and Hemingway, and they're both too involved with themselves to worry about me. And like I said, your prefect's got his own reasons for being interested in this. Whatever they are. So it made sense that the guy was a cop. But it's always good to know. You did a fine job.''

He was still a bit ruffled. ''It was not a simple thing, you know,'' he said. ''Observing without being observed. Locating a taxi before the first man slipped away—''

''I know that,'' I said. ''You did a fine job. I appreciate it.''

He sat back. ''Well.'' He looked down and he brushed a piece of lint from the material of his pants. ''I did what I could.''

''You did great.''

He looked up, smiled. ''*Bon.* And what is it we do now?''

I picked up the folder. "You said you could get this translated by tomorrow morning?"

"Certainly."

I handed him the folder, then sat down again. He set the
folder beside his hat.

"Listen," I said. "Before we go to that barge tonight, and
meet Aster Loving, I'd like to go to the bar that Hemingway
talked about. The Hole in the Wall."

"A dreadful place. Noted neither for its food nor its
safety."

"I need to go there."

He shrugged. "As you wish. When shall I come here to
get you?"

"Around eight?"

"*Bon*. That will give us ample time for dinner. And you
will rest until then?"

I shook my head. "I've got an appointment with Sybil
Norton. I used the telephone downstairs to call her."

He sat back, his lips primly pursed. "You will not need
my assistance, I take it."

"Henri, she's English. With any luck at all, she and I can
probably talk to each other. She gave me the directions to her
place. It's not far. And this is the same situation we had with
Rose Forsythe. One of us is okay, two of us is ganging up."

He held up a hand. "Yes, yes. I agree." He smiled. "And
there is the matter of the lying."

"Yeah. Okay. The guy outside. The cop. He saw you come
into the hotel? Just now?"

He shook his head. "I took precautions to prevent that.
There is a back entrance."

"Good. It might be a good idea to use it when you leave."

"And when I return this evening?"

"No. I'll meet you downstairs. There's no point tipping
them off. We're in better shape, I think, if they don't know
that we know about them."

He nodded. "We will lull their suspicions, eh?"

"And make it easier for us to dump them later, if we have
to."

He sat back in the chair. "*Mon ami*, without a question
your ancestors were French."

*   *   *

At five o'clock that afternoon I was climbing up the stairs to Sybil Norton's apartment. She lived on the top floor, the seventh, and there were a lot of stairs to climb. By the time I got to the final landing, my breath was coming and going in thoughtful little puffs.

Two doors, both painted red. On one of them, below the bell, a small brass plaque that said NORTON. Above the bell, a small circular spy hole, glowing a dull white from the light inside. I yanked on the bell.

After a moment, the spy hole darkened. Then the door opened.

"Mr. Beaumont?"

"Yes," I said. "Thanks for seeing me, Mrs. Norton."

In her early thirties, she was tall, maybe five foot eight or nine. She wore a belted black silk dress, speckled with red fleurs de lis, that fell smoothly from her broad shoulders and her deep chest and flared nicely from her narrow waist and down along her rounded hips. Her wavy hair was strawberry blond, parted on the left side and falling to just below her ears. Like Rose Forsythe, she had blue eyes, but hers were calm and steady, almost serene. She wore no makeup, and she didn't need any—her skin had the kind of complexion, pale cream and roses, that the English all take such pride in, even when they don't have it themselves.

"Do come in," she said.

She shut the door behind me. "This way," she said. I followed her. She moved with a languid ease, like a thoroughbred who had won another race today.

From the hallway we stepped into a corner of a foreign land that was forever England.

There was British bric-a-brac all around me, in the empty shelves of the dark wood bookcase, on the coffee table, on the end tables, on the chiffonier. There were commemorative mugs and commemorative plates and small porcelain statues of foxes and horses and hounds. On the wall were framed photographs of Queen Victoria and of King George V, and framed paintings of men in red hunting jackets and black caps, snorting with eagerness as they whipped the flanks of their eager snorting mounts.

And where there wasn't bric-a-brac, there were books—neatly arranged in the bookcases, piled in stacks along the tables and on the floor, left lying open and face down along the arms of the furniture.

"Forgive the mess," she said. "One attempts to keep abreast of it, but one so seldom succeeds. Please. Have a seat."

She was like Rose Forsythe in another way, too—she'd set up the coffee table for a guest. But there were no bottles of liquor here, only a teapot under a quilted red cozy, a creamer, a sugar bowl, some cups and saucers, and a silver platter of shortbread cookies.

I sat down on the sofa, a large piece of upholstered furniture decorated with an elaborate blue floral print. She sat down in a matching chair and she leaned toward me, her spine straight, her knees together and turned gracefully to the side. I noticed that she had very good legs. She noticed that I noticed this, and I noticed that she noticed that, and both of us pretended that we hadn't noticed a thing.

She smiled. "Tea?"

"Sure," I said. "Thanks."

She plucked off the cozy, set it carefully aside, and poured tea into two cups. She slipped the cozy back on. "Sugar?" she asked me.

"Please. Two."

She put sugar into my cup, stirred the tea. "Milk? Lemon?"

"Neither, thanks."

She handed me the tea. Without adding anything to hers, she sat back, her spine still straight, and she set the cup and saucer on her lap. She smiled again and she said, "You know, the character in my books is essentially an enquiry agent, and yet you're the first I've ever actually met."

I smiled. "Probably be a big disappointment."

"Oh dear," she said lightly. "One hopes not." She sipped her tea and then she raised her eyebrows and she asked, very casually, "Have you read the books?"

"No," I said. Maybe I imagined it, but I thought that her lips turned slightly downward. "I've heard good things about them, though," I added.

She smiled. "You're very kind to say so. I've some copies here, if you'd like them . . ."

The sentence trailed off and became a kind of implied question, and I said, "Sure. Very much. If it's no trouble."

"None at all," she said. "One moment." She set down her tea, and rose from the chair. She walked with her languid ease out of the room, and her dress still fit her very well. I picked up one of the books lying open and face down on the arm of the sofa. Something called *Ulysses*, by someone named James Joyce.

In a moment she was back, carrying two books. I put *Ulysses* back on the arm of the sofa. She handed over the two books.

I made admiring noises while she sat back down and picked up her tea. "I hope that *they* won't be a disappointment," she said. "I should be curious to hear what a real detective thought of them." She sipped her tea. "Now. How may I help you?"

I put the books on the sofa, beside me, and I took a sip of tea. "According to Rose Forsythe," I said, "you were having an affair with her husband."

She had raised the tea cup halfway to her lips. She stopped raising it and stared at me. For a moment, I thought she was going to ask for her books back. But then she set the cup down on the saucer and smiled. "Goodness," she said. "You don't dawdle, do you, Mr. Beaumont?"

"Not usually."

She nodded. "Would you care for a biscuit?"

"No thanks."

She raised the cup again, and this time she sipped from it. "An *affair*," she said. "The word suggests a relationship which continues, or has continued, over a period of time. One feels that its use in this context would be something less than entirely accurate."

"What would be more accurate?"

She smiled. "*Fling*, perhaps? Or perhaps *escapade*." She listened to the sound of that. "Yes. *Escapade* perhaps best describes what Richard Forsythe and I shared. You'd never met Richard, of course?"

"No."

"He was very attractive, you know. Almost absurdly attractive. I don't mean merely in the physical sense, although physically he was stunning. And he dressed terribly well, and he spoke terribly well, and he could be terribly clever and witty and amusing. But, more important, he had a remarkable *vitality*."

She cocked her head. "It was unique, really. He was possibly the only person I've ever met who seemed genuinely to live in the present. He seemed endlessly *interested* in whatever he was doing, in wherever he was, in whomever he was with. When one spoke, he *listened*, with all of his attention, and one got the feeling that he'd never been so fascinated with anyone in all his life."

"And he did that with everyone," I said.

She laughed. It was a good laugh and it had some surprise in it. She narrowed her eyes and she studied me, very briefly, a second or two. And then I think she realized that she was being rude, or being obvious, because she quickly took another sip of tea, hiding her eyes and her thoughts.

She looked at me. "Yes," she said. "Exactly. In the end, of course, one was forced to conclude that he was either a species of saint, or that he was, in emotional terms, a species of imbecile. Or, of course, that he was merely putting on an act."

"What did you decide?"

"I didn't. I still haven't, really." She smiled. "I'm inclined, now, to believe that he was almost certainly not a saint. But beyond that, he's as much a mystery to me today as he was then."

"What were you doing at the Grande Bretagne the day he died?"

She furrowed her brow a bit, not quite a frown. "You're very well informed, it seems."

"Rose Forsythe told me that you were the one who called her."

This was a frown. "I asked her not to mention my name," she said. She shook her head briefly. "Ah well," she said. "Rose. In one ear and out the other."

"Why the secrecy?"

She sipped her tea. "If you know anything about my recent history—'' She smiled. ''Yes, I see that you do. You can no doubt understand, then, why I might wish to avoid seeing my name in the newspapers again.''

I nodded. ''Fair enough. But what happened that day?''

''I had an appointment with Richard at three o'clock. There, at the hotel.''

''You'd met him there before?''

''No.'' She smiled. ''Our escapade, the single instance of it, took place here.'' She tilted her head toward the door that she'd gone through, and returned from, a few minutes ago. ''In there, to be precise.''

Whether she had intended it or not, by mentioning the bedroom as the place she'd met with Forsythe, she'd given it a significance it hadn't had before. I didn't need much imagination to imagine that there was probably still a bed in there.

She said, ''I went to the hotel to discuss a book of mine, one that Richard intended to publish.''

''Another mystery?''

''A volume of poetry.'' She indicated the two books on the sofa. ''Those are good, I believe, of their kind. I like to think that they're well written, and that they're entertaining. And that's all they were ever intended to be, really. Entertainment. A clever puzzle, something to amuse the reader. But I wanted to do something else, something more substantial. Richard had read my poetry, and he felt that he could do well with a collection of it. We would've had to publish it anonymously, or under a nom de plume, but I accepted that.''

''Why anonymously?''

''Most of the poems were''—she smiled—''well, let us simply say that most of them were very different, in tone and subject, from the books. My *readership*''—she put the word in ironic italics—''would have found them perplexing, at the very least.''

''Forsythe asked you to come to the hotel to discuss the book?''

''Yes. To go over the final selection of poems.''

''And you were supposed to be there at three o'clock.''

''Yes.''

''That's interesting,'' I said.

''How so?''

"Forsythe died at about three o'clock."

"Yes, I know. I was there when the shot was fired."

I sipped my tea. I was very civilized.

"Inside the suite?" I said.

"Outside it. In the hallway. I was just approaching the door when I heard the shot."

"And what did you do?"

"Well, I knew, immediately, what it signified."

"Which was?"

"That Richard had committed suicide."

"And how'd you know that?"

"Everyone who knew Richard, even slightly, knew that he was fascinated by the idea of suicide. As a matter of fact, he'd even asked me to join him in the endeavor."

"Just like that? Like taking an afternoon walk?"

She smiled. "Not altogether as prosaically as that, no. He made it sound—or he attempted to make it sound—terribly noble and dashing."

"And when was this?"

"The week before."

"Did he say why he wanted to commit suicide?"

"He felt it was time, he said."

"No other reason?"

"Perhaps he was bored. He'd done everything, he'd been everywhere. Perhaps there were no surprises left."

"How does that jibe with his living in the moment?"

"I imagine that living in the moment could become extremely wearisome. In any event, when I heard that shot, I was convinced that he'd finally gone ahead and done it. Committed suicide."

"But it was a gunshot fired in a hotel room. That's all you knew about it. It didn't have to be Richard committing suicide."

"Yes. Yes, I know. But at the time I felt certain that that's what it was."

"Uh huh. And what did you do?"

"I knocked on the door. There was no answer. I tried turning the doorknob. The door was locked. I went back to the lift, took it downstairs, and I left the hotel."

"But you came back," I said. "You had to. Otherwise

you wouldn't have known about the von Stuben woman being dead.''

"I returned, yes. For a few minutes I walked the streets—not going anywhere, really, just walking. In a sort of daze, I suppose. And then it occurred to me that what you've just said might be true. That perhaps something else had happened. A burglar, perhaps. Perhaps an accident. Or that perhaps Richard *had* attempted suicide, but had failed, and that he was lying there bleeding to death. So I telephoned a friend. An acquaintance of mine, in the police department."

"Who?" I asked her.

She looked at me over the rim of her tea cup. "I doubt you'd know him."

"Not if I never get a chance."

"I'm sorry, but I don't feel, really, that it's necessary for you to know."

"Maybe not," I said. "But I do."

She smiled politely. "But let us suppose, for a moment, that I don't wish to tell you."

I smiled. Politely. "Let's suppose, for a moment, that I went to the newspapers with what you've told me already."

For a moment, without expression, she looked at me. At last she said, "You'd do that, would you."

I shrugged. "It's part of the job, Mrs. Norton."

"You do know that there are laws against libel?"

"Yeah. And I know that you'd have to prove it was libel. In court."

She smiled. Ironically. "And we'd been getting along so well, I thought."

"We still are. We're having great fun, Mrs. Norton. We can keep doing this, if you want to. But you're not an idiot. You might not want to tell me. I can understand that. But you knew, as soon as you told me about the shot, that you'd have to tell me the rest."

She smiled again, irony replaced by rue. "One could easily learn to dislike you, Mr. Beaumont."

"One would have to get in line."

She laughed, and again the laughter held some surprise. "You really *are* quite good at this, aren't you?"

"I've done it before."

"Obviously." She looked down and smoothed out a section of dress that didn't really need smoothing. "Very well," she said, looking up. "I telephoned Auguste LaGrande."

I nodded.

"The Prefect of Police," she said.

"Uh huh. How'd you know LaGrande?"

"I'd met him at a dinner party, shortly after I arrived in Paris. He was kind enough to offer his assistance with some research. We became . . . friends of a sort."

"So what happened? After you talked to the Prefect."

"He told me that he'd send someone to the hotel. A police inspector. I told him I'd meet the man there."

"Why go back? Why not just go home?"

"Well," she said, "for one thing, I wanted to learn whether Richard was all right."

"And for another," I said, "you were worried about the poems. Richard had told you they were there, in the suite. And you didn't want anyone to find them."

She stared at me for a minute, and then she smiled once more. "There's really no point, is there, in asking me questions if you already know the answers."

"Those are the best kind of questions."

She laughed again. "That's wonderful. You *must* let me use it in one of my books."

"Be my guest."

She looked down at the tea cup, then back up at me. "All right. Yes. You're quite right. It was my concern about the poems, as much as my concern about Richard, that brought me back. My name was on them, on every page."

"So you went back to the hotel, and you met the inspector."

She nodded. "Outside the suite. He arrived there with two policemen and the manager. The manager used a passkey, but the door still wouldn't open. It was bolted shut. The two policemen were obliged to force it open."

She finished her tea, leaned forward, and set the saucer and cup on the table. She lifted the cozy from the pot. "More tea?"

"No. Thanks. Were the poems there?"

She poured herself some more tea, then replaced the cozy.

She sat back, holding the cup and saucer. "No," she said. "But Richard was. And the German girl."

"You had a chance to look around?"

She frowned at me. "I wasn't there to see the sights, you know."

"No, but you did."

"I had no choice, really."

"And I don't either. I have to ask you these questions, Mrs. Norton. Did it look to you as though there'd been a struggle?"

"No. Not at all. They both seemed . . . very peaceful." She glanced away, off at the past, and then she turned back to me. "But still, you know, it was all rather . . . unsettling. I knew him. Richard. In a way, I was fond of him. And I'd met the German girl. I hadn't cared for her, really, but I certainly hadn't wished her dead. And yet there she was. And there was Richard."

"Why hadn't you cared for von Stuben?"

"She was so obviously besotted with Richard. It was an embarassment, really. I'd felt uncomfortable, just watching her when the two of them were together."

I nodded. "Where were they, exactly? The bodies. Where in the room?"

She sighed. "Von Stuben was on the floor, on her side. Her legs were bent. She was lying as though she'd been kneeling before him, when it happened." She frowned. "I was surprised, you know, that there was so little . . . mess. Just that small round hole, in her forehead."

Suddenly she winced and looked back down at the tea cup.

"Where was Richard?" I asked her.

She looked up. "In the chair, sitting back."

"And the gun? Did you see that?"

"Yes. It was in his hand. His right hand."

I nodded. "How long did you stay there?"

"Five minutes. No longer than that—possibly less. The inspector thanked me and assured me that my name wouldn't be mentioned, and I left."

"And from the time you heard the shot, and left the hall-way, until the time you came back, how much time passed?"

She thought. "Fifteen minutes. Twenty, perhaps."

"So if someone else had been in there, inside the suite, he had plenty of time to get away without being seen."

She frowned, puzzled. "Someone else?" she said.

"If Richard knew he was going to commit suicide, why would he set up an appointment with you?"

"I expect that was one of his little jokes."

"Uh huh. And how was it funny, exactly?"

"I'd spurned his generous offer and elected not to commit suicide with him. He was showing me that someone else possessed the sensitivity to accept the offer."

"But that only works if you could get in there, and see von Stuben. You said the door was locked."

"It was." She frowned. "Perhaps he expected me to run for help. As in fact I did."

"Are you usually on time for appointments, Mrs. Norton?"

"Excuse me?"

"Do you usually show up for an appointment at exactly the scheduled time?"

She frowned once more, as though this were another question she didn't understand, and she was growing weary of those. "Well, I make every effort to do so." Maybe she heard how brittle she sounded, because she softened her voice. "But in Paris, as I'm sure you'll discover, absolute punctuality is sometimes rather difficult to achieve. And in Paris, to be honest, no one really expects it. Why do you ask?"

"You said you got there at three o'clock. At exactly three?"

"Three or thereabouts. I may have been a few minutes late. Not more than four or five minutes."

"And what would you have done if you hadn't heard a gunshot? If you'd gone to the door and knocked on it, and Richard didn't answer?"

She looked at me for a moment. "I should have taken the lift down to the lobby and used the hotel phone to call his room. And, had there been no answer, I should've left the hotel, I expect. Thinking that Richard had forgotten the appointment, and had perhaps left it himself . . ."

Abruptly, she added, "You're saying, of course, that I did otherwise only because I heard that gunshot. And that Richard had no way of *knowing* I was outside the door when the shot was fired."

"Yeah. Did the poems ever turn up?"

"No. I have other copies, of course, but I was quite unhappy with the idea of Richard's copies floating about. I asked Rose, and she had no idea what Richard had done with them. She couldn't say whether he'd taken them with him to the hotel. But they weren't there, at the house."

"So Richard's copies are missing."

"Yes." She sat back, sipped her tea. "Do you really believe that there was someone else in that suite?"

"It's looking more possible now than it did before I talked to you. If someone was there, and the poems were there, he could've taken them."

"Yes, but that makes no *sense*, does it? Why on earth would anyone take them? And you're suggesting that this person also killed Richard? Why? What was the motive?"

"I don't know."

"And, if what you say is true, why do you suppose that Richard asked me to the hotel?"

"Maybe you're right. Maybe he wanted you to find the bodies. But there's something off here. Like you said, if you hadn't heard the shot, you'd have gone home, probably. Forsythe couldn't be sure that you'd get into the suite. Especially with the door locked and bolted."

She looked off, thinking.

I said, "You said that you didn't normally conduct business with Richard in a hotel room?"

She turned to me. "No. Normally I met him at his house."

"Where in the house?"

"Not in the bedroom, if that's what you're suggesting."

"I'm not suggesting anything. I'm just trying to understand what happened."

She studied me for a moment. "You do know," she said, "that Richard and Rose sometimes took other people to bed with them. In the bedroom there. A *ménage à trois*."

"I've heard that, yeah."

"I was never one of them."

"I never thought you were."

She pressed her lips together, then she nodded, mollified.

"So," I said, "where in the house?"

She smiled faintly. "You don't give up, do you, Mr. Beaumont?"

"That's supposed to be a good thing in a private detective."

Another smile, this one stronger. "In the library. Upstairs."

"When was the last time you saw him there?"

She paused. "About a week before his death."

"Did Richard ever show you his pistol?"

"Richard showed everyone his pistol. Do you know anything about psychoanalysis? About Sigmund Freud?"

"Only what I read in the newspapers."

"Do you know what a pistol represents, symbolically?"

"Sure." I smiled. "But sometimes a pistol is only a pistol."

"Not in Richard's case, I suspect."

"Okay. Getting back to the hotel. You didn't think it was strange that he wanted to meet you there?"

She raised her eyebrows, held them up there for a moment, then lowered them. "Yes, I suppose that I did. I suppose that what I thought, at the time, was that Richard was interested in having another . . . escapade."

"And how did you feel about that?"

Another faint smile. "Well," she said. "I went to the hotel, didn't I?"

Six

I WAS AT Sybil Norton's for a while longer, and I asked a few more questions.

I got back to my hotel at a little before seven that night. I undressed, washed up, and put on clean clothes. If I'd known then what would happen later, probably I would have done things differently. Probably I would've crawled under the sheets, or under the bed, and stayed there.

I had some time to kill before Ledoq arrived, so I lay down and I flipped through one of Norton's books, *The Mysterious Affair at Pyles*.

A group of people are gathered for the weekend in an English manor house near the Devon coast. One of the guests happens to be the famous French private detective Pierre Reynard, an old friend of the hostess, Lady Pettigrew. People drink cocktails and say clever things to each other, but nothing much important happens until dinnertime, when Lord Pettigrew keels over into his raspberry sorbet, dead as a dodo. Everyone thinks it's a heart attack, except for Reynard, who's been around. He examines the body and spots the tiny feathered dart sticking out of the dead man's ear. When the local cops show up, they can't get a handle on the case, so Reynard figures it's up to him to set things straight. His buddy, Kippers, who's the narrator, follows him around and admires his technique. Meanwhile, the chief inspector, who's not crazy about the idea of Reynard grabbing the glory, tries to solve the crime before Reynard does.

When I left the manor house and went downstairs to meet

Ledoq, Reynard and Kippers were interviewing young Miss Pettigrew in the conservatory. The chief inspector was off talking to the servants.

My money was on Reynard. He was a peach.

"There's no autopsy report on the desk clerk," I said.

Ledoq shrugged. "There was no autopsy. It was an accident, *mon ami*. In the police report, you will note that many witnesses had seen the man, only moments before, and that he had been obviously intoxicated. Such a man would be wise to avoid the embankment of a river. This one lacked that wisdom."

We were sitting outside, beneath the awning at a bar on the Boulevard Montparnasse called Le Dôme. The night air was clear but cool and there were small charcoal braziers set between the tables to keep the customers warm. Ledoq was drinking another Ricard. I was drinking scotch. The man who had followed us here from the hotel was drinking beer. He sat about twenty-five feet away, at one of the last tables in the clutter of tables. It was another man this time and, as Ledoq had pointed out, another bad suit.

On the table in front of me were the translations Ledoq had made from the reports given to us by LaGrande, the Prefect of Police. I had been glancing through them by matchlight.

The police report of the investigation hadn't told me much, but I'd learned a few things from the autopsy report on Richard Forsythe and Sabine von Stuben. Forsythe and the woman had in fact had sex shortly before they died. Forsythe's body had contained a large amount of alcohol, while the woman's body had contained almost none. Both bodies had contained traces of cocaine.

But there was no autopsy report on the dead desk clerk.

"Henri," I said, "Forsythe made a phone call from that suite in the Grande Bretagne. This is the guy who lost the record of that call. A week later, he ends up in the river. There should have been an autopsy."

"Perhaps so," he said. "But none was performed. Perhaps tomorrow you ought to ask the inspector about the matter."

"I will."

"And you can ask him, as well, about Sybil Norton's story. If she is telling the truth, she heard the shot that killed Monsieur Forsythe."

I put the papers down on the table and I sat back. "Maybe she fired the shot herself."

"Yes, of course," he said reasonably. "She shot him in the head, and then she prevailed upon him to bolt the door behind her as she left."

I smiled. "I'm not as bothered by that door as you are, Henri."

"And why—look, that is Man Ray and Kiki. A very famous couple. He is an American, but his French is almost intelligible. She is French, of course. A model. She has no pubic hair whatever, you know."

"No," I said, "I didn't. What are they famous for?"

Watching the couple, or the female half of the couple, he smiled. "For their celebrity." Then he turned back to me. "Why are you not troubled by the door?"

"Maybe," I said, "it was never actually bolted. Sybil Norton admits that she knows LaGrande. She admits she called him on the day of the murder. She doesn't show up in police reports because LaGrande is protecting her. Hiding the fact that she was there."

"Hiding that, perhaps, yes—but protecting a murderer?"

"You think it's impossible?"

Stroking his goatee, he considered. "*Non*," he said finally. "Not for Monsieur le Préfet. And he could easily concoct the story of the bolted door. Or instruct the investigating inspector to do so. And if indeed he is protecting Madame Norton, this would explain why he has become so interested in our movements." He glanced in the direction of the man who had followed us from the hotel. He frowned. "But what would be his motive for such an act?"

"Maybe he's smitten."

"With Madame Norton?" Disbelief made his face pucker. "She is a handsome woman, *mon ami,* but hardly the sort to drive men wild. And this theory of yours faces an additional difficulty."

"Why would Sybil Norton kill Forsythe."

"Exactly, yes. Out of jealousy? She was jealous of the German woman?"

"She didn't seem to be. She didn't like her. But I don't think she liked Forsythe enough to be jealous, either."

"Did she know about Monsieur Forsythe's connection to Aster Loving?"

"She says she never heard the name." It had been one of the questions I'd asked before I left her apartment.

"Why, then, would she kill him?"

"I don't know. Maybe she decided she wanted her poems back, and Forsythe refused."

He smiled. "She is a writer, *mon ami*. She might perhaps have killed Monsieur Forsythe for *not* publishing them. But for publishing them? I do not think so."

"Maybe she had second thoughts, and she was afraid people would find out who wrote them."

"But if all this is true, if the poems constituted her motive for murder, why should she even mention them to you? Had Rose Forsythe mentioned them?"

"No. But Norton didn't know that."

"And why, if Monsieur Forsythe was holding them against her will, should he invite her to—ah! That is Nancy Cunard. Of the steamship family, eh? Very wealthy. And attractive, *non*?"

"Yeah."

"She has a fondness for Negro men."

"Yeah?"

"A great pity," he said.

"Because you're not a Negro man?"

He laughed. "Exactly!" He laughed again and then he looked at me fondly. "I believe that it was your parents who were French, *mon ami*. Both of them."

I smiled.

He took a sip of his Ricard and set the glass back on the table. "Now. If Monsieur Forsythe had refused to return the poems to Madame Norton, why should he invite her to the hotel suite?"

"Maybe he didn't. Maybe she followed him there."

He raised his eyebrows. "Ah." He sat back and pursed his lips and he considered that. "Or perhaps it was Sybil

Norton whom Forsythe telephoned from the suite.''

I thought about it. "Why would he call her?"

He shrugged. "I cannot imagine."

"Me neither. Let's say, for the sake of argument, that she followed him."

"She followed him there from the Forsythe house?"

"Maybe. Doesn't matter. She follows him. And let's say she's being clever. Let's say she's got Forsythe's pistol with her."

"And what permits us to say this?"

"She was in Forsythe's library a week before he died. She knew about the pistol. She knew—everyone knew—that he talked about committing suicide. So she decides to take the pistol."

"Very cunning of her."

"She writes mystery novels. And she did a pretty good job of setting up her husband."

"Yes. I concede the point. She is capable of cunning. And this is why you speak of her following Forsythe, rather than receiving that telephone call from the suite. Yes? You wish, for the sake of your theory, for her to be planning ahead, rather than relying upon some chance telephone call."

"Yeah."

"And would Monsieur Forsythe fail to notice, for a week, that his pistol was missing?"

"I don't know," I admitted. "I'll ask his wife."

"So. Madame Norton follows Monsieur Forsythe to the hotel. And then what?"

"Sabine von Stuben shows up. Norton knows she can't leave her around, to testify that Norton was in the suite, so she shoots her."

"And then she and Monsieur Forsythe sit there in the suite for another two hours before she kills him."

"Maybe Forsythe tried to talk her out of it."

"I see." He raised his eyebrows. "And you find this theory persuasive?"

"Not very."

He laughed. "Nor do I, *mon ami*. Why do you wish to persuade yourself of Sybil Norton's guilt?"

"I don't. I liked her. Basically, I'm trying to eliminate her."

"And not, so far, succeeding."

"No."

He smiled. "Come, let us go find our dinner."

He got me a receipt from the waiter, after I paid for the drinks.

We ate across the river, at a place not far from the Opéra. The restaurant was handsome and elegant—polished wood, draperies, white linen tablecloths, candles. I had something called *carré d'agneau à la Bordelaise*, which was a small rack of lamb, and *fenouil cru en salade*, raw fennel topped with an anchovy dressing.

Ledoq ordered *côtes de veau en casserole à la Dreux*. "You begin with some thick chops of veal," he explained after the waiter left. "These you stud with thin strips of pickled tongue and truffle. Gently, in butter, you sauté the chops on both sides until they are completely cooked. You then arrange them on a plate with a *garniture financière*. This is made from chicken quenelles, cock's combs, and mushrooms, everything bound carefully together with a *sauce financière*. The sauce, of course, you must prepare beforehand, with shredded ham, mushrooms, truffles, and madeira wine."

"Cock's combs," I said.

"Yes. These are becoming difficult to find."

"Yeah?"

"More and more now," he said, "the chickens are slaughtered before their combs reach the proper size."

"No kidding."

Ledoq looked at me and he smiled.

The food was good, all of it, and so was the wine. That was a Château Margaux "of the vintage 1920." It was young, according to Ledoq, but promising.

The man who was following us sat across the room, in the far corner. I don't know what food he ordered, but he seemed to be happy with it. He drank beer, and he seemed to be happy with that, too.

Over dinner, Ledoq did most of the talking, and most of it was about food. I learned how to make frog legs *à la meu-*

nière, loin of pork with pistachios, turkey giblets *à la bour-guignonne*, and *crêpes suzettes*. It would all come in very handy if I ever decided to get into a different line of work.

We didn't discuss the case until we'd been served our coffee and brandy.

"One thing occurs to me," said Ledoq. "Concerning Madame Norton."

"What's that?"

"If in fact she was involved in the death of Monsieur Forsythe, why should she admit to you that she was in the hotel when it occurred?"

"Maybe she was afraid that Rose Forsythe would say something. About her calling Rose. Telling Rose that Richard and the von Stuben woman were dead."

"Yes, but if she *had* killed the husband—"

"Yeah. Why call Rose at all. I don't know. Guilt, maybe."

"Enough guilt for her to place herself in danger?"

"Maybe she didn't see it that way. She'd talked to La-Grande. She knew she was covered. So long as it was only the Paris cops investigating the death, she had nothing to worry about."

He nodded. "Something still disturbs me, however—those two hours between the death of the von Stuben girl and the death of Monsieur Forsythe."

"Yeah. They disturb me too."

After dinner, we walked west along the Boulevard des Capucines, past the Opéra, which was lit up like a Christmas tree, and we turned left onto the narrow Rue des Capucines.

The Hole in the Wall was pretty much what it claimed to be—a cramped and crowded room, foggy with cigarette smoke beneath a low metal ceiling. Behind the battered zinc-topped bar, and running its entire length, about forty feet, was a tall gilt mirror that was designed to make the room seem wider than it was, and probably to let the customers know when someone was sneaking up behind them.

Mixed with the smell of old cigarettes and older cigars were the smells of old sweat and old beer, and a whiff or two of cheap perfume. A few rickety wooden tables, all of them occupied, leaned against the wooden paneling of the wall, which was painted the color of dried blood. The floorboards were buried beneath brown drifts of sawdust. Some of the boards dipped when I stepped on them.

Five minutes and only a few blocks away, people in elegant clothes were dining on veal chops studded with truffles. Most of the people here, men and women both, looked like they'd never seen a veal chop, let alone a truffle. Some of them looked like they'd never seen food.

Ledoq and I found a space at the bar and Ledoq ordered us drinks, a pair of cognacs. "Not," he said when the bartender turned away, "that the brandy in the bottle will bear any resemblance to the *marque* on the bottle."

The bartender set the drinks on the bar and Ledoq asked him something in French. I heard the name "Reilly." The bartender shook his head and said something.

"Four francs," Ledoq translated. "He says that Reilly has not yet arrived."

I pulled some money from my pocket, put four francs on the bar.

Someone tapped me on my right shoulder.

Short and skinny, he was wearing a long wool infantry field coat, stained and frayed, over a shirt that hadn't been white since the War, or maybe before it. His sunken cheeks were dark with stubble and his deepset watery gray eyes were rimmed with red. He was probably in his midtwenties, and he looked as though he would never reach his thirties.

"You're an American, am I right?" he said. From his breath, that drink in his hand wasn't his first of the day. He probably couldn't remember his first of the day.

"Yeah."

"Me too, pal. Jimmy Jepson." He set down the drink and held out his hand. "Put 'er there."

"Phil Beaumont," I said, and I took his hand. It was hot and slippery, almost feverish. "This is Henri Ledoq."

Jepson dropped my hand and reached for Ledoq's. "Pleased t'meet-cha."

"Delighted," said Ledoq dryly. He took the man's hand and quickly released it.

Jepson turned to me. "Gotta stick together, am I right?" he said. "Us Americans."

"Right."

"Especially in what you call foreign climes, am I right?"

"Especially."

He turned to Ledoq. "No offense meant, *mohnaymee*."

"And none taken," said Ledoq, smiling primly.

Jepson turned back to me. "So what brings you to Gay Paree, pal?"

"Business. What about you?"

He shrugged. "After the War, I figured I'd stay on. Here in Paris." He'd probably stayed here during it, too, as a deserter. "Lots of opportunities, a guy's got smarts."

"Uh huh."

"The thing is, I heard your friend here, talkin' to Philippe." He jerked his head toward the bartender. "You're lookin' for Johnny Reilly, am I right?"

I nodded. "You know him?"

"Me and Johnny, we're like this," he said, and he held up his hand, index and middle fingers extended and crossed. Then he lowered the hand, hooked his elbow over the counter, and leaned toward me. When he spoke, the words came floating out of him on a damp dense cloud of fumes. "Anything you want from ole Johnny, pal, I can get for you. Anything at all, you catch my drift?"

"What I need is a little information."

"Information," he said, breathing more fumes at me. "This is your lucky day, pal. You came to the right man exactly. I got plenty of that."

"You know a guy named Richard Forsythe?"

He mulled that over for a moment. "The rich guy? Faggot? Sure I know him. Showed up with a really classy little dame a couple of times. A real looker. Someone said she was his wife, but that's a crock. Hadda be." He leaned closer. I stopped breathing. "A faggot's a faggot, am I right?"

"So you've seen him here?"

He moved back and he looked at me from beneath lowered eyebrows. "Din't I just say so? Seen him with that Kraut woman, too. Von Something. Von Stupid." He grinned at his display of wit. "Frienda Johnny's."

"Sabine von Stuben?" I said. "She was a friend of Reilly's?"

"Sure. Used to come in here alla time, hang out with Johnny, before she started hanging out with the faggot. I heard he was dead. The faggot."

"He is."

"Yeah. I heard that. I heard he got croaked."

"That right? Did you hear how?"

He looked up at me, blinking. "How come you wanna know?"

"Curiosity."

He smiled slyly. "Yeah? You talkin' about real curiosity? Or only passin'-the-time curiosity?"

I reached into my pocket and pulled out a roll of francs. I counted fifty of them, put them on the bar, returned the roll to my pocket. He watched all this very carefully, as though it were a magic trick he'd never seen performed before, and he wanted very badly to figure out how it worked.

When I finished, he glanced from the money to me, then glanced back at the money. Probably he decided he couldn't snap up the cash and get around me before I grabbed him and caused him some pain. Casually he said, "You don't mind me asking, how come you're so innarested in this guy?"

"I used to do business with him. A year or two ago."

"What kinda business?"

"Chemicals."

He stared at me blankly for a moment and then he smiled slyly again. "And now you're lookin' for someone else, am I right? To do business with?"

"Exactly. So what's the story on his getting croaked?"

He glanced down at the money again, glanced up at me.

"Take it," I said.

His hand swept out across the bar, snatched away the notes, shoved them into the pocket of his overcoat. Then he turned and nonchalantly put both his hands on the bartop. Anyone in the room who hadn't seen this, and figured it out, was blind or dead. He lifted his glass, took a swallow, set the glass down. Then he leaned toward me. "What I heard," he said from the corner of his mouth, "I heard some very important people had it in for him."

"Who?"

"I dunno. Very important people, is what I heard."

"And why'd they have it in for him?"

"He was going to spill the beans, is what I heard. The gov'ment knew all about it, see. His getting croaked, I mean. The cops had orders to keep their hands off, is what I heard."

"Spill what beans, Jimmy?" I asked him.

He turned to me and suddenly his face went still.

"Jimmy, me darlin' boy," said a deep musical Irish voice behind me. "How *are* we tonight?"

"Hey, John," said Jepson. He was grinning so widely that his mouth looked ready to cramp. "How's it goin'?"

I turned.

In his forties, the man was tall, maybe six foot two, and he was big and burly inside an expensive black wool topcoat. There were velvet lapels on the topcoat and there was a red rose in the boutonniere. He was a handsome man, and a healthy man, and he looked like a man who took a lot of pleasure in being both. His grayish-brown hair was thick and parted on the left, his forehead was broad. His dark brown eyes were bright, his wide cheeks were florid with health or Irish whiskey, his smile was as pleased as the smile of a cardinal who had just backed the winning pope.

"Coupla guys to see ya, John," said Jepson quickly, the words running together like carriages on an express train. "I was just shootin' the breeze with 'em till you got here."

"Good for you, Jimmy lad," said the big man, still grinning happily. He clapped Jepson on the shoulder. Jepson sagged beneath the impact. He winced and then he smiled some more.

"And isn't that the sociable thing to do?" said the big man. His thick fingers were kneading Jepson's thin shoulder. Jepson stopped smiling and he glanced at the hand.

The big man turned to us, released Jepson, and pointed a pink finger at Ledoq. "You I know. Ledoq, is it?" And then, beaming, he said something in cheerful French.

Ledoq smiled and replied, also in French.

The big man turned to me, still beaming. "But you, now. I don't believe I've ever had the pleasure."

"Phil Beaumont," I said.

He held out his large hand. I took it. I was a bit surprised that he didn't try to show me how big and strong he was.

Maybe he didn't think he had to. "John Reilly," he said. He released my hand, and he grinned at me. "Beaumont is it? A French name, eh, but not the way you say it. American, are ye?"

"That's right."

"Glad to hear it. Glad to see a fellow countryman on these shores." He turned to Jepson, and he beamed at him. "Jimmy lad, you run along now. You and I, we'll have us a little chat later, eh?"

Jepson was already pale, but now he lost what little color he had. He tried for another smile but it blew away like a cheap mask in a wind, and suddenly the desperation showed. "John, I was only talkin' to 'em, shootin' the breeze, you can ask 'em—"

Still beaming, Reilly reached out and wrapped his hand around Jepson's upper left arm. "Jimmy, Jimmy. You're babbling, lad, and I cannot for the life of me abide a babbler." Veins rose along the back of Reilly's hand, small muscular worms squirming beneath the florid skin. Above the hand, and below it, the wrinkles in Jepson's sleeve got deeper. Jepson's mouth opened, and he hissed as he sucked in some air.

Reilly's grin hadn't wavered. "Next thing ye know," he said, "you'll be blubbering. And for a fact, lad, that'd turn me stomach altogether."

Suddenly he released Jepson. Jepson swayed slightly. His right hand moved up to his left arm, where the sleeve still held the dents made by Reilly's fingers.

His grin gone, Reilly leaned his broad back against the bar. He notched the heel of one big shoe on the foot rail, put both big elbows on the counter, and then he jerked his thumb toward the door. He looked down at Jepson like a father looking at a favored son. "Ye've got yerself a head start, lad. Better make the most of it."

Jepson looked from Reilly to me, from me to Ledoq, and then back to Reilly. Faintly, Reilly nodded toward the door. Jepson tucked in his head and walked quickly away.

Reilly watched him go, thoughtfully. He waited until Jepson was out the door and then he turned to me and smiled sadly. "He won't, ye know. The pity of it is, ye see, that he's got nowhere to go."

"I can see," I said, "that you've got his best interests at heart."

Reilly looked at me blankly for a moment. Then he grinned again. Slowly, pivoting on his right elbow, dropping his foot from the rail, he rolled his back off the bar and turned to face me directly. He put his big left hand on his big right forearm. "Yer a stranger here, Phil, so you'll not be knowin' the way o' things. Let me see if I can lay 'em out for ye." He gestured casually with his left hand, taking in all of the bar. "This is mine, ye see. I don't own it, not on paper, not in a court of law, but it's mine all the same. It belongs to me." He nodded toward the other customers. "And so do they. I snap me fingers and they jump. And that's a good thing, Phil. That way, we got order. We got discipline. Ye understand what I'm sayin' here?"

"Sure. Especially when you explain it slowly like that."

He smiled. His eyes were twinkling. He was having a swell time. "Order is important, Phil. Without it, now, we're worse off than the wild beasts of the forest. You still with me?"

"You bet."

"So what happens, Phil, when someone like little Jimmy starts shooting off his yap at strangers? It's not good, Phil. Not a-tall. It sets a bad example, it does. And, to correct that, ya see, set things right again, I got to turn around and make an example o' Jimmy. I don't like it, Phil, me hand on the Bible to that, it doesn't give me a single bit o' pleasure, but there it is."

"He didn't tell us anything."

"That's not the point, is it?" His big ruddy face went sad. "Just by talkin' to ye, the lad was steppin' over the line." He shook his head. "And, sad to say, so were you and your little Froggy friend."

I nodded. "I can see why you'd think so."

"I just want ye t'know that there's nothin' personal in this. It wouldn't surprise me none, you know, in a different life, let's say, if you and me had got to know each other—"

I didn't see much point in letting him finish. Both of us knew where this was heading.

His reflexes were probably pretty good, but he was so busy frightening me that I caught him off guard. I hit him with a good solid jab in the throat, a right. His eyes flew open and he made a gargling sound as he reached for his Adam's apple, and I came up from the floor with my left and slammed it at the corner of his jaw, putting a lot of swivel into it.

His head snapped to the side but he still didn't go down, so I kneed him, hard, and he doubled up and I grabbed him by the hair and I ran him over to the wall and introduced the top of his head to the paneling. The wood split, crackling open against the stonework it concealed, and Reilly gave a little sigh, like a man remembering the vanished joys of vanished times, and he collapsed to the floor in a heap. Sawdust billowed out from beneath him and sprayed across my shoes.

This all happened within a second or two. When I spun around, no one was moving.

That didn't last for long.

The three men at the nearest table got up and rushed me.

Dear Evangeline,

Events have rushed at me so swiftly since I last wrote that I have no idea, really where to begin.

As you can see from the address above, I'm now in St. Piat, a lovely little village some fifteen miles north of Chartres. Actually, we (clan Forsythe and I) are situated a mile or so from the village. The 'perfectly dreamy little chateau' that *Maman* Forsythe mentioned is in fact very nearly a castle, perched midway up a forested hill. From my room in the tower (a real tower!) I have a spectacular view over the billowing blossoms of the chestnut trees and out across the broad valley to the River Eure, a ribbon of reflected blue that lopes gently through pale green fields and through darker stands of alder. Here and there, scattered among the green, stands a fruit tree aswirl in a mist of flowers—white and cream and pink. It is all utterly gorgeous, Evy, something out of a fairy tale.

And (speaking of fairy tales) I've met the count and his sister, Eugénie, and most impressive they both were, too. Tomorrow Eugénie and I are off to Paris, where we'll be staying overnight at the count's townhouse on the Ile Saint-Louis. And then on Sunday, of course, I'll be attending a masquerade party at Monsieur le Comte's chateau in Chartres. Ho hum. It's all so tedious, this endless coming and going, don't you think?

Since we arrived here, I have climbed, with the children, up the narrow bell tower of Chartres Cathedral; I have read a small but an extraordinarily fine book, one of those published by Richard Forsythe, a collection of short stories written by a man named Ernest Hemingway; and I have wandered through the forests around the chateau, sighing romantically, striking poses, and harvesting fistfuls of wild flowers like the most rapacious of ingenues.

But knowing my Evangeline, I realise that she has considerably less interest in wildflowers than in counts and their sisters. So. To *le comte*, then.

The two of them arrived here last night, after dinner. Melissa and Edward were in their rooms. *Maman* and Mr Forsythe were sitting on the parlour's sofa; Neal and the nanny in chairs. The nanny had been permitted to linger over the postprandial coffee, I suspect, because Mr Forsythe, who arrived here only this afternoon, wanted to evaluate this new addition to the household. As a wealthy international banker, Mr Forsythe is a demon evaluator.

I haven't told you about Mr Forsythe.

He looks very much as one would expect a wealthy international banker to look. Pink and comfortably plump in his tweed suit, he is perhaps fifty-five years old and perhaps five foot six inches tall. (Which makes him approximately one inch taller and fifteen years older than his wife.) His smile, beneath a neatly trimmed grey moustache, is broad and quick and, in all likelihood, ultimately meaningless. He is clearly a man who has never in his life been troubled by doubt or debt; never been troubled by any trouble whatever.

He was holding forth on the subject of socialism, one topic among an infinitude of topics about which he is exceedingly—preternaturally, one might almost say—well informed.

'You take Germany now,' he said. 'That damned Weimar Republic. It's going to hell in a handbasket. Four *million* marks to the dollar. In Berlin these days you need a wheelbarrow to haul around the money to buy yourself a loaf of bread. Women—*aristocrats*, I mean—they're selling themselves on the streets.'

'Darling,' said *Maman*, with a small *moue* of distaste. 'Please.' She has completely recovered, by the way, from the stomach upset she suffered at Mont-Saint-Michel.

He grinned at her. 'Come on, Mother.' (I am not inventing this, Evy; he really does address her thus.) 'We're all grown-ups here.' He turned to Neal and winked broadly. 'Eh, kiddo?'

Neal smiled at him, rather weakly, then glanced at me and glanced quickly away. He finds his father an embarrassment, I think. One can scarcely blame him.

'But neither Miss Turner nor I,' said *Maman*, 'is interested in sordid details like that.'

Mr Forsythe looked at me. 'Straight talk bother you any, Miss Turner?'

'Not at all. But—'

'Didn't think so.' He gave his wife a look of pleased but not entirely unexpected victory. 'See that? You picked yourself a good one.'

'Well,' she said, 'I, for one, don't want to hear it.'

'Whatever you say, Mother,' he said, grinning merrily, and reached out and clapped his hand against her thigh. (A thigh that was, by the way, handsomely concealed beneath a pleated white satin skirt that went extremely well, I fear, with her navy blue satin top.) 'Whatever you say.'

He sat back. 'Now. Where was I?' He looked around him, as though he expected to discover, somewhere nearby, a familiar strand of conversation hovering in the air.

'Four million marks, dear,' said *Maman*, who is very good with figures.

'Right you are,' said he. 'And that's your Reds for you. Socialists, they call themselves. No better than damn Bolsheviks, you ask me. They're running that country right into the ground.'

He turned to me. 'You ever been to Germany, Miss Turner?'

'Yes. As a matter of—'

'Since the War?'

'No. I—'

'You wouldn't recognise it. Crime, drugs, out-and-out perversion.' He shook his head. 'Going to hell in a handbasket.'

Maman frowned. 'Then why, dear, do you keep pouring money in there?'

He chuckled indulgently. 'Not my money, Mother. The bank's. And we'll get it all back, believe me, and then some. There are still some good men over there. This fellow Messerschmidt—'

From somewhere, interrupting him, a doorbell chimed.

'That's Jean,' he said, and began to rise.

Maman put a hand on his arm. 'Peters will handle it, dear.' Peters is the butler. Like Reagan the Swine, he is English. All the servants are English, with the exception of Madame Esther, the cook. *Maman* cannot abide English cooking. This is a woman who has obviously never sampled the delights of bangers and mash.

Mr Forsythe turned to me once more and said, 'So how do you like France, Miss Turner?'

'It's lovely,' I said.

'Been here before?'

'Yes. My parents—'

'Wonderful country,' he said. 'Lots of opportunities.' He looked towards the room's entrance. 'Ah, there you are. Jean. And Eugénie.' He stood up. 'Good to see you.'

They make a striking couple, Evy. He is tall and slender, clean shaven, perhaps forty years old. His thick hair is ebony black but for a dramatic streak of silver at the temples. His eyes are nearly as black as his hair. His forehead is high, his cheekbones prominent, his nose straight. His lips are broad and so clearly defined that they might have been sculpted. Beneath them, his square chin is cleft. Jane Eyre, seeing him, might have gone a trifle swoonish. Had I not been a trained and hardened Pinkerton, I might have gone a trifle swoonish myself.

He wore a black coat, a white shirt, black trousers, black shoes. No cravat; and the slightly overlong collars of his shirt, open at the neck, suggested a kind of Byronic elegance, and an excellent tailor.

His sister's clothes, and the sister herself, were equally elegant. She wore a black silk gown, sleeveless, its neckline draped, its hem tasselled and uneven. Across her forehead, encircling her short-cropped black hair, she wore a black silk headband embroidered with bands of gold, its ends tied above her left ear and trailing down to her shoulder. She is tall, too, although not so tall as he; and she is much more slender. She is really extraordinarily beautiful, a softer, 'feminised' version of her brother. But what struck me most about her was her pallor. Her skin is very fine, poreless, but it is milky white, almost translucent. When shadows fall along her arms, along her throat, they become pale blue. She reminded me, at first, of those ethereal women who wander, as if in a dream, through the short stories of Edgar Allan Poe.

'George,' said the count, smiling pleasantly at Mr Forsythe as he shook his hand. Then he stepped toward *Maman*, took the hand she offered up to him, bent over it and kissed it. 'Alice,' he said, and smiled.

'You know Neal,' said Mr Forsythe. 'My son.'

'But of course,' said the Count. Neal was standing, as well, and now he stepped forward and offered his hand to the count, who shook it cheerfully.

'And this,' said Mr Forsythe, 'is Miss Jane Turner, the new nanny. Miss Turner, this is Jean Aubier, the Count De Saintes.'

The count smiled at me and inclined his aristocratic head. 'Charmed,' he said. I remained kissless. Few nannies (or Pinkertons, in my experience) are kissed, on the hand or anywhere else.

I inclined my own head. 'Monsieur.'

Monsieur with a courtly nod indicated the woman beside him. 'My sister, Eugénie.'

I smiled at the sister. *'Enchantée,'* I said.

Her eyebrows rose slightly. 'Oh,' she said. *'Parlez-vous francais?'*

'Un peu,' I said.

'But your accent,' she said, in a delighted French, 'is excellent.' (I translate for you, Evy, because as I recall your own French never progressed much beyond the basic culinary sort, and the even more basic anatomical.)

'Brandy?' asked Mr Forsythe, and both the count

and Eugénie agreed. 'Have a seat,' Mr Forsythe directed them, and so they did, Eugénie in the chair beside mine, the count directly across from me. Neal returned to his chair. He glanced at Eugénie, glanced at me, saw that I was watching him, and looked away again. Poor thing. I don't know how anyone, male or female, ever survives adolescence. Sometimes I'm not entirely certain that I've survived my own.

As Mr Forsythe poured the brandy, Eugénie leaned toward me and asked, again in French, 'Have you been in France before?'

'When I was a child,' I said. 'My parents and I came here every year.'

She seemed, suddenly, not at all ethereal. Smiling happily, she sat back and clapped her hands. 'But your French is splendid! How wonderful!' Her brown eyes were bright as she leaned forward and placed the tips of her fingers, briefly, along my arm. 'For me, I mean! At last, someone to talk to!'

'Miss Turner,' said Mr Forsythe. 'You sure you won't have a small brandy?'

I had declined earlier—as I felt I ought to do, both as a responsible nanny and as the Pinkerton responsible for that nanny's behaviour. 'Well,' I said, 'perhaps just a small one.'

'Oh, you must,' said Eugénie, and she smiled again, radiantly. 'For the heart, you know.'

Mr Forsythe distributed the glasses and then returned to his seat on the sofa. 'We were just talking about Germany,' he told the count.

'Ah,' said the count. 'Germany. The *bête noire* of Europe. Whatever shall we do with Germany?' His English was virtually without accent.

I glanced at *Maman* and discovered that she was eyeing the count over her brandy snifter with a curious intensity, almost an avidity. One can easily understand why, of course. But I did feel that her interest was, in a married woman, perhaps a shade inappropriate.

Neal spoke. 'Miss Turner's been to Germany,' he told the count.

The count looked at me. 'Have you, Miss Turner,' he said, and smiled with a kind of blank politeness. 'And what are your thoughts regarding that country.'

I've put no question marks in the statement because, from the way he delivered it, it was no question. It was a declaration, however outwardly polite, of almost complete indifference to me and to anything I should have to say; the indifference tempered (perhaps) by a faint hope that I should say something not only ignorant but also spectacularly stupid and therefore entertaining.

'As I knew about it then,' I said, 'or as I think about it now?'

He smiled wanly again. 'Whichever you prefer.' Both being, *naturellement*, eminently worthless.

Ah well, Evy. You will find this difficult to believe, I know, but I'm afraid that I reacted badly. I did the one thing that all my upbringing (with the exception of those years spent with the redoubtable Mrs Applewhite), and all my training as a Pinkerton, had counselled me never to do: I said exactly what I thought.

I sweetened it up a bit, of course. The family was there; and it is important for me, as a Pinkerton, to remain with them as a nanny. I smiled one of those fetching, sweetly uncertain smiles we nannies don on the rare occasions when we address Important Issues, or Important People. And I said, 'Well, Mr Forsythe was speaking a few minutes ago about the inflation in Germany. I don't know anything about economics, of course, but isn't that really the fault of the French government?'

The count smiled, a smile I fancied was somewhat less wan than his earlier attempts. 'How do you mean?'

I said, 'If it hadn't sent in troops to occupy the Ruhr—'

'But Miss Turner,' said Mr Forsythe, 'the Germans had fallen behind in their reparations. The French had no choice. They had to do *something*.'

'But why that?' I said. My smile had gone from sweet uncertainty to sweet (because utter) helplessness. You would have been thoroughly impressed, Evy.

'That's what I don't understand, you see. The French troops occupy the territory, the German workers go on strike, the German government supports the workers. But in order to do so, it needs to print more money—'

'Exactly,' said Mr Forsythe, and he smiled patiently. 'That's exactly the point, Miss Turner. They're printing worthless paper to support workers who refuse to do their jobs.'

I had slipped over into sweet befuddlement now. 'But hasn't that horrible inflation actually lowered the prices of German goods on the international markets? And hasn't that hurt the French?'

Mr Forsythe opened his mouth to say something when the count startled him—and the heretical nanny—by laughing. Everyone turned to him.

'Miss Turner is absolutely right,' he said to Mr Forsythe. 'It has. The occupation was a foolish move. The government will recall the troops within six months.'

Mr Forsythe had turned to him, frowning. 'You really think so?'

'It is inevitable. The occupation has damaged Germany, yes, but as Miss Turner points out, it has also damaged France.' He turned to me, smiling again. 'And what do you think of the reparations themselves?'

'Oh, dear,' said *Maman*, her voice infinitely weary, '*must* we talk about reparations and occupations and all those silly old political things? I'd really much rather discuss the masquerade on Saturday. Eugénie, it *is* still on, isn't it? I've been looking forward to it for months.'

'Yes, of course,' said Eugénie. Her English is less fluent than her brother's, but it has to it a sweet and a somehow vulnerable lilt. I find it charming.

Suddenly she turned to me and smiled again that radiant smile. 'But Miss Turner,' she said, still in English, 'you must be coming to ziss!' She touched my arm again. 'It will be great fun for you, yes? And for us.' Excited, she spun towards the count. 'Jean? Please? We must have Miss Turner wizz us on Saturday.'

He smiled. He has quite a repertoire of smiles. This

one was both amused and affectionate. (The count was, as you may have guessed, slowly climbing back into the nanny's good graces.) 'Of course,' he said. 'Miss Turner, will you do us the honour of attending our little affair on Saturday night?'

I glanced at *Maman* and saw that small bitter parentheses had abruptly formed at the corners of her tightened mouth. One doesn't, even when one is American, attend a party attended by one's servants. Well, one does, of course; but not happily.

I was in something of a quandary, Evy. On the one hand, the purpose of my nanny masquerade had been specifically to obtain information from (and about) the count and his sister; and opening before me was a lovely opportunity to do precisely that. On the other, by accepting the invitation (if I were reading *Maman's* expression aright), I risked having my nannyhood plucked away.

'Thank you,' I told the count. 'I'm very grateful, but I'm afraid I can't accept. I have my responsibilities to the children.' (This said, of course, with simple nannyish dignity.)

'Nonsense,' he said. 'Surely George and Alice can surrender you for an evening.'

'Sure we can,' said Mr Forsythe. 'You come along too, Miss Turner.' He grinned. 'All work and no play, you know. Can't have that. Right, Mother?'

Beside him, *Maman* smiled stiffly. I suspected that later, when the two of them were alone, Mr Forsythe would have cause to regret his liberality.

I made one more attempt. I turned to Eugénie and said, 'A masquerade? I couldn't. Honestly. I have nothing to wear.'

Eugénie turned to *Maman* and said with mock firmness, 'Alice, you must permit Miss Turner to be coming wizz me to Paris tomorrow, for zee shops. Yes? She can stay wizz me overnight, in zee townhouse.' She turned back to me, smiling happily. 'It is on the Ile Saint-Louis, and it is very, very nice. We will have a wonderful time.'

'But Miss Turner,' said *Maman*, 'is taking the children into Paris on Saturday morning.' She smiled one of those calmly reasonable smiles that often, in mothers and other maniacs, masks a fierce surge of triumph. 'It's all arranged. And she can't do that, obviously, if she's already in Paris. I'm sorry, but—'

'Surely, Alice,' said the count, 'you can make other arrangements?'

'I'd love to, Jean,' she said sweetly, 'but I really can't put Eddy and Sissa onto the train by themselves.'

'I'll take them,' volunteered Neal.

Maman's glance darted to him. Betrayed by her own flesh and blood. I expect she was seething behind the placid surface of her face.

And, as both she and Neal no doubt realised, the outing would provide Neal a thick slice of unsupervised time with the nanny. (Since we arrived here, she has been shifting us around like pieces on a chessboard.) But neither mother nor son let this knowledge show in their faces. 'We can all meet Miss Turner in Paris,' he added, with a glib innocence that is presumably hereditary. Perhaps there is hope for Neal after all.

'There,' said the count. 'You see how easily these things are done?'

'But Jean,' she began.

'Oh come on, Mother,' Mr Forsythe said. 'Neal will be fine with the kids. And it'll do him good to take some responsibility for a change.' He grinned at Neal. 'Eh, kiddo?'

'And perhaps,' said the count to *Maman*, 'you and George would join me for lunch tomorrow. I've some new paintings I'd like to show you. A Picasso and a lovely Matisse.'

'I can't make it myself,' said Mr Forsythe. 'Got to go to London tomorrow, and I won't be back 'til Saturday. I told you about it, Mother. But *you* should go.' He turned to the count. 'That all right with you, Jean?'

'But of course,' he said. He smiled at *Maman*. 'I'd be delighted to have you join me, Alice.'

Intentionally or not, the count had created a barter

situation: in exchange for the nanny's freedom, he would provide the lunch. (The ambiguity of that phrase is intentional, by the way; for I begin to suspect that at some earlier time *Maman* and *Le comte* had previously lunched with, and possibly upon, each other.)

It didn't take *Maman* long to decide. (No longer, really, than it should have taken your typical nanny.) 'I'd love to, Jean,' she said, and smiled.

'Good,' he said. 'Then it's settled.'

Eugénie touched my arm again. 'Wonderful! We shall leave tomorrow morning. At about nine, yes? I will come for you, wiz zee au-to.'

'Well, all right,' said *Maman*. She turned to me and smiled sweetly. 'I hope you have a good time, Miss Turner. But I wonder if I could ask you to do me a small favour right now?'

'Of course,' I told her.

'Could you just check on the children and make sure they're all right? Sissa sometimes has trouble sleeping in the country.'

'Certainly,' I said. It was an obvious ploy, designed to reestablish her primacy; but I had Paris in my pocket and I didn't care a fig. I smiled (sweetly) and said, 'To be honest, I'm rather tired myself. If you'll all excuse me, I'll look in on the children and then retire for the evening.'

The men all rose as I stood, and so did Eugénie. 'Tomorrow,' she said, touching my arm lightly as, once again, she smiled that bright smile.

So. I shall be in Paris. Tomorrow. The Eiffel Tower. The Champs-Elysées. The Arc de Triomphe. And the *shops*, Evy!

Enough. I must sleep.

But what a wonderful surprise it is, this trip to Paris!

All my love,
Jane

Seven

LEDOQ SURPRISED ME. As the three men rushed at me, he casually reached out his foot and tripped the first of them. The man hurtled to the floor, sawdust exploding all around him, and he came skidding through it toward me, his arms thrashing. I kicked him in the head. The second man turned to Ledoq, whipping out a very large knife, and Ledoq swung his leg up as gracefully as a ballerina and kicked him in the hand. The knife went spinning off to the left. I didn't see what happened next, didn't have time, because the third man was still coming at me. I let him come and when he reached me I grabbed the front of his coat and I held on to it as I turned and he kept going, over my hip. His back smashed against the floor. It knocked the air out of him but not the spirit because his hands scrambled for my legs. He had a lot of spirit, so I kicked him in the head. It had worked with the first man, and it worked with this one.

I was just thinking, with real regret, that I should have brought the Colt from the hotel room when someone fired a pistol.

I wheeled around. The second man was down. That made four people on the floor, including Reilly, who looked like he might be staying there for a while. Everyone else was upright, standing away from their seats and crowding the narrow room. Ledoq stood facing them, like a lion tamer facing the lions. His right hand was raised straight up, and in the hand was a silver-plated double-barreled derringer. Gray smoke drifted from the muzzle and disappeared into the tobacco haze. I looked up at the ceiling. There were three or four bullet holes up there. I hadn't noticed them before, and I couldn't tell which one of them was Ledoq's.

Ledoq lowered the small pistol, aimed it more or less at the center of the crowd, and said something in French. From the back of the crowd, a man called out, angry. Ledoq said something else. Somewhere in the crowd, a woman laughed.

Off to the right, at the crowd's edge, I could see the man who'd been following us all night. He didn't look like someone who wanted to rescue us from a mob. He looked like someone who was having a fine time being part of a mob.

Ledoq backed up, toward me, and said something else to the crowd. No one moved.

Without turning his head toward me, Ledoq said, "Phil?"

"Yeah."

"The door behind you. Open it, please, *mon ami.*"

The door was steel, painted to match the dried-blood color of the wooden paneling. I opened it. It opened inward. There was a light coming from inside.

"Okay," I told Ledoq.

Ledoq took a couple more steps backward. One of the men from the crowd began to move toward him and Ledoq said something very quietly. The man stopped moving.

Again Ledoq didn't look back when he spoke to me, "Into the next room, Phil."

I stepped into the room, glanced around. A small office—a desk, a chair, a lamp, a metal sink, some shelves, some wooden storage cabinets, a gray concrete floor. Across from me, between rows of hand-made shelving that held liquor bottles, was another door, also steel, barred from the inside. Unless that door led out onto the street, we would be trapped in the room.

I stepped back out and said to Ledoq, "Is this a good idea, Henri?"

"There is a bar for that door, *non?*"

I looked. It was leaning against the wall behind the door. Like the bar on the other door, it was a slab of wood about three feet long, six inches wide, two inches thick. On either side of the door, attached to the stonework, were L-shaped metal supports to hold it in place. I lifted the bar. The thing weighed about thirty pounds. "Yeah. I've got it."

"You are ready?"

I wondered what Pierre Reynard, the legendary French detective, would say in a situation like this. What I said was, "Yeah."

Ledoq spun around and darted for the door. The mob surged forward. Someone tossed a bottle of something. Brandy, I think.

It missed Ledoq, shattering against the wall as he jumped for the entrance. I slammed the door shut behind him and lifted the big bar and rammed it into the supports.

Something hit it from the other side.

"Hold the door, please," said Ledoq, and shoved the little pistol into his pocket.

I put my weight against the metal. Something hit it again. And then a lot of things began to hit it, loudly, some of them at the same time and some of them one after the other. The door jumped and shivered against my shoulder. On the other side of it, people were shouting.

Ledoq was running around the office, tugging cupboard doors open, pulling out drawers.

"What are we looking for, Henri?"

A locomotive crashed against the door. Or maybe it was only a table.

Ledoq dashed across the room to the other door. With a gasp, using both hands, he pushed the bar up out of its supports. He hurled it to the center of the floor and he ripped open the door. Stairs led down into darkness. "Ah." He bent forward, plucked something off the floor, then scurried with it over to the desk.

A miner's safety lamp.

Ledoq tore open the desk drawer, found a box of matches, struck one, opened the lamp's glass door, raised the safety grate, lit the wick. He shook out the match, tossed it to the floor, slipped the match box into his pocket. He lowered the grate, closed the door, and then ran with the lamp over to the stairs and turned and waved to me. "Come! Grab the other bar!"

Another locomotive crashed against the door. The support

on the right, where the door opened, jumped half an inch from the stonework.

I ran to the fallen bar, lifted it, ran to the other door. There was a smell drifting up from the stairway, an unpleasant smell, something a lot worse than the smell of musty old cellars. I nodded to the stairs. "What's down there?"

"The sewers."

"*Shit*," I said.

He nodded sadly. "*Exactement.*"

Something smashed against the other door. Any second now, that support would pop free.

We moved quickly into the stairway entrance. Ledoq held the lantern high and pulled the door shut. I swung up the bar and then pushed it down into the supports in the door jamb, and into another pair of supports welded to the door itself. The owners of the place probably thought it was convenient to be able to leave it quickly, and to bar the door behind him. I know that I did.

"Come," Ledoq said, and started down the steps. I followed. The walls and the stairway itself seemed to dip and swing as the yellow light from the lantern swooped along them. The steps were worn and slippery and the ceiling was low—as I raced downward, I had to bend my neck and my shoulders forward, throwing myself off balance. My right hand grappled for support along the damp rough surface of the stone walls. The smell that was bad at the top of the stairs grew worse with every hurried step down into the clammy darkness.

Just as we reached bottom, I heard a crashing sound from behind us, back up the stairs. I heard, too, a squeaking and a chittering on either side of us. Rats. There would be a lot of them down here.

"That door will take them longer than the other," said Ledoq. "It opens inward. They cannot simply push it open. Hold this, please." He handed me the lantern and reached into his coat, pulled out a sheet of paper, rapidly unfolded it, studied it briefly in the glare of the lamp.

Another crash from up there.

We were in a narrow passageway of stone and brick, maybe four feet wide, perpendicular to the stairway. The ceiling here was arched, but it still was too low for me to stand upright.

"That way," he said, pointing to the left, "will take us toward the river." He looked at me. "They will expect us to proceed in that direction, I suspect."

"Where'd you get the map?"

"From one of my books. It is well known that a passage to the sewers runs from the Hole in the Wall. I felt that making a copy of the plans might be a wise precaution."

"You're a prince, Henri."

"Merci." He folded the map, slipped it back into his coat pocket. "This way, then?"

I nodded. "This way."

I gave him back the lantern. If I were in the lead, he wouldn't be able to see around me. With him in the lead, I could see over his head.

The rats kept squealing as we scuttled along the passageway. Sometimes I could see them ahead of us, scurrying away from the lantern's glow, dull gray haunches darting into the gloom, long dark hairless tails sliding along behind them. I thought I could hear their tiny claws scratching on the stone, but that might have been my imagination.

Ledoq coughed once, delicately. "Quite a stench, eh?"

"Yeah." I felt like coughing, too, but I was afraid that once I started I wouldn't be able to stop.

Finally we came to the channel. Roughly semicircular, the tunnel was about seven feet wide at the bottom, three feet of water and two feet of brick walkway on either side of that. The water was black and thick and there were small shapeless things bobbing in it. The rats plopped into the water from this side and swam quickly over to the far side, then scrambled out and scooted down the other walkway, long and lean and dark, slick with slime.

"This way," said Ledoq, and turned to the left. Once again, I followed him. The ceiling was still too low for me to stand upright.

I was panting now, sucking in that foul air a lot more quickly than I wanted to.

"Where'd you get the derringer?" I asked him.

Over his shoulder, he said, "It was a gift, many years ago. I have never had occasion to use it before."

"I'm glad you brought it along tonight. You were pretty handy with your feet, too."

"*Savate*, we call it," he said. "I won several medals as a youth. And you, *mon ami*—you used your own feet rather well, I thought."

"*Kicking*, we call it."

The dark walls of the tunnel were still swaying and jerking with the movement of the lantern. The smell was so intense now that my eyes were watering.

"And, *mon ami*," he said, "you dealt with the large man, Reilly, most effectively. I confess that I was somewhat concerned." He coughed again. "I feared that the famous American sense of fair play would do us in."

"If I hadn't sucker-punched him, right now his friends would probably still be shoving sawdust down our throats."

His small head nodded. "Yes. In the circumstances, I believe that you made the correct choice."

I looked around. Rats, sewage, darkness. That unbelievable stink. "We'll see," I said.

They almost got us, a few minutes later.

We had come to a juncture in the tunnels. Our tunnel ended as it met another, this one perpendicular to it, and wider. The water channel was maybe five feet across.

"Now, I think," said Ledoq, "we go in the direction of the river." He nodded toward the left.

"Fine with me," I said.

But Ledoq was looking back the way we'd come. "What is that?

I turned on the narrow walkway. Carefully. The bricks beneath my shoes were slippery with muck.

It was a light, quivering down there in the black distance, maybe two hundred feet away. Another lantern. Too far away to see who was holding it.

"It must be one of them, eh?" said Ledoq.

And then, from a point just to the right of the lantern, another light appeared, this one suddenly there, merging with the light of the lantern, and then suddenly gone, like a match bursting into flame and snuffing itself out, and the tunnel was filled with the roar of a big pistol.

We darted around the corner.

I grabbed Ledoq's arm, stopping him, and I leaned toward him and whispered. "Give me the derringer."

"But Phil—"

"Henri, we don't have time."

"But there may be more than one of them," he said.

"That's why I want the derringer."

He reached into his pocket, pulled out the pistol, handed it to me.

"Okay," I whispered. "You keep going. I'll knock out that lantern."

"But how will you see, afterward?"

"I'll call you. You come back and get me. If I don't call, just keep going."

He stood fully upright. "I refuse."

"Henri, there's no time. Get that light away or he'll know I'm here."

He frowned.

"Go!" I said.

He took off. I watched him hurry down the tunnel, a dapper silhouette within the ring of light that wobbled against the walls and the ceiling and along the gleam of water, a ring that slowly wobbled off into the distance. The blackness and the stink settled over me.

I turned and faced the entrance to the tunnel, only a few feet away. I cocked the derringer and put my trigger finger along the barrel. There was no trigger guard, and I didn't know how much force the trigger required, so I would have to be careful.

I rubbed at my neck with my left. Now that I'd stopped moving, I could feel the pain. My head had been bent forward, to keep it away from the low ceilings, since we came down the stairway. That had been only a couple of hundred yards back, probably, but it seemed like a couple of miles.

I turned and looked toward Ledoq. The ring of light was dimmer now, farther away.

I looked at the tunnel entrance. No light showing yet.

If the guy was stupid, he would come around the corner quickly.

Firing a pistol down here had been stupid. There would be methane in the tunnels, pockets of it here and there. That was the reason for the miner's safety lantern. An open flame could ignite the gas. So could a shot from a pistol.

But it hadn't. Which meant that, if necessary, I could use the derringer.

But his firing the pistol had been stupid. He hadn't known, before he fired, that it would be safe.

So maybe he would come quickly. Quickly would be better.

Then I saw the faint glow of light, trembling on the tunnel wall opposite me. I realized that I was still panting. I took in a deep breath—not a healthy thing to do, down there—and I let it slowly out.

The light grew brighter. Soon I could see the black water beneath me, the bricks in the walkway, the bricks in the wall. No voices out there. Probably only one of them.

Then the sound of footsteps, quick footsteps, but only a single set.

He would be here any second now. I stuck the derringer into my pocket. What I had in mind would work better without it. I braced my feet.

The lantern came around the corner first, in his left hand. I grabbed his wrist with my own left hand and I slammed my right at his elbow and I whipped him around the corner, off his feet. He fired the pistol—in the crazy twirling light of the lantern, I saw that it was a big Webley—but he was in the air by then, sailing, and the shot went straight down, pocking the lumpy black surface of the water. Then the lantern hit, and suddenly I was back in the darkness, and then the man smacked against the water with a big sloppy splash. I felt something spatter wet and cold against my face, heard something spatter against my clothes, and my stomach clenched and my throat went tight, but I didn't stop to think about that because already I was shuffling slowly sideways, my back and my hands to the damp wall, toward Ledoq.

I had the derringer out again. If the man still held the Webley, and if it could still fire after being dunked in the swill, he would probably use it, even though he couldn't see me.

I knew the Webley. It was a good rugged pistol, it used a good rugged cartridge, and it would probably be working just fine. But the moment he fired, I would see him and I would use the derringer.

I heard nothing. No shot. No thrashing.

Maybe he'd hit his head. Maybe he was drowning. Maybe he was already dead.

Or maybe he was waiting for me to light a match.

I didn't have a match, and I wouldn't have lit one if I had. I kept edging away, as quietly as I could.

Up ahead, the ring of light had stopped moving. Now it began to move again, but toward me. I couldn't see Ledoq himself because he was behind the lantern now.

Stupid. He didn't know what had happened back here. I could be the bad guy, heading directly for him.

I heard Ledoq call out, *"Phil?"*

I took a chance. Raising the little pistol, I turned back toward the part of the tunnel where I thought the man was. I turned my head slightly to the side, toward Ledoq, and I shouted, *"Quiet!"*

The Webley boomed and I heard the slug screech against the wall, somewhere close, and for an instant the man was lit by the sudden glare of the the explosion, ten feet away, standing waist deep in the center of that foul black water, sludge dripping from his face and clothes. I fired the derringer.

It was a long shot for a pistol with a short, smooth-bore barrel, and I had only one bullet left. I knew that if I didn't hit him, I was dead. He would use the sound and sight of my own shot to line me up. And the Webley would have five bullets left.

I heard a dull, heavy splash. I heard something that might have been air, escaping from submerged lungs and bubbling up through thick sewage. And then I heard nothing at all.

I put the pistol in my pocket and I started moving toward Ledoq again.

"We must hurry, Phil," said Ledoq. "If the others heard those shots, they will be here shortly."

"How do we get out of here?"

"I believe that we are approaching one of the main tunnels. Is that not light up there?"

It was, and in a few minutes we came to a tunnel wider than the one we were in. Lights burned along the curved walls.

"Hullo there!" cried a cheerful British voice.

I turned and I saw, about twenty feet away, a boat coming toward us. It was rectangular, built like a small open barge. It had a blunt metal prow and it was about four feet high and fifteen feet long and seven feet wide, just wide enough to fit in the channel. There were safety lamps burning at the front and the rear of it, and in its center, at a table that held a wicker basket and an assortment of food, was an elderly couple, a man and a woman in their seventies. They were both wearing black formal evening clothes, including a frilly sort of bonnet for her and a top hat for him, and they were both sitting very upright. The man had a bright red face and a bushy white mustache that swept back to bushy white muttonchop sideburns. Behind them, sitting at the back of the boat, were two men dressed in white workcoats.

The old man said cheerfully, "You chaps lost, are you? Speak English, do you? Need a lift?"

Eight

YES, YES," SAID Colonel Mereweather, "the smell is appalling. No argument from me on that score. But we've lived with worse, eh, Mavis?"

"I should say so," said Mrs. Mereweather. She turned to her husband and she smiled sweetly. "The loo at Pondicherry Rail Station, for a start."

"Haw!" said Colonel Mereweather, smiling widely. "Right you are." He turned to me. "Now there was a pong. This is roses, my boy, next to the loo at Pondicherry Rail Station. Diabolical. We had a lad with us—subaltern, forget his name—"

"Weaver," said Mrs. Mereweather comfortably.

"That's it. Shropshire lad. Collapsed on his way *into* the filthy place. Never even made it past the door. Lay there on the tiles like an old sack of bedding. Took three sepoys to haul him back into the fresh air. Never really recovered, poor beggar." He turned to his wife, frowning. "Whatever happened to him, Mavis? Weaver?"

"He resigned his commission, dear. He returned to Shropshire, I believe."

"So he did. No stamina, poor chap. Nothing against Shropshire, mind. My experience, you get these frail types from all over. One of those family problems, no doubt. Some flaw in the hereditary thingummy. Could happen anywhere. Sure you won't have some of this pâté? Damn good stuff."

"No thanks," I said.

"More claret, Mr. Beaumont?"

"Please."

"And you, Mr. Ledoq?"

"I should be grateful, Colonel."

The Colonel poured more wine into our crystal glasses.

The boat might have floated here straight from *The Arabian Nights*. The cushioned seats were upholstered in thick red velvet. The floor was lushly carpeted. The fittings were brass, all of them polished to a mellow gleam. The safety lanterns cast a pale yellow light over the goods that the colonel and his wife had removed from their wicker picnic basket and set out along the leather table—containers of pâté, chunks of cheese, small jars of caviar, bottles of wine, loaves of bread.

The boat was called, Ledoq had told me, a *bateau-vanne*. He had turned to the colonel. "But I was under the impression that the municipality had stopped operating these tours two years ago, when the sewer system was modified to accept human waste."

"Very likely, very likely," the colonel had said. "Friend of a friend, chap in the War Ministry, laid it on for us. Always wanted to give it a go, Mavis and I. I was here during the War, with the regiment, but I'd promised Mavis I wouldn't do it without her, you see." He had smiled at his wife, and she had smiled sweetly back.

We were slowly sliding along the sluggish current down the long arched tunnel. More lamps glowed high on the wall, a procession of lights leading off into a distance that seemed infinite, the lights doubled by their reflections in the barely moving black water beneath them.

"Course," said the colonel now, setting down the bottle of wine. He tapped a long bony finger against the long bony nose that jutted out above his bushy white mustache. "Old sniffer's not what it used to be." He spread some pâté on a crust of bread. "Mavis has the same problem. All those curries, eh, my dear? All that chicken vindaloo, eh?"

At "chicken vindaloo," Ledoq glanced at him, winced once, then deliberately smoothed out his face.

Mrs. Mereweather smiled again. "Nonsense, Howard. Simple old age."

"Haw!" said the colonel, delighted. He turned to me

again. "Calls a spade a spade, eh? Always has."

I took a drink of wine. I couldn't taste it above the stench that surrounded us, but just then I didn't care.

The colonel popped the crust of bread into his mouth. He chewed thoughtfully for a minute, then swallowed. "One thing, though. Don't mean to be a nosy parker, of course. If I am, just say so, eh, and there's an end to it. But how is it you chaps are wandering about down here? Not really the place for a ramble, is it? Thing is, you see, we thought we'd heard some gunshots, little while back. Couldn't swear to it, naturally. These tunnels muck up the sound something awful. But seemed like gunshots to us, eh, Mavis?"

Mrs. Mereweather nodded firmly. "They were gunshots," she said. "I know my gunshots, Howard."

"Haw!" said the colonel and he turned to me. "She does, too, you know."

"Yeah," I said. "They were gunshots."

Briefly, I told him who we were and what had happened.

"Extraordinary," said the colonel, when I finished. "A Pinkerton, you say? Heard of you chaps, of course. But this man you shot. Dead, is he?"

"Probably, Colonel. I didn't fish him out to check his pulse."

"Quite." He nodded. "Quite." He shook his head. "Extraordinary. Well, my boy, your course is as plain as a pikestaff. Bring in the police, eh?"

"Normally I would," I said. "But I don't think it's a very good idea right now. I think that the police—some of them, anyway—are involved in all this."

He raised his bushy white eyebrows. "You don't say! Extraordinary." He frowned at his wife. "Wouldn't happen in England, would it, Mavis?" He turned quickly to Ledoq. "I say. No offense, old chap. I've nothing against the Frenchies. Very decent bunch when you get to know them. Saw a spot of action with them against the Hun. Fight like tigers when their blood's up."

Ledoq smiled. "No offense is taken." He had been saying that, or something like it, all evening.

"And these chaps, Pierre and Jacques, or whatever"—the colonel jerked his thumb back, toward the two men in the back of the boat—"damn' helpful, both of them. Salt of the earth."

He turned to me. "Anything we can do? Reconaissance? Intelligence? Eh?"

I smiled. "No, Colonel, thank you. Once we're out of here, we'll be fine."

He looked disappointed. "If you're sure." Suddenly he brightened. "But look here," he said. He reached into his topcoat, pulled out a silver card case, opened it, pulled out a card. "My card, eh? Just in case. Staying at the Ritz, Mavis and I, until Thursday. Beastly expensive, but they do a proper tea."

I took the card. "Thank you, Colonel."

"You need reinforcements, you let us know, eh?"

"I will."

He peered at me for a moment, then frowned slightly. "One thing, though. Forgive me for saying so, but you've a spot of something"—he tapped a bony finger against his sunken cheek—"just here."

I got out my handkerchief.

Fifteen minutes later we were back on the streets of Paris, near the Champs-Elysées and the river. City lights had never looked so bright—the Eiffel Tower, south of us, was gleaming like a beacon—and city air had never smelled so fresh.

We said good-bye to Colonel and Mrs. Mereweather. The colonel had refused to let us help pay the sewermen. "On me, my boy. Small contribution to the war effort, eh?"

After they drove away in one taxicab, Ledoq flagged down another. As soon as we got in, the driver took one loud sniff and immediately his face clenched like a fist. He started waving his arms and shouting in disgusted French. Ledoq waved his own arms and shouted back. Finally the driver grunted something and nodded. But he made a big point of opening both his windows before he took off. I didn't blame him.

"We are obliged to pay him an extra five francs," Ledoq told me, sitting back. "To reimburse him for cleaning the vehicle after we leave it."

"Fine."

He reached into his pocket and pulled out his watch. "Only twelve o'clock."

"Yeah," I said. "But what day?"

He smiled. "We can change our clothing and still arrive at the barge in time to speak with the Loving woman."

"There's something we should think about first."

"Yes?"

"Reilly. He knows your name. It probably wouldn't be hard for him to find you."

"Ah." Stroking his goatee, he looked out at the passing streetlights. "And he might in fact decide to do so."

"He's probably not too happy about that lump on the head."

He glanced at the cabdriver. In a conversational tone, he said, "You realize, of course, that the driver of this taxi is a pederast and a traitor to France. His wife, incidentally, is a prostitute, and syphilitic."

Nothing from the cabdriver.

Ledoq smiled at me, pleased with himself. "And let us not forget the gentleman you left reposing in the sewer."

All at once, I remembered the mad lurch of the lantern, the splash of a man into the sewage, the darkness, the sudden glare of his gun, and mine.

"Reilly," said Ledoq, "may take that as a personal affront, and feel obliged to avenge him." He thought for a moment. "Perhaps we should both change our locations."

"He doesn't know where I'm staying."

"But Monsieur LaGrande does. He has attempted to conceal certain facts, remember. Madame Norton's presence at the Grande Bretagne may be the least of these. Perhaps, if we discover others, these still less savory, he may take measures to terminate our meddling."

"Henri, I'm meeting one of his inspectors tomorrow. If he wants to run me in, he can do it as soon as I show up."

"You mistake me. I doubt, you see, that he would act openly. You are a Pinkerton, eh? Behind you stands a large and important organization. Monsieur LaGrande would be unlikely to confront it. But by tomorrow, at the latest, he will know that Reilly has an interest in locating you."

"And he could tip him off to where I'm staying. Maybe.

But I've got a feeling that LaGrande wants us to keep snooping around. He didn't need to give us those reports. He didn't need to arrange the meeting tomorrow. I think he wants to see what we come up with. Maybe he's trying to find out how well he's covered his tracks.''

"Wherever those tracks may lead.''

"Yeah.''

"But are you prepared, *mon ami,* to risk your life on this feeling?''

I smiled. "Not if I don't have to.''

"*Bon.* It so happens that at the moment a good friend of mine is in the country. I possess the key to her flat here in Paris. It is in the Eleventh, not a fashionable arrondissement, of course, but it will suit our purposes. There is room enough for both of us. And, around the corner, there is a small bistro that does an excellent *poulet sauté à l'estragon.* Chicken, that is, in a sauce of tarragon and shallots.''

"Uh huh. What's your friend doing in the country?''

"Visiting her husband.''

"Visiting?''

"He owns an estate in Normandy, and she cannot abide Normandy. She visits him in April and May, for the apple blossoms, and then again in December, for the Christmas holiday. In the summer, she goes to Cannes. By herself.''

"Interesting marriage.''

"For both of them. He has his cheerful, compliant peasant girls, redolent of apples and butter, and she has . . .'' He smiled brightly. "Well, among many other things, of course, she has me.''

"A fair trade.''

He nodded. "An entirely equitable arrangement.''

"Anyone know about your connection to her?''

He seemed insulted. "*Mon ami*, she is the soul of discretion. She is, after all, a married woman.''

"Okay. We'll try it.''

"Now,'' said Ledoq. "You must tell me what you thought of the colorful young American at the Hole in the Wall.''

"I thought that what he said was interesting.''

"Which thing he said? That very important people were

involved in Forsythe's death? Or that Sabine von Stuben was an acquaintance of Reilly's?''

"He said *friend*, not acquaintance, and, yeah, that's what I think is interesting.''

"But perhaps he exaggerated the relationship. Many of the wealthy, the aristocracy, they enjoy consorting with people like Reilly. It adds savor to their lives. A *soupçon* of spice.''

"Maybe. But the way Jepson was talking, it sounds like von Stuben consorted on a regular basis.''

"And this establishes . . . what?''

Outside, streetlights whizzed past. "I don't know. But I'd like to find out more about von Stuben.'' I turned to him. "Where was she from, originally?''

"Munich, I believe.''

I nodded. "I'll wire London tomorrow. See what the Agency can come up with.''

"And what of the very important people that Jepson mentioned?''

"I don't think that's worth much.''

He frowned. "But you wished, I thought, to establish that Monsieur Forsythe did *not* commit suicide. Jepson's claims do not provoke your interest?''

"I want to establish what actually happened in that hotel room. Jepson's a bottom feeder. And probably a junkie. Anything he knows is bound to be third- or fourth-hand.''

"A bottom feeder," said Ledoq, and he smiled. *"Très bon."* He looked at me. "But Jepson did, in fact, know that the police were less than enthusiastic in their investigation of Monsieur Forsythe's death.''

"So did we. And maybe LaGrande just wants to keep Sybil Norton's name out of it.''

We went first to my hotel. After another argument with Ledoq, the cabdriver agreed to wait. I gave Ledoq some money, then took the elevator upstairs while he handled the bill. I stripped off all my clothes, balled them up, shoved them into the wastebasket. The shoes I'd worn into the sewer were the only pair I had, so I cleaned them off as well as I could. Then I climbed into the bathtub and cleaned myself off as well as I could. If I'd had any steel wool, I would've used it.

I dressed again, put the derringer in my pocket, threw everything into my satchel, then left the room and took the elevator downstairs. As soon as I walked into the lobby, I could smell Ledoq.

When we got back into the cab, I rolled down my own window. Ledoq turned to me sadly. "It is that bad, is it?"

"Yeah. I'm sorry, Henri."

He sighed.

I turned around and glanced out the rear window. A small black car pulled away from the curb, about twenty feet behind the entrance to the hotel.

I turned around and sat back. "We're being followed."

He looked at me. "The police?"

"Probably. I doubt that LaGrande's sold us out already. Even if he has, I don't think Reilly could get someone here so soon."

"But I must go to my flat," he said. "I *must* get these things off me."

"We're going there," I said. "Doesn't matter. The cops know about you. They've probably got someone watching the place already."

He frowned.

"We'll lose them," I said. "Afterward. As soon as you get some stuff from your apartment."

Looking out the window again, he stroked his goatee thoughtfully.

I said, "I'm sorry I got you into this, Henri. The problem with Reilly. The cops."

He turned to me. "No, no, *mon ami*. I was not brooding. I was merely considering what articles of clothing I ought to pack. A difficult set of decisions, in the circumstances. Which cravat, exactly, goes best with effluent?" He laughed and he clapped me on the knee. "No, no, I am entirely enjoying the adventure, I assure you."

"Henri," I said, "I killed a guy back there."

He nodded sadly. "Yes, that was unfortunate, I agree. But much worse for him than for us, eh? And, in the meantime, we still have a puzzle to solve."

"We're not making much progress."

He smiled broadly. "But we are having a splendid time,

eh? Ratiocination, fisticuffs, nighttime dashes through the sewers of Paris. All very stirring.'' He frowned. ''Deaths aside, I mean. And also, along the way, we have shared a decent meal or two.'' He shrugged. ''Who could ask for more? Ah, here we are.''

The cab slowed to a stop in front of a building that looked pretty much like all the other buildings in this part of town. Ledoq grabbed the door handle, turned back to me. ''I shall return in but a moment.''

''Henri, you only need enough stuff for a few days.''

''I understand completely,'' he said. For some reason, this didn't reassure me.

He got out and I swiveled in the seat to look out the rear window. The small black car had pulled into the curb about a hundred feet away. I sat back and I waited.

After a few minutes, the cab driver looked up into the rearview mirror and said, ''*Vous parlez francais, m'sieur?*''

''No,'' I told him. ''Sorry.''

He nodded sadly. Like the old man at the hotel, he had expected that.

It took Ledoq about half an hour, but finally he came bustling out of the building's front door, wearing another black suit and lugging a large suitcase in each hand. From the way he carried them, they were both loaded with cannon balls. The driver muttered under his breath, opened his door, and stepped out to help Ledoq load the cases into the trunk of the car.

The two of them stood talking back there for a few more minutes. Their voices rose for a while, then softened, then rose again, then softened. Then they stopped and the driver came around to his door, and Ledoq opened his and slipped into the cab. He smelled, once again, of bay rum.

''That's a few days' worth?'' I asked him.

''Better to be safe,'' he said, ''than to be sorry.''

The driver started the car and pulled it out into the street. Behind us, the small black car eased away from the curb.

Ledoq turned to me. ''Have you two hundred francs?''

''Why?''

''To pay the driver.''

''For a cab ride?''

"We agreed to pay for cleaning the taxi. Now we must pay an additional amount, for his expertise in eliminating pursuit.'

"Yeah. I've got two hundred francs."

"*Bon*. May I have a hundred of them now?"

I pulled out the roll of francs and I used the passing lights of the streetlamps to count out a hundred of them. I gave them to Ledoq. He leaned forward, tapped the driver on the shoulder, and handed the money to the man, who took it without glancing away from the road and stuffed it into his shirt pocket.

Ledoq sat back, looked at me, and smiled. "All is arranged," he said.

Soon we were crossing the river again. Ledoq looked out the window. "Ah," he said. "Paris at night. Beautiful, is it not?"

It was. It was beautiful in the daytime, too, but in the sunlight you could see that the beauty was coated with a layer of gray. At night you couldn't. Everything seemed crisp and clear and perfect. The lights of the city, bright and filled with promise, were perfectly reflected along the smooth black surface of the water. Upriver, the red eye of a solitary barge winked shut as the boat slid around a graceful bend.

I wondered whether the sewers emptied directly into the river. I wondered whether, if they did, some kind of grating protected the openings and prevented large objects—like a human body—from shooting out into the current.

"You must pay attention now," said Ledoq. "If the driver has not exaggerated his automotive skills, which of course is possible, this next bit may prove interesting."

We were crossing the river on the Pont Neuf, the westernmost bridge on the Ile de la Cité, the island that held the Prefecture of Police and the cathedral of Notre-Dame. When we reached the Right Bank, we were on the Boulevard Sebastopol, heading roughly north. The driver drove normally as we crossed the broad Rue de Rivoli, where Ledoq and I had enjoyed our coffee this morning—it seemed like a week ago. The avenue was brilliantly lit, the streetlamps and the fronts of the cafés blazing. Even now, at one o'clock in the morning, well-dressed people sauntered happily down the sidewalks. Probably none of them gave a thought to the sewers that gurgled and bubbled beneath their feet.

A couple of blocks beyond Rivoli, the driver suddenly whipped the steering wheel to the left and the car went squealing across the oncoming traffic lane and down a narrow side street.

The driver hadn't exaggerated his automotive skills. He was good.

We raced down the street, whipping around a large, slow-moving truck, the taxi bouncing once as its left wheels climbed up onto the sidewalk, then bouncing again, jarring Ledoq and me, as the wheels jumped back to street level. The truck's horn wailed at us. I glanced through the rear window. The black car was still on our tail, coming around the truck, but it was farther back now.

Ledoq and I were tossed to the side as the car spun to the left again, down another side street. There were more trucks here, but they didn't slow down the driver. We spent a fair amount of time slamming up onto the sidewalks and slamming back down. Horns blared. The black car was still falling behind.

"We are nearing Les Halles," said Ledoq. "The central market for all of Paris. There is a restaurant nearby—open throughout the night—which serves a splendid onion soup."

I was thrown against Ledoq's shoulder as the taxi made another screeching left turn. More trucks, more sidewalks. More horns.

"The recipe," said Ledoq, "is simplicity itself. You merely slice some onions and sauté them in butter until nearly brown. You add a bit of flour, stir for a few moments, blending it in well, and then you add some white stock. There is a school of thought which maintains that you may use brown stock. I find personally—"

The taxi made still another screeching left, missing by a few inches a truck coming from the other direction.

"—that this produces far too heavy a soup. A white stock is essential. You then add a few good dashes of good port wine—"

We were up on the sidewalk again as we passed another truck. It looked familiar, and so did the street, and I realized,

as the truck's horn wailed, that it was the first truck we'd
passed. We had gone in a circle.

"—or madeira. You cook this, simmering, for approximately half an hour. Into a large crock you place a slice of
bread that has been—"

We were careening out onto a huge square that looked to
be about a mile wide, and in its center was an enormous
building of wrought iron and glass. It reminded me of Victoria Station, in London, but it was even more imposing. The
peaked roof of the center section was maybe three or four
stories high, and the flat roofs of the two massive wings that
flanked it were only a story shorter. The whole building must
have covered thirty or forty acres of land. All around it, trucks
and horse carts were everywhere, most of them pulled up
toward the building, where workers with heavy shoulders
were unloading bulky sacks and baskets and boxes in the
yellow glare of the streetlamps. But some of the trucks were
winding their way slowly through tall piles of wooden pallets
and rickety-looking stacks of wooden crates. People were
walking slowly, too, most of them carrying more of those
sacks and baskets and boxes. The cab began to dash through
all this, wheeling right, wheeling left, while the driver leaned
on his horn. Ahead, people saw us coming, stared for a minute
in disbelief, and then tossed whatever they carried, and ran.

"—dried in the oven, and *voilà*, there you have it. *Soupe
à l'oignon.* At the restaurant I have in mind, they add a nice
refinement. They grate cheese thickly over the top and—"

And now other horns were honking, horses were neighing
and tossing their heads, people were screaming at us and
shaking their fists and pulling off their caps and hurling them
to the ground. We tore around one truck and nearly collided
with another. We went into a slide, leftward, and the rear
fender hit a stack of empty crates—the taxi shivered at the
impact—and the crates went bounding skyward. The driver
recovered very nicely, swinging the tail of the taxi back into
place, and we were off again, more people scattering in front
of us.

"—broil the crock under a hot fire until the cheese has
browned."

We had nearly circled the square, leaving several hundred

very unhappy people in our wake, and a lot of nervous horses.
I looked back, but I couldn't see the black car.

"A dry white wine," said Ledoq, "goes very well with
this."

Suddenly, at the entrance to another side street, the taxi
jerked to a stop. Just ahead, beyond the street and under another streetlamp, men were unloading flat rectangular boxes
from a parked truck and stacking them on the street. The cab
driver rolled down his window, put two fingers to his mouth,
and whistled shrilly. The men looked over. One of them, a
bulky man in a black turtleneck sweater, ran over to the cab.

I looked at Ledoq.

"His cousin," he explained.

I glanced through the rearview mirror. The black car was
just rounding the corner of the square, about a hundred yards
away.

The driver rattled some French at the man in the turtleneck,
handed him my hundred francs, and then floored the gas pedal
and spun the car to the right, into the side street.

Looking back through the mirror as we hurtled down the
street, I saw the black car reach the entrance, just as the gate
of the truck swung open and fifteen or twenty flat rectangular
boxes came tumbling out, spilling their contents and blocking
the road. The contents, in the light of the streetlamps, flashed
silver and gold. The black car smacked into all that, and then
went skidding out of view.

"Fish," said Ledoq, who had also turned to look through
the window. "You must remind me not to order any tomorrow."

The taxi kept speeding down the side street, but when we
reached the next main avenue, it slowed down and we made
a normal turn to the right. We drove north for a while—I
think it was north—then came to another broad avenue and
turned right again.

I said to Ledoq, "Can I ask you a question?"

"But of course, *mon ami*."

"You didn't tell the driver to drop us off anywhere near
that apartment?"

"Naturally not. I gave him a destination some distance
from the apartment. After he deposits us there, we will take

another cab. And perhaps yet another, after that. It is beyond doubt that the police have noted the number of this taxi. Before tomorrow morning, without fail, they will arrest this madman.''

The apartment, like Sybil Norton's, was located on the top floor of the building it occupied. It was a long way up when you were carrying one of Henri Ledoq's suitcases.

"What's in this?" I had asked him at the bottom of the stairs. We had stopped for a moment to rest. The thing must have weighed over a hundred pounds.

"My dumbbells," he said. "For the physical therapy. I do it every day." He made his hands into fists and he pushed them straight into the air, over his head, to show me. "A sound mind in a sound body."

"Uh huh." I reached into my pocket, pulled out the derringer, handed it to him. "Then you can carry this up, too."

"Thank you, *mon ami*." He slipped it into his pocket.

"Thanks for bringing it," I said.

We picked up the suitcase again, and we started climbing.

The apartment was large and airy and feminine. The furniture was all antique, delicate curved wooden legs on the chairs and the sofa, and the upholstery was all flounced. There was floral wallpaper on the wall. There was fringe on all the lampshades. Over the white fireplace, in a gilt frame, hung a large painting of very well-dressed shepherds playing flutes while they lolled happily on the mossy bank of a foaming stream. Some sheep were asleep there, too. In the air of the apartment, behind the faint smell of must, was the fainter smell of expensive perfume.

Ledoq dropped the suitcase to the Persian carpet and collapsed into one of the chairs. I set down the case I was carrying and I sat down on the sofa.

"It's okay," I asked him, "to have these lights on?"

"Yes," he said. "Mathilde sometimes permits guests to stay here. The neighbors are familiar with this."

"She's not going to have any guests for the next day or two?"

He smiled. "I will telephone her tomorrow and see that she does not." He reached into his pocket and pulled out his watch. "Only two-thirty. We still have time to go to the barge and speak with Aster Loving."

"It's been a long day, Henri. Let's wait until tomorrow."

But tomorrow would be too late. It was too late right now. At two-thirty, when we were sitting there in the living room, Aster Loving had been dead for at least five hours.

BOOK TWO

Dear Evangeline,

What a day this has been! And not yet over!

I am, I suspect, the busiest human being in Paris; events are proceeding at a pace which makes it impossible for me to catalogue them. I feel rather like a rodent on a treadmill. But I expect that I am having a much gayer time than any rodent is likely to have, on a treadmill or off it.

This letter will be brief. I'll write another, later tonight, when we return from the home of Gertrude Stein. According to Eugénie, Ernest Hemingway will probably be there, and I very much look forward to meeting him. Miss Stein is a writer herself, says Eugénie, and something of an eccentric, even by Parisian expatriate standards. She is also a lesbian. But then so is Eugénie. And so, seemingly, is a large proportion of the female population of Paris.

But perhaps I have been misled. If one's guide to Paris were, for example, a dwarf, then one should meet rather a lot of dwarves, I expect.

More on this later. The lesbians, I meant to say.

To sum up my day for you: since this morning I have driven an automobile (an enormous Rolls-Royce) and eaten snails and become tipsy at lunch, all for the first time in my life; I have visited a number of wonderful little boutiques, including one owned by Coco Chanel, who was tiny and *chic* and utterly delightful; and I have roamed through Bon Marché, my favourite department store in all of Paris, like a wide-eyed Visigoth through the halls of Rome.

When I asked Eugénie if we could go there, she blinked and her normal pallor went a bit more pale. Bon Marché is, after all, the bastion of bourgeois shopping; and I suspect that Eugénie, the daughter of a count, tends to look askance at (which is not necessarily the same as down upon) the bourgeoisie in general. But when I explained that I'd gone there, years ago, with my mother, and that my memories of those visits are among my fondest, she became nearly as excited as I.

I must tell you one thing more. You recall my mentioning Phil Beaumont, the American who was responsible for my becoming a Pinkerton operative? And my mentioning that he might one day soon be returning to Europe? Well, today, as Eugénie and I wandered through Bon Marché, a sudden movement caught my eye, off to the right. I glanced over and saw a man ambling down a nearby aisle—I never saw his face, but from the rear he looked uncannily like Mr Beaumont, the same dark hair, the same broad shoulders; and for a moment my breath caught in my chest and my heart actually wobbled.

(It did. It wobbled. Left and then right. But this might, of course, have been caused by the snails.)

Just as I decided that it *must* be Mr Beaumont, smiling Eugénie asked me something—did I think this brooch was *spirituelle*?—and my attention was distracted. By the time I looked back, the man was gone.

It wasn't Mr Beaumont, of course. Had he been sent to Paris, I should have been told of it. And, you know, I really cannot imagine him in Bon Marché at all, amidst the baubles and the bangles.

But I do find it amusing that I invented his presence, and in Bon Marché, of all places. Apparently the possibility of his return has been more on my mind than I realised.

But not, I suspect, more than you did. I hate you, Evy.

Let me see . . . what else happened today? Yes. I learned something extremely interesting, possibly even extremely important, about Sabine von Stuben. You remember—the woman who died with Richard Forsythe. (The life of a Pinkerton does not always involve shopping.) And I learned something as well, and something perhaps equally important, about Sybil Norton the crime writer who comes, as I do, from Torquay. I know that you enjoy her books, but you may enjoy them less when you hear what I have to say.

Oh, and I was propositioned by an astonishingly beautiful American heiress who speaks and writes perfect French.

No time, now, to write more. I'll post this on the way out.

Much love,
Jane

P.S. I've hired a costume for the party tomorrow. But I don't believe that I'm ready just yet to tell you what it is.

Love,
J.

Nine

I SLEPT IN the maid's room. The maid was obviously a lot shorter than I was, because both my feet hung out over the end of the mattress. And the bed had no pillow, only a bolster—cylindrical, like a telephone pole, but not as soft. I dumped it to the floor, and that gave me another inch or two of bed. I still thought I wouldn't be able to sleep, but I didn't think it for long, because within five minutes I was out.

When I woke up, a thin blade of sunlight was slicing beneath the pulled-down shade and painting a band of yellow across the closed lace curtains. I heard an automobile horn honking, distant and muffled. I looked at my watch. Nine o'clock. Late.

I threw back the sheet, swung my legs off the bed, got up. Felt a sudden sharp twinge in my back, just below the shoulder blade.

Maybe it was the tiny bed. I was getting too old to be sleeping in tiny beds.

Or maybe I'd pulled a muscle last night, when I tossed that Frenchman over my shoulder. I was also getting too old to toss Frenchmen over my shoulder.

I rummaged in my valise, found my bathrobe, climbed into it, and went out to find Ledoq.

He was sitting on the living room sofa, fully dressed, holding a cup of coffee, leaning slightly forward over a newspaper opened on the coffee table.

"Ah, *mon ami*," he said, and set his cup onto its saucer. "You return to the land of the living, eh?"

"Not all the way," I said. "Not yet."

He smiled. Today he was wearing a three-piece lightweight suit of gray wool, as spotless as his suit had been yesterday, until it had gone running through the sewers. Somehow he had managed to pack the new suit, and unpack it, without putting a single wrinkle anywhere on the fabric. He was also wearing a white shirt with a stiff collar, a gray bow tie, black shoes, and a pair of white spats, neatly buttoned.

"Sit," he said, waving me down, and he stood up himself. "How do you prefer your coffee?"

"Hot. Black. Two sugars." I sat down in one of the rickety chairs. "Thanks."

"Would you care for a croissant? I went out and purchased some at the local café. They are tolerable."

"No thanks, Henri. The coffee will be fine."

"*Bon.*" He nodded and left the room. I sat back, looked up at the painting of the well-dressed shepherds. They were still playing their flutes. The sheep were still sleeping. I envied them.

Ledoq came back, carrying a cup and saucer. He handed them to me.

"Thank you," I said. As he sat back down, I nodded to the newspaper. "Anything in there about our friend in the sewer?"

"*Non.* But there *is* some bad news, I am afraid."

I drank some coffee. It was perfect, which didn't really surprise me. I figured that anyone who knew how to make frog legs *à la meunière* would probably know how to put together a cup of coffee. "What's that?"

"Aster Loving. The singer. She is dead."

"Dead?" I repeated stupidly.

"An overdose of heroin," he said. "Last night."

I lowered my coffee cup. "We should've gone to that damned barge."

"We should have been too late, *mon ami.* She died earlier in the evening." He held up the newpaper. "Shall I translate?"

"Yeah." I looked off. *"Shit."*

He sat back, looked down at the newspaper. *"Aster Loving,"* he read, *"the beautiful Negro chanteuse*—singer, that is—*whose haunting version of the lovely song 'Blackbird' had made her*—'' He frowned. "*Merde.* What nonsense.— *had made her the jewel in the crown of Paris nightlife*—'' He looked up. "Where do they find these ridiculous phrases?"

I nodded. "Go on."

He looked back down at the paper. "—*was found late on Thursday evening, dead from an overdose of heroin. Miss Loving's body was discovered at eleven P.M. by her manager, Jacques Morret, who summoned both the police and medical assistance. Efforts to revive the singer proved fruitless, and she was pronounced dead on the scene. According to reports from the police, Miss Loving died at some time between eight and ten o'clock last night.*"

He glanced down the column. "There is some biographical detail, her colorful life in the United States before she became this famous jewel in the Parisian crown, and then there is a poetic coda, in English." He looked up. '*Bye Bye Blackbird,*' it says. Shall I read more?"

I shook my head. "Damn it," I said. "That's some coincidence. We start asking questions, and the next day she turns up dead."

He stroked his goatee. "It is very curious, I agree. But how, *mon ami,* could her death be connected to the investigation? You have spoken only to Rose Forsythe and Sybil Norton, and neither knew of Madamoiselle Loving's relationship to Richard Forsythe."

"Not until I told them about it."

He thought for a moment, frowning. "But you said that you had not explained the relationship. To Madame Forsythe, at any rate."

"Rose may not be as goofy as she seems. I'm investigating her husband's death, I give her a woman's name. Maybe she figured it out. Or maybe Sybil Norton did."

"But why would either of them kill Aster Loving? And the newspaper says she died of an overdose of heroin. If she were addicted to the drug, would she not always be risking such a consequence?"

"Maybe. But always is a long time, Henri. She died yesterday. The same day I showed up in Paris. I don't like it."

Ledoq was silent. Finally he said, "It occurs to me that there is another possibility. In addition to Madame Forsythe and Madame Norton."

I had forgotten about my coffee. It didn't taste as good as it had tasted before, but it still tasted like coffee, and I still needed it. "What?" I asked him.

"Monsieur le Préfet. Let us assume that you are correct, and that Richard Forsythe's death was not a suicide. Perhaps LaGrande knew of Aster Loving. Perhaps Aster Loving was in possession of some vital piece of information regarding Forsythe's death. And perhaps LaGrande knew this. Perhaps, fearing that you might learn of her involvement with Forsythe, he decided to dispose of her."

I nodded. "Or maybe Reilly did."

He frowned.

"Maybe," I said, "Reilly knew something. About Aster Loving and Forsythe. And when he saw us talking to Jepson last night, he thought Jepson had spilled the beans."

"But Jepson mentioned nothing about Aster Loving."

"Reilly doesn't know that."

He considered this for a second. "Yes, you are correct, of course. But this is all purely speculative, is it not?"

"Yeah. Purely."

"The woman may have simply died of an overdose, self-administered. An accident."

"Yeah." I drank some more coffee. "All right," I said. "Look. We're supposed to meet that inspector at noon, at the Grande Bretagne. The one who investigated Forsythe's death. I need to go to the telegraph office and send a wire to London, see if they can dig up anything in Munich about the von Stuben woman. And I have to go to the bank, too, and arrange a check for LaGrande and his orphans. You have an address for that Society of his?"

"I will obtain it. I will make some telephone calls while you dress."

"Good. Thanks. And while I'm running around this morning, could you try to track down Aster Loving's manager? What's his name again?"

"Jacques"—he scanned the paper—"Morret."

"Could you see if he can talk to us this afternoon? Try to

set up an appointment at—what? Two o'clock okay with you?''

"Certainly. I will arrange it."

"Great. Thanks, Henri."

He waved a hand. "It is nothing."

I went back to the maid's room, grabbed a clean shirt, underwear, and socks from the valise, and tossed them to the bed. In one corner of the room there was a tiny alcove, not much bigger than a closet, that held a bathtub and a sink. Like the bed, the tub hadn't been designed for someone of my size. Sitting upright in the thing—the only possible way I could sit in it—made me feel like a bear in a bucket.

Afterward, I shaved and I put on the clean clothes and my only remaining suit. Before I left the room, I took the rest of the clothing from the valise, opened the false bottom, and slipped out the .32 Colt automatic. I slid it into my pants pocket.

I took a taxi to Barclay's Bank, where I arranged for a check of two thousand francs to be sent to LaGrande's Orphan Society. The bank was on the Rue du 4 Septembre, close enough to the Rue des Capucines and the Hole in the Wall for me to spend some time looking over my shoulder.

No one seemed to be watching me when I left the bank, so I took another taxi to the telegraph office. No one followed the cab. Inside, I sent my wire to London and I checked to see if there was a wire waiting for me, maybe another report forwarded, via the London office, from the operative who'd been placed with the Forsythe family. There wasn't.

By then it was ten-thirty. I had over an hour to kill before I met Ledoq and the inspector at the Grande Bretagne. I decided to walk it, and I got directions from the clerk at Western Union.

It was another fine day, bright and clear and warm. Despite the grime and the soot that covered it, Paris was a beautiful city. I liked the elegant sweep of the boulevards, the grace and dignity of the old buildings, the slow steady bustle of the boats along the quiet brown river.

It would be a good city to investigate, I decided, if I weren't already investigating a murder.

I stopped at a café. The waiter spoke no English, so I went inside and I got a chance to feel like a circus clown while I pointed at this and pointed at that and nodded and shook my head. I went back outside to my table and in a few minutes I got a sandwich, a coffee, and overcharged. The sandwich wasn't great. The bread was good, which almost made up for the meat. Fortunately, there wasn't much meat. The coffee was excellent.

I arrived at the Grande Bretagne a few minutes after twelve. Henri Ledoq was standing at the front desk, one hand down at his side, holding his gloves and a gray fedora, the other hand raised to his chest and cupping his watch. He was peering down at the watch.

"Hi, Henri," I said.

"Ah, there you are." He smiled and slipped the watch into his pocket.

"The inspector show?" I asked him.

"Not as yet. But I spoke, by telephone, with Aster Loving's manager, and he will meet with us at two o'clock, at his office."

"Great. Thanks, Henri."

It was a big lobby, arching columns and potted trees, expensive tapestries on the walls and expensive rugs on the marble floor, a faint smell in the air of good cigars and better perfume. There was a lot of plush, tasteful furniture scattered around, so the guests wouldn't have to go all the way up to their rooms whenever they felt like sitting down and counting their money.

If LaGrande had been annoyed at us for losing the tail last night, and for causing all the confusion at Les Halles, he could've filled the place with cops. He hadn't. But there was a man sitting by himself on one of the big sofas, and now he got up and he walked toward us. He wasn't wearing a big sign around his neck that said I AM A POLICEMAN, but he didn't need to.

He carried a black fedora and he wore a black two-piece suit, a white shirt, a striped tie, and a pair of heavy black brogues. His shoulders were broad and his body was thick and solid. His straight black hair was parted on the left. His face was fleshy, with a slightly bulbous nose and a slightly pendulous lower lip. It wasn't a handsome face, but it was an interesting face. It was a face that looked like it had been set since childhood in the expression it had now—the hooded, sleepy expression of someone who had seen all the things that people did to each other, and who had listened to the people explain why they'd done them.

"Mister Beaumont?" he said to me.

I admitted that I was.

"Monsieur Ledoq?"

Henri admitted it.

The Inspector nodded, then gave us his name. He didn't offer his hand, and neither Ledoq nor I offered ours.

"Thank you for coming," I said.

The expression didn't change. He said in flat, accented English, "Please to follow me."

Moving without hurry, he led us to the elevators. There were two, and the doors to one of them opened up, as if by magic, the moment we got there. We stepped in. The attendant, a young man dressed like a South American general on parade, said something in French. The Inspector grunted something back. No one said another word until we reached the seventh floor, got out, walked down the thickly carpeted corridor, and came to a door on the right.

The Inspector reached into his pants pocket and he pulled out a hotel room key. He turned to me. "This is not the original door. That was broken when we entered the suite."

"Right," I said.

He slipped the key into the lock and turned it. The door swung open. He stood back and, with a faint movement of his heavy hand, gestured for us to go in. We did, and he followed.

He was closing the door when I said, "Excuse me, Inspector."

He turned to me, his hand still on the door.

"May I look?" I said, and indicated the door.

He raised his eyebrows an eighth of an inch, lightly shrugged his heavy shoulders, and stepped back.

On the edge of the door were a latchbolt and a deadbolt, both set in brass faceplates. The latchbolt, like most latch-bolts, retracted whenever the door handle was turned. The deadbolt was retracted now. I asked the Inspector for the key and he handed it over, expressionless, and he put his hands into his pockets and watched me. I slid the key into the outer face of the lock and turned it to the left. The deadbolt popped out, a rectangular brass tongue.

I looked at the Inspector. "The deadbolt was locked when you arrived?"

The Inspector frowned.

I turned to Ledoq, who stood off to the side, his hands behind his back. "What's it called in French? The deadbolt?"

"Le pêne dormant," he said.

"Oui," said the Inspector, and then in English, "It was locked."

I turned the key in the other direction, two full circles, and the deadbolt retracted. I closed the door and looked at the safety bolt.

It was brass, with a rounded lever protruding from its left side, about three inches from the edge of the door. The casing on the doorjamb, into which it slid, was brass, too, screwed into the wood with six brass screws. I lifted the bolt's rounded lever and flipped the bolt into the casing. I tried the door. It didn't budge. I ran my finger along the jamb, first above the casing and then below it. About an inch and a half below it, very faintly, I could feel a large, irregular indentation in the wood—a ragged hole that had been filled with putty, sanded down, then painted over. No matter how carefully you sandpaper, it's almost impossible to conceal a repair like that.

I turned to the Inspector. "The door was bolted. When you broke it open, you ripped the screws away, and some of the wood. Here."

He nodded.

The door had in fact been bolted.

So much for my theory that it hadn't been.

Unless, of course, the cops had faked the damage.

I handed him the room key. "Thank you," I said. He nodded and slipped it back into his pocket as I turned and looked around us.

This was the living room, and it was at least twice, maybe three times, as large as the hotel room I hadn't stayed in last night. White carpeting, white walls. On one wall, beneath a familiar-looking framed print of the Eiffel Tower, was a long, off-white, thickly padded sofa. In front of that, a shiny mahogany coffee table. There were two chairs, upholstered like the sofa, each with a shiny mahogany end table beside it. Between the chairs was a tall mahogany wireless, as brightly polished as the coffee table. On the far wall was a pair of French doors. The white curtains had been drawn and I could see out to a narrow balcony with a wrought iron railing, and beyond that to the sunlit upper stories of the building across the avenue.

I turned to the Inspector. "Is everything—all the furniture—in the same position now as it was when you found the body?"

The Inspector nodded. He reached into his right jacket pocket and pulled out an old briar pipe, then reached into his left jacket pocket and pulled out a leather tobacco pouch.

I walked over to the French doors. I tried to open them. Locked. Beneath the handle was a small latch. I flicked it, tried the door again. It opened. I turned to the Inspector. "Locked?" I asked him.

He was packing the pipe with tobacco. He looked up at me and nodded.

I stepped onto the balcony, examined the exterior of the doors. No way to lock or unlock them from out there. I stepped back in, shut the door, flicked the lever closed, turned back to the Inspector. "Is it okay if I look around?"

The pipe was filled now, and he shrugged and he waved it indifferently in the air, as though he didn't much care what I did.

I crossed the carpet and I walked down the hallway. The first room was a blizzard of white. It held a toilet, a sink, a bidet, and a lot of tile, all of it gleaming as though it had just come back from the dentist. The next room held a huge enameled bathtub, another sink, and a makeup counter. Everything gleamed here, too. Then came the bedroom—more white walls, more white carpeting, two mahogany nightstands, two big mahogany wardrobes, a huge white bed in a shining brass frame. Two more French doors that looked out onto an extension of the balcony I'd already seen.

When I returned to the living room, the room smelled of burning rope. The Inspector had sat down in one of the chairs, planted his big feet on the floor, and gotten his pipe going. A wreath of blue smoke hovered above his head, like a small storm cloud.

Ledoq was sitting on one end of the couch. I sat down on the other.

I said, "The doors in the bedroom were locked, too? Out to the balcony?"

The Inspector nodded, puffing out a calm billow of smoke.

"And where was the body?" I asked him. "Forsythe's?"

He took the stem of his pipe from between his lips and pointed it toward the other chair.

"And Sabine von Stuben?"

The pipe stem pointed toward the floor in front of the chair. He put the stem back between his lips.

"Was there any kind of luggage in here? Suitcase? Briefcase?"

Still holding the pipe in his mouth, he shook his head.

"Didn't von Stuben have a purse?"

"Yes."

"What was in it?"

He took the pipe from his mouth. "The usual. Cosmetics."

"The autopsy found alcohol in Forsythe's body. Was there a bottle here?"

Slowly he crossed his legs, right knee over left knee, and he rested the pipe on his thigh. "A bottle of absinthe," he said.

"Full? Empty?"

For a moment he stared at me. Then he said, "The bottle, it was almost empty."

"Did you find out where it came from?"

"It was purchased by Mr. Forsythe. From a nearby store. Shortly before he registered in the hotel." After this flood of words he put the pipe back in his mouth and puffed on it.

"Were there drinking glasses?" I asked him.

"Two glasses. One was empty, one was half empty."

"Did von Stuben wear lipstick?" I asked him.

He puffed twice this time, watching me, before he unplugged the pipe. He rested it on his thigh. "The half-empty glass was marked with the lipstick of Mademoiselle von Stuben.''

"Did you find any drugs in the room?"

He looked down at the pipe, then looked back at me. "We found in Monsieur Forsythe's pocket a silver . . ." He hesitated, searching for the word. ". . . a silver container of cocaine. Shaped like a skull, but flat. Also, within the container, a small silver straw."

"Did you fingerprint the room?"

"Not I," he said. "The technicians."

"And they accounted for all the prints?"

He put the pipe back in his mouth, and he nodded once.

"The maids, the hotel staff?" I said.

He nodded.

"None of them," I said, "belonged to Sybil Norton."

For a moment he sat there. Then he said, *"Non."* He removed the pipe again, and he smiled without showing any teeth. "You have spoken to Madame Norton."

"Yeah. Listen, Inspector, where would you normally be about now?"

His eyebrows dipped an eighth of an inch. *"Pardon?"*

"Right about now, on any given day—where would you be? What would you be doing?"

He puffed some more, thoughtfully. After a moment, he answered, "Eating. A sandwich, perhaps, at the Brasserie Dauphin, near the Quay d'Orsay. Perhaps drinking a beer."

"I can understand why you might be angry at me for taking you away from your sandwich. I can understand why you might be angry at me for asking questions about your investigation. I'm sure you did your job as well as anyone could have done it."

I took a deep breath. "But I've got a job to do, too. Richard Forsythe's mother doesn't live in Paris. She doesn't know anything about the Paris police department, and she doesn't know anything about you. All she knows is that her son is dead. She wants to find out why. I think that's understandable. She hired the Pinkertons to look into it, and the agency sent me here."

Another breath. "I know that Sybil Norton was here that day. But there are a lot of things I don't know, and you're the only one who can tell me about them. I'd appreciate it, Inspector, if you cooperated with me.''

He didn't react at all during my little speech. He just sat there, calmly puffing away. When I finished, he took another puff, then plucked the pipe from his mouth and rested it once again on his thigh. Once again, he smiled without showing his teeth.

''I like this very much,'' he said, ''the way you—'' He turned to Ledoq, shot a French word at him.

''*Appeal,*'' said Ledoq.

The Inspector turned back to me. ''—appeal to my heart with this story of the mother.''

I smiled. ''I was hoping it would make up for a sandwich.''

''And a beer,'' he said.

''I'll buy you a beer. I'll buy you a sandwich.''

Another faint smile. He put the pipe back in his mouth, puffed once, twice, then removed it and put it back on his thigh. ''You must understand. I am an Inspector only. A small fish. Over me, above me, swim many others. Bigger fish. Some want this, some want that. I must keep them all happy, eh? Perhaps there are questions I cannot answer for you. You understand me?''

''Yeah.''

He nodded. ''But I will try.''

''Thanks,'' I said. ''And I'll still buy you a sandwich and a beer.''

He waved his hand wearily. ''No, no. Thank you, but no. When we finish here, I will go home for an hour. My wife has made *coq au vin,* and I look forward to it.''

''She uses red wine?'' asked Ledoq.

''No,'' said the Inspector, looking over to him. ''She uses white. A Riesling.''

''Ah. She uses *lardons*?'' He turned to me. ''Strips of salt pork,'' he explained.

''Thanks,'' I said. Since they were both speaking English for my benefit, it seemed unfair to interrupt them.

''No,'' said the Inspector. ''She browns the chicken in lard, and then she removes them from the pan. Then she adds some carrot, some shallots, and some garlic. These are all finely chopped, of course.''

''Yes, of course,'' said Ledoq.

''She browns all this, then returns the chicken to the pan, and then she adds equal amounts of the Riesling and of chicken stock.''

''Ah. I see. Stock. And does she add any additional flavoring to the sauce?''

''After she has thickened the sauce with egg yolk, mixed with a little cream, she adds some lemon juice and some sloe-berry brandy.''

''Sloe-berry brandy. Yes. Interesting.'' Ledoq nodded primly. ''Thank you.''

''My pleasure,'' said the Inspector. He put the pipe into his mouth, and he turned back to me. ''You mention Sybil Norton,'' he said around the stem. The words came on a small puff of smoke.

''Yeah,'' I said.

''She tells me she came to the room of Mr. Forsythe at three o'clock. She heard the shot. She believed Mr. Forsythe was committing suicide, she tells me. She left. But then she changed her mind and she telephoned to a friend who is . . . let us say, an important person. He telephoned to me.'' He smiled again. ''I am very famous for my discretion, eh?''

I nodded.

''I collect some officers and I come here. She is downstairs. We all come up in the lift together. The door is locked. We break it down. There''—he pointed again with the pipe-stem—''are Mr. Forsythe and Sabine von Stuben, both of them dead. Mrs. Norton gives me some information about the two. I ask her some more questions, I thank her, and I tell her she may leave.''

He shrugged again. ''The rest is as I said.''

''Did Sybil Norton go into any of the other rooms?''

The pipe had gone out. He was fumbling in his jacket pocket for matches. ''Into the bedroom. I was with her. She was looking for some papers. They were hers, she said.'' He got out a match.

''Did she find them?'' I asked.

"Non." Holding the bowl of the pipe in his left hand, he scraped it with the back end of the match.

"Did you check out her story?"

He tamped down the tobacco with his thumb, then he put the pipestem between his teeth, struck the match, held it to the bowl of the pipe. "Yes," he said. The flame popped and snapped. Puffing at the pipe, he shook out the match. He leaned to the side, dropped the match into the ashtray on the endtable.

"The desk clerk," he said, "and one of the maids, they said that she arrived here, in the hotel, just before three o'clock. Another maid said that she left a few minutes later, and then returned after fifteen minutes. We arrived soon after this."

"So theoretically she could've killed Richard Forsythe."

"Yes. Theoretically. But she was not seen before three o'clock, and von Stuben was dead by then. And it would be very foolish of her, I think, to kill Forsythe and then to telephone . . . her important friend."

"Maybe she knew she'd been seen. Maybe she was protecting herself."

A puff, a shrug. "Perhaps. But there is still the matter of the dead von Stuben."

I nodded. "The desk clerk," I said. "That's the one who made that phone call for Richard Forsythe."

"Yes," he said. He puffed on the pipe. "That is the one."

"Does the desk clerk normally handle telephone calls?"

"Only at that time of day. When the usual operator goes to lunch."

"Did anyone see him handle it?"

"Another maid. She was the one who told us about it. He had not mentioned it until then. He said he had forgotten. When he looked for the record, it was gone. According to the maid, the call was made shortly before one o'clock."

"Around the time of von Stuben's death."

A puff. "Perhaps before. Perhaps after. We do not know the exact time of death. Not the very minute."

"And the desk clerk couldn't remember who the call was made to."

"Non."

"And there was no way for you to find out?"

He placed the pipe on his leg again. "The telephone company examined their records. A number of telephone calls were made from this hotel that afternoon, between twelve o'clock and one. One call was made to a small tobacco shop, on the Left Bank. It is possible that this is the call made from Monsieur Forsythe's room. The owner of the *tabac* could not remember the call."

"Is that very likely?"

Once again he smiled that humorless smile. He shrugged. "The man refused to change his story."

"What's his name? The owner of the shop."

"Martin Sardou. But he has left Paris. We cannot find him."

"And that doesn't bother you?"

"It bothers me, yes."

"When did he leave?"

"Two weeks after the death of Monsieur Forsythe. He sold his shop, and he simply vanished."

"Okay. Back to the maid. She knew about the one call. She was there at the time. But there could have been other calls made from the Forsythes' suite, calls she didn't know about."

"Between twelve and one, yes. At one o'clock, the operator returned to the switchboard. There were no more calls from the suite."

I nodded. "How did the clerk manage to lose the record of the call?"

"He said he wrote it down on a sheet of paper and placed that in the account book. The paper, it must have slipped out, he said."

"Did you believe him?"

He shrugged. "Like the other, he refused to change his story. I had no way to prove he was lying."

Which didn't exactly answer my question. "He died about a week later," I said.

He put the pipe back into his mouth. "Yes."

He was getting curt on me again. "And you investigated his death."

"Yes."

"It was an accident."

"He was seen drunk, earlier. He was seen walking near the river. When seen next, he was in the river. Dead." The Inspector shrugged. "It has happened before."

"There was no autopsy performed."

He took the pipe from his mouth, and he pressed his lips together bleakly. Except for the smile without humor, this was the first sign of emotion he'd made. *"Non."*

"Why not?"

He put the pipe back, puffed a bit, took it out again. "It was felt not to be necessary."

"By you?"

"By me, no. I suggested that one be performed."

I nodded. "Anything unusual about the accident?"

"Not the accident itself. Again, it has happened before, this type of accident. But that night he had been spending a large amount of money. And on the previous nights, also, he had been spending large amounts of money."

"You never found out where it came from?"

"No."

"Okay," I said. "The woman. Sabine von Stuben."

"Yes?"

"Who collected her body?"

He lowered the pipe, and he nodded faintly. "That is a very interesting question," he said.

"Why?"

He smiled that small smile. "Because it has, I think, a very interesting answer. The body was collected by two men. Friends of the family, they said. Germans. From Munich. They were soldiers, officers. They were not dressed as soldiers, but from the way they walked, the way they talked . . . they were German officers. I was in the War. I know German officers."

He puffed at the pipe. "And they refused to answer any of my questions. They were . . . rude. I asked that they be detained." He pursed his lips again. "This was not possible."

"Why did you want them detained?"

"From stories I had been told, Sabine von Stuben was the daughter of a German aristocrat. A baron. I spoke to the German ambassador and learned from him that no such baron existed. He was very cooperative, the ambassador, on the day I spoke with him. The next day he was not so cooperative. He telephoned me to say that two men would be collecting the body. Like the German officers, he refused to answer any more questions. I believe he was nervous. I believe he was frightened.''

''Of what?''

He shrugged. ''Of whatever it is that frightens ambassadors.''

''The body was released without any problem?''

''Without problem. Without delay.'' He pulled out his watch, glanced at it, slipped it back. ''I think that I have said enough. Perhaps too much.''

''Inspector,'' I said, ''do you know who Aster Loving is?''

''The singer who died? Yes. It is not my investigation, but I know of the death.'' Then he looked at me sharply. ''Why?''

''She was involved with Richard Forsythe.''

''Oh?'' he said, and once again his eyebrows raised an eighth of an inch. ''At the time of his death?''

''I don't know yet. But I will.''

''Good. And when you do, you will tell me.'' It wasn't a question.

''Yes,'' I said.

''Good.'' He stood, and so did we. He reached into his coat, pulled out his wallet, opened it, found a business card. He handed it to me. A simple card with only his name and a telephone number. I slipped it into my coat pocket.

He put his wallet back and for a moment he looked at me. ''I believe that you should be very careful, Mr. Beaumont.'' He smiled that small smile again. ''I have heard last night of an adventure in Les Halles. It may be that not everyone who is interested in you, and your questions, will be so easily diverted by a truck filled with fish.''

''Thank you, Inspector. One more question?''

The eyebrows raised a fraction. ''Yes?''

''Do you believe that Richard Forsythe committed suicide?''

He smiled the smile. ''I could not prove otherwise.''

Ten

HE BELIEVES," SAID Ledoq, "that Richard Forsythe did *not* commit suicide." There was a sliver of surprise in his voice.

We were standing in front of the Grande Bretagne, and we had just watched the Inspector drive off.

"Yeah," I said. "I've got to go back to the telegraph office."

He frowned at me. *"Pardon?"*

"I believe the Inspector. That door was bolted. If Richard Forsythe didn't commit suicide, then the person who killed him, whoever it was, managed to walk right through the door, bolt and all. I want to find out how he did it."

"And how will you do this?"

"I know a guy who can tell me. Harry Houdini."

Ledoq raised his eyebrows. "The magician? You know him?"

"Yeah." I waved at a cab and it swerved through the traffic and pulled over to the curb in front of us. "I worked with him once."

I opened the door and gestured for Ledoq to go in. I followed him and pulled the door shut behind me. Ledoq gave some instructions to the driver and then sat back.

"Worked with him where?" he asked me.

"In England. A couple of years ago." With a lurch, the cab pulled away from the curb.

"I am impressed, *mon ami*. I have read some of his books,

of course, but I have never met the man. He is perhaps the greatest magician who ever lived.''

''Yeah. That's what he says, too.'' I swung around in the seat to look out the rear window. ''Could you ask the driver to make a turn? Let's see if we picked up any lint.''

He leaned forward, said something to the driver, then sat back and said, ''What is all this, do you suppose, with that von Stuben girl? And those German officers. And the ambassador. What does it all signify?''

''I don't know, Henri. But like the Inspector said, it's interesting.''

The cab turned sedately to the left.

''You sound pleased,'' he said.

A black car turned into the same street, following us. ''Not pleased, exactly,'' I said. ''But interested. Things are a lot more complicated than they seemed. Could you ask him to make another turn?''

He said something to the driver, then swung around in the seat, so he could look out the window, too.

''But even the Inspector could prove nothing,'' he said. ''Officially, Forsythe's death is a suicide.''

''The Inspector couldn't prove anything because someone, maybe LaGrande, didn't want him to. I don't have to listen to LaGrande. He can't fire me.''

The cab made another left turn.

''No,'' said Ledoq. ''He can merely arrest you. Or have you killed, of course.''

I glanced away from the window to smile at him. ''I sure hope that doesn't happen.''

Behind us, the black car turned again, still following our cab.

''Police, do you think?'' said Ledoq.

''Probably.'' I sat back. ''We'll lose them after the telegraph office.'' I looked at him. ''But no Keystone Kops stuff today. Ask him to drop us somewhere we can lose them on foot. We'll grab another cab from there.''

''Precisely what I intended.''

''You're a champ, Henri.''

''*Merci*. But, to be honest, I was rather looking forward to another automobile race through Paris.''

"Next time," I said.

"Bon." He sat back and remained silent for a few moments. I watched Paris pass us by. Then he turned to me and said, "What is it that could frighten an ambassador?"

I looked over at him. "The same thing that frightens everybody. Someone bigger."

"But who?"

"I don't know, Henri. But it looks like maybe we've been focusing on the wrong person."

"On Richard Forsythe, you mean. Rather than on Sabine von Stuben."

"Yeah."

Ledoq waited in the cab outside the telegraph office. I ran in, sent the wire to Houdini in New York, then ran back out to the car. The driver took off.

We crossed the river on the Pont Neuf again, and went south on Rue Dauphine until we turned right on Boulevard Saint-Germain. We drove a block or two, then turned left onto Rue du Four, a narrow street that suddenly widened up when it became Rue de Sèvres. We crossed Boulevard Raspail and slowed down as we passed a bright green, neatly tended park where women pushed baby carriages and old men sat on wooden benches, tossing bread crumbs to the pigeons. We pulled up at the next corner, in front of the building that stood opposite the greenery. Maybe fifty yards back, the black car pulled up alongside the park.

I paid the driver—six francs—and Ledoq got me a receipt.

We climbed out of the cab, and I looked at the building. Gray, like all the buildings in Paris. It was a department store, four stories tall, bigger than Harrods in London and at least as big as Macy's in New York. Windows filled with stiff, well-dressed mannequins flanked a columned entrance that rose forty or fifty feet to an arch that held a couple of statues who sat back lazily and watched the traffic go by.

"This is Bon Marché," said Ledoq. "Come. Let us stroll."

We strolled along the wide sidewalk of Rue de Sèvres and we turned right onto Rue du Bac. Cars passed us on the left, but none of them was the black car that had been following us.

"Bon Marché," said Ledoq conversationally, "was the first department store in the world. It is still among the largest." He seemed in no hurry. He peered into the windows of the store as we slowly passed them, studying the displays of luggage, of jewelry, of furniture and bedding and cookware. More mannequins, male and female, stood inside there, frozen in poses that very few real human beings would ever get their bodies into. "It was built," said Ledoq, "in 1869. Zola did research here for his book *Au bonheur des dames*. Rather a mediocre novel, of course, like most of Zola's *oeuvre*, but it does contain some amusing observations. He compared the great department stores to the cathedrals of the Middle Ages. In the end, he said, they contain all the drama of life, with a promise of a beautiful hereafter."

"No kidding," I said.

He turned to me and smiled. "We shall be going inside at the next entrance. Do not move quickly until I tell you to do so."

"Right."

And so we strolled inside at the next entrance, into the smells of department stores everywhere, of leather and perfume and cash, and we turned right and we strolled through the displays of merchandise, past the counters piled with goods. Soft sunlight filtered down from huge opaque skylights three floors above, and electric lights glittered to the left and right, and together they made everything seem even more dazzling and precious than it already was. The customers may have been French, but they weren't much different from the customers in Macy's. They wandered through it all as though they were stunned by the splendor around them. Their bodies moved mechanically, and only their glistening eyes were alive—darting back and forth as they took in one bright shiny thing after another.

Neither Ledoq nor I looked back. We came to a large graceful circular stairway with ornate wrought iron railings that had been painted a pale green. Slowly, casually, still just strolling, we began to climb up the stairs, leaving the counters and the customers below.

Maybe ten feet from the end of the stairway, Ledoq said, "When we reach the top, we will walk slowly for a few feet, and then we will begin to move very quickly indeed."

"Got you," I said.

We strolled to the top of the stairway and for six or seven feet across a parqueted landing. And then Ledoq began to move very quickly indeed, a bit like Charlie Chaplin chasing a train. I followed him. Past some startled shoppers, through a small service door, down a narrow corridor, through another door, and then down some narrow, dimly lit wooden steps. Our footsteps clattered in the confined space. Ledoq's head bobbed beneath me as we raced down one flight, then another, then another.

Finally we reached bottom and came to another doorway. Ledoq slammed this open and we flew out into another service corridor. Ledoq spun to the right, and I kept following. We whipped by some doors until we came to the final door, at the end of the corridor. Ledoq tore this open and we went clattering up another narrow set of stairs.

Up one floor only this time, to still another service door. Ledoq grabbed the door handle and turned to me. He was panting. So was I. "Calmly, now," he said.

"Yeah."

He pulled open the door and we stepped calmly back into the store, into the rich smells of leather and perfume. Calmly panting, we strolled through the aisles of merchandise, hundreds of bracelets and necklaces and rings, and then down another aisle, and then through an elegant pair of entrance doors and out onto the busy sidewalk. The small park was opposite us now. We had emerged on the other side of the store.

We crossed the street, dodging a car or two as we calmly strolled, and then we calmly walked along the edge of the park for fifty or sixty yards back in the direction of Rue de Sèvres, to a Métro station entrance surrounded by a pale green wrought iron railing like the one in Bon Marché. As we began calmly climbing down the concrete steps, Ledoq glanced back. No one was following us.

He turned to me. "Success, *mon ami*." It came out through his smile in a breathless rush.

"Yeah," I said. Like him, I was still panting. "How'd you know about those stairs?"

"I was once . . ." he panted, "very friendly . . . with a woman whose husband . . . was on the board of directors."

"And she used the stairs?"

"Non." He gulped some more air. "The husband's mistress did . . . She told the wife about it at a later date."

"Monsieur Morret," said Ledoq, "strongly disapproved of Mademoiselle Loving's relationship with Monsieur Forsythe. He says that he warned her about him many, many times."

Jacques Morret said something in French, his face red with anger, his hands waving. In the ashtray on his desk, his cigar burned away like a slow fuse.

The small office looked like the offices of theatrical managers all over the world, except that everything here was French. On the walls were posters and playbills and signed photographs, some tinted in pastels that made their subjects look like they'd just been embalmed, and badly. Probably the people were all theatrical big-timers who had known Morret at one time or another, or who had at least signed the pictures, or who had at least posed for them. Scattered around the top of the battered wooden desk were invoices and receipts and letters and scraps of paper that looked like they might be Morret's notes to himself. A single window looked out onto the empty stone wall of another building, across a narrow gray courtyard. We were somewhere in the Sixth Arrondissement, not far from the Odéon Théâtre.

Morret himself was a small, squat man in his forties who smoked cigars. He had a round balding head, slightly protruding blue eyes, deep creases between his eyebrows, and a wide pink mouth. All of that made him look a bit like a thoughtful bullfrog. His jacket was hanging from a small coat rack beside the door. He sat opposite us, behind the desk. His collar was open and his tie was pulled down to one side, and his brown hair, what there was of it, was messy because he ran his fingers through it whenever he got upset, and he got upset fairly often.

Ledoq said, "He says that Monsieur Forsythe was an adulterer and a pervert. He says that he told Mademoiselle Loving that Forsythe was merely using her.''

Morret nodded emphatically and turned to me and said, in very heavily accented English, ''He was a *peeg*.''

''Was she still involved with him at the time he died?'' I asked him.

''Non, non, non!'' said Morret. He picked up the cigar, turned to Ledoq, rattled off some French. Then he stuck the cigar in his mouth, chomped down on it, and he put his hands flat on the arms of the chair and swiveled the chair so he could look out the window.

''Their relationship,'' said Ledoq, ''ended at the beginning of the year. In January. Thank God, he says. And he repeated the observation about Monsieur Forsythe being a pig.''

''Why did it end?'' I asked Morret.

Still staring out the window, Morret didn't answer. Ledoq spoke to him in French. Morret shrugged and then, without looking at us, said something to Ledoq.

Ledoq translated. ''Mr. Forsythe obtained a new paramour. A German woman. He told Mademoiselle Loving that he would no longer see her. She was desolated.''

''Did you ever meet the German woman?'' I asked Morret.

''Non,'' he said to the window.

''Do you know anything about her?''

He shrugged and spoke, without looking at either of us.

''Only,'' said Ledoq, ''that she was rich, and the daughter of a baron.''

Morret spat out some more French.

''She was white as well, of course,'' said Ledoq.

Still looking out the window, Morret took the cigar from his mouth and he said something else.

''He asks why,'' said Ledoq, ''it is always the most helpless of women who become associated with the most ruthless of men.''

''I don't know,'' I said. ''Sometimes they seek each other out.''

Morret glanced at me, looked back out the window again, and faintly nodded. Once again he spoke without looking at us, then he shook his head sadly.

Ledoq said, ''He loved her like a daughter, he says.''

Morret blinked a few times, sighed, and then raised his hands and rubbed quickly at his eyes, as though they were tired.

"Mr. Morret," I said. "I know you've suffered a great loss, and I apologize to you for asking questions at a time like this. I'm very sorry. But there are some things I need to know."

Morret ran his hand through what was left of his hair and swiveled his chair around to face me. He was about to speak when the telephone rang. He stuck the cigar between his teeth, and he snatched up the machine. Holding the stalk of the mouthpiece in his left hand, the earpiece against his ear with his right, he said, *"Oui?"* He listened. *"Oui,"* he said, and then he said some more things, including a lot more *oui*s. He ran his hand through his hair again. He plucked a black pen from an onyx stand on his desk and he wrote something down on a scrap of paper.

Ledoq turned to me. "He is thanking someone for offering condolences."

Morret said something else, then hooked the earpiece back on the telephone and propped the thing back on his desk. He took the cigar from his mouth, looked at me, looked at the phone. "All the day, it rings. Different peoples. Rich, poor. Famous, not famous. They all having grief. They all love her." He pressed his wide lips together. *"I* love her."

I nodded. "Mr. Morret, did Miss Loving have any other men friends?"

"Non." He shot something in French to Ledoq.

"Not since the pig Forsythe," Ledoq told me.

"For how long had she been taking heroin?" I asked Morret.

He sat back. "The feelthy heroin. Yes. For ever. Always she is taking it. She learns this in New York." He started to say something, then turned to Ledoq and said it in French.

Ledoq translated. "He attempted many times to persuade her to stop using the drug. But she was poor and she was black. When she was younger, the heroin had been the means by which she escaped from these facts."

Morret said something more, tapping at the center of his plump chest with two blunt fingers of his right hand.

"She was no longer poor," said Ledoq, "but she was still black. And in her heart, she still dwelt in a kind of poverty. Our childhood never leaves us." Ledoq smiled faintly to me. "I am translating now, you understand, not venturing my own opinion."

I nodded. "Did she ever overdose before?" I asked Morret.

Morret looked at Ledoq. Ledoq translated. Morret looked at me. *"Oui,"* he said. "Two times. Once . . ." He turned to Ledoq, spoke in French.

"On one occasion," Ledoq said, "he was obliged to telephone a doctor. On the other, she recovered on her own."

"The newspaper article," I said to Morret, "mentioned that the police figure she died sometime between eight o'clock and ten o'clock. Do you know how they got those times?"

Morret turned to Ledoq and answered. Ledoq turned to me. "The neighbors in the adjoining apartment, they heard her playing music on the gramophone. The music stopped at a little after eight."

"It was a hand-cranked gramophone?"

Morret frowned, and Ledoq asked him.

"Oui," said Morret.

"Did they hear anything else? Voices? Anyone in there with Miss Loving?"

"Non," said Morret. Once again he turned and spoke to Ledoq.

"He says that the apartment was a good one," Ledoq told me. "Not far from here, with excellent walls. They never heard conversation, even when Madamoiselle Loving had visitors. They heard the music only because she often played it quite loudly."

Ledoq asked Morret something else and listened to the answer. "I asked him about the concierge. Most apartment buildings in Paris have one, a person who manages the building, who watches the door. This is often a woman. There is a concierge at Madamoiselle Loving's building, but Monsieur Morret says that she is a drunk. Often she is gone, in her own apartment, and often she is asleep in her office. And, also, there is a rear entrance to the building. Mademoiselle Loving sometimes used this.''

"So someone," I said to Morret, "could have gone up to that apartment without being seen?"

"Oui." He turned to Ledoq, spoke in French.

Ledoq turned to me. "But the police are persuaded that she died of an accidental overdose. From the body, they believe she died some time after the gramophone stopped playing. Closer to nine o'clock than to eight."

I started to say something, but Morret interrupted.

Ledoq listened. "He says that everyone loved Mademoiselle Loving. The only person who might possibly want to do her any harm, the only person in the world, was herself."

I turned to Morret. "What music was playing on the gramophone?" I didn't really need to know. I was curious.

Morret looked at me sadly. "Her own recording. A song she love. 'Bye Bye Blackbird.' " He looked down at his desk and he sighed, a deep long ragged sigh. *" 'Pack up all your cares and woe,' "* he said, and then he sat there for a moment. He pursed his wide lips together, tightly. And then, as though the pressure of his lips had somehow pinched it out, a solitary tear rolled down his cheek.

"The police are convinced," said Ledoq.

"I'm not," I said.

We were walking along the Rue de l'Odéon, downhill, away from the the grand gray theater and toward the busy Boulevard Saint-Germain.

"Nor am I," said Ledoq. "I agree that the woman's death is entirely too convenient to be merely coincidental, but—ah, look, that is James Joyce."

He nodded toward a tall man stepping into a bookstore across the street. He was so thin that he looked as though he had been put together with coat hangers. He wore a dark suit and a bow tie and, beneath the left lens of his spectacles, a black eye patch. A sign above the store's big double window said SHAKESPEARE AND COMPANY.

"He is Irish," said Ledoq, "and perhaps the most talented of the expatriate writers in Paris. He wrote a book called

Ulysses, a very scandalous but fascinating piece of work. Very accomplished, very intelligent.''

"Sybil Norton has a copy," I said. "I saw it at her apartment."

"You surprise me. I should not have thought that a crime writer would read this book."

"Depends on the crime writer, I guess."

"As it happens, it was published by Sylvia Beach, the woman who owns that book shop."

"Yeah?"

He smiled. "You do not concern yourself with such matters, *mon ami*?"

"Not when I've got other things on my mind."

He nodded. "I, too, am distracted. I have eaten nothing since those croissants this morning. Fortunately there is, very near to us, a passable brasserie."

At the restaurant, I explained to Ledoq that I wanted a steak. A thick steak. A rare steak. No cream sauce. No wine sauce. A thick rare steak, cooked all by itself. With maybe some fried potatoes and a salad. He didn't really approve, but he ordered it for me anyway, and it took him less than half an hour to explain it to the waiter. For himself he ordered the day's special, *tournedos Rossini*. "These are small *filets mignon* sautéed in butter, topped with two slices of sautéed truffles and a slice of *foie gras*, goose liver. After the meat is cooked, one deglazes the pan with a good madeira, and one pours the resulting sauce over the meat. You are quite certain that you will not reconsider?"

"Yeah. Quite."

"It is an extremely tasty dish. And they do it very well here."

"A thick steak. Rare. No sauces."

He sighed. "As you wish. One can lead a horse to *tournedos Rossini*, but one cannot make him eat." He smiled suddenly. "In some restaurants, however, an especially fortunate horse may himself become a *tournedo*."

"Not in this restaurant."

"*Non.*" He smiled. "If you like, we could bring our custom to such an establishment."

"Later, maybe."

"Very well." He glanced down at the menu. "For the wine, I suggest we have the Chambolle-Musigny, of the vintage 1919. It is an excellent burgundy, one of the best, and it will complement both our meals very nicely."

"Fine."

He looked at me and narrowed his eyes. "You are quite certain that your name is Beaumont?

"That's what my parents told me."

"Ah," he said. "It must be true, then. For parents never lie."

For a while, as we ate, we talked about Aster Loving and her death, but neither one of us had a brainstorm. If someone had killed her, which seemed likely to me, I had no way of knowing who it was, or why he—or she—had done it.

There was no point in our going to the police and trying to find out what they knew. We'd been avoiding them for two days, vigorously, and I didn't think that any of them would be eager to share information with us.

Except maybe for the Inspector we'd met at the Grande Bretagne. He might be able, and might be willing, to help. And I had promised him that I would let him know what I learned about Aster Loving.

"I'll call him," I told Ledoq, "when we get back to the apartment. I want to take another shower before I go to Gertrude Stein's place."

"Ah yes," said Ledoq. "You will be attending her *salon* tonight, with the widow Forsythe. Perhaps I shall see you there. I often attend her little gatherings. But if I may make a suggestion, *mon ami*?"

"Sure."

"It might be wiser, perhaps, for you to call the Inspector from some telephone other than the one in Mathilde's apartment."

"The cops?"

He nodded. "They know that you spoke with the Inspector today. Perhaps they expect you to contact him again. Perhaps his telephone is being . . . overseen."

"Can they do that?"

He shrugged. "I am not an expert at telephony. But if it

is possible, it is no doubt being done. We can use the telephone in some *tabac*."

"Okay. You about ready to go?"

He nodded once, finished his coffee, and stood.

As we rose from the chair, I noticed a man getting up at the back of the restaurant, off to my right.

Under his breath, barely moving his lips, Ledoq said, "You saw him, *mon ami*?"

"Yeah. Let's see if he sticks."

He did, and so did his partner, who'd been waiting outside the restaurant.

"They were watching the office of Monsieur Morret," Ledoq said to me as we walked east on Saint-Germain.

"Yeah," I said. "Interesting, isn't it?"

We walked them around for a while, north on Monsieur-le-Prince, past the hotel I'd almost stayed in last night, then past the School of Medicine, and we turned left on Racine and walked along that to Boulevard Saint-Michel. We grabbed another cab there and we took it across the river to another department store, Samaritain, and we got out in front of the building.

And then we did another department store getaway. We ran around for a while, up some service stairways and then down some service stairways, the way we had at Bon Marché, then calmly strolled past the linens and the jewelry and the ceramic crocks. By the time we left, we had lost the cops. To make sure, we found ourselves another cab, and we took it over to the Left Bank. No one followed us. We located a tobacco shop, I paid out some francs to the taxi driver, and I got another receipt. I was building up a nice collection of receipts.

Inside the tobacco store, I called the Inspector. He was in his office.

I told him what I'd learned—that, according to her manager, Aster Loving hadn't been involved with Richard Forsythe for some time. He'd already learned that, he told me. He said that the inspector responsible for the investigation of her death was satisfied that she had died of an accidental overdose.

"Are you satisfied?" I asked him.

"I am never satisfied," he said. "If you learn anything, you will let me know." Once again, it wasn't a question.

"Sure," I told him.

"And I say again, Monsieur Beaumont. Be careful. I have heard of your adventures this afternoon. Soon you and your friend will have used up all the department stores in Paris."

I smiled. "Thanks, Inspector. I'll talk to you later."

We went by cab back to Ledoq's friend's apartment, across the river. By then it was nearly six o'clock. I took a shower, changed my shirt, climbed back into my suit. Ledoq was sipping tea in the living room. He had decided, he said, that he would take a short nap. "And possibly, afterward, I shall join you and the lovely Mrs. Forsythe at Gertrude Stein's."

"Maybe you'd better give me the phone number here," I said. "In case something comes up."

"Certainly." He told me what it was, and I memorized it. He reached into his vest pocket and pulled out a key. "And perhaps you should take this, as well. It is a spare key to the apartment." He smiled. "If you are kidnapped by the widow Forsythe, you may require it."

I took the key. "Thanks. Listen. The people who'll be there tonight, at Stein's. Do they know that you sometimes work with the Pinkertons?"

"No," he said. "Such work as I have done for your Monsieur Cooper, it has never involved any of them."

"The only person who's seen you with me is Hemingway. And you knew Forsythe, so it makes sense that I'd be talking to you. Maybe we shouldn't advertise the connection between you and me. Maybe you'll pick up something on your own that we wouldn't get together."

He nodded. "Yes. This is possible."

"Okay. I'll see you later."

"Very likely, *mon ami*."

I left, found another cab, and took it across the river to Rose Forsythe's house.

She opened the huge wooden door before I finished knocking on it. Her face was alight and her blue eyes were shining.

Maybe she was delighted to see me. Maybe she had just taken some cocaine.

"You're on *time*," she said. "That's *wonderful*!" I was a few minutes early.

She stepped out onto the landing and she pulled the door shut. It closed with a heavy, final sound, like the door to a bank vault, or a crypt.

Smiling up at me, she offered me her small, perfect right arm. I took it, and she looked me up and down. "Goodness," she said. "Were you this tall yesterday?"

"And the day before."

She giggled. "You're *very* tall. Here." She slipped her right hand down to the crook of my elbow and she put her left hand against my upper arm and she patted me. "But I *like* tall men."

She was wearing a black silk dress with a low waist, buttoned up to a straight, Oriental-style collar, and a black silk shawl, thick and glossy, long enough to be loosely wrapped around her twice. Beneath a black wool hat, her short black hair was thick and glossy, too. A small black leather purse hung by a leather strap from her left shoulder. Her nails and her lips were painted the same matching red they'd been painted yesterday, and once again she smelled of gardenias.

"We can get a cab down at Saint-Pères," she said as we walked across the courtyard, the heels of her shoes clicking on the flagstones.

"I've still got to ask you some questions, Rose." We turned left on the Rue de Lille.

A shadow crossed her face. "Oh, do we *have* to do that? I thought we'd finished all those up yesterday."

"I've got a few left."

"But I wanted this to be a *fun* evening. For the *two* of us. I haven't been out much since Dickie died—hardly at all, really." Still smiling, she squeezed my arm. "This is my first big *rendezvous*."

"The questions won't take long," I said. "We can probably finish before we get to Miss Stein's house."

She signed elaborately. "Oh, all right." Squeezing my arm again, she looked up at me with mock sternness. "But no questions at Gertrude's. We've got a deal?"

"Deal," I said. "Richard's pistol. The Browning. When was the last time you saw it?"

"When the police gave it back to me. A few weeks after Dickie died."

"I meant before that. Before Richard died."

"Oh." She pursed her red lips and she looked down at the sidewalk for a moment. She looked up at me. "Is it important?"

"Maybe."

She frowned. "Let's see." She lowered her head again, then suddenly raised it. "*I* know. It was when some people came over, Kay Boyle and Bob McAlmon. Kay's a writer, or she wants to be, and Bob's a publisher like Dickie was—only his books aren't as nice as Dickie's, I think. Dickie did such a *marvelous* job with his books. The paper, the binding—"

"And Richard brought out the gun? While McAlmon and Boyle were there?"

She nodded. "We were in the study, the four of us. And, yes, Dickie got out the gun—he used to keep it in the drawer there, in the desk—and he shot at this big old stuffed bear we have. It was a joke he had." She giggled. "I don't think Bob liked it, though. The joke, I mean. He didn't laugh, anyway. But Bob doesn't have much of a sense of humor."

We had reached the Rue des Saints-Pères, opposite the School of Fine Arts. "Which way are we going?" I asked her.

"What? Oh. To Rue de Fleurus." She pointed to our right. "That way."

I looked to my left and saw a taxi coming. I waved my arm. "And when was that, Rose?"

She frowned. "*When* was it? Let me see. About two weeks before everything happened. Before Dickie died, I mean." She cocked her head and she looked off for a moment. "Is that right?"

She looked up at me as the cab pulled over to the curb. "Yes. Absolutely. It was just after Dickie's birthday, the day after, and his birthday was on the ninth of March. He was twenty-five. And he died on the twenty-third." She nodded. "So about two weeks before that. On the tenth."

I opened the door to the cab and held it for her as she

slipped into the seat. She slid over gracefully, and I got in.
She was leaning forward to give directions to the driver.

"And you didn't see the pistol again?" I asked her.

She sat back. "No. Not until the police gave it to me."

"In those two weeks, did anyone besides Richard go into
the study?"

She looked at me. "You mean with Dickie?"

"With him," I said, "or without him."

We turned left on Rue Jacob.

She blinked. "Why would anyone go up there on their
own?"

"I don't know, Rose. To get some papers, maybe?" I
glanced back, out the rear window. No one was following us.
I thought that this was fairly interesting.

"No. I can't imagine—oh, wait! Sybil did. Sybil Norton?
I told you about her? The woman who writes those mysteries?"

We turned right on Rue Bonaparte.

"She went in there with Richard?" I asked her.

"No, no. By herself, like you said. She and Dickie were
doing this book, a collection of poems, I think, and we were
all downstairs in the living room, and Sybil said she'd re-
written one of the poems—it *was* a collection of poems, *that's*
right—and she asked Dickie if she could have her original
back. The original version, I mean. And Dickie was going to
go get it—it was upstairs in the study, on his desk—but Sybil
said not to bother, she'd run up there and get it herself."

Rue Bonaparte crossed a big square with an old church
facing it and became Rue Guynemer.

"And when was that, Rose?"

"When? Oh, I don't know. About a week before it happened?" Again she frowned and looked off. "Is that right?"
she asked herself.

We crossed Rue de Vaugirard. To our left was a broad
green formal park, acres of grass and huge stands of tall blos-
soming chestnut trees. The sunlight was fading now and the
blossoms were painted a faint shade of pink.

"That's the Luxembourg Gardens," said Rose. "They're
very pretty, don't you think?"

"Very. A week before?"

She flapped her hand impatiently, as though she wanted to wipe the concept of ''time'' from the air. ''Something like that. I don't know. Five days, six days.'' Her face brightened. ''Not more than a week, though. I remember because it was on a Sunday night, and Dickie died on Friday. The next Friday. So that would be—what? Sunday, Monday, Tuesday—''

''Five days.''

''That's right. *Exactly*. Five days.''

The car pulled over and began to slow down. ''And did Richard use the study much in those five days?'' I asked her. ''Did he take the gun out?''

''Here we are,'' she said. ''It's just up that street.''

I leaned forward to look at the meter. Three francs. I gave the driver a five-franc note and I waved away the change.

I opened the door, held it for her while she stepped out onto the sidewalk, slammed it shut.

''It's just up there,'' she said, and nodded to our right. ''We have to cross the street.''

She took my arm again and we crossed the street. ''Did Richard take the pistol out again?'' I asked her.

She frowned, irritated now. ''Not until the day he used it.''

''Friday, you mean.''

''Uh huh.''

''Did you see him take it that day?''

We were walking up the left hand side of the street, past a number of books set in a display window on the ground level of an apartment building.

''No, of course not,'' she said. ''If I had, I would've *asked* him about it. Dickie was *much* too clever to let me see him take it.''

''Is it possible,'' I said, ''that Richard hadn't seen the gun during that time? From the time he fired it, when Boyle and McAlmon were there, to that Friday?''

She blinked, puzzled. ''Why do you ask?''

''I'm curious.''

''Well, of *course* it's possible. He kept the gun in a drawer all by itself, down at the bottom of the desk, and he only opened the drawer when he wanted to shoot at the bear. And he *didn't* shoot at the bear again, not after he shot at it when Kay and Bob were there, so probably he *didn't* see the gun. Until he took it out on Friday, I mean. Here we are.''

She dropped her hands from my arm, and she turned to face me, holding on to her purse with both hands. We stood at an archway that opened onto a small paved courtyard.

''No more questions now, all right?'' she said. ''You promised.''

''I think that'll do it,'' I said.

''Good,'' she said, and she smiled brightly. ''Thank you, darling.'' She took my arm again and she led me into the courtyard.

I had noticed the ''darling,'' but it didn't bother me much. It was probably what she called any man she went out with. And she hadn't been out with one, according to her, for quite a while.

Across the flagstones, walking to the right, we came to a pair of large wooden doors in a small two-story addition built up against the main apartment building. Rose knocked on one of the doors. After a moment, it was opened by a small, almost gaunt woman in her forties whose black hair was cut in a short pageboy. She had large, deepset brown eyes, angular cheekbones, a large hooked nose, and a wide mouth in a dark, narrow, almost Gypsy face. She was wearing a long dark dress with a white ruffled collar, long sleeves and white ruffled cuffs. There was a faint shadow along her upper lip that might have been a mustache, or might have been only a faint shadow.

She looked from Rose to me and back to Rose again, and she smiled. It was a nice smile, and it softened the hard features of her face. ''Hello, Rose.'' Her voice was very soft.

''Hi, Alice. This is Mr. Phil Beaumont, from America. Mr. Beaumont, this is Alice Toklas, Gertrude's friend.''

''How do you do,'' Miss Toklas said to me. ''Please come in.''

We stepped in, she shut the door, and we followed her. Hands folded together at her chest, she walked slowly and evenly, without moving her upper body at all, and not moving much of her lower body. It was as though she were floating a few inches above the floor.

The room was filled with paintings and people and cigarette smoke. The paintings were hanging on the wall, everywhere, and the people were standing on the floor or sitting in the chairs, everywhere.

And then I saw, beyond the crowd, a woman I hadn't expected to see.

Rose Forsythe's eyes, when I first saw them, had reminded me of a woman in England. The woman was Jane Turner. The last I'd heard, she was still in England.

She wasn't in England at the moment, because she stood across the room from me in the apartment in Paris, France.

Dear Evangeline,

Phil Beaumont is in Paris. Presumably that *was* he I spied this afternoon, prowling through the aisles of Bon Marché.

Seeking out gewgaws for his floozy, I imagine.

I don't wish to speak ill of him. I don't wish to speak of him at all, in fact; or of the floozy, or of Gertrude Stein's soirée, which is where I saw the two of them.

I did meet Ernest Hemingway while I was there. He was not—NOT—at all as I imagined him. When he was alone with me in Miss Stein's kitchen, he—well, I don't wish to speak of that, either. Not at the moment.

I met Gertrude Stein, too, of course. I liked her very much. And I met Erik Satie, and I met some other writers and some Parisian painters. One day I will tell you about them all. And about what happened in Miss Stein's kitchen.

Oh, and I met a Frenchman who is working with Mr Beaumont; and who told me something else about your friend Sybil Norton, something fascinating. I'll tell you about it when I tell you the rest.

Do you remember Theda Bara as the 'vampire' in *A Fool There Was*? (*'Kiss me, my fool!'*) Well, that apparently is the 'type' which attracts Mr Beaumont—the slim and sleek (and in this instance of it, really terribly short) seductress.

Do you know who she was, the floozy? No, of course you don't.

It was Rose Forsythe, the widow of the man whose death I'm investigating. There she was, dressed to the nines, slinking about Paris in a short dress (drop-waisted, with a mandarin collar) before her husband was even cold in his grave.

Well. All right, yes, I suppose that after two months in there he's probably achieved a certain level of chill. I grant you that. But you ought to have seen her, Evy—

wrapping herself around Mr Beaumont as though she
were a clematis. And Mr Beaumont seemed not to mind
at all. In fact he seemed to be quite enjoying himself.

Now you may tell me, as I told myself, that Mr
Beaumont is likely working on the same case that I am,
and that he was accompanying the floozy in order to
elicit information from her. But I saw them, Evy. I saw
how they acted. And, incidentally, I can assure you that
eliciting information from the woman does not present
an insuperable difficulty. The insuperable difficulty lies
in bunging off the relentless flow of it. I couldn't believe the things she said of him while he was chatting
with Miss Stein.

I don't wish to speak of it.

No, I shall speak, rather, of my afternoon visit with
Eugénie to the salon of Virginia Randall. Miss Randall
is an American who has been living independently in
Paris for some ten years, since she was eighteen. She
is magnificent. Slender and tall (unlike certain other
people), she is a graceful woman with a wild mass of
titian hair that tumbles to square shoulders and sur-
rounds a beautiful oval face. Her eyes are huge and
violet (yes, violet), her mouth is sculpted, her skin is
utterly without pore; or, I suspect, peer.

The eyes of the really terribly short floozy are blue,
by the way; and not, I admit, entirely unattractive. Especially if you ignore, as Mr Beaumont evidently has,
the feverish, predatory gaiety that burns, like a bordello
lamp, within them.

Enough.

Miss Virginia Randall is something of a seductress
herself, but she is also thoughtful. And clever. And cul-
tured and poised. She paints, and she does so with a
very real talent. She speaks flawless Parisian French,
and writes poetry in it as well.

(Did I mention that she was tall?)

In sum, she is precisely the sort of person, wealthy,
beautiful, and gifted, whom I should immediately hate—
had she not been from the very start so exceedingly
kind to me.

Her house—a mansion, really—is on Rue Jacob. It's

been designed to look like a Renaissance palace, and at
this it succeeds wonderfully. The high white ceilings
are intricately moulded, the floors are tiled with satiny
grey marble, the stuccoed red walls are bedecked with
antique portraits in lovingly wrought gold frames. The
furniture is extraordinary: burnished Chippendale and
Hepplewhite and some achingly lovely Louis XVI
chairs and tables. And in all the rooms are plump plush
sofas and divans and love-seats, everything piled high
with embroidered cushions and draped with leopard
skins and velvet throws. Each item, individually, is perfectly elegant and perfectly priceless; but scattered
about as they are, in that lovely and (nearly) accidental
jumble, they create such an atmosphere of snug, cosy
informality that one (nearly) fails to register their value.

When Eugénie and I arrived there, at a little past
three this afternoon (fresh from Bon Marchè and my
near encounter with the bothersome Mr Beaumont), the
entire house was crowded with people and hubbub.
Guests were chatting everywhere, some sitting, some
standing, some milling from room to room. For a moment I noticed nothing unusual, except that a few of
the men, in their tailcoats and breeches, seemed perhaps
a shade overdressed for an afternoon get-together. But
as Eugénie led me through the crowd to greet our hostess, I realised that the men were not men at all. They
were women dressed as men. Most of them wore short
hair, cut and pomaded in the masculine fashion. Some
wore frock coats, some wore dinner jackets. One wore
a small black moustache of mascara, carefully painted
in a curlicue up along her cheeks. Frenchmen take their
moustaches very seriously, even when the Frenchmen
are Frenchwomen.

There were no Frenchmen in the room, no men of
any sort.

I turned to Eugénie. She was watching me, smiling.
'Oui,' she said simply.

'And . . . you?' I asked her. This was in French, naturellement. I haven't spoken a word of English since I
left St Piat.

Still smiling, she shrugged lightly. 'But of course.'

'Ah,' I said. Mrs Applewhite would have beamed at my *sangfroid*. She always felt, you'll recall, that my *sangfroid* needed working on. Now, probably, in an orgy of approbation, she would have covered me with ribbons from head to foot.

To be honest, Evy, it was less *sangfroid* than simple shock. I hadn't, for a single moment, suspected. This does not, perhaps, bode well for my detecting skills.

But Miss Randall. She was sitting on a divan in the sun room, talking to one of the *faux* Frenchmen. When she saw Eugénie, she opened wide her violet eyes, smiled with delight, patted the other woman on the hand, and then rose and swept through the crowd, her proud head slightly canted, her long arms open. She wore a long belted skirt of purple silk, and a billowing lavender blouse, also silk, with puffed sleeves and a large collar, open. At her throat was a gold choker that held, in its centre, a single large amethyst. Not many women of red hair would venture so much purple, but the violet of her eyes allowed her to carry it off, and superbly.

They embraced, Eugénie and she—very chastely, I must tell you, with no more than typical French enthusiasm: a quick amiable hug, a quick amiable peck on each cheek. But standing there together, they made a striking couple: both beautiful, but one pale and delicate and Parisian, the other bright and vibrant and flamboyantly American.

'It's been so long,' said Miss Randall in French, holding Eugénie's hands. 'You look ravishing.'

'Thank you,' said Eugénie, smiling. 'You are, as always, splendid. Virginia, this is my good friend, Jane Turner, from England.'

'Ah,' said Miss Randall as she turned to me. Her violet eyes blazing into mine, she offered me her hand, as a man might, and I took it. 'I'm *so* pleased to meet you,' she said. Her grip was strong, her fingers warm. 'Eugénie spoke of you in such ardent terms this morning, on the telephone. I never doubted that you were as clever and as charming as she claimed—Eugénie is never less than truthful.' She smiled. 'Some flaw in her character, I suppose. But she never mentioned how very lovely you were.' She released my hand.

I was glad that my hair covered my ears, for they felt suddenly like slices of fresh toast. 'Thank you,' I said. 'But Eugénie exaggerates my virtues, I'm afraid.'

'Now that I *do* doubt. And certainly she didn't exaggerate the fluency of your French. You've lived in France?'

'No. I merely visited from time to time, when I was a child. Years ago.'

She smiled. 'Not so very many years, I think. And you speak the language like a native.'

'Thank you. But I speak it nowhere near so well as you.'

'Nonsense. Now—would you like something to drink? Some champagne? Perhaps some food? There are tons of it in the dining room.'

'Thank you, but we ate only a few hours ago.'

'Well, come, then. You must let me show you around the seraglio. Eugénie, you'll permit me to kidnap your friend for a moment?'

Eugénie smiled. 'Only if you swear you'll bring her back.'

'I never swear to anything,' said Miss Randall, lifting her sculpted chin. 'Life is much too whimsical to provide us with certainty—and why should I be different?' Then, smiling, she reached out and touched Eugénie's shoulder; and somehow this simple gesture—so similar to the manner in which Eugénie has herself reached out and touched me—seemed infinitely more intimate than their earlier embrace. 'But I'll do my best,' she promised.

Gracefully she slipped her arm through mine and led me into the crowd.

She is exactly the same height as I, at least four or five inches taller than most of the other women there. I was very conscious of the glances aimed in our direction, some quickly averted, some lingering, some becoming outright stares—speculative, appraising, occasionally even hostile. I felt abruptly as though I had stepped out onto a stage, and into a role about which the audience knew everything, and I nothing.

She showed me the dining room, where a lace-covered trestle table swayed beneath what truly did look like tons of food: silver buckets dripping with dew and packed with shaved ice and gleaming bottles of champagne, silver salvers heaped with caviar and *foie gras* and salmon and sturgeon, a roast of beef, an enormous country ham, a plump turkey, a leg of lamb, four or five wicker baskets stuffed with baguettes, two or three trays of cheeses—wheels of brie and camembert, stout white loaves of *chèvre*. Had I had not already gorged myself at lunch, I should have made an utter pig of myself.

She showed me her bedroom—more velvet, more tiger skins, more framed portraits on the wall, an immense antique cherrywood four-poster—and then the bathroom with its mirrored walls and its sunken marble tub and golden faucets. And then she took me outside, into the garden, where, amidst the rose bushes and the brambles and the ivy, she has had constructed a small, delightful marble temple in the Doric style. It is used, she told me, for the presentation of plays written and performed by her friends. (Plays which I suspect are not very different, in theme and content, from those which we performed, you and I, on those warm, giggling nights at Mrs Applewhite's.)

Had she been, I believe, even very slightly different from what she was, I might have found all this opulence, and perhaps found her, rather oppressive. There was enough food on that table to feed a Welsh mining village for six months. The money that might be realised by the sale of furniture from but a single room of that house could feed the same village, and possibly the whole of Wales, for the remainder of the year. Wealth such as hers makes me at best uneasy, at worst belligerent. Too often during those early years in London I felt, at the back of my neck, the chill dank breath of

Poverty. It is a breath that Miss Randall has never felt, and perhaps never imagined.

But she took such complete and obvious pleasure in her life and the things with which she decorated it, and such pleasure in offering them to her friends (and to her newfound spinster acquaintances), that she completely disarmed me. I found myself absurdly pleased with her company. That a beautiful, talented, intelligent woman seemed quite sincerely pleased with mine had, of course, nothing whatever to do with my response.

'Come,' she said, and she took my hand in hers and led me down a pathway between two sedate ranks of Italian cypress to the south side of the house, where stood, nestled among some more rose bushes, a tiny whitewashed cottage of stone and thatch. Here in the centre (both geographical and cultural) of Paris, the little house was a marvel: it might have been magically transported, only a moment before, from the Cotswolds.

'My studio,' she told me, and opened the door and gestured for me to enter.

Inside, the single room was spare, almost spartan: a few simple throw rugs on the slate floor; a stone fireplace, blackened from use, in one corner. Apart from the easel, there was but a plain wooden cabinet, two plain wooden chairs, and a plain wooden table, the surface of this cluttered with curled tubes of pigment, brightly tinted rags, stoppered bottles, and slender wooden brushes, stained but tied into neat bundles. In the air was the cloying chemical smell of paints and thinners, and all around us were paintings, perhaps hundreds of them. For the most part, they were portraits. None were framed, and they varied in size from quite small—miniatures, very nearly—to medium, perhaps two feet by three. Many had been hung, in what seemed to be no particular order, on all sides of the room; but many more stood on the floor, propped against the walls.

(The walls of Miss Gertrude Stein's atelier are similarly lined with paintings, I later learned; and I was able to examine many of these, even after my attention was distracted by the arrival of Mr Beaumont and his slim, sleek, really terribly short floozy. On balance, I should say that I prefer Miss Randall's paintings to most of those owned by Miss Stein. Of course, my opinion of the latter may be somewhat coloured by my mental and physical state at the time I viewed them. I may, just possibly, have been suffering from fatigue. Or from chagrin. Or from floozy poisoning.)

I stood there for a moment, looking round the room.

'My friends,' said Miss Randall, smiling, and I didn't know then whether she meant the people represented in them, or the paintings themselves. In retrospect, I know that she meant the paintings.

Standing off to one side, she watched me as I moved slowly along one wall and examined her work—as though I were someone actually equipped to pronounce judgement upon it.

I am not, as you well know. But I very much liked it. She has clearly studied with the Impressionists, and, like many of them, she uses quick, elegant dabs of colour to suggest subtle shadings of light; and, perhaps more important, and certainly more difficult, to suggest subtle shadings of character. I had a sense, peering at the portraits, peering into them, that I could recognise these people, recognise the squint of greed in the eyes of this portly gentleman, recognise the smirk of self-indulgence in the rosebud mouth of that young *gamine*.

And then I came to a portrait whose subject I did, in fact, recognise. Surprised, I turned to Miss Randall. 'This is Richard Forsythe,' I said.

She frowned slightly, as though herself surprised, and then she smiled. 'Of course. Eugénie mentioned that you were connected to the family.' (I noted, naturally, her use of the gracious 'connected to', in lieu of the rather more accurate 'working for'.) She frowned again. 'But surely you couldn't have met him.'

'I've seen photographs,' I said. I looked more closely at the portrait. He was wearing a red robe of what appeared to be satin, opened to reveal a bare, pale, patrician throat. His dark shiny hair was brushed back, but on both sides of his wide white forehead a few loose, raffish strands were curling toward his dark brown shiny eyes. He was as elegantly handsome as he had been in the photographs, as polished, as princely. A lazy smile had etched an ironical shadow in the right corner of his mouth. But there was something wrong with those shiny brown eyes.

I turned again to Miss Randall. 'He seems somehow desperate.'

She raised her russet eyebrows, then smiled again. 'Eugénie was right, as usual. You *are* a woman of insight.'

'But you painted him,' I said (barely flushing at all, and blinking only once or twice). 'The insight is yours.'

'But you saw what I painted,' she said. 'You saw what I saw. Very few people have seen that. Almost no one. Not in the portrait, and not in Richard.'

She stepped across the narrow floor, stood beside me, folded her arms beneath her breasts, and for a moment she gazed at the portrait. Finally she said, 'Poor Richard.'

I turned to her. 'Poor?'

Still staring at the painting, she said, 'He was brilliant. He was charming. And he had everything he wanted. Except talent.'

She turned to me. 'And of course that was the thing he wanted most. He was a dilettante.' She smiled. 'As I am.'

'But your talent is very real,'' I said. I glanced around the room. 'These are . . . lovely. All of them.'

'Thank you.' She inclined her head briefly, and her wild red tumble of hair shivered, but when she raised her head again, her smile was rueful. 'I have a small skill, perhaps. At something a bit like caricature.' There was a very faint self-mocking tone in her voice. And perhaps she'd heard it herself, for she quickly glanced back at the portrait and said, 'Richard lacked even that. And it rankled him.'

She looked at me. '*Desperate* is the proper word. He wanted desperately to be an artist. He tried poetry, he tried painting. He failed at both. He tried publishing. Art as commerce, commerce as art. He published beautiful books. No one bought them.'

Lightly, very much in the French manner, she shrugged. 'Art requires self-deception. You must persuade yourself, as an artist, that what you create is somehow useful to the rest of the world. It isn't, of course. The world doesn't give a damn. But you plod along anyway—because ultimately, deep down, beneath another level of self-deception, you really don't give a damn about the world. And if you're good, or if you're blessed, you do create something useful, something beautiful. Richard wasn't good, not very, and unfortunately all his blessings had fallen elsewhere. His tragedy, I think, was that he'd lost the ability to deceive himself. At any level.'

She looked back at the painting.

'Do you really believe that?' I said. 'That the world doesn't care about art?'

She turned to me again. 'Not beyond the fleeting moment.' She smiled. 'But that's all there are, really, don't you think? Fleeting moments. We must enjoy them while we can.'

'And Richard didn't, you're saying?'

'Richard couldn't, I'm saying.'

'His suicide wasn't a surprise, then.'

'No.' She looked off, and for a brief moment her eyebrows lowered. Then she looked back at me. 'Have you seen pictures of Sabine? You do know who she was?'

'Yes,'' I said, and I lied, 'But I've seen no pictures of her.'

'Over here.' She took my arm and led me to the opposite wall.

'There,' she said. 'In the centre.' She smiled—sadly, ironically, I couldn't determine. 'Directly opposite Richard,' she added.

The photograph of Sabine von Stuben which I'd seen in London had failed to do her justice. The woman in the photograph had been attractive; the woman in the painting was ravishing. Her blond hair, bobbed and fringed, was so pale it that it was white, as white as snow. Her large, almond-shaped eyes were the deep, impenetrable blue that one imagines of Arctic waters. Her cheekbones were high and prominent, her nose was strong—almost too strong, really, and on a different face it might have overwhelmed the other features. But on hers it was exactly right. Her wide lips were red and glistening, as though she had just applied rouge; or had, only a moment before, slowly licked them moist.

As in the portrait of Richard Forsythe, however, there was something unsettling about the painting and its subject. Those lips were parted in a kind of hushed expectancy, small white teeth glimmering between, and the woman was leaning forward, the décolleté of her black gown offering the curves of her full white breasts and the deep blue shadow that lay between them. Her eyes were gazing off to the left at something in an attitude, or so it seemed to me, of supplication, almost of adoration.

I turned to Miss Randall. 'At whom was she looking?'

Miss Randall laughed. 'At Richard.' She laughed again. 'Very good. You knew it was a person.'

'But what else could it have been?'

'A god, perhaps. One of Sabine's gods. She worshipped gods before she worshipped Richard.' She smiled. 'After Richard arrived, she would have no god but him.'

'Which gods?'

'Ah,' she said wryly. 'Sabine's gods were many and various. But they were all dark.'

I glanced at the painting that hung beside the portrait and saw that it, too, was a representation of Sabine. But this was no portrait. She lay nude (extremely nude) on a black silk sheet in a bed that was unmistakably the four-poster I had seen in Miss Randall's room. Hands clasped behind her head, she had drawn up her long slender right leg to rest the sole of her foot against the sheet. Her left leg was splayed out at an angle along the silk. Her body was very white, nearly as white as her bobbed hair (the colour of which, by the way, was demonstrably natural). She was staring towards the viewer, or towards the artist, whose position was at the bottom of the bed, and on her face was the most wanton, the most wicked smile I had ever seen.

Miss Randall had noticed my glance. (And possibly my reaction, a quick intake of breath which lacked virtually all *sangfroid*. I tried to conceal it with a small cough, but I expect that this made it only more obvious. So much for my ribbons.)

'That was painted,' she said, 'before Sabine met Richard.'

'Ah,' I said. A Pinkerton is never at a loss for words. I turned to her. I don't believe that I was blushing. 'You knew her, then.'

'I knew her.'

I looked at the painting, looked back again at Miss Randall. 'What was she like?'

Miss Randall tilted her head to the side. 'Do you really wish to hear about Sabine?'

''Yes,' I said. 'Very much.'

'Simple curiosity?'

I think I did blush then. But a blush at this point would have been appropriate, I expect, even if I hadn't been a Pinkerton. 'Perhaps,' I said. 'I've heard something of Richard, of course, from his family. Not a great deal—they're very secretive about him. But I've heard nothing of Sabine.'

She studied me for a moment, as though I were a painting. Then she nodded. 'All right. But first, I think, a glass of wine.'

She walked over to the wooden cabinet, opened it, and removed from it a bottle of red wine, a corkscrew, and two stemmed crystal glasses. The studio was not so spartan as it seemed.

She turned to me and said, 'Come. Sit.'

'But your guests,' I said.

'Can take care of themselves. Come.'

As I sat down, she placed the bottle and the glasses

on the table and then cleared away some of the paints and brushes. Her movements were quick and direct— not masculine, and in no way unfeminine; but they had an assurance to them, a swift confidence, that I found admirable.

Still standing, she ran the tip of the corkscrew round the lip of the bottle, neatly cutting through the foil. She set the scrap of foil aside, inserted the point of the screw into the cork, rested the base of the bottle on the table; and then, while holding the corkscrew steady, she slowly and smoothly and carefully (and in exactly the manner I remember my father doing it, back in Torquay) turned the bottle round. After a moment she stopped turning the bottle and she began to twist the corkscrew. In another moment, pop, the thing was done.

Like a sommelier, she poured a small portion of wine into my glass, and stood there while I tasted it.

I looked up at her. 'It's wonderful,' I told her, truthfully.

She smiled. 'Chambolle-Musigny. My favourite.' She held out the bottle, I held out my glass, she filled it, then filled her own, returned the bottle to the table, and sat down. She lifted her glass and held it out to me. 'Cheers.'

'Cheers,' said I, with the *insouciance* of a nanny who quite often drinks an afternoon glass of wine in a Cotswold cottage in Paris with an entity like Miss Randall. We clicked glasses, we each took a sip of wine, and then her violet eyes looked at me in a glance that was as direct as her movements.

'She and I were close for a time,' she said.

'Yes,' I said.

'We were, for a time, lovers.'

'Of course,' I said. I thought that I delivered this rather well; but, from the crinkling at the corners of her eyes I sensed that Miss Randall was amused.

Naturally, as subtle as this was, it suggested that Miss Randall *wanted* me to know she was amused.

'She was,' said Miss Randall, 'or she appeared to be, a very sensual woman.'

'Appeared to be?'

Miss Randall took a sip of wine. 'Few of us are who we seem to be. Sabine was even less so. I thought for a time that I knew her. We enjoyed each other, or so I thought. I don't mean merely in the physical sense.''

I nodded.

She smiled. 'Although, as you can probably tell from the painting, that was a part of the relationship as well. A large part.'

'Yes,' I said, and I was very conscious of not blinking.

Another smile as she sat back in the chair. 'Do I embarrass you, Jane?'

'No, no. Not at all.'

She laughed, lifting her head for a moment and showing her slender throat. The amethyst on her choker trembled, winking in the light, and then she lowered her head. Her violet glance found mine again. For just an instant her eyes narrowed, as though she were trying to peer beneath the surface of my own. 'You intrigue me, Jane. There's something very English about you—I don't mean that badly, please don't misunderstand me—but there's something else there, something I can't quite put my finger on.'

My Pinkerton identification papers, perhaps. These are in London, safely hidden away from prying eyes, and prying fingers.

I smiled. 'Few of us,' I said, 'are who we seem.' (From off in the wings, I could hear Mrs Applewhite's delighted applause.)

'*Touché*,' said Miss Randall. Watching me, she raised her glass, sipped her wine.

'She lied to you?' I asked her.

She pursed her lips and considered that for a moment. At last she said, 'She was, herself, a lie. The person whom she claimed to be, that person didn't exist.'

She leaned towards me, and now her smile was teasing. 'Do you want to know what she was doing here? In Paris?'

'Yes, of course.'

She sat back again. 'Well. She said that she was here because Munich bored her. She said that her father, a baron, was thinking about investing here. She said that she might buy a small house, somewhere on the Ile Saint-Louis.'' She took a sip of wine, glanced over at the paintings of Sabine, looked back at me. Her smile was brief. 'She said a great many things. And all of them were lies.'

''Why, then, was she here?'

She looked down at my wine glass, which I hadn't touched since that first sip. 'I thought you liked the wine.'

'I do. Very much. It's just that I drank quite a lot at lunch.'

'Oh, Jane, *please* don't be proper. Don't be *moderate*. Not here. Not with me. I can accept excess, I can accept abstinence, but I cannot accept moderation.'

I laughed. I took a sip from the glass. 'It's lovely wine.'

She nodded with slow elaborate grace, her hair spilling forward. 'Thank you. And thank you for humouring me.' She took another sip of hers. 'She was here to collect money for a political party in Germany.'

'In Germany?'

'There's a German party called the National Socialists Workers party. Do you know of it?'

'I've heard of it. And, yes, I recall someone telling me that Sabine was a member.'

Her eyebrows arched slightly. 'Really? Who?'

'I don't recall.' But you will, Evy, if you've been paying attention. It was Neal Forsythe. 'Someone connected to Richard's family.'

She nodded. 'But she wasn't merely a member. She worked for them. She was channelling funds from France to Germany.'

'But whose funds? Why would anyone in France give money to a German political party?'

'Do you know what the National Socialists stand for? What their beliefs are?'

'Only in the vaguest way. They're against the Bolsheviks, aren't they? And the Jews?'

'Virulently. Against both. Like everyone else, the
Germans tend to blame others for their own misfor-
tunes. The workers, many of them, blame the Jews, who
they like to believe are running the country. The indus-
trialists and the army, who actually are running the
country, blame the Bolsheviks. The bourgeoisie blame
France. The National Socialists appeal to everyone. And
they appeal, as well, to the that tiresome strain of mys-
ticism in the Germans, their worship of their dreary
Teutonic past. Blood unity. National identity.'

'*Der Volk.*'

This time it was one of her eyebrows that arched.
'You speak German?'

'A little,' I admitted.

Amused again, she raised her glass and sipped from
it. 'You're quite the dark horse, Jane.'

Best to ignore that, I thought. 'But where does the
socialism come in?'

She smiled. 'An elusive dark horse,' she said.

Best to ignore that as well. Innocently I said, 'But I
don't understand why they call it socialism.'

She laughed suddenly, vastly entertained, tossing her
head back once again. And then she levelled her gaze
and studied me for a moment, smiling. She nodded. 'All
right, Jane. We'll stick to the subject shall we?' Another
smile, another light shrug. 'Why call it socialism? Probably because they think that the workers will like the
sound of it. What's the English phrase? "It'll go over
a treat." But you're quite right. It isn't socialism. National Socialism means that everyone, workers and in-
dustrialists and bourgeoisie alike, works together for the
glory of the New Germany.'

'But why would anyone in France wish to help
them?'

'There are people here who share that horror of the
Bolsheviks. They despise the Weimar government—socialist, as you must know, in theory if not always in
practise—and they're delighted to help support a party

that promises to destroy it. And destroy the Bolsheviks into the bargain. And, you know, they wouldn't mind terribly if somehow, along the way, the Jews were dealt with, too.'

'But France and Germany have always been enemies. What would happen if the National Socialists did succeed in coming to power?'

'As indeed they might. Well, I'm sure the French supporters tell themselves that they'll cross that bridge, or burn it, when they come to it. The revolution in Russia has terrified them all. You know that the Bolshevik leaders, Lenin and Trotsky, were living here in Paris before the revolution?'

'Yes.'

'These people, these French supporters, they fear a strong Germany far less than they do a revolution.'

She glanced once more at the painting of Sabine and then sipped some wine. She sat back. 'Anyway, as I say, it was from people like them that Sabine was receiving money.'

'You knew about it?'

'Not at first. We spent very little time discussing politics. I ought to have known about it, though. From things she said. But for a long time I deliberately ignored those things. She was very young, just twenty years old, and the young are passionate about their politics. And I was a tiny bit infatuated, you see.'

She poured some more wine into my glass, which was still nearly full, then poured some into hers, which was nearly empty. She put the bottle back, raised her glass, sipped from it. 'And then, one day, I discovered that she'd forged my name to a check. I confronted her. It was an . . . unpleasant moment. She said things to me that were really quite vile. Among them, that she'd merely been using me all along. My position. My access to certain people. She said outright that she'd been involved with me, a woman, only because she wished to help the party. She said—' She smiled wryly. ''Well, she said some very vile things.'

'I'm so sorry,' I said.

For a moment—an instant only, for far less time that it takes to tell of it—she went stiff, her eyes narrowing, her mouth tightening. I knew at once that I'd said something foolish. Beneath that sophistication of hers was a fury, a rage, that I should never have suspected. (It may be that I ought find some other sort of work.) Miss Randall did *not* want pity from anyone.

But then, as suddenly as it had appeared, the stiffness left her. She lifted the glass, drank some wine. 'I said some vile things as well. I attacked her precious party. She threw some names back at me—people here in France who felt differently about it.'

'Which names?'

She shook her head. 'It doesn't matter now. It's all in the past.'

Drat. 'And afterward,' I said, 'she became involved with Richard.'

'Yes.'

'For the same reason, do you think?'

'I thought so, initially. I hired a private detective— what do you call them in England? Enquiry agents?'

'I believe so,' I said smoothly. (More applause from off in the wings.)

'After we . . . after we separated, I hired one, to investigate her. It transpired that nothing of what she'd told me was true. Her father was no baron. She was being supported by the party, as a payment for channelling the funds from France to Munich. I learned, too, more about the party. It's quite evil, really. I told Richard everything I'd learned—we've never been close friends, but I felt he deserved to know. He told me that he already knew. She'd told him, he said. I asked him whether it didn't bother him, knowing that she was helping support those people. He said she'd given that up. He said he'd presented her with a choice, the party or him, and that she'd chosen him.'

'Do you think that was true?'

'Yes, I do. You had only to look at her, when he was present, to see that she was lost.' She sipped some wine. 'It was something beyond infatuation. She was besotted.'

'And yet you painted them. Both of them. Wasn't that difficult for you?'

Her smile was wry and very faint. 'The most difficult thing was not putting into the painting everything I knew about her. Not painting her as she was, but as she seemed.' She shrugged once more. 'Richard asked me to paint them both, and I owed him a favour. But it was all a joke. One of Richard's final jokes.'

''What do you mean?'

'He was supposed to pick up the paintings on the day he killed himself. He knew, I think, when he made the arrangements, that he'd never be coming for them. That he'd be leaving them here, for me.'

I looked over at the painting of Sabine. 'Why was she so attracted to Richard, do you suppose?'

'There was a darkness in him, for all his charm. And Sabine was drawn to darkness, like a moth to light. It was the darkness of the National Socialists—their hatreds, their blood myths, their hunger for power—that brought her to them. Evidently, Richard fulfilled her needs—those needs—better even than the party did.'

'How extraordinary.'

'People come together for all sorts of reasons, Jane. And frequently the reasons have little to do with sweetness and light.'

'No, of course not,' said I, the voice of authority.

Still smiling, her elbows on the table, she leaned forward, raised her hands, linked her fingers and notched her chin against them. Framed by that aura of red hair, her remarkable eyes looked into mine. 'And what about you, Jane?'

'Me? How do you mean?' Perhaps Mr Darwin's theories are correct; but I've never understood what useful evolutionary function is served by the human blush.

'Have you someone special in your life just now?' she asked me.

'I? No. Not really.'

That violet gaze was almost palpable. It seemed to

have a weight to it, a force; I could feel its pressure against the skin of my face.

'I'd very much like,' she said softly, 'to paint you.'

And lying between us, as though they were physically present on the table, were all the possibilities that this implied.

It would have been so easy, Evy. I believe that if I had simply moved my hand a fraction of an inch in her direction, her hand would have floated down and covered mine, like a blanket settling over a bare shoulder.

A part of me was tempted, I must tell you. She is, as I've said, an exceptional woman.

And my acting as nanny to two children has done very little to soothe that loneliness which hides away, like some sad black beast, in the secret corners of the heart, and which, on empty rainy days, or in the long reaches of the night, sometimes shuffles forward to show its bleak familiar face. The time I've recently spent with Eugénie, which has been great fun, and which ought to have soothed it, has instead only aroused it. My time with Eugénie will be over soon. And I am with her on false pretences.

Furthermore, as to Miss Randall's offer itself—and no one knows this better than you—it's not as though I haven't had some small experience along those lines.

But, Evy, those long-ago fumblings, those midnight grasps and gasps, those clever little tricks you taught me—sweet as they were (and are), and as much as I cherish them (and as much as I cherish you), I've always thought of them as, well, practise of a sort. An experiment. A game. (And I know from what you've told me about the dashing Mr Hammond that your feelings cannot be too different, *n'est-ce pas?*)

If—shall we say *when*—I dispense with, or dispose of, this burdensome 'treasure', I should like to do so in a situation that bears at least some resemblance to my own dreams and hopes and fantasies. I have been hopelessly corrupted by the Brothers Grimm. I cannot shift my allegiance, this late in the day, to Sappho.

(I confess to you, however, that I did feel somewhat

differently about everything a few hours later, when I was confronted with Mr Beaumont and the slim, sleek, terribly short floozy.)

In any event, I sat there for a moment. The spoken question, and those unspoken, trembled in the air as we stared at each other across the table. Finally I said, 'Thank you. I'm really very flattered. But I've so much to do. I honestly don't think I could ever find the time.'

Her gaze didn't waver. 'What a pity,' she said. She sat back, lifted her wine glass, sipped from it. 'Shall we go back and join the others?'

If this were a novel, that would be an excellent place to end a chapter, don't you think?

Ah, but there's more. As I keep reminding you, I am not only a *femme fatale*, I am also a Pinkerton.

As we were passing between the cypresses again, I asked her, 'These people who were giving money to Sabine . . .'

She had been staring down, as though watching the pathway spool away beneath her feet. Now she turned to me and laughed. 'You don't give up, Jane, do you?'

'But I find it such a strange notion—Frenchmen giving money to a German party.'

She smiled. 'Not all of them were French, and not all of them were men. One of them was the writer, Sybil Norton.'

'Sybil Norton!' I was astonished. 'But she's British!'

'She is, yes,' she said, smiling, 'but clearly some of her sympathies lie in Germany. And the sympathies of her lover, as well.'

'Her lover?'

She touched my arm lightly, much as she had touched Eugénie earlier. 'Yes, but Jane, you mustn't breathe a word of this to anyone. Her lover is the Prefect of Police. He's a very dangerous man.'

And with that I think I *will* end the chapter. It's just gone two in the morning. I am utterly exhausted and I must try to get some sleep.

Goodness. Something just occurred to me—just now, as I was about to lay down my pen. If Sabine von Stuben deserted Miss Randall for Richard Forsythe, then Miss Randall may very possibly have had a motive to kill them both. And I have no way of knowing whether what she told me today, any of it, is true.

Enough. I shall grapple with it all tomorrow.

All my love,
Jane

Eleven

STANDING BENEATH A large painting, Miss Turner and another woman, a pale attractive brunette dressed in black, were talking to Ernest Hemingway. Just as I caught sight of her, Miss Turner looked over to her left and across the room, directly at me.

Behind her wire-rim glasses, her eyes narrowed slightly and her glance slid from me to Rose Forsythe and then back to me. I gave her a small shake of my head and I looked away as Rose and I followed Alice Toklas, who was still floating along above the floor.

Cooper, in London, should have told me that Miss Turner might be here. She was a Pinkerton operative, and she was probably working on a case—and maybe the Forsythe case. Cooper sometimes doesn't let the right hand know what the left hand is doing. Sometimes Cooper doesn't let the right hand know what the right hand is doing.

But both of Rose Forsythe's hands were cooperating pretty well. She was using them to hang on to my arm as though she were planning a set of chin-ups. "Isn't this *nice*?" she said. "Oh, look, there's Pablo. He's Spanish but he's been in Paris *forever*. He's a painter and I *love* some of his earlier stuff, mandolin players and things, they're *awfully* sad and romantic. Very Spanish." She leaned toward me and tugged at me, bringing my head closer to hers. I could feel her warm whispered breath against my ear and I could smell the hothouse scent of her perfume. "But the stuff he's doing right now is just *crazy*."

Miss Toklas led us toward the fireplace. Beside it, a heavy-set woman wearing a black circus tent was talking to a thin young man with floppy brown hair. The young man, who wore a black suit, sat forward in his wooden chair, leaning into the conversation. The woman sat back comfortably in hers, an upholstered chair, with her hands folded on her broad lap. In her forties, maybe, she looked as serene and as immobile as a Buddha. Her black hair was wound into a thick topknot. Beneath a broad, powerful nose, her mouth was thin and narrow, almost pinched.

"Joyce is good," the woman was saying. She spoke slowly and precisely, like someone patiently explaining obvious things to an idiot. "He is a good writer. People like him because he is incomprehensible and nobody can understand him. But who came first, James Joyce or Gertrude Stein? Who started the whole thing? Do not forget that my first great book, *Three Lives*, was published in 1909. That was long before *Ulysses*."

She looked up at Miss Toklas and us, and she smiled. It was a good smile, relaxed and open and pleased. "Ah," she said. "Rose. Rose is a rose is a rose." I wondered if she'd been drinking.

"Oh Gertrude," said Rose, and laughed. She turned to me and said, "She always says that." She turned back to Miss Stein. "Gertrude, this is Mr. Beaumont. He's a private detective for the Pinkertons. He—"

There was a sudden loud crash from across the room. We all turned. Hemingway was staring down, looking puzzled, at a small table that had somehow toppled to the floor and spilled knickknacks across the Persian carpet. Miss Turner and her friend watched him as he bent foward. His elbow banged against the frame of a picture hanging on the wall and the picture jerked to the side and began to swing rapidly, like a metronome, smacking into the paintings on either side of it. He lurched forward to steady it, but the other paintings were moving now and one of them swung back and slammed into his fingers. He snapped his hand away and shook it quickly up and down. Except for Miss Turner and her friend, all the people around him were busy looking away, or over at Miss Stein.

Miss Stein sighed. "Go to Hemingway," she said slowly, "would you, Alice? Go to Hemingway and take him into the kitchen. Keep him well away from the china, but feed him something. Yes, feed him the *coq au vin*. He likes *coq au vin*. Feed him that, would you?"

Miss Toklas smiled and turned and drifted off.

Miss Stein looked up at Rose again. "A Pinkerton, you said?" She turned to me. "An actual Pinkerton of the genuine kind?" She spoke to me—she probably spoke to everyone—with the same slow precision.

"Yes," I said.

"Ah, but are you the sort of Pinkerton who chases after cowboy desperadoes, or are you the sort of Pinkerton who chases after tenement gangsters? Or are you in fact the sort who breaks strikes by hitting poor starving workers on the head with big thick sticks?"

"We don't do that anymore. Break strikes."

"So cowboys, then, and gangsters. You chase them."

"Whenever I can."

She laughed—a solid, up from the belly laugh. "Wonderful. You must sit down and tell me about it. This is Desmond Spottiswode, from Oxford in England. I have become very famous in Oxford for my work. They very much admire my work in Oxford, and this provides me with great hope for the British Empire. Desmond has come here all the way from there, from Oxford, to ask me penetrating questions."

The young man stood up, blinking furiously, and he offered me a languid hand. I was careful not to hurt it. He kept blinking anyway. "Charmed," he said.

"Do pull up a chair," Miss Stein told me.

"Darling," said Rose, and squeezed my arm, "I just saw a *wonderful* friend. I've *got* to run over and say hello." She loosened the shawl at her throat. "You have a fun time with Gertrude, all right? I'll be back."

Smiling, Miss Stein watched her. Faintly, she shook her head. "Rose is a rose," she said again. She looked up at me. "A chair, Beaumont. You must find yourself a chair and you must tell me all about these cowboys." She turned to the young Englishman. "This will be good for you, Desmond. Very good, I think. You shall observe me in discussion with a fellow American, and he and I shall be discussing interesting American things such as cowboys. This will be very useful for your article.''

The young Englishman nodded, blinking. ''Yes, of course.''

There was an empty chair a few feet away. I grabbed it, swung it around, and sat down. I looked over at Miss Turner. She and the pale brunette were listening to Rose Forsythe.

''Now,'' said Miss Stein to me. ''Have you come to Paris in search of cowboys? We have not a great many cowboys here, I should warn you. We do have Apaches, and very colorful they are, too, although they are very different I suspect from the Apaches of your acquaintance. But we suffer from a serious deficiency of cowboys. A definite dearth, I should say, of cowboys.''

''I'm investigating the death of Richard Forsythe,'' I told her.

''*Are* you?'' she said. ''Are you indeed? Well, I think that this is an excellent thing. I think, yes, that this is truly an excellent thing. Someone who is capable of mounting an investigation, a penetrating investigation, should certainly be investigating the death of Richard Forsythe. I have never believed, for a single instant, that the man committed suicide.''

The young Englishman leaned forward, blinking, and he coughed politely and then said, ''Excuse me.''

Miss Stein turned to him. ''Yes?''

''Who was Richard Forsythe?''

Miss Stein's plump right hand lifted a few inches from her lap and brushed dismissively at the air. ''A publisher,'' she said. The hand settled back onto her lap and she nodded toward the far side of the room, where Rose stood with Miss Turner and her friend. The three women had been joined by a short, bearded man in a fussy black suit, who was talking to them all. Rose looked like she was waiting for him to stop talking and let her start. ''Her husband,'' said Miss Stein. ''Rose's.''

She turned to me. ''Now. Do you know why I say this? Why I say that Richard Forsythe did not commit suicide? Why he could not commit suicide?''

''No,'' I said. ''Why's that?''

"Because," she said, "he was yellow."

"Yellow," I said.

"Exactly. He was yellow." She turned to the Englishman. "He was a coward," she explained.

She turned back to me. "Suicide is a form of cowardice, of course. It is the result of the fear of living overpowering the fear of dying. But there is a paradox here, you see. In a strange way, the fear of living becomes an inverted kind of bravery."

"Yeah. Ernest Hemingway said pretty much the same thing."

She nodded. "Yes, of course," she said. "He got it from me. He gets everything from me. He is my pupil and he is an apt pupil. Have you read his work?"

"No."

"It is very promising. Have you read my work?"

"Not yet."

She laughed again, her big body shaking. "A diplomatic Pinkerton. I would not have thought it possible. Would you, Desmond?"

He leaned forward, blinking, but before he could answer, she said to me, "When you do read my work and you compare it to Hemingway's work you will clearly see his debt to me. He is an apt pupil and I am very pleased with him. But we were talking about Richard Forsythe. I have never been pleased with Richard Forsythe. We had business dealings, you see, and he cheated me."

"Yes, I heard that you had a disagreement with him."

"We were in disagreement together. He was in the wrong and I was in the right, and therefore we were in disagreement together. He tried to steal some books of mine."

"I thought he'd published some books of yours."

"He did, he did publish some books of mine, but then he tried to steal them. He refused to release my copies to me. We had a disagreement about this and he won. Publishers always win. This is a fact of nature, like the moon revolving around the earth. And, as a fact of nature, I accept it."

Across the room, someone began playing on the piano. Miss Stein glanced in that direction. "Satie. He is an interesting man. And an interesting composer. This is one of his own pieces.''

I looked. It was the short, bearded man in the fussy suit. Jane Turner and her friend stood off to one side. Rose Forsythe was still standing with them, and she was talking again. The two women had their heads bent forward, toward Rose, but both of them kept glancing toward the piano.

Then Miss Turner glanced at me. I turned back to Miss Stein. ''You were saying that Richard Forsythe was yellow.''

She nodded. ''He was yellow, yes. He was incapable of bravery of any sort, even the inverted sort. He would not have killed himself.''

''His wife believes he did.''

''Rose? Rose is very nice, I think. She is in her own way a very nice woman. But Rose does not believe things. She merely repeats them.''

''The police say that he committed suicide.''

''The police *say* that he committed suicide. That is not the same thing as believing that he did.'' She smiled. ''You are a Pinkerton. Do you always say what you believe, and do you always believe what you say?''

''Always,'' I said.

She laughed again, pleased. ''And so you prove my point.''

''What about Sabine von Stuben?'' I asked her. ''Could Forsythe have killed her?''

''I have no difficulty believing that Richard Forsythe could have killed her. I have no difficulty believing that anyone could have killed her. She was eminently killable, I would say. She was forever going on about her dreadful Nationalist party and her dreadful racial theories. I did not like her, I did not like her at all, and indeed I have no difficulty believing that I could have killed her myself. But I did not.'' She smiled at me. ''Do you want to hear my alibi?'' She turned to the young Englishman. ''Alibis are of the utmost importance in these situations.'' He blinked and she turned back to me. ''Do you want to hear it?''

''Sure.''

''I was here all day, all the day that the two of them died. Alice was here with me.''

I nodded. "Which dreadful Nationalist party was that? The one that von Stuben was going on about?"

"It was some nasty German political party. I did not pay much attention. I have no real interest in politics, no interest in politics at all. Except in the historical sense. Historically, politics can be very interesting."

"Right. So if Forsythe didn't commit suicide, who do you think killed him?"

"I do not know. He used drugs. He used quite a lot of drugs. Perhaps it was someone from that milieu. Or perhaps it was a writer. He was a publisher, after all."

"Do you know Sybil Norton?

"*Of* her I know. She is a popular writer. I use 'popular' in the sense of 'common,' which is to say appealing to the common people. Among the uncommon people, on the other hand, I am myself a popular writer, in the sense of 'esteemed' or 'beloved.' It is important, with words, to be accurate."

"Did you know that she and Forsythe were involved?"

She raised her eyebrows. "Were they really? I find that very interesting." She looked off for a moment, probably thinking about how interesting that was. "But now that you tell me, I am not much surprised. Richard Forsythe was very common himself, I think. He tried very hard to be uncommon, he made a great effort to be uncommon, but of course this in itself is evidence of his commonness." She nodded. "Yes, I see now that his commonness would be compatible with the commonness of Sybil Forsythe."

"Darling?" It was Rose Forsythe, and she had her hand in my hair. "Come along for a minute. You really *must* meet Eugénie. Excuse us, would you, Gertrude?"

"I can excuse almost everything," said Miss Stein. "That is the sort of person I am." She turned to me. "Remind me, later, and I will give you some examples of my work so that you may read them. If you would like something to drink, there is wine in the kitchen."

"Fine," I said. "Thanks."

"You are quite welcome."

I got up and and Rose tucked my left hand under her right arm and held it with both her hands and she began to tow me through the crowd. Breaking her wrists would have been rude.

Jane Turner and her friend watched us approach, both of them holding glasses of white wine. The table that had fallen over, a narrow table of cherrywood, was back up now, against the wall. Off to the left, the small bearded man was still playing the piano. He played it well, and people had gathered around the old upright, listening with solemn faces.

"Here he is," said Rose to the two women. "My big brave Pinkerton. Isn't he *gorgeous*? Phillip, darling, this is one of my *very* best friends, Eugénie Aubier. You remember, I talked about her—she and her brother, the count, they have that *wonderful* house in Chartres."

Miss Aubier held out her hand, horizontally, so I could kiss it, if that was what I had in mind. I shook it, gently, and I said, "Hello."

"I am very pleased to meet you," she said with a strong French accent. She was thin and pale, as though she'd been ill. But she had the kind of calmly feverish beauty you sometimes see in consumptives, when the flesh is wasting away and the spirit is becoming visible.

Rose was still holding on to my left hand with both of hers. "And this," she said, "is her friend from England, Jane Um . . ."

"Turner," said Miss Turner. She held out her hand and I took it. It was cool from the glass of wine. "Jane Turner," she said, and she smiled.

"Hello," I said.

Miss Turner was tall and her eyes were nearly level with mine. Rose Forsythe's bright blue eyes, when I first saw them, had reminded me of Miss Turner's. I realized now that Miss Turner's eyes, behind her glasses, were different. They were fresher. They had seen less, and probably they could see more.

Her thick brown hair was long and loose, falling to her shoulders. She was wearing a simple dark blue dress with a matching jacket. She had always been a handsome woman, and now, next to Rose, she looked even more handsome.

"Darling," said Rose, "Eugénie and Jean are having one of their *marvelous* masquerade parties tomorrow, out in Chartres at that *wonderful* house. It'll be *the* event of the season, *everyone* will be there, and we really *have* to go, don't you think?''

I looked at Miss Aubier and at Miss Turner, who was sipping from her glass of wine. ''We'll see,'' I said.

Miss Aubier smiled. ''You would be most welcome.''

''Thank you,'' I said. To Miss Turner I said, ''Will you be going?''

''Yes,'' she said.

''Darling,'' said Rose, her hands climbing up my arm, ''I've got to run to the little girls' room. I'll be right back.'' She turned to Miss Aubier. ''Now don't let *anyone* steal him away.''

Miss Aubier smiled politely. ''*Non.*''

Rose gave my arm a squeeze and then she turned and fluttered off.

Miss Aubier and Miss Turner watched her go, and then Miss Aubier said to me, ''She is a woman of zee enthusiasm, no?''

''Yeah,'' I said. ''And then some.''

''She has recovered admirably from zee sad dett of her husband.''

I looked at her more carefully, but I couldn't tell if she was being ironic. ''Yeah. She's bounced right back.''

Miss Turner took another sip of wine. Maybe she needed it. She was probably as surprised to see me in Paris as I was to see her.

Looking up at me, Miss Aubier tilted her head. ''She says, Rose, zat you are investigating zis. His dett.''

''That's right. His death and the death of Sabine von Stuben. Did you know them?''

''Only a very little. It was a terrible sing, a tragic sing. But zis is an amazing coincidence.''

''How so?''

''Because Jane here, she is working wiz the family of Richard Forsyse. Wiz the family of his uncle.''

''Is that right?'' I said, and I looked at Miss Turner.

''Yes,'' said Miss Turner. ''I'm the children's nanny.''

''Isn't it wonderful?'' said Miss Aubier. ''Does Jane look to you like a nanny?''

"No," I said, and I smiled at Miss Turner. "But I haven't met many nannies."

"But I sought," said Miss Aubier, "zat Richard Forsyse died a suicide." She turned to Miss Turner. "You remember, Jane? We were speaking of zis."

"Yes," said Miss Turner. "I recall." She took another sip of wine, emptying the glass.

Miss Aubier said to me, "It was not a suicide?"

"I don't know. That's one of the things I'm trying to find out."

"But if not a suicide, zen zey were *killed, non*?"

"Right."

"But who could do such a sing?"

"That's the other thing I'm trying to find out."

The piano music stopped just then and people applauded. The two women set their glasses on the table, and they applauded, too.

When the clapping died down, Miss Aubier said to me, "Have you done zis work for a long time?"

I was about to answer when a big brown hand landed on my shoulder. "Hey, Beechum, great to see you!"

It was Hemingway, big broad chest and and sparkling brown eyes and flashing white teeth. His mustache was shiny now and there was a gray chunk of something, probably *coq au vin*, trapped between two of the flashing white teeth. He held a large glass of wine in his left hand.

I smiled. "Beaumont."

His hand fell away and he grinned. "Right, right, great to see you. You know Jane and Eugénie?"

"We've just met."

He turned his grin toward the two women. "You girls want to be careful with Beaumont here. He's a Pinkerton, you know. Don't wash the dirty linen in public, hey?"

Miss Aubier smiled. "He has told us of zis, Ernest."

Miss Turner picked up her wine glass, saw that it was empty, put it back down.

"Say, Jane," said Hemingway. "You're out of wine. I'll get you another one, hey?" He reached for her glass, and some wine from his own glass spilled out and spattered onto the carpet. He didn't notice. Miss Aubier did, and she took a delicate step backward.

Miss Turner snatched up her glass. "No, no," she said quickly. "Thank you, really, but I'll get it myself." She fanned herself lightly with her hand. "I could do with a bit of air. And I should like to find Monsieur Satie, and thank him. Would you care for something, Eugénie?"

"Sank you, *non.*"

"Mr. Beaumont?"

"No thanks."

"C'mon," said Hemingway. "I'll show you where it is."

Miss Turner glanced at Miss Aubier, then turned back to Hemingway and smiled. "Thank you."

Hemingway led her off. Along the way, he stepped on my foot. He didn't notice that, either.

"So," said Miss Aubier, "for how many years have you done zis work?"

"Since after the War."

"And you enjoy it?"

"Darling?" said Rose Forsythe, clamping onto my arm. "Do you know Ernest Hemingway?"

"We've met."

Rose's blue eyes were brighter than they'd been when she left. "Wasn't that Ernest I just saw, going off with Miss Tanner?"

"Turner," I said. "Yeah, it was."

She turned to Miss Aubier and she said in an excited mock whisper, "Does the poor thing know that Ernest is married?"

"Yes," said Miss Aubier. "And I believe zat Jane can . . ." She paused, frowning, as though trying to remember the word. ". . . fend? Yes, fend for herself."

"I hope so," said Rose. "Ernest can be *extremely* charming." She leaned toward the other woman, lowering her voice and her eyebrows. "If you know what I mean."

"Yes," said Miss Aubier, without lowering anything. "I expect I do." By now I was pretty sure that she had a nice turn in irony.

Rose turned to me and squeezed my arm. "Come along, darling. There are *thousands* of people I want you to meet." She turned back to Miss Aubier. "It's such a treat to see you,

Eugénie. You look *divine* in that Chanel. And I can't *wait* for tomorrow. I know *exactly* what I'm going to wear.''

"I look forward," said Miss Aubier, "to discovering zis.''

"Well, then, *au revoir*. Until then.''

Miss Aubier nodded to Rose, nodded to me.

"Nice to meet you," I said.

She smiled. "For me as well.''

After we were a few feet away, Rose looked up at me and said, "She's lovely, isn't she?''

"Yeah.''

"But so *pale*. Men don't like that in a woman. And that dress of hers didn't suit her at all.'' Playfully, she jerked at my arm. "What did you think of her English friend?''

"I didn't get much of a chance to talk to her.''

"They're so *cold*, aren't they, those English women? Dickie used to say that they had icicles in their panties.''

"He was a clever guy.''

"He was *brilliant*, darling. Oh, there's Juan.''

Rose hauled me around the room and she introduced me to people. She was as pleased as punch to have me with her, or she seemed to be, and I felt like a very large marlin who'd been landed in a very small boat. I met Juan and Bob and Kay and Pablo and Man Ray and Kiki and Djuna, and Rose would say pleasant things about most of them beforehand and unpleasant things afterward. A lot of the people told me that it must be fascinating to be a Pinkerton, and I told them that it certainly was.

From time to time I glanced around, looking for Miss Turner, but she and Hemingway had disappeared. Finally I saw her again, talking to the small bearded man, the piano player.

After a while, Rose fluttered off to the bathroom once more, leaving me with a tall, bulky Englishwoman who looked like Jack Dempsey and who wore a tweed skirt and jacket, a white shirt and black tie, and big polished brogues. She explained to me why the English were better off than the Americans. "You Americans, with your airplane minds and their shining, dynamic velocity, find us so stodgy and stolid, but generations of experience have taught us not to become easily upset, and all of our classes have born in them the tradition of noninterference.''

"Right," I said. "Excuse me. I see a friend."

It was Ledoq, and he had been slowly circling around the room, working it like a Tammany politician, smiling, nodding, chatting.

When I came up to him he was talking to Bob and Kay and he was saying, "Yes, Marxism is a science. Much like phrenology."

"Excuse me," I said to Bob and Kay. "Mr. Ledoq, I wonder if I could talk to you for a minute."

"Ah, Monsieur Beaumont. What a surprise!" He shook my hand. "Do you know Robert and Kay?"

"We've met, yes."

"Well then, of course, Monsieur, I am at your disposal." He turned to Bob and Kay and made his pert little bow.

"Listen, Henri," I said when I had him over in an empty corner. "You see that tall woman over there? In the blue dress? Talking to the man with the beard?"

"Erik Satie, yes. An amusing composer." He stroked his goatee. "She is English, I should think. Quite attractive, really, in that sedate English way. Without the spectacles, and with a dab or two of makeup, she would be quite stunning. I cannot introduce you to her, *mon ami*. Sad to say, I do not know her."

"I do. Her name is Jane Turner and she's the Pinkerton operative who's working with the Forsythe family."

He raised an eyebrow. "Truly?" He glanced over at Miss Turner, looked back at me. "My opinion of Monsieur Cooper has just risen by several degrees."

"I don't want to be seen talking to her," I said. "Not alone. There are too many people on my tail right now. And it's possible that someone here knows LaGrande. Can you do me a favor?"

"But of course."

"Try to talk to her. Alone. Explain who you are and tell her what we know so far. And find out what she's learned."

"But Monsieur LaGrande is aware that I am working with you."

"Yeah, but would he be surprised if he found out that you

spent some time talking to an attractive woman?''

He nodded sagely. "No. Of course not.'' He looked over at Miss Turner, looked back at me, and then said happily, "It will be a great pleasure, *mon ami*.''

I smiled. "You'll be professional about it, right?''

"But how can I be professional when I am, like the celebrated Pierre Reynard, merely an amateur sleuth?''

"Do your best.''

"Ah,'' he said, and nodded. "I comprehend. There is a connection there. Between you and the woman.''

"No. I'm just guessing that Cooper would be pretty unhappy, with both of us, if he found out that you hadn't been professional.''

He nodded again. "Yes. Yes, of course.'' He frowned. "But how shall I persuade her that I am in fact your emissary?''

"Mention 'Maplewhite.' It's the name of the place I met her. An estate in England.''

"Maplewhite,'' he repeated.

"And give her the phone number of the apartment,'' I said. "Ask her to call me tomorrow, if she can get to a private line.''

"Very well. Is there anything else?'' He smiled. "Are you sure, *mon ami*, that there is no *billet doux* for me to deliver? No quickly scrawled endearment?''

"No. Thanks, Henri. I'm going to try—''

"*There* you are. And *Henri*, what a *pleasure*! How *are* you? I haven't seen you for *ages*.''

Ledoq smiled. "And I have spent all of them, my dear Rose, pining for the sight of you.''

"Isn't he *terrible*?'' she asked me, delighted. "You're *incorrigible*, Henri.'' She squeezed my arm and looked up at me with those bright shiny blue eyes. "Having fun, darling?''

I think that Ledoq's mouth may have twitched a bit at the "darling.''

"Yeah,'' I said. "But I've got a lot to do tomorrow. I'm sorry, Rose, but I'll have to take off. Will you be able to get a taxi?''

"But darling, there's no need for that. I was *just* going to suggest leaving myself. We'll go together—let me say good-bye to Gertrude. I'll be right back.''

Ledoq watched her walk away, then turned to me. "I see that there will be no need for me to purchase extra croissants in the morning."

"Yeah there will. And could you get some milk, too?"

"Milk?" He frowned. "Are you planning to adopt an infant?"

I smiled. "When do you think you'll get back to the apartment?"

"Within an hour or two, I imagine. After I confer with your Mademoiselle Turner."

"I'll be at the apartment."

"We shall see."

"Ah, Beaumont." It was Miss Stein. I was a bit surprised to see her upright. "Hello, Henri," she said. "Very nice to see you." She turned back to me. "Rose told me that you were leaving and I did want you to have this." She held out a book. "*Tender Buttons*. You will find it very enlightening. It is perhaps my most important work. One of them, anyway."

"Thank you," I said, and I took the book. If I kept meeting writers, pretty soon I could open up a lending library.

"And may I have a private word with you?"

"Sure. Will you excuse me, Mr. Ledoq?"

"But of course. Perhaps we will meet again, before you leave Paris."

"I hope so."

Ledoq smiled his prim smile, turned, and walked away. I glanced around the room, found Miss Turner, saw that she was back with Miss Aubier. And I saw that Rose Forsythe was with them. She was leaning forward, smiling with pleasure, as she spoke.

"Now, Beaumont," said Miss Stein. "It is of course none of my business, and normally I would say nothing about it, but you see I quite enjoyed speaking with you and I quite enjoyed speaking with her. I liked her very much, and I like you very much, and I would like to offer my help."

"Excuse me? Are we talking about Rose?"

"No. We are not talking about Rose. We talked about

Rose earlier this evening, and I believe that I said everything that I would want to say about Rose. At the present moment we are talking about Miss Jane Turner."

"The Englishwoman?"

"Beaumont, please do not insult me. I am a writer, you know, and as such I am gifted with a deep insight into the human character. I saw the way that you looked at her when you arrived, and I saw the way that she looked at you, and I have seen the way that the two of you have continued to look at each other over the course of the evening. It is very clear to me that you know each other. Now. Let me ask you this. Is Miss Turner in some kind of trouble?"

"No," I told her. "Not right now. But she might be, if anyone else found out that I knew her."

"They will not learn of it from me. You have my word on it. And I do not think that you need to worry about someone else noticing tonight what I noticed. Few people are as perceptive as I am, you see."

"Right."

"I do not want to know more about this matter now, although naturally I would appreciate a full explanation at some time in the future."

"When I can, I'll tell you."

"Very good. Now. Is there some way in which I can be of assistance to you, or to her?"

"I don't think so. But thank you, Miss Stein."

"You are quite welcome. When you finish the book, please do tell me how much you liked it. Will you be going to the party on Saturday, at Eugénie's house in Chartres? We could discuss it then."

"Nope. Sorry. I won't be going to the party."

"Well, I shall be at home tomorrow, if you would like to give me your reaction by telephone."

"Fine. If I finish it by then, I'll let you know."

"Good evening, then."

"Good evening."

And slowly she turned and then slowly she moved away through the crowd, like an ocean liner through a fishing fleet. Rose was coming from the opposite direction, and she inclined her head toward Miss Stein and she said something quick and enthusiastic in passing, and Miss Stein slowly nodded. Rose fluttered up to me, her face shining as she arranged the shawl around her shoulders.

"Shall we go, darling?"

In the cab she held my hand tightly while she chattered away about Pablo and Juan and Bob and Kay and the others, and I sat there and I made agreeing sounds and watched the city slide by the window. And then, as we turned onto Rue de Lille, I realized that something was different in her voice.

I looked at her. She was still chattering away as though nothing had changed, but in the shifting light from the street-lamps I could see the two tracks of tears that trembled down her cheeks, leaving dark wavering trails of mascara.

"Rose?" I said, and suddenly her voice cracked and she gave out a single sob, almost a cough, and then she bent forward, her small hands balled into tight fists against her face, and she pressed her head against her knees.

Her shoulders rose and fell, jerkily. When she spoke, her voice was muffled. "I *miss* him," she said, and her shoulders convulsed again. "I miss him so *much*."

I reached out and put my hand on her back and quickly she raised her head and turned and came into my arms. As frail as a small child's, her body shook against my chest. After a moment she raised her head slightly, took a couple of deep ragged breaths, trying to get her control back. But she broke down again, coughing those harsh, racking sobs.

We had reached number 27. The driver pulled over and waited. He didn't mind waiting. He was on the meter.

She sucked in a deep breath. "He was always *there*," she said into my neck. "I could look over, from anywhere in a room, and he'd be standing there. And when—" she took another deep breath—"and when he saw me watching him, he'd smile at me. That wonderful smile of his." She coughed out another sob and she collapsed against me.

I stroked her narrow back for a few minutes. Slowly, the sobs grew softer. Finally she sniffled once and she pushed herself off my chest. She turned her head away. "I'm sorry, darling," she said, keeping her head averted as she opened her purse and searched inside it. She sniffled again. She found a handkerchief, blew into it, dabbed it at one eye, then the other. "I must look a mess."

She turned to me. Mascara was still smudged along her cheeks. "And I just can't make love to you, darling. I know you'll think I'm a *terrible* tease, the way I've been acting all night. I *did* want to do it, I was looking forward to it *ever* so much. I thought it would help me—help me stop thinking about Dickie. But I know it won't. Nothing will. I'll never stop thinking about him."

She looked down, looked back up. "I want to do it, darling, I still want to, honestly I do, but I know I can't. I'm so sorry."

"It's okay, Rose," I said.

"It's just that I need to be alone right now."

"Sure."

"And darling, I really don't think that I'll be up to that masquerade party tomorrow night. At Eugénie's. Do you mind terribly?"

"No. It's okay, Rose."

She took my hand. "We'll get together some other time? Maybe you'll be in Paris again someday?"

"I'm sure I will."

"And you'll telephone me?"

"Of course." As Miss Stein suggested, a Pinkerton doesn't always say what he believes.

"And we'll laugh at how silly I was. And we'll have a *wonderful* time together, I promise. None of this *melodrama*."

"Is there anyone you can call, Rose? Tonight? Someone who can come stay with you?"

She shook her head. "I don't want to see anyone." She squeezed my hand. "I'll be all right, darling. Honestly. I've got something to help me sleep. I'll be much better tomorrow. I'll be fine tomorrow." She squeezed my hand again. "Thank you."

She leaned forward, kissed me quickly on the cheek, and then she swung around and opened the door and climbed out of the taxi. She shut the door, looked down at me through the window, held up her small, perfect hand and waved goodbye, moving just her fingers up and down, opening the hand

and closing it. Then she drew the shawl more tightly about her, and she turned and walked into the courtyard.

"M'sieur?" said the cab driver.

"Champs-Elysées," I told him. He took off.

I glanced through the rear window. No one was following. But I was still playing it safe—when I got to the Champs-Elysées, I would get another cab and then return to the apartment and wait for Henri Ledoq.

I sat back in the seat and I wondered what Miss Turner was doing right now.

Dear Evangeline,

If you open this letter first, before the other, please put this one aside until you've read that one. It is important, I believe, that you read my ravings in their proper order, and so gain an accurate picture of my rapid descent into lunacy. After you've read them both—if, that is, you can bring yourself to read them both—please feel free to burn them.

I could, of course, tear open the envelope containing the first letter and append these ravings to those. But the envelope (and this stationery) is Eugénie's, and it's so lovely that I cannot bring myself to damage it. A lunatic I may be, but I am a frugal lunatic.

It is now after three in the morning. I doubt that I shall ever sleep. And I am to meet the children in only seven hours, at the Gare du Montparnasse. Perhaps they can hire a cart, hurl me into it, and haul me directly to the sanatorium.

I know that I am being ridiculous. But am I being ridiculously ridiculous or am I being only moderately ridiculous? I know that I have no claim whatever on Mr Beaumont. But I was caught utterly off my guard by his appearance at Miss Stein's. With that woman attached to him like a lamprey eel.

She was so *obvious*, Evy.

I expect that I would feel less upset about her being obvious if she had also been plain and drab and grotesquely overweight. She was none of those things, alas.

She was, however, as I said, terribly short. I believe, as a general principle, that terribly short women, no matter how *chic* and how attractive, ought never accompany tall American Pinkerton operatives. It is unbecoming. It is unseemly. It is unfair.

I suppose that I should tell you about the evening. Better to scribble about it than to lie here fretting over it. You will want to learn, I think, what occurred between me and Ernest Hemingway in the kitchen. And certainly you will want to learn what I've discovered about your friend Sybil Norton.

It was, all in all, quite an eventful evening.

We arrived at Miss Stein's atelier at about six in the evening. It is located in a courtyard on Rue de Fleurus, not far from the Jardins du Luxembourg. We were admitted by Miss Stein's companion, Alice Toklas. According to Eugénie, the two of them have been together, here in Paris, for many years, since long before the War. Both of them are American.

I liked Miss Toklas. Very thin and frail-looking, a woman of some forty-five years with exotically dark skin and almost Asiatic features, she spoke perfect French in a very soft voice. She wore her black hair in a short pageboy that was not, I felt, entirely becoming; and her longish black dress was several years out of fashion. But I don't believe that Miss Toklas much cares for fashion.

I know that Miss Stein does not. Approximately the same age as Miss Toklas, she was wearing a shapeless black velvet affair, designed, no doubt, to conceal her bulk, which is considerable. But then so is her presence. She has the face of a Roman emperor, strong and forceful, almost masculine; but, with her dense black hair drawn up into a loose bun, she resembles nothing so much as the matriarch, sedate and sage, of some Mediterranean village. For most of the evening she sat nearly immobile in a padded chair near the fireplace, greeting her guests as they wandered over, dispensing observations and opinions and smiles. She has a great many opinions, but she has quite as many smiles. And she has really a wonderful laugh, hearty and jolly and full, like a lorry driver's.

There were only a very few people present when we arrived, and Eugénie and I sat for some time with Miss Stein. She speaks v-e-r-y s-l-o-w-l-y, and with deliberate, almost ponderous conviction, like some Delphic priestess. She was pleased to learn that I was English.

'I very much like the English people in general,' she said. 'The English people in general exhibit very good taste and very good judgement. They very much admire my work, for example. As it happens, I am to be interviewed tonight by a young man from Oxford, in England, about my work. He has studied it intently, and he recognises its great importance. Have you been to Oxford?'

'Years ago,' I told her. 'It's a beautiful city.'

'Yes, it is. It is a beautiful city. I have been asked to go there and speak about my work, and perhaps one day I shall do so. This would of course make them very happy in Oxford. But it is very difficult for me to leave Paris nowadays. Alice and I were forced to leave it during the War, and I find nowadays that I do not want to leave it at all. Do you like Paris?'

'I love it. I love everything about it.'

'This afternoon,' said smiling Eugénie in French, 'we went to Virginia Randall's house. Virginia was quite taken with Jane.'

Miss Stein nodded. 'I am not at all surprised to learn that Virginia was quite taken with Jane.' She smiled at me. 'But from what I know about human nature, and I know much about human nature, I would be very surprised to learn that you were taken with Virginia in precisely the same way.'

I felt my ears becoming toast once more. 'She was very kind to me.'

'She is a kind person. She is a very kind person. But I have noticed that her kindness is more often than not extended toward beautiful and intelligent young women.'

'I am, then, one of the exceptions.'

She laughed. 'You are modest. I admire modesty in other people, perhaps because I have none myself. But the modesty of many modest people is in my experience quite appropriate. They possess nothing at all of which they may rightly be proud, except of course the modesty itself.' She smiled. 'But you, I think, have much of which you may rightly be proud.'

Possibly it will not surprise you to learn that I found myself warming to Miss Stein.

Just then, behind me, someone pronounced her name in a thin but very proper English voice.

'Ah, Desmond,' said Miss Stein. 'There you are. Desmond, this is Eugénie Aubier and Jane Turner. And this is Desmond Spottiswode, an interesting young man who has come all the way from Oxford to ask me questions about my work. Will they be penetrating questions, Desmond? I have a great fondness for penetrating questions.'

'I certainly hope so,' he said. He was in his early twenties, tall and willowy, fair-haired, clean shaven, nicely dressed in a black suit; but he possessed, the poor man, a facial tic which kept his eyes blinking uncontrollably.

He turned to Eugénie and me and said, 'How do you do?'

We said our hellos, and then Eugénie stood up. 'We'll leave you for a time, Gertrude,' she said, again in French. 'I'll show Jane your paintings.'

'I am sure that she will enjoy them,' said Miss Stein. 'All of them are very good and some of them are extraordinary. But do not run off, either of you, without saying goodbye. If you would like something to drink, there is wine in the kitchen. You must help yourselves. My cook is at her mother's house today.'

'I felt so *sorry* for him,' said Eugénie when we were a few paces away. 'In another minute I should have been blinking as well, in sympathy—and without end, I fear. I could not have helped myself.'

I haven't really told you about Eugénie, have I? Perhaps, while Mr Beaumont and the floozy are amusing themselves offstage, preparing themselves for their entrance, I ought to do so.

She is simply wonderful, Evy. She is clever and amusing and gay. Yes, of course, she is rich; richer even than Miss Randall. But, like Miss Randall's, her wealth has not tainted her; it has not hardened her. She derives as much happiness from the curl of a rose petal as she does from the drape of a dinner gown. Her full name is Eugénie Aubier De Saintes—but she never uses the last part and will not permit anyone else to use it either. Titles, she says, are *passé*. She is kind, and she is compassionate. And she is very French. (One aspect of her compassion is that she feels genuinely sorry not only for hapless young Englishmen, but also for everyone in the world who has had the misfortune to be born elsewhere than France.) I like her very much.

As a source of information about Richard Forsythe and Sabine von Stuben, however, she is something of a disappointment. She scarcely knew them; and what she knew *of* them, she says, had not inclined her to learn more. Her brother, the count, knew them better, she says; and for a time he was, shall we say, particularly well acquainted with Miss von Stuben.

But this relationship, which Eugénie describes as '*insignifiant*', had ended some months before Mr Forsythe and Miss von Stuben died. And the count was with Eugénie in Chartres on the day of their deaths, she informs me; and so could have had nothing directly to do with them.

Perhaps tomorrow, at the party, I shall be able to learn something from him.

I had so been looking forward to the party. (And, I confess, to the count.) But now—if I didn't feel that I possessed several good Pinkerton reasons for going there, I should prefer to spend tomorrow evening in bed.

This evening, I mean to say.

I should prefer, actually, to spend all of today in bed. And possibly the remainder of my life. I am so tired, Evy.

But I have yet another reason for preferring beds to parties, and we shall come to it shortly.

Back to our drama. Scribble scribble.

For a few moments Eugénie and I wandered the room, looking at the paintings. (As I said before, I preferred the paintings of Virginia Randall to these, most of which were portraits of Miss Stein.) More guests had arrived. They had gathered in the corners and in small clusters throughout the room. The smell of cigarette smoke was drifting along the air, through wavering ribbons of chatter and slender threads of laughter.

Eugénie introduced me. I met Pablo Picasso, who spoke lovely French with a lovely Spanish lilt to it. I met Juan Gris, another Spaniard. I met two American writers, Robert McAlmon and Kay Boyle. And then I met Ernest Hemingway.

I had told Eugénie how very much I had enjoyed those short stories. At the time, she had smiled and said that I might have an opportunity to meet the author. And now, when she saw him amidst the crowd, she went off, smiling again, and brought him back to me.

He is, quite simply, astonishing. He is big and robust and strikingly handsome. Not handsome as the count is handsome, in that dark, poetic, romantic, European fashion. He is handsome in a vibrant, vigorous, dimpled, curiously boyish American fashion. He is perhaps six feet tall, broad-shouldered and broad-chested. His swarthy face is broad as well, with a thick thatch of dark brown hair, a dark brown moustache, and dark brown eyes that scrunch up at their corners when he smiles, which he does often, and charmingly, showing a very large number of very white teeth.

Charming, yes: he was at first quite unbelievably charming. Standing before him, in the full glare of that beaming smile and those beaming eyes, all that churning male energy of his, was a bit like standing before a blast furnace.

His clothes, I should tell you, were unprepossessing: the sort of clothes that might be worn by a gamekeeper on a Sunday visit to his wife's relatives: heavy shoes, brown trousers, a grey wool jumper over a plaid shirt, a slightly rumpled and slightly stained brown wool coat.

Initially, it seemed to me hardly possible that this vigorous, slightly rumpled, and aggressively handsome gamekeeper could be the same person who wrote the beautiful evocative prose of the stories. Within a few moments, it seemed still less possible.

He fairly glowed as he shook my hand. 'Great to meet you, Jane. English, hey? I've got a lot of English friends. Terrific people, the English. Eugénie says you liked my work?'

'I thought,' I said, 'that the short stories I read were beautifully written.'

His glance dipped to my bosom. 'That's great. Always good to hear.' He turned his beam onto Eugénie. 'Especially from a beautiful girl, hey?'

She smiled.

'They were very sensitive,' I said. 'And very honest, I thought.'

He turned back to me. Lowering the intensity of his beam, he nodded seriously. 'That's what I'm shooting for. Honesty. That's the hardest thing. Getting rid of the crap. When I sit down, I try to write one honest sentence, one sentence that's good and honest and true. Doesn't matter if it takes me all day.'

'But surely,' said Eugénie, with a faint smile, 'you cannot stop at merely zee one sentence.'

'I *start* with one,' he said—a bit irritably, I thought. 'And then I write another one. The important thing is the battle with the truth. And the battle *for* the truth.' He turned to me and, turning up the intensity, he said, 'So, Jane. Been in town for long?'

'Only a day or two.'

'Having a good time?'

'A wonderful time. I love Paris.'

Briefly he examined my bosom once more, perhaps to satisfy himself that it had not ambled off since his last survey, and then he beamed into my eyes again. 'It's great, hey? It's a feast, Paris.'

'Yes,' I said, 'but it's a sort of moveable feast, isn't it? It leaves you with memories so powerful that you can never really forget them. They stay with you forever.'

He nodded seriously again. 'You do any writing yourself?'

I laughed. 'Not at all.'

He beamed again—as though relieved, I thought. 'Makes you the only person in Paris, probably, who isn't looking for a book contract. Listen, I'm going to go grab some wine. Gertrude's always got good stuff. Can I bring you some?'

'I oughtn't, really. I've drunk quite a lot of it today.'

He grinned. 'You're in Paris, hey? And it's free. C'mon.'

'Well, perhaps a very small glass.'

'Great. Eugénie?'

'Yes, please, Ernest. Thank you.'

'Okay. Be back in a minute.'

When he turned, his arm brushed against the side of a small table standing against the wall. Some statuary on it wobbled. He seemed unaware of this.

As his broad back lumbered off through the crowd, I turned to Eugénie. She was smiling at me. 'You must trust the Art,' she said, 'and not the Artist.'

'Hey?' I said.

She laughed. 'But he is, you must admit, a very handsome man.'

'He's striking. I'm surprised he's not married—well, on second thought, perhaps I'm not surprised.'

'But he is married. At the moment, his wife is pregnant.'

'But why, then, is he . . . acting that way with me?'

Another smile. 'As he says, this is Paris.'

A few moments later he returned with three glasses, carrying them as carefully as a miner might carry dynamite. He offered one to Eugénie, one to me, kept one for himself, and then raised it, beaming. 'Cheers, hey?'

'Cheers,' said Eugénie and I.

He drank, and a small gout of wine shot past his mouth and down his left cheek and splattered onto his shoulder. He lowered his glass, put it into his left hand, and brushed at the shoulder carelessly with the back of his right. I looked politely off—and directly into the eyes of Mr Beaumont.

With him, of course, was the slim, sleek, terribly short floozy, wearing her sleek silk dress and a black cloche hat and, wrapped around her tiny shoulders, a black silk shawl. They had just entered the room, and they were following Miss Toklas.

He had clearly recognised me. But, with a small, quick, peremptory shake of his head, he signalled me to ignore him. He continued to follow Miss Toklas, the floozy clinging to his arm as though she had just been dragged from the roaring surf.

Mr Hemingway was prattling about bullfights—he had been to one, or he had been in one—and his face was very serious once again as he spoke of bravery and grace with that tedious solemnity which men often adopt when they discuss the killing of innocent animals. But I was thinking about Maplewhite, and the days there, two years ago, when I first met Mr Beaumont.

He and the floozy were talking to Miss Stein when Mr Hemingway, attempting to demonstrate the correct way to perform some intricate bullfighting movement, a toreador or a corridor or something, brushed his arm against the table again, with more force this time. The table swayed for an instant, then swung away from the wall and hurtled to the floor. Statuary rolled helter-skelter across the carpet—Mr Picasso, I saw, was struck in the ankle by a bust of Hadrian.

Nothing was seriously damaged, except possibly Mr Picasso, who began to limp to the far side of the room, glancing back warily over his shoulder; but Mr Hemingway hadn't finished yet. As he lunged for the table, his elbow had slapped against one of the wall paintings—which jerked to the side and slapped against another painting. For an instant I had a terrible vision: all the paintings in the room, from one wall to the next, slapping at each other in series, like large dominoes.

Attempting, no doubt, to avert this very disaster, Mr Hemingway reached forward—and was immediately thumped in the knuckles by a painting on its return arc. It was a heavy painting, a portrait of Miss Stein, and the blow probably smarted. He stepped back and shook his hand rapidly.

'Are you all right, Ernest?' Eugénie asked him.

He stopped shaking his hand. Beaming, he shrugged with heroic nonchalance. 'It's nothing, hey? I got a lot worse than this in the War.'

In a moment Miss Toklas had arrived to make small cooing noises over Mr Hemingway's injury. She prescribed a large serving of *coq au vin*: a peculiar course of therapy, I thought, but one to which Mr Hemingway readily agreed. As she led him off to the kitchen, he beamed at me over his shoulder. 'Back in a minute.'

Within less than a minute, who should suddenly come swirling out of the crowd, her tiny eyes wide and her tiny red mouth gaping in a smile, but the slim, sleek, terribly short floozy herself, calling out Eugénie's name.

'*Merde,*' said Eugénie under her breath. But she greeted the woman politely enough: 'Rose. How nice to see you.'

They embraced, brushing cheeks and pecking at the air, and then Eugénie introduced me: 'Rose, zis is my friend Jane Turner, from England. Jane, zis is Rose Forsythe.'

That came as a shock. I knew her name, of course, and I had seen her picture, in London; but I simply hadn't recognised her. Of course, I hadn't expected to see her flitting about Paris, one tiny hip glued to the side of Mr Beaumont's knee.

We said hello. I even managed a smile. Eugénie had not mentioned my connection to the family of Mrs Forsythe's husband, and I saw no reason to do so myself.

Eugénie said to her, 'I have not seen you since Richard's death. I was very sorry to hear of zis.'

'Yes, *thank* you,' said Mrs Forsythe. Sadly, she said, 'You're very kind, as always. It was a horrible thing. I was a *wreck*.' She smiled suddenly. 'But guess what? Tonight I'm doing something about it. Did you see that *beautiful* man I came with? Over there, talking to Gertrude? Not the blinky one—the other one. Isn't he a *dream*? He's a Pinkerton from London—a private detective—and Claire's hired him, Dickie's mother, because she *still* can't believe, poor thing, that Dickie killed himself.'

'He is English?' asked Eugénie.

I nearly blurted out his nationality myself, but Mrs

Forsythe said, 'No, he's from the States. Isn't he *delicious*?'

'And he is here officially tonight?'

'He's in *Paris* officially,' said Mrs Forsythe, and she added, with a conspiratorial smile, 'but he's with *me* tonight. He's got a teensy-weensy little crush on me, to tell you the truth. And, just between you and me—'

'Ah,' said Eugénie abruptly. 'Excuse me, Rose.' She turned to me and said in French, 'Didn't you say that you enjoyed the music of Erik Satie?'

'Yes,' I said. 'Very much.' *A teensy-weensy little crush*?

'He is here,' said Eugénie. 'I will introduce you.'

And she moved off, leaving me with Rose Forsythe.

'You speak French, do you, Miss Tanner?' she asked me.

I plucked another smile from my rapidly dwindling hoard. 'It's Turner, actually. Yes, I do. And you?'

'Not a single *word*. Dickie was always telling me—that's my late husband—that I should learn it, but I just never had the *time*. There were always so many things to *do*. Dickie spoke it fluently, of course. But Dickie did *everything* well.' She glanced over at Mr Beaumont, who still sat with Miss Stein, and then turned back to me. Smiling, her voice lowered, she said, 'But my Pinkerton has a few talents of his *own*, if you know what I mean.'

I was saved from apoplexy, or arrest, by the return of Eugénie, who brought with her a man of perhaps fifty years. Slight and short, he wore a Vandyke beard and a black velvet suit, beautifully tailored but a bit worn and frayed. He carried a walking stick with a round silver head, and he peered at the world through wire-rim spectacles with small brown bitter eyes, like a professor who had never found a promising student, and who had finally stopped looking.

He was rather intimidating. But normally, even so, I should have been thrilled to meet him. You know how fond I am of his music. Mrs Forsythe's presence, however, blunted my enthusiasm considerably.

'Erik,' said Eugénie, 'this is Mademoiselle Jane Turner. You know Rose, of course.'

'I know,' said Monsieur Satie *en francaise*, 'that she cannot speak French.' His hands on the head of the walking stick, he bowed stiffly to Rose, then turned to me. 'And you, Mademoiselle?'

'I speak it, Monsieur.'

'And where are you from?'

'From England.'

'Oh yes? I admire all things English. Their clothing, their architecture, and most especially their cooking.'

'English cooking?'

'They have brought the art of boiling to the peak of its perfection. They boil everything, vegetables, fruit, meat, bread, and often at the same time, in the same pot. It is classical in its simplicity. You need only a pot, a fire, and water. It can be done anywhere, and under the most trying of circumstances.'

I smiled. 'Have you been to England, Monsieur?'

'Never. The reality, I fear, would undo my fantasies—and how, then, could I ever trust them again?'

'Jane,' said Eugénie, 'is a great admirer of your music.'

All the while, incidentally, Mrs Forsythe had been looking back and forth between us, a hopeful smile upon her tiny face, shifting her weight impatiently from one tiny foot to the other, like a child outside a locked lavatory. A lesser person than I might have snatched some petty satisfaction from this.

'Oh yes?' said Monsieur Satie. 'You have heard me playing it, then, from across the Channel?'

'My mother played it for me, when I was a little girl. She purchased the sheets of the *Gymnopédies* on one of our visits to France. I've loved them ever since.'

'Ah,' he said.

'Would you play something, Erik?' asked Eugénie.

'Oh no,' I said. 'Not here. It will be buried beneath all the conversation.'

He smiled. 'That is its intended purpose. It is fur-

niture music, designed to be part of the room, but un-
noticed.'

'You do yourself a great injustice, Monsieur.'

'I am not the first. But I should be happy to play
something.'

He gave each of us another small, stiff bow. He
walked to the piano, rested the stick against its side,
and sat down before it. Raising the keyboard cover,
with no preparation whatever he began to play one of
the *Gymnopédies*.

And immediately this was buried beneath the conversation of Mrs Forsythe. 'He's such a *funny* little
man, isn't he? Dickie thought he was a *genius*, though,
so I guess he's got *something* going for him.'

On and on she babbled about Dickie and about her
gorgeous Pinkerton. I was perversely fascinated, of
course, by her Pinkerton comments; but at the same
time I was trying desperately to catch a strain or two
of music. At last she said to Eugénie, 'You've *got* to
meet him. I'll go get him, all right?'

Eugénie nodded. 'But of course.'

'Be *right* back,' she said. She raised her tiny right
hand and fluttered her tiny fingers, and then off she
went.

Monsieur Satie was playing another of the *Gymnopédies*.

I have loved this music for most of my life—its
abrupt shifts from lyricism to irony; its playful parodies,
its whimsy; its sweetness, its mystery.

Now, although Monsieur Satie performed it very
well, as I awaited the arrival of Mr Beaumont the notes
seemed flat and dull. They brushed against me, lifeless,
and fell to the carpet at my feet like brittle leaves.

And then he was there, having been towed across
the room by Mrs Forsythe. I can scarcely recall a word
of what I said. I know that my hands were chill, as
though they had been plunged into ice water.

Eugénie and Mr Beaumont did most of the talking,
while Mrs Forsythe stood there gleefully fondling him.

She is a champion fondler. If ribbons are given for fondling, she has mountains of them.

She did, however, in the midst of the fondling, wheedle from Eugénie an invitation for Mr Beaumont to the masquerade party.

And isn't that grand? More fondling tonight. Another reason, as I said, to remain in bed.

After a few moments, mercifully, she dragged herself away from him and set off for the 'little girls' room'. Eugénie and he talked briefly about the death of Richard Forsythe, and I believe I mumbled a phrase or two, and Monsieur Satie finished the piece, and we all applauded, and then Mr Hemingway reappeared. (We are approaching the famous kitchen scene.) He had met Mr Beaumont before, and knew that he was a Pinkerton. For a time he beamed at everyone—unaware that a morsel of *coq au vin* was lodged between two of his teeth—and, after a short time, he offered to refresh my wine, which at some point, quite unwittingly, I had finished.

I saw this as a chance to escape, and said that I would find my own—'I could do with a bit of air'— but Mr Hemingway insisted upon guiding me to the kitchen, as though it were located somewhere in Equatorial Africa; and, reluctantly, I accepted.

This was, I'm afraid, an error.

Inside the small, empty kitchen, beaming furiously, he poured me some wine, poured some for himself, and handed me my glass. Holding his in both hands, he leaned back against the counter. I heard, behind him, something clatter as it fell. He failed to notice this. 'So, Jane,' he said. 'What brings you to Paris, hey?'

I was in no great hurry to rejoin Mr Beaumont; and by now, probably, Mrs Forsythe was back at her fondling. 'Just a brief visit. Excuse me, but you've a small piece of something stuck to your tooth.'

'Yeah?' He scraped at his teeth with his index finger, sucked on the finger, ran his tongue along the teeth, and then displayed them in a stupendous grin. 'Gone?'

'Yes.'

'Thanks. So you're a good friend of Eugénie's? Close, I mean?'

He was trying, of course, to determine whether I shared Eugénie's preferences.

'I like her very much,' I said.

'Great girl,' he said, beaming. 'Great girl. So where'd the two of you meet?'

'She is a friend of the family for whom I work. I'm a nanny.' This, I felt, might dim his beam somewhat.

It did. He frowned. 'A nanny?' He looked me up and down, blatantly, and then he beamed again. 'You're pulling my leg.'

I smiled. 'I work for the Forsythe family. Do you know them?'

He seemed puzzled. 'Richard didn't have any kids.'

'Not Richard Forsythe. His uncle's family.'

'Oh yeah. Right. The banker, hey? You're really a nanny?'

'Yes. It was Richard who published those stories of yours, wasn't it?' You see how, in my cunning Pinkerton manner, I am manoeuvring him away from the subject of the nanny and towards the subject of Richard Forsythe.

'Yeah,' he said. 'But I never liked the guy.'

'Why is that?'

'He cheated me on that book deal. And besides, he was a fairy. A homosexual.'

'But, from what I've heard, he was . . . attached to any number of women.'

He waved his hand. 'Window dressing. The French don't like fairies, hey? They hate 'em. Even rich American fairies. So Forsythe put on a big act. But that's all it was, an act.'

'Why do you suppose he committed suicide?'

'Forsythe? What I think it was, I think he just couldn't get a . . . I think he was impotent. That day, I mean. Because he was a fairy, hey? And he went nuts. Killed the girl, the German girl, and then he killed himself.'

'I see.'

'So,' he said. 'Which one of the stories did you like best?'

' "The Big Two-Hearted River'', I think. It was lovely. Did you know Sabine von Stuben?'

'Yeah, that's a good story. One of my best. I'm glad you liked it.'

'I understand that she was involved with some German political party?'

'You didn't like "The Doctor's Son''?'

'I did, yes. I thought it was very fine. Did you know her at all?'

'Unh unh. It was kind of autobiographical. "The Doctor's Son''. I don't know if you got that.'

'I'd thought as much. I've heard from a friend that she wasn't—'

'Yeah?' he said, beaming. 'You saw that? Great.' He drank some of his wine. 'Say, listen. Why don't we go somewhere, you and I, and sit down and talk for a while?'

'I'm sorry, but I really couldn't leave Eugénie.'

'She'll be fine. She's a tough girl, hey? I know a little place, not far from here. Nice wine, not too expensive. We could get to know each other better.'

'I couldn't. Honestly.'

He inhaled deeply and the small kitchen grew abruptly smaller as his chest expanded. He narrowed his eyes and the beam became a smoulder. 'Jane, do you believe that two people, a man and a woman, can meet and see, right away, that there's something honest and true between them?'

'I don't, actually.'

'I could tell, just looking at you, that you were something special. And listen, that little place? With the wine? There's a great little hotel right next door.'

And he winked at me.

'When, exactly,' I said, 'will your wife be having the baby?'

He leaned back, suddenly scowling. To be accurate, it was more of a pout than a scowl. And he was pouting more in annoyance than in embarrassment; and I was not, I soon discovered, its source. 'Isn't that a kick in the head? Hey? Isn't that a punch in the gut? I mean, can you see *me* as a papa?' He pouted again. 'I'm not ready for that crap. I don't know how the hell it happened.'

'Perhaps you could consult a good medical guide.'

'Oh, I know *how* it happened. That's not what I mean. It wasn't *supposed* to happen. Not now.'

'You have all my sympathy, of course.'

Irony was lost on him. 'Thanks,' he said. 'I appreciate it.' He winked again. 'So what do you say? Let's blow this joint.'

'Are you mad?'

'Mad?' He pouted again. 'You said you liked my stuff.'

'I do, very much, but that doesn't mean that I'm going off with you to some hotel.'

He glared at me for a moment. Then he lifted his wine glass to his mouth, drained it, set it down on the counter, looked at me with utter contempt, and said, 'Women.' And with that he lumbered from the room.

Evy, it's nearly seven in the morning. I must bring this—

I haven't told you about Monsieur Ledoq and Sybil Norton.

Very quickly:

I returned to the salon. Mr Beaumont and Mrs Forsythe circulated for a time, and then departed for God knows where, she clinging to him once again like a drowned swimmer. I chatted remotely with people, here and there, and then suddenly I noticed, at my side, a dapper Frenchman. With his neatly trimmed goatee, he reminded me a bit, actually, of Monsieur Satie; but he was rather younger and rather taller. He wore no spectacles, and his suit, while beautifully tailored, was wool and not velvet.

'Mademoiselle,' he said, 'a friend from Maplewhite has asked me to give you his regards.'

'Oh?'

'Yes. May we speak in private?'

'Certainly, Monsieur.'

And, no, Evy, Mr Beaumont had not seen the error of his ways, flung Mrs Forsythe into a nearby hedge, and sent Monsieur Ledoq—for this was he—into the atelier to fetch me. While Mr Beaumont was making merry with the widow, he wanted Monsieur Ledoq to determine what I had learned thus far in my investigation, and to apprise me of what they had learned.

Briefly, regarding the deaths, they had learned:

1. That it was Sybil Norton who discovered the bodies of Richard Forsythe and Sabine von Stuben. She had gone to the hotel room to discuss the publication, by Mr Forsythe, of a volume of her poetry; and you may feel somewhat differently about the creator of Pierre Reynard when you learn that the poems were erotic. (!)

2. That the Prefect of Police, Monsieur Auguste LaGrande, has kept removed from all accounts any mention of the presence of Mrs Norton in the hotel room.

3. That Aster Loving, the Negro jazz singer, died on Thursday night. (Had I found time to read a newspaper, I should have known this myself.) The police believe her death to be an accidental overdose of heroin. Mr Beaumont is dubious, but there seems to have been no connection between Miss Loving and Mr Forsythe for some time.

I cannot think how this brings us any closer to a solution of the mystery. But then at the moment I cannot think.

What I have learned regarding the deaths, all of it, you have read in these interminable letters; and I acquainted Monsieur Ledoq with it, all of it, and provided the names of my sources. I didn't mention the remarkable scene with Mr Hemingway.

I must go. I am a shambles. Perhaps some coffee will help.

I wonder what Mr Beaumont and Mrs Forsythe are doing just now.

All my love,
Jane

Twelve

I WAS WRITING my reports in the living room when Henri Ledoq returned to the apartment. Writing the reports wasn't hard work. There wasn't much to write.

Ledoq was carrying a couple of paper bags, and he seemed surprised to see me. "Ah. You *are* here, *mon ami.*" He smiled. "I had thought that you might not return for a week or so. And that, when you did, you would require the services of a physician."

"I'm here," I said. "Did you talk to Miss Turner?"

"I did, yes. And I was, I assure you, the very essence of professionalism. This was not easily accomplished, I might add. She is a very attractive woman. Are you at all hungry?"

"Yeah, I am," I admitted. I hadn't eaten anything since the steak at lunch. "What did she have to say?"

"Come join me in the kitchen and I shall give you a full account."

In the kitchen, I sat down at the small wooden table while he stood and unpacked his bags. "Wine," he said. "Two bottles of Sancerre, not a noteworthy marque but very drinkable. Cheese. A camembert, one hovering at the exact peak of ripeness—a lovely cheese. And here we have a splendid baguette . . . some Normandy eggs . . . Normandy butter as well . . . and some romaine for the salad." He frowned. "A trifle bruised, I am afraid. But the inner leaves will be fine." He rubbed his hands together. "We shall dine simply but well."

"Miss Turner?" I said.

"As I say, a very attractive young woman." Carefully, he removed his suit coat and draped it over the back of the other chair. "I found her extremely engaging." He walked over to a small door set in the wall and opened it. From a peg inside, he lifted a white apron printed with tiny rosebuds. He slipped the neckband over his head, flattened the material down along his vest, pulled the strings around behind him and tied them in front, at his stomach. "For how long has she been a Pinkerton?"

"A year or two."

He pushed the left sleeve of his shirt up along his arm. "An extremely engaging woman." He pushed the right sleeve up, then tugged open a drawer, peered in, shut it, tugged open another, took out a corkscrew. "Here, *mon ami*, would you do me a great kindness and contend with the wine?"

I took the corkscrew and fiddled with a bottle while Ledoq washed his hands in the sink. He glanced back at me, probably to make sure I wasn't breaking anything. "And extremely competent, she appeared to me," he said as he dried his hands on a towel hanging from a drawer handle.

I got the cork out. "And what was it she said?"

He opened a cabinet and removed a pair of wine glasses. "She is not, as I first suspected, a member of the lesbian sorority." He set the glasses on the table. "She is staying in Paris, you know, with Eugénie Aubier, the sister of the Count De Saintes. Who is, as I believe I told you, a lesbian."

"I remember." I poured some wine into the glasses, put down the bottle.

He picked up a glass and raised it. *"Salut,"* he said.

I took the other glass, raised it. *"Salut."*

He smelled the wine delicately, then took a sip, rolled it around inside his mouth, sucked in a tiny bit of air, swallowed. He thought about it for a moment, and then he said, "Drinkable."

I tasted the wine. It was wine.

"You know," he said thoughtfully, "I do not really approve of lesbianism."

"No? Why's that?"

"It is so unnecessary. There is nothing that one woman

can do for another that a skillful and sympathetic man cannot also do.''

"A man like you, for example."

Smiling, he shrugged. "Well, yes. For example."

"Suppose the woman just happens to like women better?"

"But in such a case I should bring along another woman, a cooperative friend. And the three of us could, together, investigate the possibilities."

"Uh huh. It's a pretty interesting idea, Henri. You get many takers on that?"

"Unfortunately," he said, "no." He sipped at the wine, swallowed, shook his head sadly. "It is such a waste."

"About Miss Turner," I said.

"She is not a lesbian. I am convinced of this, and I am invariably right about such matters."

"I was wondering what it was she told you."

"Ah. My account."

He gave it to me while he prepared the meal. He knew his way around a kitchen, and he moved smoothly as he set out the plates, washed and tore the lettuce, arranged the leaves in a wooden bowl, cracked six eggs, one at a time and one-handed, into an earthenware bowl and then beat them with a fork.

One thing Miss Turner had told him was that Aster Loving didn't like to inject her own heroin. She liked having a man do it for her. "Which would suggest," said Ledoq, looking into a cabinet, "that there might have been a man present that night, in her apartment. Where *does* she keep the bloody mustard? Ah."

"If there was a man there, he could've given her more heroin than she was used to. Accidentally or deliberately."

"Exactement."

"And Miss Turner got this from Forsythe's cousin?"

"Yes." Carefully, he poured some vinegar into a bowl. "Monsieur Forsythe confided in the boy, it would seem." Carefully, he shook some powdered mustard into the bowl.

"But he doesn't know who the man might've been."

"Non." He added some salt. "As her manager told us, Monsieur Forsythe had not seen Mademoiselle Loving for several months before his death." Using a small wooden pep-

per mill, he ground some pepper into the bowl.

"So that doesn't help us much," I said.

"Non." With a fork, carefully but quickly, he stirred the mixture. He poured some oil into the bowl and then stirred the mixture again.

"What else did she have to say?"

He dipped his pinky finger into the mixture, tasted it. *"Bon."* He poured the dressing over the romaine and handed me the bowl. "Could you blend this, *mon ami*? Gently. We do not wish to wound the lettuce."

I took the bowl and he handed me a wooden fork and spoon. I started to toss the salad. He watched me.

"Don't worry, Henri," I said. "I almost never wound the lettuce. What else did Miss Turner say?"

He took a sip of wine. "She told me something fascinating about Sybil Norton and Sabine von Stuben."

"Yeah?"

He put down the wine glass, plucked a box of matches from the counter, opened it, pulled out a match. He struck it, turned on one of the stove's gas burners, and lit the flame. From the row of pots and pans hanging above the stove he took a small copper saucepan and set that on the burner.

"She told me," he cut a thick pat of butter, "that Madame Norton," he tapped the butter lightly into the saucepan, "was giving money to Mademoiselle von Stuben." He shook the saucepan.

"Money?" I said. "Why?" I finished tossing the salad and I ferried a bunch of it onto one plate, then a bunch onto another.

Ledoq was staring down into the saucepan. "It transpires that Mademoiselle von Stuben was collecting money, here in France, from people who sympathized with a political party in Germany." He looked at me. "The German National Socialist Workers party. I have read of them. They are right-wing swine of the very worst sort."

I could hear the butter sizzling. "Why would Sybil Norton give them money?"

He lifted the bowl that held the beaten eggs, poured some of the liquid into the saucepan, put down the bowl. "She is, one must conclude, a right-wing swine herself." Moving the pan quickly with his left hand, he used a fork in his right to play with the eggs. "And Mademoiselle von Stuben was also receiving money from Monsieur LaGrande, our illustrious prefect."

I nodded. "Rose Forsythe told me, the first time I talked to her, that LaGrande was hanging around von Stuben at some party at the Count De Saintes's."

"You know," said Ledoq thoughtfully, "it occurs to me that perhaps this—the money—would also explain Monsieur Reilly's connection to Mademoiselle von Stuben. You remember that the young man in the bar, Jepson, mentioned that they knew each other."

"Somehow I don't see Reilly contributing to a political party."

"Possibly he was contributing someone else's money."

Gently, he slid the omelet onto a plate, and it folded over itself perfectly.

"That's a nice idea, Henri. But whose money?"

He handed me the plate. "I do not know. Do you believe that Monsieur Reilly might still be looking for us?"

"Just because he hasn't found us doesn't mean he's not looking. It probably only means he doesn't know where to look."

"Yes. How very annoying. Oh, by the by, Mademoiselle Turner confirms that Madame Norton was in fact having an affair with Monsieur LaGrande. Eat, *mon ami*. I shall join you in a moment."

"Where did Miss Turner get all this?"

He sliced another pat of butter, tapped it into the saucepan. "From Virginia Randall, an American who has been living for some time in Paris." He poured the rest of the eggs into the saucepan, moved the pan, played with the eggs, and looked over at me. "It is good?"

I hadn't tried it. I took a bite. It was very good, and I said so. "But where did Virginia Randall get it?" I asked him.

"From Sabine von Stuben. Mademoiselle Randall had an affair with her."

I smiled. "Another lesbian?" I took a bite of omelet.

Ledoq shrugged. "There are probably no more of them here in Paris than there are male homosexuals." He slipped the omelet from the pan to a plate, stepped over to the table and put down the plate. Easing down his right sleeve, he said, "But there is less onus on them." He eased down his left sleeve, untied the apron strings. "The French will tolerate lesbians, so long as they remain somewhat discreet." He pulled the apron over his head, carried it back to the cabinet from which he'd taken it. "Mademoiselle Randall does not, but then she is rich. And she is an American." He hung the apron inside and he smiled at me. "We expect eccentricity from Americans. Male homosexualism, however, American or otherwise, is a very different matter."

He returned to the table, lifted his suit coat from the chair, put it on, adjusted it, sat down. He picked up a fork and looked at me. "What are your feelings now, regarding Madame Norton?"

"She never mentioned anything about giving money to von Stuben."

"She simply forgot to do so, no doubt." He took a bite of salad.

"No doubt."

"Here is another interesting item," he said. "According to Mademoiselle Randall, shortly after Mademoiselle von Stuben became involved with Monsieur Forsythe, she ended her involvement with the party." He took a bite of salad.

"How would Randall know that?"

"From Richard Forsythe. He told her that he had given Mademoiselle von Stuben a choice between the party and him, and that she had chosen him."

"Looks like she made the wrong choice."

He frowned. "You say that, *mon ami*, because you are not familiar with the vermin who populate the party."

"Maybe. But Rose Forsythe said pretty much the same thing—that von Stuben had given up on politics after she met Forsythe."

"Perhaps, then, it is true." He took a bite of omelet.

I drank some wine. "What would happen to LaGrande if people found out he was giving money to a German political party?"

Ledoq swallowed. "Yes. An excellent point. I should not be surprised to learn that among people of the right, here in

France, there are many who secretly sympathize with these German swine. But to be seen doing so, publicly, would be a catastrophe. The War is over, but Germany is still the enemy. LaGrande's career would be destroyed."

"And Randall says that LaGrande and Norton were having an affair?"

"Yes, but we already knew this, did we not?"

"Suspected it, yeah. I asked Rose tonight whether Norton had access to the pistol."

He sipped his wine. "Yes?"

"She had access. Five days before he died, Norton was up in Forsythe's study by herself. Rose says that Richard didn't use the gun during those five days. Norton could have taken it, and no one would've been missed it."

"But why would she have done so? We are back to the same question—why would she wish to kill Richard Forsythe?"

"Maybe he was just in the way. Maybe the person she wanted to kill was Sabine von Stuben."

"But again—why?"

"Von Stuben knew that LaGrande and Norton were giving money to the Germans. And she probably knew about Norton's affair with LaGrande. How would Norton's readers feel when they heard about all that?"

"Blackmail. But you are aware, of course, that England, like France, has its share of right-wing swine. These would no doubt applaud Madame Norton's connection to the party. And, as to the affair, from what I know of the people who read crime novels, I expect that another scandal would increase, rather than diminish, Madame Norton's readership. And you are forgetting something, *mon ami*."

"LaGrande."

"Precisely. He is a powerful man. Had he felt threatened by Mademoiselle von Stuben, or felt Madame Norton to be in jeopardy, he could have dealt swiftly with the problem. Mademoiselle von Stuben might simply have disappeared."

"I haven't forgotten him. I'm trying to find a way around him."

"And there are two things more."

"What?"

"Ah." He smiled. "So you cannot invariably read my mind."

"Sometimes I can't read my own. What?"

"First, the fact that Madame Norton was not seen at the hotel until three."

"Maybe the dead desk clerk saw her. Maybe that's why he's dead."

"Perhaps. And, second, the interval between the deaths. If she killed Mademoiselle von Stuben at one o'clock, what were she and Monsieur Forsythe doing for the next two hours? Not dallying, I expect. I hardly think that even Monsieur Forsythe would be up to dallying with the woman who had just killed his mistress."

"I don't know, Henri. Maybe he was trying to talk her out of shooting him."

"Do you believe that?"

"No." I finished off the glass of wine. "Looks like I'll be talking to Sybil Norton again."

Ledoq poured more wine into my glass. "I suggest that you be extremely careful, *mon ami*. You may be right in what you said previously—that Monsieur LaGrande is deliberately allowing us to proceed with all this, simply to see what we learn. If he discovers that we know about his donations to those German pigs . . ." His raised his eyebrows and he shrugged elaborately.

I said, "I think LaGrande's decided that we're not worth bothering with. He's called off his tails. No one followed me from Rose Forsythe's house. If LaGrande wanted to find me again, that'd be the obvious place to pick me up."

"Perhaps he has other plans."

Ledoq was right. LaGrande did have other plans for me. But I wouldn't find out about them until the next day.

We talked for a bit more that night. Ledoq told me that he had given the apartment's phone number to Miss Turner, and that she would try to call me here tomorrow afternoon, after an outing with the Forsythe children.

He asked me if I'd need him tomorrow—he was supposed to attend the masquerade party at the count's house in Chartres. I told me I thought I could take care of things on my

own. In that case, he said, he planned to leave for Chartres
early enough to find himself a hotel room. The party wasn't
until nine tomorrow night, and the last train from Chartres to
Paris left at seven-thirty in the evening. After the party, he
would be staying overnight. But he enjoyed Chartres, he said.
There was a restaurant down by the river that served an es-
timable duck.

He asked me to join him, but I pointed out that I had to
talk to Sybil Norton, and I had to check the telegraph offices
for wires from Houdini and from London.

Before I went off to bed, I asked him to tell me a little
about the National Socialist Party, and he did.

I was up at eight the next morning, and half an hour later I
had showered and dressed. Ledoq was in the living room,
wearing another gray suit and reading another newspaper.

"Any surprises in the paper today?" I asked him.

"Non. Coffee, *mon ami*?"

"Please, Henri. Thank you."

He put the paper aside and stood up. "Sit, sit. I shall bring
it. And I obtained some fresh croissants. I was also, with great
difficulty, able to locate some milk. What does one do with
it, exactly? Bathe in it?"

I smiled. "Thanks, Henri. I'll have a glass of that, too."

He shuddered delicately and walked off.

I glanced up at the painting of the shepherds. They were
still playing their flutes. The sheep were still sleeping. I still
envied them.

A few minutes later, Ledoq brought out a tray that held
coffee, croissants, and a glass of milk. He set it down on the
table and said, "I forgot to ask you last night, but what did
you think of Gertrude Stein?"

I stood, took a cup of coffee, sat back down. "I got a big
kick out of her."

He lowered himself to the sofa. "She can be an amusing
woman. Much more so than perhaps she realizes. Did she
explain to you her philosophy of writing?" He picked up his
coffee cup.

I drank some coffee. Once again it was good. "She said
that with words, you had to be accurate."

"Very profound. It is a pity she did not provide you with her entire doctrine. It is very entertaining. Writers who create a philosophy of writing invariably create one which, magically, transforms their own deficiencies into strengths."

"She gave me one of her books."

"You must tell me how you like it."

"That's what she said."

He smiled. "Of course."

I pulled out my watch, looked at it.

"When are you leaving," he asked me.

"Ten minutes, maybe. You?"

"I have not decided. Soon, possibly. In time to obtain the luncheon duck. But I shall telephone you this afternoon, from Chartres, and give you the name of my hotel."

"Don't use the phone there. Call from a tobacco shop. Let's not leave any obvious record of phone calls to this place."

He frowned. "It will be hugely expensive." He nodded. "But perhaps you are right."

Suddenly he raised his head. "But if you do not attend the party, you will not see my costume."

I smiled. "I guess not."

"One moment." He set down his cup and saucer, stood, and walked off.

Five minutes later he returned. He had taken off his suit coat and replaced it with a long, dark, caped overcoat. On his head he wore a deerstalker cap, and on his face a flesh-colored half mask that gave him a large, beaked nose. He turned to the side to show me his profile, and he put the stem of an enormous calabash pipe between his teeth.

I laughed.

"It is good, eh?" he said.

"It's great, Henri. But what about the goatee? You going to shave it off?"

He stood upright. "Of course not. It is poetic license. But are you certain that you will not change your mind about attending the party? I feel sure that we could locate a costume for you." Beneath that beaked nose, he smiled. "Perhaps Dr. Watson?"

I smiled back. "No thanks."

"You do know that Mademoiselle Turner will be there?"

"Yeah. Listen, Henri. You're taking along the derringer, right? To Chartres?"

"I very much doubt that I shall require it in Chartres. Except possibly at the restaurant, should they ruin the duck."

"You think Reilly's people won't be watching the train station?"

Below the mask, his lips pursed. "Yes. Once again, you are right. I shall bring it. And you, *mon ami*? Might they not be watching the telegraph office also?"

"I've got a Colt," I said.

"But of course," he said.

I didn't need the Colt at the telegraph office. No one was waiting for me there, and neither were any telegrams. I took a taxi to Sybil Norton's apartment, climbed up the seven flights of stairs, and jerked the bell-pull. After a moment, there was a darkening in the door's spyhole. The door opened.

"Mr. Beaumont." She smiled. "What a pleasant surprise."

She was wearing another belted silk dress today, this one gray.

"May I come in?" I said.

"Of course." She stepped back to let me in. She still moved with the languid ease of a thoroughbred. "Please," she said, and gestured for me to enter the living room.

Queen Victoria and George V hadn't moved from their position on the wall, but today there seemed to be even more books piled around the room.

She reached up and she briefly touched her strawberry blond hair, as though making sure it was all there. "May I get you some tea?"

"No thanks. This won't take long."

She smiled. "Goodness. That sounds terribly ominous. Perhaps you ought to sit down."

I sat on the sofa again, and she sat in the same chair she'd used before, her knees together and turned gracefully to the side once again. She still had very good legs.

On the arm of the sofa, the copy of *Ulysses* was in exactly the same spot it had been in yesterday. Maybe Ledoq was right and she wasn't actually reading it. Maybe it was only a prop.

"What is it, then?" she said.

"You didn't tell me," I said, "that you've been giving money to the German National Socialist party."

Her gaze remained level, but now her smile was puzzled. "Wherever did you hear such a thing?"

"No," I said. "The right way to do it, see, is you ask me what the German National Socialist party is."

She stared at me for a moment, and then she said flatly, "I'll make a note of that. I'm sure it will prove useful. And from where, exactly, are you obtaining your information?"

"Doesn't matter. You just confirmed that it's true."

"My politics are, of course, none of your business. Nor are my finances."

"My business is finding out why Richard Forsythe died."

She smiled dryly. "Then my politics are completely irrelevant."

"Maybe not. Sabine von Stuben stopped collecting money for the party, didn't she? After she got involved with Richard."

"Even if she had—and I don't for a moment admit any of this—how could that possibly have had any connection to Richard's death?"

"Von Stuben died, too."

"Yes, and?"

"And maybe she died because someone wasn't happy about her stopping. Someone in the party."

Her face twisted with scorn. "That's preposterous."

"Is it? From what I've heard about them, they're not a very forgiving bunch. They don't mind a little violence now and then."

"Nonsense. Bolshevik propoganda. They're the only group, in all of Germany, who stands between it and communism. And if Germany goes communist, so will Austria. And then France, and then England. Do you know how many people the Bolsheviks have murdered in Russia?"

I noticed that she'd stopped being coy about her connection to the party.

"Millions," she said. "Property seized, homes looted.

Women and children raped and slaughtered. And not just aristocrats, mind you. Farmers, peasants, members of the precious *proletariat*." She said the word with a sneer.

"Moscow's a long way from London," I said.

"Not when Britain is rotting at the core. Not when the British Labor party is riddled with Bolshevik sympathizers and growing every day more powerful."

"Mrs. Norton. I don't want to argue politics with you."

"Just as well," she said. "I suspect that you're extremely ill equipped to do so."

"Maybe. But I do know that a couple of years ago I was in a war. I don't want to be in another one."

"You almost certainly will be, however, if the communists take over Europe."

"Uh huh. And if the National Socialists take over Germany?"

She raised her chin. "There will never be another war between England and Germany. They share a common heritage."

"Yeah. I noticed that in the last one."

Her face twisted again. "You're a very silly man, Mr. Beaumont. One day, perhaps, you'll wake up and see what's right before your face. I only hope that it's not too late."

"Did Sabine stop collecting money after she got involved with Forsythe?"

Her face was closed. "I have nothing further to say."

I stood up. "Thanks. I'll find my own way out."

"And please don't bother to return."

"I think I can manage that," I said.

I left the apartment, climbed down the seven flights of stairs, hailed a taxi and took it back to the telegraph office.

I still had the Colt with me. But when they came at me, I never had time to use it.

Thirteen

THEY WEREN'T VERY subtle.

Outside the telegraph building, I paid the driver and sent the cab off. I planned to walk back to the apartment. I had nothing much to do right then, and it was another fine day—warm and sunny, with a few pale white clouds floating high up there in the pale blue French sky. I thought that it was time for me to see some more of Paris.

Inside the telegraph building, after standing in line for ten minutes, I learned that there was still no wire from Houdini, and still no wire from London about Sabine von Stuben.

I came down the steps to the Rue du Louvre and I turned south, toward the river.

This was the Right Bank again, grand old buildings on either side of the street, expensive suits and dresses parading along the sidewalk.

I had gone only a block or so when they came at me. If I'd been on the other side of the street, and they'd come at me from behind, they probably would have pulled it off.

It was a boxy black Renault, and its passenger window was down and leaning out of that was a man with a beret on his head and a gun in his hand. The gun was a nine-millimeter Luger, eight rounds in the clip, and I just had time to recognize what it was before I was diving for the concrete and going into a roll. From then on, everything moved with the logic of a dream.

I heard the gun crack three or four times, maybe more, and I heard the ping and wail as slugs ricocheted off the pavement, and I heard someone scream, a woman, high-pitched and terrified, and then I heard the roar of the engine as the car raced away. I was still rolling but I hadn't felt the hard fast punch of a slug, and I decided that I was probably alive and that I might as well get up from the sidewalk.

My pants were torn at the knee, and the palms of my hands were scraped raw, but I was okay.

No one had been hit, which seemed impossible. It's not easy to hit a moving target from a moving car, but it doesn't take much effort to hit a bystander.

People were speaking in excited French and holding on to each other, and a young, very pretty girl was crying in her pretty mother's arms, and a woman was still screaming, or maybe it was another woman now, and some men were shouting and waving their arms. And then, before I could slip away, suddenly there was a young cop on the scene, spic-and-span in his blue uniform with its dashing cape and its dandy little cap, and he was holding on to a club in one hand and using the other to hold the whistle he was blowing. It was the loudest whistle I'd ever heard.

He finished with the whistle and he talked to some people and they pointed to me and he came over and looked concerned while he spoke at me in French. And then there was another cop there, an older cop, and bigger, and he spoke English. He had a club in his hand, too.

"You are unhurt, Monsieur?"

"I'm fine," I said. "A little banged up." I showed him my hands—the palms had been scraped. I noticed that my fingers were shaking.

"Do you have your papers with you, Monsieur?"

"Sure." I reached into my coat pocket and took out my passport and I handed it to him. He opened it.

If he had been given the name "Beaumont" earlier in the day, even just a couple of hours ago, he might not have reacted at all. But I imagine that this was the first passport he'd looked at today, and I saw the tiny flicker at the corner of his eye, and I knew that LaGrande had just put out the name, probably in the past few minutes.

I had left Sybil Norton's apartment no more than half an hour ago. But that had given her time to call LaGrande, and it had given LaGrande time to notify the troops.

I hadn't said anything about LaGrande and his party con-
tributions to Norton, but it looked like he wasn't taking any
chances. If I knew about hers, I might know about his.

The cop was good, despite that little flicker. He nodded as
he casually slipped the passport into the side pocket of his
coat, and then he smiled at me, very friendly, and said, "If
you will just come with me, Monsieur. We will have some
questions for the report."

I hesitated. I didn't know what LaGrande had in mind, but
it probably wasn't talking about orphans.

The cop made another mistake then. He saw the hesitation
and he brought up the club.

I was still juiced with adrenaline and I made what was
probably a mistake myself. I blocked the arm with the club,
and I hit him below the rib cage as hard as I could. He said
"Ooof," and he bent forward and I pounded the back of his
neck with my fist and turned to the young cop. He was bringing up his club, but I don't think he really believed that any
of this was happening. I didn't either, but I clipped him anyway, a good hook along the edge of the jaw. As he headed
for the sidewalk I started to run.

There was a crowd by now and a few people grabbed at
me, but I pulled myself loose. Someone shouted, a man this
time. I could hear more whistles blowing, behind me.

" 'Allo?"

"Inspector?"

"Mr. Beaumont! Are you *insane*?"

"What the hell's going on?"

I was calling from a tobacco shop on the Left Bank. Running from the Rue du Louvre, I had ducked into the street
entrance of a hotel bar, then suddenly slowed down like a
drunk in a Mack Sennett short, walked through the bar and
out into the lobby, and through the lobby to the front entrance.
The doorman didn't much like the tear in my pants but he
liked my five-franc note well enough to take it and wave
down a cab. I got into it and said "Boulevard Saint-Michel."
One we reached it, I had made the driver stop at the first sign
that said TABAC.

"You are wanted for questioning," said the Inspector. "It was very foolish of you to strike those officers. What were you *thinking*?"

"What kind of questioning?" I asked him.

"Your violence has been reported. Do you understand what this means? When you are apprehended, you will be dealt with . . . in an unkindly manner. If you will come to my office and surrender yourself, it may be that I can help you."

"Maybe," I said. "What kind of questioning?"

"Concerning the death of a Paul Trebeque."

"And who is Paul Trebeque?"

"A man who was found shot in the sewers last night. He had been dead for at least twenty-four hours. A witness has identified you as the man responsible."

"What witness?"

"His brother."

"And that's what you've got? For evidence?"

"The coat to your suit was found at the scene."

"That's impossible," I said, but even before I finished saying the words, I realized that it wasn't. I had tossed the coat and the pants and all my clothes into the wastebasket at my hotel, before Ledoq and I had moved to the apartment.

"And," I said, "someone found the pants at the Hotel Victorien."

"Yes. The stains on them clearly match the stains on the coat. And your name is in the guest register."

"Why would I leave my suit coat in the damn sewer?"

"I do not know. Mr. Beaumont—"

"What were Paul Trebeque and his brother doing down there?"

"It was a joke, he says."

"And why did I shoot Trebeque?"

"The brother does not know. Suddenly, he says, you appeared and fired wildly."

"Was I alone at the time? I forget."

"According to the testimony of the brother, yes."

It had to be Reilly and LaGrande who'd cooked this up, together. Maybe Reilly hadn't mentioned Ledoq to LaGrande. If he hadn't, that was pretty sporting of him. But then Ledoq hadn't run Reilly's head into a stone wall.

Or maybe LaGrande wanted to handle Ledoq in some other way.

LaGrande had the evidence from the hotel, Reilly had the body. Whenever he wanted to, LaGrande could have used both. Maybe, if I hadn't questioned Sybil Norton again, he wouldn't have used them, wouldn't have bothered. But so long as he had them, he had me.

That was why he hadn't wasted time trying to pick me up, why there hadn't been a tail waiting for me at Rose Forsythe's house. Whenever he wanted to bring me in, he could produce the body and the suit, and send the whole Paris police force out looking for me.

"You find a weapon?" I asked.

"The sewers are being searched."

And probably they would find the Webley. And probably it would turn out that Trebeque had been shot with that, and not with a derringer. And probably, sooner or later, once the cops had me, my fingerprints would be found on the gun.

If they didn't find the Webley, they would find something else.

A good police lab might poke holes in the whole thing. A good lawyer might tear the case apart in court. But LaGrande was in charge of the people who were in charge of the police lab. And if LaGrande got me in custody, I doubted that I'd ever live to see a lawyer—or a court.

"Mr. Beaumont," said the Inspector. "I ask you, please, to surrender. Anything else is madness. We have your passport. You cannot leave the country. You cannot leave Paris. You are being searched for, everywhere. If you come to me, I will do what I can do. You have my word."

I believed him. But he was a cop, and just then I remembered what Ledoq had said about the police telephone line being "overseen." I hung up.

I was watching from around the corner, a minute later, when the three cop cars arrived.

I used three different taxis to get within two hundred yards of the apartment building, and I walked the rest of the way. I was lucky. I didn't see any cops. By the time I arrived back at the apartment, it was nearly twelve o'clock and Ledoq had already left.

I sat down in the living room, and I looked at the possibilities.

The people who had come at me, outside the telegraph office, had to belong to Reilly. But how had they gotten that car there? How had they set that up?

Someone, one of Reilly's people, had seen me going into the building, and made a phone call. The Hole in the Wall wasn't far from the Rue du Louvre. If Reilly were using it as a headquarters, he could have sent the car to the telegraph building while I was waiting in line.

But why bother? He and LaGrande had already cooked up the frame.

Probably because the frame wasn't good enough for Reilly. LaGrande might not use it. So, in the meantime, Reilly would keep his people looking for me. And if they found me, he would forget about the frame and deal with me in his own way.

They had found me, and he had dealt with me, or tried to.

Reilly on the one hand, LaGrande on the other. For this time of year, France was getting very warm.

I could call the Inspector again and tell him what I knew about LaGrande and the donations. But I had no proof—it was my word against LaGrande's, and I was a murder suspect. Would Virginia Randall, the source of the information, back me up? I didn't know her, but I doubted it. If she lived in Paris, she had to know how powerful LaGrande was.

At the moment, all things considered, getting out of the country seemed like a very good idea. I had the phony passport and plenty of cash in the valise.

Using a car—even if I could rent one, or steal one—was probably not a very good idea. I didn't know my way around the city, and there could be roadblocks anywhere.

A bus might work, but I didn't know anything about the buses in Paris—when they left, where they left from.

A train, it seemed to me, was the best bet.

It would seem that way to the cops, too.

There would be cops at all the train stations, but maybe most of them would focus on the Gare du Nord, where the trains for London left. I could use another station, and go east. Into Germany, to Frankfurt, and from there take another train, back west through Holland to the coast.

They had my passport photograph, and they could copy that, and maybe they could deliver copies to the cops at the train station before I got there. But it was—it had been designed to be—a bad photograph.

They had my description, but that would fit a lot of people.

I didn't speak any French—or German, either—and I was no master of disguise, but I thought that I might be able to make it.

I didn't really have much choice. I knew that I could handle the problem better from the Pinkerton office in London than I could from a jail cell in Paris.

But I couldn't leave without letting Ledoq know what had happened.

And I couldn't leave without talking to Miss Turner. She knew about LaGrande and his donations to the party. If she mentioned that to anyone else, and if it got back to LaGrande, she would be brought in for "questioning."

Ledoq had said that he would call. He had said that she would call.

So I waited.

The hours passed. One o'clock. Two o'clock.

At two-fifteen, finally, the telephone rang. I grabbed it.

"Hello."

"*Mon ami,* how are you? I have just finished a superb duck. It was lovely. And, for dessert, I consumed an enormous portion of—"

"Henri," I said, "listen. We're in trouble."

"Trouble?"

"You're not calling from the hotel room?"

"*Non, non.* As you suggested, I am using the telephone in a *tabac.* The proprietor is smiling a dreamy smile. By the time I finish, I will have bought him a farmhouse in Normandy. What trouble?"

I told him all of it.

"Yes," he said, when I finished. "You are right. You must leave the country. *Merde.* What a disaster."

"As soon as I hear from Miss Turner, I'll make a run for the train station."

"The longer you delay, *mon ami,* the more time you give LaGrande to tighten the net."

"I can't leave until I talk to her."

"*Non,* of course not. I will telephone Eugénie Aubier. If Miss Turner is there, I will ask her to telephone you immediately. If she is not, I will leave a message saying that she must do so at the very moment she returns. And if she is not there, I will myself telephone you immediately."

"Fine. But after that, don't call here again. I want to keep the line open."

"Ah, *mon ami*! An idea occurs! I will be seeing Mademoiselle Turner tonight, at the masquerade. If for some reason she does not telephone you, I could take her aside and tell her everything."

"You're still going to the masquerade party?"

"But of course."

"I don't think you should, Henri. LaGrande may be there. He knows the Count De Saintes. LaGrande was at that other party, the one Rose Forsythe mentioned."

"But Monsieur LaGrande is not within his jurisdiction here. And you said that my name has not been broached."

"Not yet. But if LaGrande sees you—"

"You forget, my friend, that I am going in disguise." He laughed. "It will be an adventure!"

"I don't think it's a good idea."

"But what adventure is? And by going, I can guarantee that Mademoiselle Turner learns about LaGrande."

He was right. "All right. I still don't like it. But when you see her, make sure she knows not to talk to anyone about LaGrande."

"But of course. Do you feel it is safe for her to remain in France?"

"No. I think she should get out."

"I agree. Perhaps—*non, non,* it would be too dangerous for you."

"What?"

"I was thinking that perhaps she could join you in Paris tomorrow, and that the two of you could leave it together.

The police are not searching for a couple. But tomorrow, I think, will be too late. You must leave Paris as soon as possible.''

"Yeah. And the cops don't know about her now. If she and I were together, and they spotted me, then they'd have both of us. She should get out on her own."

"But what, then, of the investigation?"

"We'll send someone else. What about you, Henri? I think you should stay out of Paris for a while."

There was a brief silence on the line. "What I shall do, I believe, is take a train for the south tomorrow. I have friends in Pau. I shall remain with them until I learn that it is safe to return to Paris. If I determine that I am in danger, perhaps I shall leave the country myself. Perhaps I shall join you in London. Yes, London is very nice in the spring. Perhaps you and I can enjoy a whiskey at the Dorchester."

"Maybe. But listen. I want to thank you for your help. I wouldn't have gotten anywhere—"

He laughed again. "*Mon ami,* you speak as though we will not see each other again. You are going to London, are you not? Very likely I shall see you there within a week or two."

"All right, Henri. But give me the name of your hotel there, and the address of your friends in Pau."

He did both, and I wrote them down.

"If you need help," I said, "get in touch with Cooper."

"I shall. And now I shall telephone Mademoiselle Aubier. This will fill the proprietor with joy. He is about to obtain some livestock for his farm."

"If I don't talk to you again, Henri, for a week or so, like you say, then good luck."

"And to you, *mon ami. Bonne chance.*"

He hung up.

I started pacing the floor. I didn't get in too many paces before the phone rang.

It was Ledoq again. "I am sorry, *mon ami,* but she has not yet returned to the house. Shall I telephone again?"

"You left the message?"

"Yes."

"Don't call again. It's probably a bad idea to make too

many calls to that number. If LaGrande starts looking for you, and he looks in Chartres, he might find that tobacco shop.''

''And the telephone records, yes. Very well. Shall I give you Mademoiselle Aubier's telephone number? Ah, but the maid speaks no English.''

''And I don't want to make any calls from this number. The cops may locate the apartment. I'm still hoping that Miss Turner will call. But in case she doesn't, just make sure that when you see her, you tell her to take the first train to London. And tell her . . .''

''Yes?''

''Tell her to be careful, Henri.''

''I will do so.''

''Thank you. You be careful, too.''

''And you as well, *mon ami*. I will speak with you soon. In London.''

''Right.''

When we hung up, I started pacing again.

Ledoq had been right. The longer I stayed in Paris, the less chance I had of getting out. If LaGrande were serious about this, and so far it looked like he was very serious, by now the cops were trickling into the train stations. By now they were talking to cab drivers. Ledoq and I had been careful, but if the cops found two drivers who'd brought us to roughly the same location, they would start moving in, going from house to house. And by now they all knew that I'd roughed up those other cops, on the Rue du Louvre. As the Inspector had said, if I were apprehended, I would be treated in an unkindly manner.

I knew I should leave. I knew I should make a run for the station, before it was too late.

But what if something happened to Ledoq? What if LaGrande already knew that Ledoq would be there tonight, at the party? LaGrande knew the count. Maybe he knew who the count's guests would be. Maybe he had a surprise planned for one of them.

And if I didn't speak to Miss Turner, and if Ledoq couldn't, then she was in danger.

I told myself that I should have gotten Miss Aubier's

phone number from Ledoq. I could leave the apartment, call
it from a tobacco shop.

But the police would be going into all the tobacco shops,
talking to all the owners . . .

I went over and over all of this for another hour, and I did
a lot of pacing, and then, at six o'clock, the telephone rang.

I snatched it off the receiver. "Hello?"

"Beaumont?"

"Miss Stein?"

"Yes. I am very glad that I found you. Something has
happened to Miss Turner. I think it is important, yes, I think
it is very important that you come to my house immediately."

"What's happened to her?"

"She has been shot at. But she is all right, I assure you,
and she is safe now. She is going out to Chartres with Eugénie
and she will be safe there. But I think it is very important
that you and I speak with each other."

I thought for a moment. Would LaGrande have cops
watching Miss Stein's place? Probably not. I hadn't been followed when I went there with Rose Forsythe last night.

"Beaumont?" said Miss Stein.

"I'll get there as soon as I can," I told her, and I hung
up.

I changed into the last pair of pants I had and I took the
phony passport and the money from the suitcase. Whatever
happened, I wouldn't be coming back to the apartment.

"Oh dear," said Miss Stein. "Oh dear. I *insisted* that she
attend the masquerade party. I am not usually a foolish person, but that was a very foolish thing for me to do."

"You didn't know," I said.

I had taken another cab, this one to within a few blocks
of Rue du Fleurus. Once again I had been lucky and I hadn't
been spotted by the cops. I was beginning to wonder how
much longer my luck would hold out.

Miss Stein had spoken with Miss Turner only an hour or
so before, at Eugénie Aubier's house. Miss Turner had been
wounded when someone had attacked her and the Forsythe
children. She had told Miss Stein, just as she'd told Henri

Ledoq, everything that had happened to her since she began working for the Forsythe family.

Miss Stein and I talked for a while in her living room, with Miss Toklas sitting beside her, listening in, and it didn't take too long for all of us to realize that there was a big problem, and that Miss Turner was in serious trouble.

Miss Stein had pointed out a few things, and I had pointed out a few things, and Miss Stein had said, "But how could Henri Ledoq not have realized that?"

That didn't matter now, I had said. Right now we had to figure out what to do.

We tried calling Miss Aubier's place, but everyone had already left for Chartres.

"I've got to go out there," I said. "To Chartres."

"But what of the police?" said Miss Stein. She was wearing another circus tent. Beside her, Miss Toklas was wearing another black dress. "You did say, did you not, that Monsieur LaGrande might be there?"

"He might be, yeah. But, like Ledoq said, he's out of his jurisdiction there."

"Yes, but he is certainly influential enough to get the police in Chartres to arrest you. Or the *gendarmerie*."

"What *gendarmerie*?"

"The country police. They are a branch of the army."

For the first time, Miss Toklas spoke. "I have an idea," she said softly.

"So do I," I said.

Dear Evangeline,

Neal has been shot. He is not seriously injured, thank God. He is in hospital at the moment, and his parents will be taking him to London tomorrow.

I have been wounded as well, but in only a very minor way, little more than a scratch.

The doctor informs me that Neal and I are extremely lucky. To be honest, I should have preferred for both of us to have been lucky by just a tiny fraction more, and not been shot at all.

I have also been dismissed: I am no longer a nanny. Mrs Forsythe was, very properly, outraged.

She stood there at the foot of the bed (I had returned to Eugénie's by then) and shouted at me, 'How could you *do* that? How could you possibly bring *children* down there? Are you out of your *mind*?'

Beneath that perfect blond hair of hers, her face was bright red.

'Didn't you *think*?' Some white flecks of spittle flew. If women remembered how unbecoming anger is, we should all become saints. 'Didn't you *care* what happened to them?'

'Yes, of course,' I said weakly.

Mrs Forsythe is a woman who seldom takes 'yes' for an answer. 'Didn't you realise how *damaging* a place like that can *be* to young children? How it could affect them for the rest of their *lives*—even if poor Neal *hadn't* been nearly killed?'

'I'm so very sorry, Mrs Forsythe. Truly I am.'

'Sorry? *I'll* say you're sorry. You're a sorry excuse for a nanny, *that's* what you are. I knew it the minute I laid eyes on you. One of those hoity-toity British *bitches* who thinks she's better than—'

'I sink zat is enough, Alice,' said Eugénie, who had entered the room behind her.

The presence of aristocracy, whether French or En-

glish, has invariably a soothing effect on Americans.
Mrs Forsythe turned, put her hand to her breast, and
took a deep breath. 'Yes,' she said. 'Yes, you're right,
Eugénie. Of course.' She breathed again. 'It's just that
I'm terribly upset about poor Neal.'

'We all are upset. Jane, too. And Jane was hurt, also,
by zis person.'

'Yes, yes, I know. And naturally I'm sorry about
that.' This she said without a glance at me, her sorrow
well concealed. 'But after all, it was her responsibility
to watch the children. If she'd followed my instructions,
if she'd done what I told her to do, this never would've
happened.'

She turned to me stiffly and raised her chin. 'Miss
Turner, I'm afraid I'm going to terminate our arrangement. As agreed, you'll receive two weeks' pay in lieu
of notice.'

She frowned; her sorrow about the two weeks' salary
was less well concealed. 'You can let us know, by mail
or telephone, where to send it. We'll send your things
there, too, if necessary. Or you can arrange for someone
to come get them. Obviously, it would be best for the
children if they didn't see you again.'

She straightened her jacket (rose-coloured linen).
'And I hope that you'll be . . .' She paused, searching I
believe for a word that would sting me and yet not
offend Eugénie. ' . . . thoughtful enough not to appear
socially at any event attended by my husband and myself.'

'If you are speaking of zee masquerade,' said Eugénie softly, 'you know, I hope, zat it is I and my brozer
who decide who comes to zis.'

'Yes, of course,' said Mrs Forsythe, leaning slightly
towards her. 'Of *course*, Eugénie. Believe me, I didn't
mean for a *minute* . . . I just meant that under the circumstances, Miss Turner might find it . . . well . . . she
might find it an embarrassment to be there tonight.'

Eugénie moved her shoulders. 'Zat, of course, will
be Jane's decision.'

'Yes, of course.' She straightened her jacket again
and, glancing down, she briefly tightened her mouth.

'Yes. Well. I just hope that she makes the right one this time.'

Eugénie smiled faintly. 'Come. You will want to be wiss Neal.'

'Yes, poor Neal. Thank you, Eugénie.'

Eugénie turned to me and said, '*Un moment.*' And then she led Mrs Forsythe from the room. Mrs Forsythe never looked back.

I knew—I *know*—that her wrath was perfectly understandable. Neal might have been killed. But the knowledge didn't make my being the brunt of it, defenceless, any more pleasant. By the time Eugénie returned, I was weepy and a-sniffle, soaking my handkerchief.

She sat on the edge of the bed. 'The woman,' she said in French, 'is impossible.'

I sniffled. 'But she's right, Eugénie. She has every reason to be angry with me.'

'Yes, if you insist. But no reason to take such pleasure in it. No reason to use it as a mask for her jealousy.'

'Jealousy?' Sniffle. I stopped wiping my nose to consider this unlikely but appealing notion. 'She? Jealous of me?'

Eugénie smiled. 'You are younger. You are more attractive. You—'

'She's *beautiful*!'

'An artificial beauty. From bottles and jars. Yours is real. And her children love you.'

Blushing and sniffling, lovely indeed, I said, 'Oh, they like me well enough, I know that. But—'

'And young Neal, he has a passion, eh? For the nanny?'

'Neal? He's only a boy.' Not much escapes Eugénie.

'Yes,' she said, 'but he is *her* boy, *n'est-ce pas?* And she knows.'

I thought of Neal, his bravery down there. I thought of Edward and Melissa and realised that I should never see any of them again, and I went weepy once more.

'And she knows you care about them,' said Eugénie.

'She is using your affection as a weapon against you.'

I could feel my throat tightening. I said something which I should never have believed I should say, back when I began my nannyhood: 'I shall miss them horribly.'

More weeping then, buckets of it.

And I know that I *shall* miss them, even though the entire catastrophe was their fault, the little swines.

It began as such a beautiful day, Evy. The sun was splashing through the streets of Paris when the taxi carried me to Gare Montparnasse. People filled the sidewalks, all of them furiously busy with their furiously French business. The sky was one of those beautiful spring skies, high and pale, only a very few thin white clouds drifting absentmindedly across it.

The train from Chartres was late; and for a while I stood in the midst of that wonderful hurry and expectancy of all great rail stations, the crowd hustling and jostling around me, and I studied the schedule, read the bold white names on the big black board—LE MANS, LAVAL, RENNES, NANTES. Wonderful names: poetry. I imagined myself travelling by train to all those places, in a private compartment, of course, mysteriously veiled and gazing (tragically, it goes without saying) out the window as the fields and forests and villages rumbled by. And, *naturellement,* in the very next compartment would be a Handsome Stranger; and, as we passed in the aisle, his dark, penetrating eyes would glance into mine . . .

The reality, tomorrow, will doubtless be a second-class seat on the train to London, beside a grocer from Dover. I have lost, with my employment, my usefulness as a Pinkerton. Mr Cooper will be very disappointed.

I believe that Eugénie exaggerates the children's fondness for me—except for Neal's—but, certainly, when they finally arrived, they did seem pleased to see me. Neal (all in black again) stood off to the side, blinking and smiling, while Edward jumped gleefully up and down and Melissa rushed at me with her arms wide. I bent down to hug her, and she grinned up at me hugely. 'Hi, Miss Turner!'

It was Melissa who informed me that they had, among them, revised *Maman*'s carefully conceived itinerary, with which I had been provided before I left St Piat. This included a tour round the Tuileries, two hours at the Louvre, and a 'light' lunch at the Ritz ('and no spicy food for Eddy'). All very edifying and stimulating, you'll agree.

Would that we had held to this schedule.

But, as I say, the children had other plans. 'We've already *gone* to the Louvre,' complained Edward, screwing up his small face. 'It's just a bunch of boring old pictures.'

'And you can't really see much of it,' came Melissa's more persuasive argument, 'in just two hours.'

'What is it, then,' I said, 'that you wish to see?' As I understood *Maman*'s intention, her itinerary was a (perhaps fairly firm) suggestion; but it was not a command.

Thus does a nanny's downfall begin.

'Some *cemeteries*!' said Edward.

'Yes,' said Melissa. 'Père-Lachaise would be really nice. And Montparnasse. And Montmartre, if there's time before the Catacombs.'

'The Catacombs? I don't believe, really, that the Catacombs are a good idea.'

'*I'm* not scared,' said Edward, peering up bravely from beneath his brown fringe.

'They're very fascinating,' said Melissa. She cocked her head, and her pale blond hair brushed along the fitted shoulder of her jacket. (Linen, nearly a duplicate of her mother's, but blue.) 'The bones and skulls and things were all moved there hundreds of years ago, when Paris was getting bigger.'

I glanced at Neal. This macabre snippet of lore, and in fact the entire new itinerary, had a definite Neal-ish tang to it. For a moment he looked back at me, the picture of innocence, but then he blinked and looked away.

'Well,' I said, 'as to the Catacombs, we shall see. But of course we can go to Montparnasse Cemetery. It's quite close. We can walk there. But you must promise me, both of you, to remain together. No running out into the street.' I looked sternly at Edward. 'Any of that, and it's back onto the train.'

'Sure,' he said. 'I promise.'

I looked at Melissa.

'Well of *course*,' she said.

And so we strolled down the Avenue du Maine and turned left at Rue Froidevaux and ambled along the tall grey wall that conceals the cemetery. Neal and Melissa, being the older and more sophisticated, walked slightly ahead, Neal glancing back at me from time to time.

With utter naturalness, Edward reached out and took my hand and wrapped his fingers round mine. 'Miss Turner?' he said.

'Yes?'

'How long are you gonna stay with us?'

'*Going to*.' As the twig is bent. I was still a nanny then.

'Going to, I mean.'

'I honestly can't say, Edward.' Neither of us knew, of course, that I should be with them for only a few hours more. But I knew then, and he did not, that once the investigation was completed, I should be returning to the Pinkerton fold. In a way, it is—it was—more difficult to lie to the children than it was to lie to Miss Randall. Difficult there, as I said, because her trust is not freely given. Difficult here, because theirs is.

'And one day, you know,' I said, 'you'll grow up, and you won't be needing a nanny any longer.'

'You could marry Reagan, Dad's driver, and then you could stay with us forever.'

'Marry Reagan?' I laughed. 'I think not, Edward.'

'But—*Hey!*' he shouted at his siblings. 'Wait up!'

They had indeed increased the distance between us, and were turning into the entrance to the cemetery. They waited, and, as we approached, Melissa rolled her eyes.

'Why do you have to walk so *slow*?' she asked Edward.

'*Slowly*,' I said.

Cackling, curling over with pleasure, he pointed a finger at her.

And, in a gesture uncannily like her mother's, she raised her chin. 'You're so immature.'

'Hey!' he said, indignant. 'That's 'cause I'm a little kid.'

'*Be*cause,' she said. 'Right, Miss Turner?'

'Yes, but why don't we decide where we'll start? Neal, did you know that Baudelaire was buried here?'

He blinked. 'Oh yeah?'

Melissa hooted. 'You big liar!' She turned to me, excited, as she revealed the truth. 'He already told us about Baudelaire.'

Neal was blushing. 'I said I *thought* he was buried here.'

'*Liar*.'

'Please, Melissa,' I said. 'Now, if I recall correctly, Baudelaire's grave is just down this way.'

We found Monsieur Baudelaire's grave, and then we meandered for a while down the broad gravel alleyways between the ornate crypts. Most of these, as perhaps you know, are tall and narrow; but a few are sizeable enough for the occupants, should they wish, to invite all their friends and hold a large tea party.

The air was balmy, strung with the scent of flowers; and, because it was a bright Saturday morning, other families were meandering as well, mothers and fathers and their children. It was hushed but not sombre; it was quite peaceful, quite lovely.

'Eddy,' said Melissa, 'do you know how many people are dead in here?'

'How many?'

'All of them,' said Melissa, and giggled.

Edward looked at her for a moment, and was then suddenly overtaken by a convulsion of laughter. '*All of them*,' he said, clutching at his sides.

I suppose that already I'm seeing the children, the

three of them, through the rose-tinted spectacles of re-
membrance; but it seems to me that this was a very
sweet moment: Edward helpless with laughter; Melissa
still giggling, holding her hand to her mouth now,
nearly helpless herself; Neal smiling indulgently, then
(once again) glancing at me and glancing away.

Is this how parents do it? How they survive? By
ignoring the day-to-day tedium and the weekly disasters; by simply clutching at each sweet moment as it
arrives? Swinging staunchly from one sweet moment to
the next, like chimpanzees after bananas—forgetting
the brambles, the predators, the danger of the drop?

I don't know, Evy. But it seems to me a terribly
difficult occupation. More difficult than being a Pinkerton. More difficult than being a nanny—and we know
how supremely well I've done at that.

Actually, we don't, or rather you don't; not yet.

We were merely a few blocks from the entrance to
the Catacombs, at Denfert Rochereau; but I didn't mention this. I was still unsure about bringing the children
there. We took a taxi from Raspail over to the Eleventh,
on the Left Bank, and to Père-Lachaise.

This is my favourite of the Paris cemeteries. I like it
better even than Montmartre, which, while lovely, is a
trifle too florid for my tastes.

Neal, of course, wanted to see the grave of Oscar
Wilde.

We meandered up and down some more alleyways—
it had been years since I'd been there.

Edward had taken my hand once more. He said,
'Hey, Miss Turner, you know how many people are
dead in here?'

'No, Edward. How many?'

'*All of them.*' He clenched up, cackling again. Melissa rolled her eyes.

After several minutes, we found the grave.

Curiously, there was a tall American cowboy staring
at the monument, from somewhat off to the side. I assume, at least, that he was an American cowboy: he
wore, below a white shirt and a black weskit, a pair of

blue denim pants and those odd, uncomfortable-looking boots with the pointed toes and the high heels.

I was wondering what interest such an individual could have in Oscar Wilde when Edward suddenly raised his arm, pointed at the monument, and said, quite loudly, 'Hey, look! Someone stole his pee-pee!'

Melissa hooted again, and glanced at the cowboy, who apparently hadn't heard, and who must therefore have been deaf.

The monument depicts, in bas-relief, a naked male sphinx; and in fact someone had broken off what Mrs Applewhite would have called its progenerative organ.

Neal was blushing, Melissa was giggling and glancing at the cowboy. Edward looked up. 'Why'd they do that, Miss Turner?'

The cowboy smiled at me, as though pleased that he himself wasn't required to answer that question, and then he turned and shuffled off. Seeking out Indians, presumably, or cows.

'I don't know,' I told Edward. 'But it wasn't very nice, was it?'

'It sure wasn't. Is that Oscar Wilde?'

'No, dear. He looked rather different.'

Melissa said, 'Okay. Let's go to the Catacombs.'

'Melissa,' I said, 'I'm not certain that the Catacombs are appropriate. They're not really designed for children.'

'*All* my friends in London have been there.'

Substitute 'Torquay' for 'London' and you have precisely the declaration I had made to my father in Paris, years ago, when I was Melissa's age and he had expressed, to me, the same reservations I had just expressed.

'*I'm* not scared,' said Edward.

Neal said nothing. Hardly voluble when we are alone, he is usually altogether silent when the other children are present.

'April Haverly,' Melissa informed me, 'says it's really not all that scary.' This, too, had a familiar ring.

'I'm not *scared*,' said Edward. 'Honest.'

'If *someone* does get scared down there,' said Melissa, with a meaningful glance at Edward, 'we'll turn around and come back. Okay?'

'Please?' said Edward. '*Please,* Miss Turner?'

I looked at Neal. Innocently, as though baffled by all this, he shrugged.

'*Please,* Miss Turner?'

Perhaps if I had not been so exhausted after my sleepless night, I should have done things differently. But what I did was sigh and say, 'Very well.'

Thus was sealed the nanny's fate.

I cannot remember, Evy—have you been to the Catacombs? The entrance is not at all impressive: a small, simple stonework building on the south side of the square. Beside it sits a smaller wooden shack. From an open window of this, a frail old woman in widow's black (perhaps the same frail old woman who had been there fourteen years ago) takes your two francs and gives you a small candle and a box of matches.

The candle flickering weakly in your hand, you proceed down the narrow stone stairway. And you continue to proceed down the stairway, which slowly, slowly spirals hundreds of feet into the earth. You must walk most carefully, for the stairs are steep; and, with any sudden movement, your candle will gutter out.

Edward's candle guttered out before we had gone down forty feet. There was just room along the stair for him to walk beside me, and, since we'd entered, his fingers had been tightly clenched around mine.

'I think,' I said, 'that we should return to the street.'

'*No,*' said Edward. 'Please, Miss Turner. It was the wind! Please?' Eagerly he held out his candle, wanting me to relight it from mine.

Neal and Melissa were following behind. I looked back at them. Their faces trembled in the yellow candlelight. Neal said, 'He's okay.'

'I'm *okay,*' said Edward.

'Let's keep *going,*' said Melissa, her eyes wide.

With misgivings, I held my candle to Edward's, lighted it, and gave his tiny hand a squeeze.

And so we continued—down, down, farther away from the sights and sounds and smells of Paris, farther away from the sun, moving through the absolute darkness in our little wavering pocket of light. The air was cold now, and dank.

'How far down are we?' Edward asked.

'Miles,' said Melissa.

'Not miles,' I said. 'I don't recall exactly how deep we go. We'll purchase a pamphlet when we get back up.'

'It *seems* like miles,' said Edward.

And then at last we reached the bottom. The tunnel in which we found ourselves was perhaps five feet wide and six feet high. We walked along it for a few paces, and came to the first of the burial chambers.

'Wow!' said Melissa.

This chamber alone, beneath a gently arched roof some twenty feet long, must hold the bones of several hundred people. Along the front, the dark brown skulls and femurs had been carefully arranged in a kind of mosaic wall, the skulls placed in geometrical patterns— crosses and circles and squares. But beyond the wall, which was perhaps four feet high, beyond the feeble flutter of light from our candles, more bones were piled higgly-piggly, skulls and femurs and everything else, literally tons of bones, thousands of bones, perhaps hundreds of thousands of bones.

Edward's hand was clamped to mine.

'Edward,' I said.

'Huh?' He stared straight at that wall of skulls as though hypnotised.

'Do you know how many people are dead in here?'

He looked up at me and said solemnly, 'All of them?'

'Yes. And dead people can't hurt you. Only living people can do that.'

'Except for,' said Melissa, and then lowered her voice, 'the *Headless Horseman. Waaarrrgh!*'

Edward's glance darted to her.

'Cut it out, Melissa,' said Neal.

'Now,' I said. 'I really think we've seen enough. The rest is more of the same. And it's quite a long walk to the other entrance. I suggest we simply go back up the way we came.'

'But what if someone's coming down?' asked Edward.

'Yeah, the *Headless*—ouch! Miss Turner, Neal hit me.'

'Neal, don't hit your sister. And Melissa, do stop that.'

'Can I touch one?' asked Edward.

'Pardon me?'

'Can I touch one? One of the skull things?'

'Why do you want to do that, Edward?'

'To see if it's real?'

'Well. Edward, you must remember that while these can't hurt you, these bones, they once . . . belonged to people, and for that reason they deserve our respect. How would you feel if, after you died, someone came along and wanted to touch you?'

'But they can't feel, can they? Not now, I mean.'

'No, of course not. It's the idea, you see.'

'But if I was dead, and I couldn't feel anyway, and it was just a little kid who wanted to touch me, and just for only one time, I think it'd be okay. I really do.'

'Yes,' I said. I nodded. 'I expect you're right. Very well, then. But be careful.'

And carefully, tentatively, he reached out and placed his index finger against the cheekbone of a skull. He held it there for a moment. Behind him, grinning insanely, Melissa raised her hand and moved it towards his throat. Before I could say anything, Neal grabbed at her arm and pulled her away. She wrenched her arm free, looked at me, saw me frowning, and looked down, rubbing at the arm as though she had been mortally wounded.

Edward let his hand fall away from the skull. 'Okay,' he said. He nodded and then looked up at me. 'Can we go the rest of the way?'

'Are you quite certain?'

'Uh huh. Yeah. I really want to.'

'*Hsshhh!*' said Melissa, glancing back toward the stairway. 'What was *that?*'

'Melissa,' said Neal, as sternly as any nanny could have said it.

'No, really! I *heard* something. From the stairs.'

'It's only someone else,' said I, in my infinite wisdom, 'come to see the Catacombs. Are we going on, then?'

'Yes!' This from Edward.

So we continued along the tunnel, past chamber after chamber, each walled across its front with that barrier of geometrically arranged skulls; each, beyond that, piled nearly to the rooftop with bones.

After a time, the sheer abundance of the bones actually rather diminishes their fearsomeness. You begin to think of all those skulls and femurs less as human remains than as part of a complicated engineering problem. How many people were required to move these here, to pile them in the chambers, to arrange the skulls in those patterns?

'Miss Turner?' said Melissa, her voice soft.

'Yes?'

'Look.' She pointed back the way we'd come.

Stopping, I turned to look. Far off in the darkness—I cannot say how far off—a single distant candle glimmered, moving slowly towards us. And then, as though keeping pace with us—for all of us were now standing still—it stopped moving forward. We could make out merely the faint glow of the candle, not the person who held it.

'Yes. As I said, some other visitor.'

But in truth, although naturally I didn't admit it to the children, I had found that single candle somewhat chilling. I should not have been disturbed by two candles; but I was disturbed by one. I knew that, alone, I should never come down into the Catacombs. And yet someone had seemingly done so, and was now following us.

But perhaps, I told myself, it is two people with one candle.

It was not.

'Come along,' I said, and started along the tunnel again.

'Do a lot of people come down here?' asked Edward. His grip had once more tightened on my hand.

'Thousands of them,' I said. 'In the summer, I expect that there are huge crowds.'

'We should've come in the summer,' he said.

'I believe that the exit isn't much farther along,' I said, with more hope than conviction.

I glanced back. The distant candle was moving forward again, still keeping pace with us.

'It's probably just some boy with his girlfriend,' said Melissa. 'I'll bet that a lot of boys bring their girlfriends down here.' I heard in her voice the same hope I had heard in mine.

'I'm sure you're right,' I said.

I glanced over my shoulder. The candle had disappeared. Possibly its owner had turned back. Or had stopped, beyond a bend in the tunnel, to admire one particular geometric pattern or another.

I felt absurdly relieved. We should be safe now, I thought.

We came to another chamber, this one empty of bones.

'What's that?' said Edward, and started into the chamber. I glanced back. Still no candle.

'It's an altar, Edward. They sometimes have religious services here. Come along.'

'Look, somebody wrote something.'

Still no candle. We all moved toward Edward.

Melissa suddenly spun round. *'What was that?'*

What happened next, Evy, happened so quickly that I am still not entirely clear about it all.

Suddenly, from the utter blackness at the entrance to the chamber, a figure appeared—man or woman, I could not determine. Above the shoulders of a long swirling black coat, it wore a black muffler and a low, flat-brimmed black hat. Except for the eyes, dark and narrowed, its face was concealed.

Melissa shrieked and dropped her candle. The figure darted forward, directly towards me, reaching for my handbag.

In London, while I was training to become a Pinkerton, I learned from a retired army sergeant several wonderful ways to injure an attacker. These had quite deserted me now: I stood there, frozen.

Neal—splendid Neal—leaped at the figure, grappled with it, and all at once there was a blast, deafening in that enclosed space, and a bright burst of light, whitening the walls like a photographer's flash. Neal made a sound, a grunt, and collapsed to the floor. The figure spun about, coming for me again, but Neal's courage had enkindled my own, and I tossed my candle into the muffled face. The figure batted it aside but I dropped my handbag and stepped slightly to the right, just as I had in gymnasium with Sergeant Bellows, and I snatched at the figure's right arm, the arm that held the weapon, and, whirling my back to the figure, using the figure's own momentum, I swung it up over my shoulder.

Neal and Melissa had dropped their candles, I had hurled mine. The only light in the chamber came from Edward's candle; and, at just this moment, it went out.

In the darkness, I heard the figure smack to the stone floor, heard its breath hiss out explosively, and then my legs were swept from beneath me. As I hurtled to the floor, the gun fired again—another bright white burst of light, the figure suddenly illuminated, grotesquely sprawled along the stone, its arm raised—and I felt something sear across the back of my hip. I crashed to the stone and then something—a fist, a knee, an elbow, I do not know—struck me on the cheek, very powerfully.

Stunned, I rolled to the side. Somewhere Melissa was sobbing, but above the sobs I heard a scrambling, and then the click of heels—oddly, I thought then of the cowboy—and the shuffle of feet.

It was leaving, the figure. It was leaving us.

Melissa was still sobbing.

'Edward,' I called out.

Nothing.

I patted about on the damp stone until I located my purse. I fumbled inside it for the matches, found them, struck one.

In its thin light I saw Edward sitting on the floor, his knees drawn up, his head tucked against them, his arms wrapped around them. Melissa was against one wall, her back to me, her face in her hands, her shoulders shaking. And Neal, Neal was on his knees, holding on to his side with one hand and trying to push himself off the floor with the other.

The match went out, I lighted another. I found my candle, lighted that, and went to Neal.

He had been wounded in the side and there was quite a lot of blood down his trousers and on the floor, black and shiny in the candlelight. He was breathing through clenched teeth.

'Gotta get up,' he said.

'Yes, yes, here, give me your arm.' I took his arm over my shoulder and helped him up—awkwardly, because I was still holding the candle. I walked him to the wall. 'Here,' I said, and handed him the candle. 'I'll be back.'

I ran to Edward, who was beginning now to stand up himself. He scrambled into my arms, wailing. 'Shhh, shhh,' I said as I patted him along the spine. 'Come along, Edward. It's all over. You stay with Neal—'

He wailed.

'For only a moment. I must see to Melissa, and then we'll all leave. All right? For only a moment. Come along. Neal, here, take your brother's hand. Edward, you must help Neal, he's been hurt.'

I went to Melissa, put my hand on her back. She turned, and, like Edward, came wailing into my arms. I stroked her and I whispered, 'It's all right now, everything's all right, but we must get Neal to hospital and I need your help. Melissa? I need your help with Edward. Can you be very brave and help me?'

She nodded against my throat.

'Good, thank you. Come along. Edward, Melissa's going to help you.'

Neal's wound was still bleeding, and I tore a piece of fabric from my petticoat and slipped it inside his shirt. He gasped.

The bullet had gone through him, and there was another wound at his back. I bandaged that, as well. I am no nurse, but the wound seemed to me not a fatal one: only a very small portion of his side was involved.

But he must have been in great pain—even by candlelight he looked extremely pale; and, despite the chill air, he was perspiring heavily.

He was splendid, Evy, there is no other word for it. He never complained.

They were all splendid. None of them complained as we made our way back to the surface, Neal supporting himself on my shoulder, Melissa holding Edward's hand.

There is not much more to tell. When we returned to street level, I hobbled with Neal into the nearest café. The proprietor was wonderful: he scurried about, muttering in French, seemingly at a loss; but somehow he managed to telephone for the police and an ambulance, and to provide a brandy for Neal and me, and lemonade for the children; he did everything he could to help.

The police arrived, two of them, and questioned me—or attempted to, for I refused to answer any questions until we had got Neal to hospital. The ambulance arrived and two medical people carried him into it on one of those pallet things, and the rest of us clambered in beside him.

At the hospital, Neal was taken into the emergency ward (I did not know that this would be the last time I should see him). The children and I sat and talked with the police, first the original two officers and then some others. Over and over I told the same story. Yes, the man had reached for my handbag. Yes, Neal had tried to prevent the theft . . .

All of them were polite but somewhat harried. (I

overheard a pair of them talking, and today had apparently been a busy day for the Paris police department. Not only had someone attacked Neal and me, but some American madman had apparently attacked two of their colleagues. From the manner in which they spoke of this, I shouldn't wish to be in that gentleman's shoes when they capture him.)

More policemen arrived, including an inspector, a very pleasant person, a bit worn-looking for such a young man but exceedingly kind, and he asked the same questions I had already answered, many times, for the other policemen. It was he who noticed that I was bleeding.

''It's nothing,' I told him.

'But you will see a doctor at once.'

And so I saw the same doctor who had treated Neal, and he told me that Neal was not in danger.

As I said, my own wound wasn't serious: a mere scratch on what we will continue to call—and I insist upon this—the back of my hip.

I rejoined the children, who were being entertained by the Inspector with recipes invented by his wife, and then Eugénie arrived—I had given her telephone number, and that of Mr and Mrs Forsythe, to the first policemen.

It was her idea that we should all repair to her house on the Ile Saint-Louis. I wanted to stay with Neal, but, as she pointed out, I could do nothing for him now. The Inspector agreed with this, and apologised to me, on behalf of all Parisians, for my having suffered at the hands of 'this snatcher of handbags.'

And so I returned here, I and the children in Eugénie's colossal Rolls-Royce, and Eugénie bundled me off to bed, and promised to keep the children occupied until their parents arrived.

Mrs Forsythe landed perhaps an hour later, with the results I have already described.

And I have not been able to communicate any of this to Mr Beaumont. Monsieur Ledoq, the Frenchman who is assisting him, gave me a telephone number where I might reach him, and I have attempted several times to do so, but with no success. I tried once in the morning, before I left for Gare Montparnasse; and I have tried twice since I returned to Eugénie's, but no one has answered.

I suppose that, if I did attend the masquerade, I could speak with him there. Assuming that I could pry him away from the terribly short floozy.

But I am so tired, Evy. And Mrs Forsythe is right—in the circumstances, I would in fact be embarassed to be seen there.

Even if nothing had happened today, I don't believe that I have the energy to attend the silly thing. I know I don't have the energy to witness any more fondling on the part of the floozy. I can give Eugénie a letter to present to Mr Beaumont.

As for learning anything from the count, I no longer have any confidence in my ability to do so. I've made such a muddle of everything else.

Eugénie thinks I ought to go.

'But of course you will go,' she said, after I had completed another bout of sobbing.

'Eugénie,' I said, 'I *couldn't*. Mrs Forsythe is right. How would it look, after all that's happened?'

She smiled. 'It is her own son who is in the hospital, and yet she will be there.'

'But—'

Goodness. What an astonishing woman she is. Miss Gertrude Stein, that is to say. She has just left me, after having engaged me in the most curious of conversations.

About an hour ago, as I was scribbling away at this, there came a firm knock on the bedroom door. I called out 'Come in,' and the door opened and there she stood, wearing another loose-fitting black dress, a sort of man's grey jacket over that; and, on her head, an extraordinary hat that resembled a bouquet, but one constructed by a mad florist.

'I am not disturbing you?' she said.

'Not at all, Miss Stein. Please come in.' I set aside these pages.

She shut the door and marched slowly across the room to a graceful but somewhat spindly Louis XV chair, eyed it sceptically for a moment, and then turned and cautiously lowered herself onto its delicate seat.

'Are you writing something?' she asked me. 'A novel?'

I smiled. 'No. It may appear to be, but it is merely a letter to a friend.'

She nodded. 'It is good to write letters to one's friends. I wish that I myself had time to write letters to my friends, but unfortunately the demands of my work are such that I cannot.'

She arranged her purse on her lap. 'Well,' she said. 'I will get immediately to the point. That is the sort of person I am, the sort of person who gets to the point immediately, without any dilly-dallying. I am very cross with your Mr Beaumont, I am very cross indeed. He assured me last night that you were in no danger, no danger at all, and today I understand from Eugénie that someone has shot at you with a gun. To be shot at with a gun is in my opinion very dangerous, and so I am very cross with your Mr Beaumont.'

'Do you mean the American Pinkerton who—'

She held up her hand. 'Please. As I told your Mr Beaumont, as a writer I am gifted with a remarkable insight into human nature. I observed the two of you last night and it was very plain to me that you knew each other. I spoke of this to Mr Beaumont before he left and he admitted as much, and he assured me that you were in no danger. And yet here you are. Shot at, with a gun.'

'I'm not hurt seriously, though. I'm really quite all right.'

'And I am very pleased to hear it.'

'Mr Beaumont admitted that he knew me?'

'Yes. And, since Mr Beaumont is a Pinkerton agent investigating the death of Richard Forsythe, and since you have been only recently employed by the Forsythe family, and since you and Mr Beaumont know each other, I have deduced that you are a Pinkerton agent also. I am correct about this, am I not?'

'Miss Stein, if I were, I expect that I shouldn't be allowed to tell you so.'

'Of course not. And in the normal course of things I would not ask you to. But this is not the normal course of things. In the normal course of things, attractive young women, even when they are Pinkerton agents, do not get shot at with guns. And yet you have been shot at. This offends me deeply. Does Mr Beaumont know that you have been shot at?'

'Miss Stein, you put me in a difficult position . . .'

She placed both of her plump hands along her purse. 'Jane,' she said, 'you must trust me. I believe that I can help you. If I did not believe that I could help you I would not offer to do so. I would still have come here, of course, to make sure that you were all right, and to offer my condolences upon your having been shot at, but I would not be offering my help as well. So I would be grateful if you would tell me whether Mr Beaumont knows that you have been shot at.'

I ought not have done so, perhaps. But already she knew of my connection to Mr Beaumont. And the simple truth was that I did trust Miss Stein. And, having botched everything on my own, to be honest I was very glad of her help. 'No,' I said. 'He doesn't.'

'I see. Do you have a telephone number at which you can reach him?'

'Yes, but he hasn't answered.'

'I see. And Mr Beaumont, as recently as last night, felt that you were in no danger. Do you know what all these facts suggest to me? They suggest to me that there is some failure in your communication with Mr Beaumont. I am now no longer cross with him, and this is a fine thing because I do not like to be cross. Have you communicated with Mr Beaumont at all?'

'Not directly. Through a third party.'

She nodded. 'That would be Henri Ledoq. Last night I wondered why you were spending so much time with

Henri. He is a charming man, he is a very charming man, but he is not, I believe, *your* sort of charming man. He is providing the channel through which information flows between you and Mr Beaumont?'

'Yes.'

She nodded. 'You could do much worse. I like Henri very much and I believe that he is basically sound. But you must not forget that he is French. No one is second to me in admiration of the French. I admire the French people, I admire them very much. But they are an excitable group, Jane. They are a very excitable group of people. I believe that what we need here is an Anglo-Saxon sensibility, in fact an American sensibility, in fact my own sensibility. Now, you will be going to the masquerade party at Eugénie's tonight, in Chartres?'

'I don't believe so, Miss Stein.'

'Nonsense. You must go. Eugénie has told me of your recent encounter with Mrs Forsythe. You must ignore her. She is a nincompoop. All of the Forsythes are nincompoops. It runs in the family.'

'The children are really very sweet.'

'That may be, but sooner or later they will become nincompoops. You must ignore what their mother said. You must always ignore anything said to you by a nincompoop. And, let us not forget, you will be safer in Chartres. If you stay in Paris, this person who shot at you with a gun may attempt to shoot at you again.'

'The police believe that he was trying to steal my handbag. He *did* seem to be after it.'

'Did you inform the police that you were a Pinkerton agent investigating the death of Richard Forsythe?'

'No, of course not, but—'

'The people in Paris who steal handbags do not possess guns. Now, this is what I propose. It is, I think, a brilliant proposition, but you must tell me what you think of it. First of all, you will tell me what you have experienced and encountered and learned since you began to work on this "case". Then you will go to Chartres with Eugénie. Then you will attend the masquerade party. Eugénie tells me that your wound will not pre-

vent this, and you are a young woman, and young
women should attend masquerade parties. In the meantime, I will communicate with Mr Beaumont, and I will
find out from him what he has experienced and encountered and learned.'

'But I've already done that with Monsieur Ledoq.
And Mr Beaumont will be attending the masquerade. I
can ask Eugénie to deliver a letter to him.'

'Mr Beaumont will not be attending the masquerade.
He informed me of this last night. And as for Henri, it
may be that in his French excitability he has neglected
to inform you, or to inform Mr Beaumont, of some
small but very significant fact. And perhaps new information has come to light. What harm could it do? And
then tomorrow, when you return to Paris, we shall all
get together and see what we have.'

Mr Beaumont not attending the masquerade? Have
he and Mrs Forsythe eloped? Are they now on board
my train to Nantes?

But, as to my telling Miss Stein of my experiences
and encounters, she was right. Certainly my confiding
in her, I felt, could do no more harm to the investigation
than I had already done to it.

I did tell her everything—not only what I had
learned on my own, but what I had learned from Monsieur Ledoq. I gave her, too, the telephone number for
Mr Beaumont.

At the end, she nodded. 'Very good. So you will do
all this? You will go to Chartres? You will attend the
masquerade party?'

'I'll be going to Chartres. But I don't know whether
I'll attend the party. I'm exhausted, Miss Stein.'

'Jane,' she said. 'You are young. You are in France.
These are the days about which, years from now, you
will say those were the days. You must accumulate as
many pleasant memories as possible, so that you will
have something to look back upon. Eugénie tells me
that you have rented a costume. You must use it. You
must attend the party.' She pursed her lips. 'Consider,

too, that if you do not, that nincompoop Alice Forsythe will have won.'

I smiled.

'You will go?' she said.

'Yes. I suppose so.'

She nodded. 'Very good. And I thank you, Jane, for trusting me. I believe that you will not regret having done so.'

With a small sigh, and some effort, she stood up from the chair. 'I will telephone you tomorrow, in Chartres.'

And with that, she nodded once again and marched back to the door and out of the room.

Do you know, Evy, I think I *will* attend the party.

In fact, I must get ready for it at this very moment. I shall post this on the way out.

All my love,
Jane

Fourteen

MY IDEA WAS to make a phone call. It took me a while to get through to the person I wanted, but finally I managed it.

Miss Toklas's idea was a little more complicated. "We can use those blue pantaloons of Jane's," she said to Miss Stein. She turned to me. "Not your Jane, not Miss Turner. Another Jane."

She turned back to Miss Stein. "Do you remember? She spilled cocoa on them when she was here that weekend? And we sent them to the cleaners? She never picked them up. And there's that huge white silk shirt that Leo gave you. And we can use that material of Virginia Randall's. The red velvet."

Miss Stein nodded. "Yes," she said. "Yes, I think that you have hit upon a very good plan, Alice. You have hit upon an excellent plan."

She turned to me. "What do you think, Beaumont?"

"I think you're right," I said.

She nodded as though this didn't surprise her much. She rose from the chair and looked down at Miss Toklas. "You help Mr. Beaumont prepare himself, would you, Alice? In the meantime, I shall get my own costume ready."

"Oh, Gertrude," said Miss Toklas, concerned. "Do you think you should go out there? Won't it be dangerous?"

"Not at all," said Miss Stein. "If it becomes necessary for anyone to provide derring-do, then I am sure that Beaumont will provide it. I will provide only the official invitation. It is in my name, Alice, and no matter how well we prepare

Beaumont, I do not think that we can prepare him so well that he could masquerade as me. Even if he attempted to masquerade as me when I am masquerading as someone else.''

"Oh," said Miss Toklas softly. "Oh my." She looked as though she regretted having come up with the idea.

"Miss Stein won't be in any danger," I told her.

"Oh my," she said.

"We haven't time for that now, Alice," said Miss Stein. She looked at me and she smiled grimly. "The game is afoot, eh, Beaumont?"

And she wheeled slowly about and she strode from the room.

Half an hour later, standing in the center of the living room, I was almost a pirate. The blue pantaloons were long enough but they were very wide around the waist—I wondered what their owner looked like. We used my belt to hold them up, and over that we tied the sash that Miss Toklas had cut from a long swath of red velvet. The silk shirt was loose and full, with a big floppy collar. It was a bit short in the sleeves, but pirates, as Miss Toklas pointed out, usually wore their sleeves rolled up when they went about their pirate business, and that was the way I wore mine.

From a piece of black cotton fabric she cut an eyepatch and a band to hold it on. She made me sit down so she could tie the band, and then she stepped back and looked at me critically.

"You need a mustache," she said. "But we have only one in the house, and Gertrude's using it. For her costume, I mean."

Suddenly her face brightened. "I know! Wait here."

She hurried off. Even when she moved quickly she seemed to be floating above the floor.

She floated back a minute later, carrying an eyebrow pencil delicately between finger and thumb, as though it were a dead lizard. "This isn't mine," she said. "Someone left it here. Sit still now."

I could smell the faint lavender scent of her perfume. Carefully, stroke by stroke, almost whisker by whisker, holding on to my chin as though she were steadying a canvas, she drew a mustache along my upper lip. She took her mustaches as seriously as a Frenchman, and she worked on me with her dark eyes narrowed and the pink tip of her tongue caught between her small white teeth.

She had just finished it, and she was stepping back to eye me, when Miss Stein came into the room.

She carried a furled umbrella under her arm and she wore a man's black suit and a man's bowler hat. Most of her hair was tucked up into the hat, but what you could see of it had been powdered to make it look gray. Her big handlebar mustache matched her hair. Perched on her nose was a pair of wire-rim glasses.

Miss Toklas giggled and she clapped her hands. "Gertrude, it's wonderful."

Miss Stein smiled at her and then turned to me. "What do you think, Beaumont?"

"Who are you supposed to be?" I asked her.

"Ah. Of course. You would not know him. I am Ford Madox Ford. He is a literary figure here in Paris, a German who likes to pretend that he is English." Beneath the big mustache she smiled. "He may actually be there tonight, at the masquerade. I wonder if he will recognize himself."

Miss Toklas asked her, "What about Mr. Beaumont? How do you like his costume?"

Miss Stein looked me up and down. Finally she said, "It is very good, Alice. It is wonderfully good. But something, I think, is missing."

"Boots," said Miss Toklas. "But we haven't any."

"What about those old Wellingtons of Leo's? I remember seeing those old Wellingtons somewhere. In the kitchen, was it, under the sink?"

"But pirates don't wear Wellingtons," said Miss Toklas.

"Not as a rule," agreed Miss Stein. "Not as a rule, Alice. But pirates do wear boots. Pirates are never without boots of one sort or another, and in an emergency such as this, the Wellingtons will simply have to do."

Miss Toklas floated off to get the boots.

Miss Stein looked into a mirror on the wall, and she

twirled her mustache. She smiled at herself, looking very pleased.

The car was a plain Ford two-seater runabout. The dashboard was empty—no clock, no ashtray, no cigarette lighter. The car was nude, said Miss Stein, and that was why she called it Godiva.

We left Rue du Fleurus at seven that night. The sun had gone down, the streetlights were on, but there was still some light in the sky, gray overhead, pink to the west of us. Dark clouds were beginning to roll across the southern sky, in the direction we were headed, and it looked like we might run into rain.

The masquerade party started, Ledoq had told me, at nine. According to Miss Stein, it would take us almost two hours to get to Chartres from Paris.

We had tried once again to telephone the count's house in Chartres, but there was still a problem with the line. I still didn't like that.

Miss Stein drove, wearing her Ford Madox Ford outfit, her bowler hat clamped tightly onto her head. I sat beside her in my pirate outfit, the hems of my blue pantaloons stuffed into the top of a pair of tight-fitting Wellingtons. Miss Stein had given me a large carving knife to stick in my sash, but I had put it under my seat, where it wouldn't cut off my leg.

The passport and the money and my watch were in the left pocket of the pantaloons. The Colt was in the right. My street clothes were in a paper bag in the Ford's trunk.

I've ridden with some bad drivers, but Miss Stein was probably the worst. We took Avenue du Maine south for a while, and she talked the entire time, telling me about Paris before the War, and during it. She couldn't talk without looking into the eyes of the person she was talking to, even when those eyes were mostly shut because the person didn't want to watch the way she was driving.

Maybe she always drove like that. Or maybe she was driving like that now to keep her mind off the idea that Miss Turner was in danger.

And Miss Turner *was* in danger, so I kept my mouth shut,

along with my eyes. Miss Stein knew Paris, and she knew
the way to Chartres.

We turned right onto Avenue de Châtillon, and it was a
few blocks later, just before Porte de Châtillon, that the traffic
slowed down and I knew we were coming to a roadblock. By
then the cars were piling up behind us and it was too late for
us to turn back and try to find another route out of the city.

They had parked a couple of police cars across the road, leaving room enough for only one vehicle to get through at a
time. Horns were honking, Frenchmen were shouting.

We lost fifteen minutes waiting in line. Miss Stein fiddled
with her mustache.

Finally we reached the roadblock. Beneath the streetlamp,
cops were everywhere—leaning against their cars, standing
up against the buildings, watching and waiting. All of them
had their clubs out.

It was a young cop in his twenties who walked to the
window. I don't know what went through his mind when he
saw the couple inside the Ford, but nothing showed on his
face.

Miss Stein rolled down the window and plucked off her
mustache and waved it at him. *"Bon soir, monsieur,"* she
said cheerfully.

He said something in French and Miss Stein turned to me
and said, "Your passport."

I handed it to her and she handed it, with her own, to the
cop. She was answering his questions, in French, and I heard
her say *Chartres* and I heard the names *De Saintes* and
LaGrande.

As she talked, the cop examined the passports. The phony
stamp in mine said that I'd entered France two weeks ago.

The cop bent down to look inside the car, at me, and Miss
Stein said, "Say something piratical. And do please smile."

I smiled at the cop and I said, "Yo-ho-ho."

The cop looked at me for a minute and then he smiled
back. He handed the passports to Miss Stein, touched the brim
of his hat, and then stood upright and waved us through.

Miss Stein handed me the passports and then drove us

between the two cop cars. She turned to me and smiled. "I thought that we did that very well."

"Yeah."

She set the mustache on the dashboard and rubbed at her lips. "I do not understand how men can wear those silly things. They itch terribly."

For a long time, on the road between Paris and Chartres, Miss Stein told me about herself and her place in English Literature. Basically, there was William Shakespeare, and then there was Miss Stein. She explained to me why this was so.

We hit the rain when we were about fifteen miles from Chartres. One minute the road was clear, a pale yellow strip in the beams of the headlights, narrow between the dark stands of forest, and the next minute it was a blur beyond the windshield.

Easing up on the gas, Miss Stein turned on the wipers. She stopped talking and she hunched herself over the wheel, peering forward, her eyes narrowed beneath the brim of her bowler. We had been traveling at about thirty-five miles an hour. Now we were traveling at twenty. I looked at my watch. A quarter to nine.

After a moment or two, this time without taking her eyes off the road, Miss Stein spoke. "Beaumont?" she said.

"Yeah?"

"Are you a good driver?"

"Yes."

"Are you a *very* good driver? What I mean to say is this. Can you drive Godiva more rapidly than I am driving her? In this nasty, filthy, insufferable rain? And can you do it without damaging her? Or, for that matter, without damaging us?"

"Yes," I said.

She nodded, still squinting out at the road. "Then I think that you should," she said, and she slowed down and pulled the car over to the shoulder and she stopped it.

"I'll come around," I told her. "You move over here."

I shoved open the door and I jumped out. The cold rain pelted me as I darted around the front of the car. The driver's door was swinging open and I grabbed it and pulled myself

in, slamming it shut behind me. Miss Stein was arranging
herself in the passenger seat.

I released the emergency brake, shifted into first, and I
floored the pedal. The tires spun and the rear end skittered a
bit, and then the car shot forward. Miss Stein gasped. I
glanced over her. Her hand was flat against her chest and her
eyes were wide.

"It'll be okay," I told her.

"Yes," she said. "Yes, of course."

I wiped rain from my face with the back of my hand.

"Here," said Miss Stein.

I glanced over, saw that she was holding out a pocket
hankerchief, and I took it. I wiped the water from my forehead, from my eyes.

"Thank you," I said.

"Please do not mention it," she said. She leaned forward,
pulled a knob. After a moment, warm air filled the car.

We went ripping through a turn and the tires slipped, but
I eased up on the gas and they snagged the road again. I
accelerated.

"Oh," said Miss Stein. She closed her eyes. She didn't
say much after that.

I had to go more slowly when we came to the towns and
villages—Maintenon, Mevoisins, St-Piat, Jouy, St-Prest,
Lèves, Mainvilliers—but when the road was open, I drove as
fast as I could. What kept down my speed was the speed of
the wipers. They didn't move very quickly, and when I tried
to go over forty, I lost sight of the road. I took a few chances,
but I knew I couldn't take many of them.

Beside me Miss Stein sat stiffly, her hands gripping each
other in her lap. She was silent except for a quick intake of
breath once in a while, on the turns. I think that her eyes were
closed again.

And then Chartres was up ahead. I could see the lights of
the city.

"Miss Stein," I said.

"Yes?" Her voice was small.

"I'll need your help now."

*   *   *

The count's house was a big place near the cathedral, three
or four stories tall and almost as wide as the block it sat on.
It was an old building, thick brown beams visible as they
crisscrossed against the white plaster of the walls.

In front, the narrow cobblestone street was crowded with
cars, and I had to park the Ford a couple of blocks away.

"Why don't you give me the umbrella?" I said to Miss
Stein.

She handed it to me. "And you must not forget this," she
said, and handed me the carving knife.

I stepped out of the car, got soaked again as I opened the
umbrella. Shoving the carving knife into my sash, I walked
around to get Miss Stein. I held the umbrella over her as she
climbed down onto the road. She straightened her suit coat,
and I saw by the light of the streetlamp that she had put her
mustache back on.

I pulled out my watch, looked at it. Ten minutes after nine.

We set off, moving quickly toward the count's house, or
as quickly as Miss Stein could move. The rain was still lashing at the streets, but the umbrella was big enough to shelter
us both.

At the house, the servant who opened the door looked like
he'd just pranced off a wedding cake. He wore a powdered
wig that was tied in a ponytail behind his head, a long jacket
brocaded in gold, a white shirt with lots of ruffles, a white
cravat, tight white leggings, tight white stockings, and delicate little golden slippers. But he wasn't very delicate himself,
and he wasn't very little. He was as tall as I was, and beneath
all the trimming he looked like somebody who could handle
an intruder without getting his ruffles wet.

Miss Stein handed him her invitation and he glanced at it
and bowed and then he reached toward me for the umbrella.
Miss Stein said something in French, snatched the umbrella
from me, closed it partway, bounced its tip on the floor to
shake the water off, and then furled it shut and snapped the
retaining band. It was a part of her costume and she wasn't
going to hand it over to anyone.

Holding it as though it were a cane, handle in her hand,
tip against the floor, she turned to me. "Shall we find her,
then?"

I nodded.

She spoke in French to the servant, nodded at his answer, then turned to me again. "This way," she said.

From the foyer we turned right and went up a broad wooden stairway carpeted in red. Coming down the stairs was a robed sultan and a bare-breasted slave girl. They nodded to us politely.

Directly opposite the top of the stairs, across a hallway, was the broad entrance to the main room. I could hear the sound of jazz. The party had just started but already the room was packed.

"Do you know what Miss Turner's wearing?" I asked Miss Stein. "Her costume?"

"No. We must find Eugénie. Eugénie will know."

The room was two stories tall and it smelled of perfume and cigar smoke. The jazz was coming from a Negro band at the far end, about a hundred miles away. Some of the guests were sitting at tables and some were milling around. Miss Stein and I edged through the crowd, looking for Miss Aubier.

It was quite a crowd. Beneath the sparkling electric chandeliers there were cavemen and cavewomen. There were Oriental potentates and Oriental princesses. There were pharaohs. There were priests and nuns. There were tigers and leopards and a gorilla or two. There were clowns large and small, and there were jesters and tramps and gypsies. There were even a few pirates, but none of them was wearing Wellington boots.

I thought that even if LaGrande were here somewhere, I was probably safe. He wouldn't be expecting me to show up, for one thing. For another, there were just too many people around.

But I knew that I could be wrong. LaGrande might be here, and he might have spotted me already.

Miss Stein talked to some people she recognized and she asked about Miss Aubier, and she talked to some other people, and finally we found her.

She was near the bandstand and she was dressed like a very prosperous shepherdess, holding a golden shepherd's crook in one hand and a glass of champagne in the other. She was watching the dance floor. There were only two couples out there, a cowboy and an Indian squaw, and a man in a striped shirt and black pants and a black beret who was dragging a woman around by her hair.

"Ah, Gertrude," said Miss Aubier, and smiled.

"Jane," said Miss Stein. "Where is Jane?"

Miss Aubier looked from Miss Stein to me. She frowned. "Monsieur Beaumont?"

So much for my disguise. "Miss Aubier, we've got to find Miss Turner."

She frowned again. "But . . . zair was a message. From *you*, Mr. Beaumont. A note for her. Henri and Jane and I were talking, and one of zee servants brought it. Henri and Jane went to meet wiss you." She propped the shepherd's crook against the wall and she glanced around the room. "I will find zee servant."

"Doesn't matter," I said. "I know who wrote the note. Where was I supposed to be?"

"Zee cathedral. In zee crypt."

I turned. She put a hand on my arm. She nodded toward the left. "No. Zis way. It is faster." She set her glass on a nearby table. "Come. I will show you."

I followed her past an armored knight and around an Eskimo couple. There was a wooden door set into the corner of the stone walls and she opened it and slipped inside. I was right behind her as she clattered down a wooden stairway.

She looked up at me, over her shoulder. "Henri and Jane, zey are in danger?"

"Yeah," I said.

"But from whom?"

"It's a long story."

At the bottom of the steps we dashed through another door. We came out into a huge kitchen, broad sweep of tile flooring, pots and pans hanging everywhere, an immense butcher block table, an enormous cast iron wood stove. We raced across the tiles, and Miss Aubier had her hand on the knob of another door when someone called out "Halt!"

I turned. It was Louis the Fifteenth. Or maybe Louis the Sixteenth. Tall and slender and very handsome, he wore a colossal wig of cascading black curls. His jacket was more elaborate than the doorman's and his leggings were tighter. There was a sword belt around his waist, but the scabbard was empty. The sword, a rapier, was in his hand.

"Jean!" said Miss Aubier. "We must help Jane! She—"

"Do not believe anything this man tells you," the man said. I had figured out by now that he was the Count De Saintes. "He is wanted by the Paris police." He smiled at me. "The local police are being summoned, monsieur. You cannot escape."

I reached for the Colt.

He was very fast. Before I could get the gun out, he had danced across the room in what seemed like a single swift movement. Suddenly the sharp point of the rapier was needling my throat. He was balanced nicely—his left hand raised behind him, his right foot forward. One simple poke and I would be dead. He smiled again. "You will raise your hands, Monsieur."

I raised my hands.

"Eugénie," he said. "Please remove any weapon from the man's pocket. And also that ridiculous knife."

"*Jean!*" she said, and there was anger in her voice. "Jane is in *danger*!"

The count scowled. "He is a communist, Eugénie."

"Jean, forget your silly politics! He is here to help Jane!"

"*Eugénie!*" He started rattling some French at her but he stopped suddenly, frowning, to bat aside Miss Stein's umbrella, which was spinning across the room toward his head.

Miss Stein stood in the doorway, panting. She'd lost her bowler and her mustache somewhere—maybe on the stairs as she ran down them—and her thick dark hair spilled over the shoulders of her suit coat.

As soon as the man moved his sword and swatted the umbrella, I stepped forward. Rapiers are for stabbing, not cutting, and their blades are sharpened only toward the tip. I grabbed the blade in my left hand and when his head swiveled back to me, looking annoyed, I hit him very hard on the nose with my right.

He flew back against the wall, letting go of the sword. He looked at Miss Stein and he snarled *"Jew bitch!"* I dropped the sword and I hit him a few more times and he fell down.

"Miss Stein," I said, "get out of here. Get back to Paris."

"But—"

"Please, Miss Stein. Any minute now, things are going to get very complicated."

"Yes, yes," she said. "Good luck, Beaumont."

"Same to you, Miss Stein. And thanks."

She nodded once and then turned and disappeared back through the doorway.

I looked at Miss Aubier. "Where's the crypt?"

She glanced down at the count, then looked back up at me. "Come," she said. She hurried back to the door and she pulled it open and together we ran out into the night and the rain.

The stone stairwell of the crypt was dark and it smelled of wet earth, like a grave. I had the Colt in my right hand, and I used the left to feel my way along the rough damp walls. I was damp myself now, and cold. The run through the rain had drenched me.

I had tried to send Miss Aubier back to the house, but she wouldn't go. She was waiting at the top of the stairs.

I finally came to the bottom. From up ahead, maybe fifty feet away, maybe farther, I could make out a frail light burning in the huge empty darkness. A candle.

Carefully, still feeling my way along the wall, I moved forward.

Soon—it seemed like an hour but it was probably only a few minutes—I could make out the people sitting there. Miss Turner and Henri Ledoq.

I was the audience, they were the play. Out beyond the thin wobbling circle of the candle's light, I was invisible. But I could see them.

I could hear them, too. Ledoq was saying, "But I want you to *understand* me, mademoiselle." His voice sounded hollow. It was a big crypt.

"I have no interest in understanding you," said Miss Turner. She was angry. "If you're going to shoot me, then by all means shoot me. But please don't attempt to justify it."

She was dressed like an eighteenth-century French noblewoman. From a huge blond pompadour wig, yellow ringlets tumbled down to her bare shoulders. Her low-cut dress, scarlet and gold, was tight in the chest but billowed out at her waist, puffy with all the petticoats beneath it. The material had flattened a bit at her lap, where her hands were resting. She wasn't wearing her glasses.

Opposite her, sitting on a block of stone, Ledoq was wearing his Sherlock Holmes overcoat. He wasn't wearing the hat and he wasn't wearing the mask. He was holding the derringer and it was pointed at Miss Turner.

Moving as quietly as I could, I eased closer.

"Mademoiselle," said Ledoq. "I am a man of honor."

"*Honor!*" said Miss Turner. "Was it honorable to shoot Neal Forsythe this afternoon? A defenseless young boy? You call that *honor*?"

"I call it regrettable," said Ledoq. "I had no—" He stopped talking and cocked his head.

I stopped moving.

Ledoq smiled at Miss Turner. "It seems, Mademoiselle, that we are no longer alone." He looked out into the darkness, an actor peering out over the footlights. "Is that you, *mon ami?*" He kept the derringer aimed at Miss Turner.

I said, "Yeah, Henri, it is."

Miss Turner, like Ledoq, peered out into the darkness.

"Somehow I knew you would come," said Ledoq. "The police pursue you, Reilly pursues you, I destroy the telephone lines into the count's house. And yet I knew, somehow, that you would come."

"I've got the Colt, Henri. It's pointed at your heart."

"And my weapon is pointed at Mademoiselle Turner's." He lowered his eyebrows. "How did you know, *mon ami?*"

"You made mistakes. You made a lot of mistakes. But your biggest mistake was telling Miss Turner that Sybil Norton had written erotic poetry. Syblil Norton never said that to me, and I never said that to you. The only way you could've known what they were, Henri, was if you'd read them."

"Ah," he said.

"Why'd you steal them, Henri? Why'd you take them from the suite?" I was down in a squat, moving slowly to my right, like a crab.

In the flickering candle light I could see his faint smile. "They were dreadful. I had some notion, I believe, of preventing their publication. With Forsythe dead, someone else might have published them. I burned them, later."

I was directly in front of them now. I said, "What's it all about, Henri? What happened in that hotel suite with Richard Forsythe?"

He glanced down. Miss Turner made a small movement, and he looked at her sharply. "Please attempt nothing, Mademoiselle. I am still tender from your gymnastics in the Catacombs."

"What happened, Henri?" I lowered myself to a seated position, my knees drawn up. Now I braced my arms against my legs and lined up the Colt.

Ledoq looked out into the darkness. "Forsythe did intend to kill himself after he shot Mademoiselle von Stuben. And she believed that he would do so, after he did shoot her. Their suicide pact was genuine. But Forsythe doubted himself. He was uncertain whether he could bring himself to end his own life. He and I made an arrangement. If he found that he could not commit the act, he would telephone me at the number of a tabac on the Left Bank. It was owned by a man I knew."

"The Inspector mentioned him," I said. "Martin Something."

"Sardou, yes. If Forsythe were to telephone me, I would go to the hotel and I would help him . . . finish it. Using Sardou was my idea. I wanted no phone call made from that hotel to my apartment."

"You had to know the desk clerk, too. The one at Forsythe's hotel."

"Yes. I knew him."

"There's something else, isn't there, Henri?"

He frowned. "What do you mean?"

"Why should you help Forsythe commit suicide? He had something on you."

He sighed. "He did, *mon ami*. He knew of a certain . . . indiscretion."

"An indiscretion? Why would—" And then I realized what it must have been. "An indiscretion with Forsythe, you mean, don't you, Henri?"

Maybe I imagined it, but it seemed to me that in the candlelight Ledoq's face flushed. He glanced at Miss Turner, looked back out into the darkness. "Yes," he said. "A single indiscretion, and he held it over me. Had he revealed it, he would have destroyed me."

"Detroyed your reputation, you mean."

"Precisely."

"So you went there and you shot him. You murdered him."

He shrugged. "He wanted to be shot. It was hardly murder."

"You sure about that, Henri? You sure he didn't want to change his mind? It was pretty convenient for you, wasn't it? You had a gun handy. Everything was set up for a suicide. All you had to do was pull a trigger, and no one would ever know about that indiscretion of yours."

He pursed his lips and said nothing.

"And what about the desk clerk?" I asked him. "Did he want to get pushed into the river?"

"He wanted more money. He threatened to go to the police."

Miss Turner was staring at him.

The barrel of the Colt was aimed directly at his chest. If he moved the derringer away from Miss Turner he was a dead man. I said, "And the door, Henri. The locked door at the hotel. You've read Houdini's books. You actually told me that—another mistake—but I didn't even think about it at the time. You got some gimmick out of the books."

He nodded. "A very simple technique. Laughably simple. A strong length of thread, waxed. You loop it around the lever of the bolt, close the door, and pull from the outside. The bolt is drawn into its sleeve. Then you merely tug on one end of the thread, and it comes free."

"I've been an idiot, Henri. You were the one person whose alibi I never checked. I never even asked for it."

He nodded. "I was rather disappointed in you. I had prepared an excellent one."

"And Aster Loving. You killed her because you found out—because I *told* you—that she'd known Forsythe. You were afraid that Forsythe had told her about you and him. If he had, and she told me, then maybe I'd have figured out why Forsythe and the desk clerk had to die. You were using one murder to cover up another. Why not kill everyone, Henri? All of Forsythe's friends.''

"But them I knew. And I knew that he had told them nothing.''

"Where'd you find the heroin?''

"I have many friends of my own, *mon ami*. Some of them use the drug.''

"You knew about her, you probably knew that she was an addict. You had to know. You learned her address, you got some heroin, and you brought it to her. She liked to be injected, and you obliged, and you killed her. You tried to screw up the time by putting on that phonograph record after she died. And then you ran over to my hotel room. But the next day I noticed that her manager's office was near the hotel. And he told us that her apartment was nearby, too. I was an idiot again. I didn't think twice about it.''

He nodded. Sadly, I thought. "The apartment is only a block or two away from the hotel.''

"And Neal Forsythe,'' I said. "He had to go, once you found out that Forsythe had confided in him.''

He nodded again.

"And Miss Turner, too,'' I said. "Because maybe Neal said something to her today. As of last night, he *hadn't* said anything—you knew that because you talked to Miss Turner at Miss Stein's house. But now that she'd met you, she might mention your name to Neal, and he might've heard it before.''

"Once again, *mon ami,* I could not take the chance.''

"It's all over, Henri.''

He smiled. "I still have two bullets left. One for Miss Turner, one for you.''

"You know that it won't work out that way. You're not a very good shot, Henri. That's why you had to get so close to Miss Turner today, in the Catacombs.''

He said nothing. But the gun in his hand didn't waver.

"Henri,'' I said, "whatever else you did, that was the worst. You were going to kill them both and then leave those children there, in the darkness. With the bodies. So that when they were found—if they were found—they could tell their story about you going for Miss Turner's purse.''

He glanced down. But the barrels of the derringer were still pointing at Miss Turner.

''And I think you know that,'' I said. ''I think you know how rotten that was, Henri. I think you're beginning to unravel. If you weren't, you would've used another gun. You only fired two shots in the Catacombs because a derringer only holds two shots. With another gun, you could've killed them both, even in the dark. Using the derringer was another mistake. Even Miss Stein wondered about it. And if I'd ever found out about the two shots, I would've made the connection to the gun.''

He lifted his head slightly. ''I did not intend to miss.''

''Henri, the cops would've found the slugs. They'd know that they came from a derringer.''

''It would not have mattered, *mon ami*. Only you knew that I possessed a derringer. And I felt I could persuade you that another derringer must have been involved. And, as it happened, when I spoke to you this afternoon, you were planning to leave Paris.''

''That worked out pretty well for you, didn't it?''

He smiled. ''Not as well, in the circumstances, as I had hoped. For here we are, *mon ami*.''

''You couldn't have known, when you planned it, that LaGrande would be after me. You weren't thinking, Henri. And you're not thinking now. How were you going to explain Miss Turner's body?''

Miss Turner looked at him as though she'd been wondering about that herself.

''She was attacked by the same person who attacked her before,'' said Ledoq. ''I attempted to prevent this, but he overpowered me. I was going to use the second bullet on myself.''

''Nice, Henri. You ever shot yourself before? That's something that not everyone can do. And what about the servant with the letter? He had to see you.''

''I'm—'' He frowned. ''The servant will be dealt with.''

''Jesus, Henri, another one? That's an awful lot of dead bodies.''

He frowned again.

"Henri," I said. "It's all over."

He looked out toward me. I think he sighed. He said—and I think he was saying it to me—"It is a great pity," and then he turned to Miss Turner and said something in French. Then he leaped up and he fired the derringer out into the darkness.

Both of his shots missed, wildly. Mine didn't. Ledoq took a single step backward and then went down.

I pushed myself off the floor and ran toward Miss Turner. She had jumped to her feet and some of Henri's blood had spattered her chest. She was looking down at it. I took out Miss Stein's sodden handkerchief. "Here."

She took it, moving very slowly. "I—"

I stepped over and bent down to check Ledoq's pulse. He didn't have one. I pulled out my watch. Quarter to ten.

Still moving slowly, Miss Turner was wiping at the skin of her breasts.

I grabbed the candle. I said, "This isn't over yet, Jane. We've got to get out of here."

"Yes," she said. "Yes. I'm all right. Really I am." She reached up and pulled off her wig, tossed it into the shadows. She fluffed her hair with both hands and she made a face. "I must look a fright."

"Give me your hand," I said.

She did, and it was cold. But so was mine.

We shuffled together toward the entrance.

"What did he say?" I asked her. "Ledoq, when he spoke to you in French."

"*They cannot take away my panache.* It's from *Cyrano de Bergerac.* In a way, Ledoq killed himself, didn't he?"

"Yeah," I said. "I think he did."

Outside the cathedral, things had gotten complicated. The rain was still coming down and there were cop cars parked helter-skelter in the square, and cops lined up beside them. La-Grande was with them. He had been one of the clowns at the masquerade, a very large clown, but his makeup was gone now, and he was a very unhappy clown.

Opposite the cop cars there were two army trucks, and standing beside these were about thirty soldiers, their rifles at port arms. A shepherdess suddenly came running from the middle of them all. Miss Aubier. *"Jane!"* she called out.

The two women embraced and then Miss Aubier turned to me. "Zair is a man—"

"There you are, Beaumont," said Colonel Mereweather, striding toward us in his dinner jacket. His white hair was plastered to his pink skull, but he moved through the rain as though he were on parade. "Jolly good," he said. "This the lady in question, eh? Delighted, m'dear. Glad you're safe. Come along, both of you. Got transport laid on, over here."

I looked over at the cops. None of them moved. The three of us followed the colonel, back toward the trucks.

"Don't worry about those chaps," said the Colonel. "Duchamp's lads will sort them out. My friend in the Ministry of War. Took me a while to reach him, and he was a bit grumbly at first—who could blame him, eh? Amazing story. But he spoke to that lady you mentioned, Miss Randall, guaranteed her safety, and she backed you up. A very sound cove, Duchamp. Well, here we are."

Parked behind the army trucks was a long black Bentley. Colonel Mereweather reached into his pants pockets, pulled out a set of keys, handed them to me. He glanced at the car, a bit wistfully.

I said, "Thank you, Colonel. I'll get her back to you safely."

He clapped me on the shoulder. "Know you will. Pinky— that's Duchamp—he thinks you'd best go east. Frankfurt. Lay low for a while. This blighter LaGrande, who knows what friends he has, eh? Oh. Nearly forgot." He reached into the dinner jacket, pulled out a sheaf of papers. "Passes. Pinky signed them. In case there's any trouble at the border." Grinning, he clapped me on the shoulder again. "Well, off you go then."

"Colonel," I said, "I'm very grateful."

"Not another word. Loved it, every minute. Excitement, eh? Don't get much of that at my age." He turned to Miss Turner. "Very pleased to meet you, m'dear. Hope we meet again." He pulled open the passenger door of the Bentley. "Into the car with you now. Out of this damnable rain." He looked up at the sky, his face streaming, and he scowled.

Miss Turner turned to Miss Aubier, hugged her, then climbed into the car.

The colonel turned to me. "Damn' handsome woman," he said. "You take care of her, Beaumont. And drive carefully."

"I'll do that, Colonel," I said.

May 13th

Dear Evangeline,

As you see, I am in Frankfurt, as is Mr Beaumont. So much has happened, and I have so little time, that I cannot explain everything; or much of anything, really. A longer letter will follow, from Munich.

Yes, we are off to Munich, both of us. We have been assigned by Mr Cooper to work together on an investigation. Someone, it seems, has attempted to kill the leader of that German political party I mentioned, ages ago, and reams ago, the National Socialist Party. The party has called in outside help; and we, Mr Beaumont and I, are it.

I am curious to see whether the party is dark as and threatening as Neal Forsythe and Virginia Randall suggested it was.

We did discover who killed Richard Forsythe, and I shall reveal that person's identity when next I write. I know that you are the sort of person who, whenever she picks up a crime novel, immediately opens it at the last page, to determine the identity of the killer. Well, I am terribly sorry, Evy, but I am afraid that in this case you will have to wait. All things in due course.

By the way, Mr Beaumont and I will be travelling as husband and wife. This may prove rather interesting.

More later.

Love,
Jane

P.S. My costume? Marie Antoinette. Eugénie had told me that her brother would be dressed as Louis XVI. Unfortunately, however, I never saw him; nor he me.

Mr Beaumont did see him—I asked him (with the utmost casualness)—but he seems, for some reason, reluctant to discuss his encounter with the count.

Could it be possible, do you suppose, that Mr Beaumont is perhaps just the tiniest bit . . . jealous? What an intriguing notion.

Perhaps he will have cause for jealousy. From something Eugénie once said, I gather that the count's various business dealings often bring him to Munich . . .

J.